DEBBIE MACOMBER

AND

LEE TOBIN McCLAIN

The Night We Met

mira

Recycling programs for this product may not exist in your area.

ISBN-13: 978-0-7783-0935-2

The Night We Met

Copyright © 2020 by Harlequin Books S.A.

Starlight
Copyright © 1983 by Debbie Macomber

The Soldier's Secret Child
Copyright © 2017 by Lee Tobin McClain

This edition published by arrangement with Harlequin Books S.A.

For questions and comments about the quality of this book, please contact us at CustomerService@Harlequin.com.

Mira
22 Adelaide St. West, 40th Floor
Toronto, Ontario M5H 4E3, Canada
www.Harlequin.com

Printed in U.S.A.

CONTENTS

STARLIGHT

Debbie Macomber

To my daughters Jody and Jenny, who have
always wanted me to name characters after them.

One

Karen had dreaded the party for weeks. Her father was sure to use it as another opportunity to find her a husband. She almost cringed at the thought of what lay before her—a succession of eligible men, abrupt introductions, and pointed questions. Yet she loved her godparents and wouldn't offend them by not attending their annual Christmas party.

"Are you ready, lass?" Matthew McAlister let himself into her apartment without the courtesy of knocking.

"Honestly, Dad, one of these days you're going to walk in here and find me stark naked," Karen admonished with a sigh.

Matthew chuckled.

Karen laughed, too, for it was difficult to maintain an injured air when her father was in this mood.

Stepping back to survey Karen, Matthew's eyes lit up in appreciation. "My heart swells with pride at the sight of you, lass," he said in a strong Scottish brogue.

Karen forced herself to smile. His speech always began the same way. After admiring her beauty, he would recount the days he'd courted her mother and their marriage when Madeline was nineteen. From there he'd reiterate his growing desire for grandchildren, most particularly a granddaughter. It was always the same, to the point that Karen could have mouthed the words along with him.

"Dad," she interrupted, "we'd better go. Snoqualmie Falls is a forty-five-minute drive."

Surprisingly, Matthew insisted Karen drive. She did so willingly, but glanced apprehensively at her father. He looked tired and a bit ashen.

"Are you feeling okay, Dad?" she asked, hiding the concern in her voice.

"Of course I am." He rallied somewhat. "I'm just saving myself for the grand affair. Certain demands are made of a widower these days, and the ladies are expecting a good time."

They were greeted at the large rented hall with soft Christmas music. The room was lavishly decorated with hundreds of large, glittering snowflakes suspended from the ceiling. The reflective glow of the turning flakes cast the dimly lit room into a winter wonderland.

The hall was already crowded. Several others had arrived and were milling around, chatting in small groups and sipping champagne.

Evan Forsyth raised a welcoming hand when he saw Matthew and Karen enter, and walked purposefully toward them. The two men clasped hands with the enthusiasm of many years of devoted friendship.

Her father and Evan had been friends since their school days, and although they held separate stations in life, their friendship had never wavered. Evan For-

syth was the president of the University of Washington at Tacoma, an honored and respected man, while Matthew McAlister was a small-businessman dealing in plumbing supplies. For as long as Karen could remember, her father and godfather had played chess every Thursday night.

The annual party had begun many years before, when Karen and her sister, Judy, were small. Evan and Milly Forsyth invited a few intimate friends into their home to share the joy of the holiday season. Over the years, as Evan's position became prominent, the size of the affair had grown to include business friends and faculty members. This year, the party was so large the Forsyths had rented a hall, their spacious home no longer large enough to hold the growing number of guests.

"Welcome, welcome," Evan said and smiled warmly. His wife, Milly, followed close behind and embraced Karen fondly.

"I'm so pleased you could make it, my dear."

Evan leisurely surveyed Karen, noting how the red velvet gown molded to the slender curves of her womanly figure.

"I swear you get prettier every year, Karen," he said with a hug.

"And I swear your tongue grows smoother every year."

Evan chuckled with delight while Milly tucked an arm around Karen's waist to give her a slight hug. "He's right, dear. You look radiant. And your gown suits you beautifully."

Karen returned the hug and smiled. "It should, considering what I paid for it."

Karen had gasped when the salesclerk had told her

the price, and disregarded the woman's complimentary words as an effective sales pitch. But now she willingly conceded that the effect of the simple but elegant style had been worth the price.

The four chatted until social obligations demanded the Forsyths' attention. After sampling several of the hors d'oeuvres and speaking with acquaintances, Karen and her father watched as the floor was cleared to make room for dancing.

Matthew surveyed the crowd while gently directing Karen as they danced the first waltz. His eyes glowed with amusement as he remarked, "There are several available men here. Take advantage of the opportunity to snare yourself a husband."

Karen stiffened and pulled away from her father.

Almost angrily, Matthew continued, "I can't understand what's the matter with men today. You're lovely, Karen."

"Dad, please…" A note of helplessness entered her voice. Karen was so weary of this argument. A thousand times she'd explained that the problem wasn't with men; it was with her. So many of the men she'd dated over the years were self-centered and egotistical, seeking easy conquests and one-night stands. It was almost to the point that she'd rather not date at all. Her natural good looks and vivacious personality invited the attention. But Karen had yet to discover what it was about herself that attracted the least-desirable males.

"I'm perfectly content with my life as it is." Karen sighed with impatience, tilting her chin defiantly.

"But I want grandchildren…"

"You have grandchildren," Karen reminded him coolly. "What do you call James and Carter?"

"I want a granddaughter." Matthew flashed her a disputatious look.

"Dad," Karen pleaded, "let's not argue tonight. You have grandchildren, and more than likely you'll have your precious granddaughter." Karen didn't know how much more she could endure. Matthew had applied constant pressure on her to marry for the past six months. The argument had nearly ruined their close relationship. Unable to endure his interference with her life, Karen had moved into her own apartment. It was a move long overdue. It'd been convenient to live at home and easy to rationalize her father's need for her after her mother's death. Much to her chagrin, Matthew sold their home and moved into an apartment in the same building as Karen. If anything, matters had gotten worse.

As they continued to waltz across the room, Karen caught sight of Mabel Jackson, an aging widow who'd made no effort to disguise her attraction to Matthew. *Turnabout is fair play,* she mused, and giggled devilishly.

"Do you find something amusing, lass?" Matthew asked curiously.

"No. Excuse me, Dad. I see someone I'd like to talk to." Cleverly, she wove her way through the thick couples toward the widow.

"Mrs. Jackson, you look lovely tonight," Karen greeted sweetly.

Mabel Jackson ignored the greeting and craned her long neck to stare into the dancing figures.

"Is your father here?" she asked with obvious interest.

"He sure is. In fact, it was my father who commented on how radiant you look. Dad said he'd never seen anyone more lovely."

"He did?" The woman beamed and smoothed the hairs of her lopsided wig.

"You know, Mrs. Jackson, my father is a lonely man. He'd never admit it, of course, but Dad needs a woman. A real woman." Karen stared into the crowd, unable to meet the widow's triumphant gaze.

Mabel Jackson positively glowed. "My dear child, I'm so glad we've had this little talk. Leave your father to me."

Karen smiled broadly and felt that even if she ended up disinherited, the taste of revenge was indeed sweet.

In a matter of minutes, several men were vying for Karen's attention. She danced with a number of partners, young and old, her infectious laughter ringing through the hall as she surrendered to a swelling tide of triumph. Not once was she interrupted by her father's forcing what he considered eligible men on her. An hour later, she managed to catch Matthew's eye and winked wickedly as he waltzed by in the arms of Mabel Jackson. Matthew cast her a look that threatened bodily harm, and Karen burst into helpless giggles.

A moment later, she caught sight of her father's angry stride as he wove through the crowd toward her. Wishing to avoid the taste of his Scottish temper, she hastily sought an escape. A curtained glass door leading to a balcony caught her attention. Unnoticed, she quietly slipped into the dark, leaving her father perplexed by her sudden disappearance.

Peering through the sheer curtain, Karen waited impatiently for Matthew to abandon his search.

"I beg your pardon," came a deep voice from behind her as she backed into a solid form.

"Oh! Excuse me." She fumbled and quickly straightened. "I didn't realize there was anyone out here."

"Obviously," came the clipped reply as he stared into the dark. Karen watched him for a few minutes, but he made no effort to meet her gaze.

"Would you mind sharing your hideaway for a minute?" she asked sweetly, and deliberately blinked her long, curling lashes at his impassive expression. Men were usually quick to respond to her expressive brown eyes.

"Suit yourself," he retorted unenthusiastically, and continued to stare into the night.

Undaunted by his lack of welcome, Karen joined him at the railing and searched the sky to discover what was so fascinating. The night was cold, crisp, and clear; the stars shone with a brilliant intensity.

"Leave it to my godfather to order a star display for the night of his party," Karen murmured. Her gaze returned to the stranger's face and swept his appearance. He wore a trim-fitting, dark wool suit that hugged his slim hips and long legs. The harsh contours of his face remained blank under her examination.

"Look!" Karen exclaimed, pointing her finger to the sky and counting the stars. "It's Perseus. I can't remember when I've seen the constellation stand out so clearly. You do see it, don't you?"

"No, I'm afraid I don't," he remarked dryly.

"Sure you do. Just look a little to your left," she persisted.

"Listen," he snapped impatiently, "whatever your name may be—"

"Karen McAlister," she interrupted, "and you're…?"

"Randall Prescott," he replied in a voice that spoke plainly of trepidation.

"Well, look again. It's up there plain as day." She pointed to it again for his benefit. "Really, it's very clear, if you'll just look…"

"Mrs. McAlister…"

"Miss," Karen informed him cheerfully.

"Miss McAlister…" he tried again.

"Please call me Karen."

Drawing in a breath as if to hold on to his limited patience, he began again. "Karen… Miss McAlister… whatever it is you wish to be called, I cannot view your precious Perseus, and I shall never view it. I'm blind!"

Karen felt the full impact of shock. After a moment of startled silence, she blurted out, "Oh, dear, Mr. Prescott, I do apologize."

"Randall," he interrupted.

"I had no idea, Randall. I…"

"Please call me Rand," he taunted softly.

"All right, Rand," she replied, a smile evident in her voice, "but please accept my apology."

"An apology is unnecessary; my blindness cannot be attributed to your faults," he countered stiffly.

"No, of course not, but I was being obtuse."

He turned toward her then, allowing for the first time a clear view of his rugged features. He certainly didn't fit her image of what a blind man might look like. His face was boldly defined, almost ruthless. There was a magnetic quality about his dark brown eyes that captured her gaze.

"I don't suppose you came out here without your

coat to view the stars?" he asked roughly, as if aware of her eyes studying him.

"How do you know I'm not wearing a coat?" she asked. Was this unnerving man playing her for a fool?

A sardonic smile touched the corners of his mouth. "I don't. But I suspect the slight quiver in your voice is from a chill."

Karen suddenly realized she was cold. Snoqualmie Falls was only a few minutes from the summit of Snoqualmie Pass, over the Cascades. The bitter December wind bit into her.

"Why are you hiding?" he asked, more gently. "Is someone bothering you?"

"Oh, heavens, no!" she quickly assured him, but paused. "Well, yes and no. I routed a persistent widow toward my father and was sure to taste his anger had I remained inside."

Rand smiled at her predicament, his roguish features relaxing his expression. "I'm sure the whole incident has been forgiven. You can't stay here. You'll freeze."

It was clearly a dismissal, and Karen felt strangely disappointed. She wanted to stay and learn more about this enigmatic stranger. He was the first man to really interest her in a long while. She hovered in the doorway, hoping to find an excuse to remain, but found none.

"Are you coming, too?"

"Later," he replied indifferently, and appeared bored with her company.

Karen could only leave. "Then perhaps we'll meet again," she said softly.

"It's unlikely," he mumbled, as if he hadn't intended her to hear. She watched as he returned to the railing.

Karen didn't immediately see her father once she'd entered the warmth of the large reception hall. Mrs. Jackson was standing near the orchestra, waving her hand impatiently in an attempt to gain the conductor's attention.

"Here you are."

The voice startled Karen, and she jerked around to see her godfather. "Uncle Evan." She placed a trembling hand over her heart to dramatize her fright. "You're worse than a thief in the night."

Evan Forsyth's eyes twinkled. "Your father's looking for you."

Karen lowered her gaze, a little ashamed of her ploy. As much as Matthew irritated her, she loved him and realized he had only her best interests at heart.

"I suppose he's still angry?" she asked.

"Let's put it this way," Evan said, chuckling. "He hasn't had a free second since you spoke with Mabel. He's hiding in the men's room. I think we'd better dance before he decides it's safe to return."

"Oh, dear, I'm in for it now," she mumbled as her godfather led her to the dance floor. It was a waltz, which gave her the opportunity to speak. "I'm afraid I made a blunder with one of your guests."

Evan's eyes rounded, feigning shock. "You seem to be making a night of it, my dear. Want to talk about it?" His position with the university and in the community made him a ready listener to the troubles of others.

Karen felt uneasy. "I'm afraid I literally bumped into Randall Prescott—"

"Ah," Evan interrupted her. "I imagine he was rude. He tends to be the prickly sort. Damn good professor, though, the finest. We offer the best business program in the state due to him. Prescott could teach anywhere. The university is lucky to have him." He hesitated, his thick brows knitting his forehead. "Was Cora with him?"

"Cora? No. Who's she?" It hadn't occurred to Karen that Rand was married. The thought deflated her.

"That's unusual. Rand rarely attends any social functions without her."

"Is Cora his wife?" Karen hoped to hide any telltale inflection of curiosity from her voice.

"No, she's a business associate. They've collaborated together, books and the like."

Karen felt herself relax, an excitement flowing through her limbs.

Sensing her interest, Evan felt obliged to add, "I wouldn't discourage you, Karen, but Randall Prescott is a bit of a cynic. A difficult man to get to know. He's independent and proud, highly defensive of his blindness. He's not your normal chivalrous hero…tread carefully."

"Who says I'm interested?" Karen asked defensively.

Evan chuckled. "Karen, I've known you all your life. Certainly I know you well enough to recognize that gleam in your eye."

Several minutes later, Karen saw Rand sitting unobtrusively in the rear of the hall. She had been waiting for his appearance, silently searching faces. Now she wondered how to gain his attention. In answer to her problem, the orchestra conductor turned to face his audience and announced the first ladies' choice of the evening.

Mabel Jackson, with a satisfied smirk, made a beeline for Matthew, who had recently reappeared. Karen groaned in sympathy and walked toward the back of the reception room and the mystifying Randall Prescott.

Without introduction or preamble, she curtsied. "May I have the pleasure of this dance?"

Rand sat up abruptly and stiffened. "Miss McAlister?"

"Karen," she corrected impishly.

"All right, *Karen*. Let's not go through that again." A smile threatened the stiff line of his mouth.

He hesitated so long, Karen grew uncomfortable. "You did hear them mention it was ladies' choice, didn't you?"

He held his shoulders stiff and formal. "I'm honored, but no." His mouth remained inflexible.

Karen would have been surprised if he'd accepted. "Well, that's fine; my feet are beginning to ache, anyway. New shoes," she explained before taking the seat beside him.

If he was surprised, he didn't show it. "Have a seat," he offered sarcastically.

Karen ignored his derision. "Thank you, I have."

Apparently, he felt no inclination to speak, and Karen was courteous enough not to press. After a dance or two, she discovered that she was completely content to sit with him, not talking, if he wished. She hummed and watched the dancers as they waltzed through the wintry scene. She could almost see Rand relax his guard and accept her company.

"Aren't the decorations magnificent?" she asked thoughtlessly, then gasped, recognizing her blunder. How stupid could she be? "If my new shoes are tight, I needn't worry," she apologized. "After they've been in my mouth a couple of times, they'll fit fine. That was stupid. Please excuse me," she added soberly.

"Don't worry," he assured her, almost enjoying her discomfort. "It's a common mistake. Describe the decorations, will you?"

It was a pleasure to narrate the lovely scene portrayed by the dangling snowflakes. With her natural flair for theatrics, she described the hall in graphic detail. In afterthought, she added interesting tidbits she knew about some of its occupants.

"It's almost impossible to tell when Uncle Evan is angry or upset, but he has a telltale twitch in his upper lip. If you see it move, watch out. And then there's Clayton Dunbar, a distant relative of the Forsyths'. He's about as subtle as a garden serpent and has the sincerity of a used-car salesman. He marks his conquests on his bedpost to brag to his friends."

"Do I detect a note of mockery?"

"No use hiding the fact that I detest the man. He's about as obvious as a Sherman tank." It was unlike Karen to be catty, and she immediately felt guilty. Besides, was she being any less obvious about her interest in Rand? "That's unfair. I'm sure Clayton has several good qualities…somewhere."

Rand gave a hearty laugh. "You're apt at describing others. How would you depict yourself?"

"I couldn't," she protested automatically. "How do you picture me?"

"You have an intriguing voice." He paused, thinking. "But I'm not referring to the tone quality. You possess an unshakable resolve. I doubt that you've ever failed in any pursuit. You're upbeat, cheerful."

"Heavens," Karen said dryly, "you make me sound like a high school cheerleader."

"Definitely not high school. You must be all of nineteen, maybe twenty."

Karen laughed lightly. "I'm a whole world away from high school or college. I'm twenty-three."

Rand grinned, then added, "You must be five-seven, five-eight at the most."

Impressed, Karen lifted her brows expressively. "Five-seven."

"Long dark hair and metallic-blue eyes."

"Short dark curls, equally dark eyes."

A hand cupped the back of her neck; his fingers twisted the pliable curls. Karen was too startled by the sudden action to protest. Her heart rate soared as a languorous warmth spread from her neck.

He chuckled softly and said, "Yes, short, but soft and inviting. Your eyes must be expressive, promising." He relaxed against his chair, the dim light illuminating his strongly defined features. Again, Karen experienced the full impact of his masculinity.

"That's not quite right, but I'm not going to disillusion you with the truth." She laughed because she'd always thought her dark eyes, the color of bitter chocolate, were plain. Rand made them sound exciting and enticing.

"Give me your hand," he said suddenly. When she complied, his fingers gently examined hers. "You're not a secretary, or your fingertips wouldn't be this smooth. Nor do you walk with the crisp purpose of a nurse."

"That's a chauvinistic attitude. All women aren't secretaries or nurses. I'm not a teacher, either."

"Aha!" He laughed again. "You're employed in a man's field."

Karen smiled at his novel methods of deducing her occupation, but the smile died quickly as she spied Clayton Dunbar eyeing her from the edge of the dance floor. She stiffened instinctively, her reluctance obvious.

"Is something wrong?" Rand questioned.

"My wicked past is about to catch up with me. Dad's revenge is here." Karen had dated Clayton only once and spent the entire evening fighting off his sexual advances. She hadn't told her father for fear of offending the Forsyths; now she recognized her error.

"Karen, baby, it's good to see you. I see you've been waiting for me. Let's dance."

Karen's mind whirled, searching for a plausible excuse to refuse as she stood.

Suddenly, Rand rose beside Karen, his imposing frame dwarfing Clayton's. "Excuse me," he said stiffly, "but you'll have to wait your turn. This dance is mine."

In his eagerness to corner Karen, Clayton hadn't noticed her formidable companion. His smug expression instantly turned to that of a deprived child.

Karen's mood lightened immediately. Placing her hand in Rand's, she led the way to the dance floor. With a devilish gleam, she turned back and smiled cheerfully. "Ta-ta, Clayton."

Rand took the lead, guiding her firmly but cautiously through the array of dancers. The dance floor was unfamiliar territory, but his movements were made skillfully and with confidence. He held her lightly, and a warmth flowed through her.

"How are we doing?" he questioned.

"Fine," she assured him. "You don't like to dance, do you?" He so obviously didn't, Karen wondered what had made him offer.

"Let's just say I have an easy enough time making a fool of myself without doing it purposely."

Impulsively, Karen raised her head and gently laid her lips against the rough line of his jaw. "Thank you," she whispered softly.

He drew her slightly closer, and her mind whirled in a confused mixture of emotions. Surely she hadn't imbibed that much champagne. A glass or two, three at the most. Why should this one man affect her like this?

"I didn't want to let you go," he whispered into her hair, as if admitting to a fault, his voice low and husky.

"I didn't want to go, either." She sighed and rested her head against the velvety texture of his suit jacket.

His fingers spread across the small of her back, molding her slender figure against him. The beat of his heart sounded in her ear, telling her he was as affected by their closeness as she. Slowly, his hand stroked the back of her neck, his fingers entwining with her hair.

It wasn't necessary to talk. Karen hummed the melody as the musicians played, but the tune was inaudible compared to the glorious song her heart was singing. Somehow she'd always known it would be like this. Matthew had claimed he met Madeline and decided to marry her all in the space of one day's time. Karen had secretly scoffed. Choosing a life partner wasn't something one did after only a few hours' acquaintance. Now Karen realized her father had spoken the truth. Just as he had known, she knew now. She didn't love Rand; not yet. That would come later. But Karen had never been more certain of anything in her life. It was crazy, unorthodox.

"You're smiling, aren't you?" Rand asked after some time.

Karen had a difficult time finding her voice or thinking coherently. When she did answer, her voice was weak and low. "Yes, I am. How...how did you know?"

"I just do. I can feel it."

Karen didn't want to talk, afraid words would diminish the wonder of this enchanted evening. Instead, she surrendered to the tide of contentment that engulfed them both.

He squeezed her, and his strong hand cut into her waist, arching her even closer, as if he feared letting her go. "This is insane." His lips touched the crown of her hair, his breath stirring her short curls. But he didn't loosen his hold, nor did he give an indication of wanting to let her go.

Evan interrupted them with the news that Matthew was ready to leave. "He's waiting for you at the front entrance," Evan told Karen.

Reluctantly, Karen withdrew from Rand's arms.

"Dad and I rode together," she explained unnecessarily.

"Stay," Rand murmured. "I'll take you home."

"Fine, fine." Evan gave Karen a boyish wink. "I'm pleased you two are enjoying yourselves."

Slowly, Karen led the way off the dance floor, giving Rand time to reorient himself.

"I'll only be a minute." She left Rand beside the chairs they'd shared before dancing and hurried to meet Matthew. Without bothering to explain, she gave her father a peck on the cheek and told him she had a ride home and would talk to him in the morning. Leaving Matthew looking slightly perplexed, Karen rushed to the main part of the reception hall and Rand.

But Rand was nowhere to be seen. For an instant, panic filled her until comprehension came. This time she was wise enough to seek her coat before venturing into the cold.

Opening the glass door of the balcony, she saw him standing at the railing as before. He didn't turn toward her, although she was sure he'd heard the door open.

"Rand," she whispered, suddenly nervous.

He turned to her then, his face a mask of indecision and inner turmoil. Karen yearned to run to his arms and kiss away his misgivings, to assure him that this unfathomable feeling between them was right and good. But she was frozen, overcome by her own apprehensions.

"Rand, please," she pleaded, "don't shut me out."

At the sound of her trembling voice, Rand's hard features softened, and he opened his arms to her.

Hesitatingly, she came, sliding her hands around his middle. "I know it's crazy. I don't understand it, either," she admitted, her voice low and faltering.

"I've never experienced anything like this." His voice was a strange mixture of anger and wonder.

Karen wanted to assure him this phenomenon was as much a mystery to her. "Me either, never."

"Oh, what the hell," he groaned out before his mouth crushed down upon hers in a kiss that was both fierce and hungry. His arms, folded tightly around her, relaxed as the kiss continued. Their reaction shocked them both. It was as if a charge of lightning had arced between them, jolting them. They broke apart abruptly, and Karen's breath came in uneven gasps. Had she been less unnerved, she might have noticed Rand's breathing was just as uneven.

Gently, Rand pulled her back into his arms, as if he needed to further test this sensation. This time, his kiss was tender and sweet, his mouth settling firmly over hers, drawing from Karen her very soul. When he finished, she was trembling and weak.

"Dear heaven," he moaned into her hair, "what's happening?"

Karen laid her head against his shoulder. "It's an enchanted evening, and you're the gallant Perseus," she whispered a little breathlessly, still caught in the wonder of his kiss.

"I'm hardly the gallant one," Rand said with a hint of sarcasm. "It's more like a bewitched Perseus held captive by the charms of the Lady Andromeda." His finger and thumb stroked her chin sensuously.

Mentally, Karen recalled the mythological tale. "Perseus rescued Andromeda, remember? She was doomed without him." Breaking from his hold, Karen examined the sky. "Rand, Andromeda's there." Excitement crept into her voice as she needlessly pointed to the heavens.

Rand's arms surrounded her again. "Of course Andromeda's there. Perseus needs her," he murmured, as if admitting to his own lacking. "It's been said she's very beautiful. May I examine her?"

Karen didn't understand his meaning until his fingertips began gently caressing the contours of her face, causing her to blush. Her eyelashes fluttered downward in confusion.

"Not only soft and delicate but very, very lovely." His husky voice was filled with reverence. Tucking a hand beneath her chin, he lifted her face while his mouth made an unhurried descent to claim her lips. Again, Karen's mind whirled to a new height of sensual awareness.

"I can see a distinct advantage to your blindness," Karen mumbled once the rapid beat of her heart stilled. "I'm no raving beauty."

Her hands, pressing against his back, could feel his corded muscles tense. It was wrong to mention his handicap. "I shouldn't have said that," she began haltingly, uncertain. Her teeth bit into her bottom lip as if she wanted to bite back the thoughtless words. "I have much to learn, Rand. I guess I'm afraid of making another stupid blunder."

"That was a compliment," he said stiffly. "You spoke to me as you would any other companion. You didn't attempt to rescue me or fall into the traps others do. People tend to think that because I'm blind I must also be mentally retarded. Nothing on God's earth irritates me more. Treat me as you would any other man."

"Why are you so angry?" Karen asked, attempting to hide the hurt in her voice.

Rand forcefully released his breath before a smile lifted the corners of his mouth. "I guess I do tend to stand on a soapbox every now and then. What I'm trying to say is that I don't want to be treated like a blind man."

"That won't be difficult for me. I have a hard time remembering. You move with confidence and show none of the outward signs. I thought the blind used white canes or Seeing Eye dogs."

"I have partial vision," he explained, and his mouth returned to an inflexible line. "A bad case of the measles as a child ruined my vision, and it's grown steadily worse over the years."

"Then you can see some things?" she questioned.

"Very little. Soon it will be as you mentioned—the white cane or the dog."

With infinite tenderness, Karen's hands cupped his jaw to bring his face downward so she could very gently kiss each closed eye.

Rand groaned and pulled her tightly against him, his breathing ragged. "Oh, Karen," he murmured, holding her fiercely.

"Andromeda," she corrected with a smile.

They danced in each other's arms until there was no more music. They spoke little, embraced by the marvel of the night, creating their own world on a starlit balcony.

Rand was met outside the hall by a lanky, older man who stared curiously when he saw Karen was with Rand.

"Carl." Rand's grip tightened around Karen's waist. "I'd like you to meet the Lady Andromeda."

Without the slightest hesitation, the man grinned, showing crooked teeth but a ready, warm smile. "Pleased, I'm sure," he greeted her formally.

"I'm pleased, too, Carl. But to set the record straight, the name is Karen."

Carl grinned again and opened the back door of the car for them. "Where to?" he asked cheerfully as he started the engine.

"Karen," Rand whispered, "your address."

"Oh, of course." She supplied the information and

leaned against the back of the seat until Rand's arm cupped her shoulder, drawing her close to his side. They rode in silence, bathed in a rare kind of contentment.

Sooner than Karen wanted, Carl arrived at her apartment complex. Rand walked her to her door.

Gently, her hand stroked his face. "Thank you for the lovely, enchanted evening, Perseus."

Rand's kiss was tender and fierce all at the same time. Karen clung to him and moaned as the dizzy weakness spread through her limbs. A smile tugged at the corners of her lips, and she closed her eyes, surrendering to the charge of emotion Rand wrought in her.

Again, his mouth parted hers with a kiss as searing as it was devastating. "Goodbye, my lady," he murmured, and pressed his lips against her fragrant hair.

Karen opened the apartment door and floated inside, her heart singing a glorious melody.

Two

Karen woke to the smell and sounds of perking coffee. Reluctantly, she rose, looping the tie of her velour bathrobe around her slender waist. Stifling a yawn, she sauntered from her bedroom; the aroma of the coffee guided her into the small kitchen. She took a mug from the cupboard and poured herself a cup, ignoring the fact that the coffeepot was still perking.

"Ye shouldn't be doing that." A foggy voice broke through her consciousness. "You'll get grounds in your cup."

Surprise snapped Karen's eyes open. "Dad! What are you doing here?"

An injured look narrowed the faded hazel eyes. "'Tis a fine greeting for your father."

Karen lowered herself into the large overstuffed chair opposite Matthew. "Dad, as much as I love you, I must insist you stop entering my apartment like this." She schooled her expression against the pleading puppy-dog look her father gave her.

"Forgive an old man's curiosity." He lowered his gaze, suddenly looking lost and aged beyond his years.

"All right, Dad, you're forgiven. Gosh, you look awful."

His mouth deepened into slanted grooves of amusement. "Too many dances with a demanding widow." The look he cast her sent Karen into helpless giggles.

"Serves you right, old man."

"You're the bane of my life, you wicked child," he teased lovingly. "Now, tell me about the fellow you met last night. Do you like him?"

Self-consciously, Karen centered her attention on the steaming mug cradled between her hands. "Very much."

When she didn't volunteer any further information, Matthew probed again. "Well, go on. What's his name? When will you be seeing him again?"

"Dad, honestly." Karen stood abruptly, her fluid movements displaying a subtle grace. "Did you suddenly join the FBI? I don't like being interrogated. When will you realize I'm not your little girl anymore?" She didn't mean to sound so angry.

"Lass," Matthew pleaded, "you'll always be my little girl."

Karen's mouth thinned defensively until she realized her father's silver head had possessed only a salting of gray three years ago. He was aging right before her eyes. So much had changed in both their lives since her mother's death. Matthew had lost more than his wife and best friend. In the months that followed Madeline's unexpected death, Matthew's appreciation for life, his aspirations, even his personality had altered dramatically. Seeing her father now would have shocked someone who had known him three years before.

Shrugging in a gesture of defeat, Karen lowered

herself into the chair and said, "His name is Randall Prescott; he's a professor at the university. I like him, Dad, better than anyone I've met." She paused, watching Matthew's reaction. "Rand is blind."

Matthew's eyes clouded with uncertainty. "Blind." His tongue tasted the word as if he found it unpleasant. "Lass, are you sure of your feelings?"

"I'm not sure of anything," Karen murmured dryly. "All I know is that I found him to be the most intriguing man I've ever met. Something happened last night, to Rand and me." She was quick to include herself.

"Something unusual. I can't even put it into words. It was almost as if our spirits communicated." She gave a short, embarrassed laugh. "I know that sounds crazy. Rand is tender and sensitive, but I don't think he exposes that side of his nature often. I... I think I was privileged to see that in him. And, Dad, he listens."

Matthew nodded. "I understand the blind often have an extremely good sense of hearing."

"Not hearing," she corrected. "He listens. He's not so caught in his own ego that he felt the need to impress me. He was interested in me as a person, my thoughts, opinions. That's listening, and there's a world of difference."

Matthew was studying Karen when she raised her eyes to his. "Yes, lass, that there is."

"Maybe it was the music or the champagne; I don't know." Her mind whirled with the memory of the electricity that had sparked between them.

"I think the lad was responding to the sensitive chord in you, Karen. Do you remember as a child you were always the one to rescue lost or injured animals? And several people, too, as I recall."

"Oh, Dad, I'm not rescuing Rand. For one thing, he doesn't need it. He's independent and proud. You've got to promise me you won't tell him about those things. He'd think I'm making a charity case of him. He'd hate that."

Matthew's eyes showed understanding. "I won't say a word," he assured her. "A man needs his pride."

Karen relaxed against the back cushion of the chair and sighed gratefully. "Thanks, Dad."

"As for Rand being blind, I would wish a sighted man for you, but that's my own selfishness. You're twenty-three now, and if you aren't an able judge of character, your mother and I have failed. I trust that in you, Karen. Your mother and I taught you well."

An overflowing love for her parents warmed Karen. "That you did, Dad. That you did."

Karen watched the phone all day, almost willing it to ring. She needed Rand to call just to confirm that last night had been as real to him as it was to her, and that the night hadn't been a romantic dream she'd conjured up with the moonlight. When he didn't, she couldn't contain her disappointment.

The next morning, Karen met her friend Audrey in a small coffee shop for their midmorning break. Both girls were employed by Tacoma's largest cable television service. Karen was the supervisor for the data processing department. Audrey had also been a candidate for the position but was relieved when Karen had it. Of the two, Karen had been the natural choice, having displayed tact, discretion, and forethought in a multitude of situations. Hiring a female supervisor had been only a token gesture by the company toward equal rights. Karen had stepped into a cesspool of re-sentment from her male counterparts. But it wasn't long before she grudgingly won their respect. She was good at her job and knew it.

"Do you realize I only have fourteen more days to finish my Christmas shopping?" Audrey announced as she set her cup opposite Karen's on the small table.

"Luckily, I did mine weeks ago," Karen said with-out meaning to sound like the methodical, organized soul she was. "I guess it helps when things have to be mailed."

"You'd have had it finished, anyway." Audrey sighed jealously. "I don't suppose I could interest you in fight-ing the crowds with me tonight? I thought we might have dinner out."

"Not tonight. Sorry, Audrey. I'm expecting a phone call."

"Someone I know?" Audrey quizzed with unleashed curiosity.

"No," Karen said pointedly.

Rand dominated her thoughts. Was he experienc-ing doubts about their evening? Had he decided this thing between them was the result of too much wine and music? Karen could only venture a guess at his musings. She had never longed to hear from someone so badly. Randall Prescott had her feeling very much like a schoolgirl praying that special boy would ask her to the prom. The melodious song in her heart was now replaced by an aching void of unanswered questions.

The phone was ringing when she let herself into the apartment that night. Karen dropped her purse and rushed to answer it, her heartbeat accelerating wildly. It was a carpet-cleaning salesman with a pitch for steam-cleaning her rugs. She definitely wasn't interested.

Audrey was at Karen's desk first thing the next morning. "Did you get your important phone call?" she asked before adding another pile of papers to Karen's workload.

"No, I'm afraid not." She tried to sound nonchalant and didn't bother to look up from her paperwork.

"I don't think you have much to worry about," Audrey said kindly. "He'll phone; only a blind man would be immune to your charms." Shock held Karen rigid. "I'll bet he phones tonight."

But Audrey was wrong. Rand didn't contact Karen that night or the next.

Friday night, Matthew was in Karen's apartment, waiting for her.

"Dad!" she admonished irritably. "The next time this happens, I'm going to have my lock changed."

"As soon as ye know why I'm here, you'll be singing my praises."

Feigning indifference, Karen hung her coat in the closet and went into the kitchen to make coffee.

"Don't you want to know what I found out about Randall Prescott?"

"Not particularly," she lied with an ease she didn't feel. Walking into her bedroom, she examined the contents of her closet.

"Karen, lass." Matthew followed her, his voice full of exasperation. "Hold still a minute. I want to talk to you."

"Sorry, Dad, I haven't got time now. I've got a date."

Matthew's puzzled features relaxed. "Ah, you're meeting Rand again."

"Not Rand." She pulled a crisp taffeta blouse and black velvet skirt from the closet, laying the outfit across her bed. "Jim Malloy is picking me up in an hour."

"Jim Malloy? What happened to Randall Prescott?"

Her throat muscles were so tight Karen could barely speak. "I... I decided not to see him again. You were right about my feelings for him. Randall Prescott is just another lost kitten I wanted to rescue." She hesitated, then added, "Maybe it was a latent Florence Nightingale complex."

For several minutes, Matthew said nothing. "All right, Karen, you have to decide what you think is best."

"I have," she mumbled, returning to the kitchen to take the coffeepot from the burner. "Help yourself to coffee if you like. I've got to shower."

Scratching his head, Matthew watched Karen head for the bathroom. "Women," he mumbled. "They'll be a mystery to me on my dying day."

Karen had dated Jim Malloy before. He was what she considered a safe date. He was friendly without being pushy, considerate without being condescending. Jim's only problem was that Karen found him unforgivably boring. A hundred times during the dinner and movie, Karen wished she could change her feelings. What was she waiting for? Jim may not be a knight in shining armor, but he was nice. She was being stupid, she told herself as he politely escorted her to her apartment. Meekly, she submitted to his kiss. But it was hardly a kiss at all, more a brushing of lips.

Frustrated with herself, Karen opened her mouth

slightly to deepen the contact, then moaned in disappointment. Why couldn't she feel what she had in Rand's arms? Why was she left with this void, this aching feeling at the touch of another man?

Jim reacted urgently to her initiative, crushing her against him. His hands fumbled with the opening of her coat, seeking her breasts.

Karen jerked away. "Stop it," she demanded. Her shoulders heaved with emotion, finding his touch repulsive.

"Come on. What am I supposed to think with a come-on like that?" His eyes were glazed with passion. "Let's go inside, talk this out." He pulled her back into his arms, his lips nuzzling her neck.

Again, Karen fought him. "No," she said sternly. "Not tonight. Not ever."

His dark, beady eyes filled with contempt. "You're nothing but a tease. Do you get your jollies by turning men on and then——"

"I think you'd better leave," Karen interrupted him, her voice steady and cold. Placing her apartment key between her middle and index fingers so its steel edge could inflict harm if necessary, she stared directly into his anger-filled eyes.

Jim didn't ignore the warning. "All right," he spat viciously, "have it your way." He left in a hot temper, and Karen heard the squeal of his tires as he pulled from the parking lot.

After letting herself into the apartment, Karen leaned heavily against the closed door. What was the matter with her? A feeling of desperation encompassed her. She had led Jim to believe she wanted more than a good-night kiss and couldn't blame him for his re-action. For a fleeting second, she almost hated Rand.

"Damn you," she whispered harshly, and sat in the still apartment, staring into the darkness. She didn't move for a long while.

The next week passed with intolerable slowness, although Karen made an effort to keep busy. But each time the phone rang, her heart would beat expectantly. Each time, she tasted bitter disappointment.

Five days before Christmas, Karen received a long-distance call from her sister in Texas.

"Judy?" she asked with surprise. "Is everything okay?" With a limited budget, Judy rarely phoned unless it was important.

"I've got news too good for a mere letter," she began.

"You're pregnant?" Karen guessed immediately. "Well, for heaven's sake, have a girl this time, would you? Dad is driving me crazy for a granddaughter."

"Would you kindly shut up?" Judy chided with a laugh. "I'm not pregnant! I'm calling because Mike's being transferred to McChord."

"McChord Air Force Base?" Karen asked in disbe-lief. "In Tacoma?"

"Yes, silly."

"Oh, Judy, I'm so glad. You don't know how Dad and I've missed you."

"How is Dad?"

"Wait and see. I swear he's getting crazier by the day. Everything's changed since Mom died, especially Dad."

"I know." Judy sobered. "Even his letters are getting weird. There's a bit of bad news, too. Mike's being stationed in Thailand for a year."

"Judy, no." Karen's voice filled with sympathy. Her sister and husband had been separated before. It was a miserable time for them both.

"I guess I should be used to it by now. But at least this time I'll be by family."

"I'm so glad you're coming home." Karen tried to disguise the unhappiness in her voice.

"You don't sound right. What's wrong?" Judy and Karen were too close to hide anything from each other. Judy quickly detected the tiniest voice inflection and knew immediately things were not well with her sister.

Karen hesitated. How could she possibly explain? "I can't talk now. I'll tell you everything later. I promise," she said in a long, uneven breath.

"Count on it, sis," Judy said softly.

Judy's news was just the tonic needed to brighten Karen's Christmas. The news did a world of good for Matthew, too, Karen noted as they traveled to the Forsyths' on Christmas afternoon. Matthew seemed happier than Karen could remember since her mother's death.

At first Karen was a bit uneasy at her uncle's, fearing he would mention Randall Prescott, but the day passed comfortably, with no allusion to him or the party.

Everything moved very quickly after Christmas. Within a week, Judy and her family had arrived and moved into government housing. Mike, an aircraft mechanic, was due to fly out Monday afternoon, and he worked around the clock to settle his family before departing.

Karen volunteered to keep the boys Saturday night so the couple could spend the evening alone.

"Are you sure about this?" Judy questioned hesitantly. "James and Carter can be a handful."

"Of course I'm sure. I've been looking forward to this all week. If I were you, I'd make the most of my generous offer." She batted her eyelashes seductively and watched her sister blush.

"I know, but—"

"No buts. Dad and I've got everything planned. We're going to have a great time, aren't we, boys?" Immediately, the two lively youngsters flew into the room, bounding with energy.

"Will you buy me a squirt gun, Aunt Karen?" six-year-old Carter asked.

"Carter," Judy warned in disapproval.

"We'll see." Karen affectionately ruffled the top of his blond head. "Get your sleeping bags loaded into my car. I'll be there in a minute." She placed her empty coffee mug in the kitchen sink and gathered her coat and purse. "Dad and I've got everything arranged. I'm taking the boys to a movie this afternoon, and then we're picking up Dad at the chess club. He's playing in that tournament this weekend," she explained needlessly. "From there we're going to have Chinese food."

Judy walked down the steps with her. "The boys will love it." Her expression softened. "Mike and I appreciate this more than you know."

Karen gave her sister an affectionate hug. "The pleasure's mine."

Judy laughed slyly. "Tell me that tomorrow afternoon; then I'll believe you."

"Come on, Aunt Karen. We're ready," the boys

called from her compact Dodge, having rolled down the window.

"See what I mean?" Judy said.

The movie was a western comedy the boys ate their way through. After three bags of popcorn, two soft drinks, and a candy bar each, Karen wondered where they'd put the meal she'd planned for later.

"When's dinner?" James asked on the way to the parking lot.

"Dinner?" Karen gasped, then laughed, shaking her head at her nephew. "I can see I'm going to need groceries before we pick up your grandpa."

They made a quick trip to the neighborhood market, buying breakfast items and a few between-meals snacks, just in case the boys got hungry during the night, they told her.

Twenty minutes later, they arrived at the chess club. James and Carter looked around, curiously watching the players sitting at the long tables. Although the club was filled to capacity with nearly a hundred occupants, the noise level was surprisingly low. Glancing about the room, Karen easily caught sight of her father. He sat at one of the tables, intently involved in his game. She pointed him out to the boys and explained why they must be quiet and wait patiently. They sat in the back of the room, watching as each of the players made his move, then hit the clock, setting the other player's timer. The boys asked a couple of questions, but otherwise were content to sit and watch.

Briefly surveying the room again, Karen's attention moved to a table with three players. Instinctively, she stiffened, her emotions muddled and confused. "Rand." She spoke his name softly, her voice barely above a whisper. James and Carter glanced at her questioningly, but she didn't notice.

Rand lifted his head briefly, as though he'd heard, paused, then returned his attention to the game. But it wasn't possible for him to have heard her at this distance. His back, facing her, was held rigid and determined.

Drawing a deep breath, Karen's first reaction was anger and resentment. Yet there was a flooding relief, an elation just in seeing him again, even from a distance.

Karen continued to watch him for several moves with wry amusement. If he couldn't see the chessboard, how could he participate? It was soon evident Rand didn't use the board; the figures were moved for him on command by the third party. The entire game was played in his mind.

She experienced a twinge of pride when he won the match. Her gaze followed him as he left the table and sauntered toward her.

"I'll be right back," she instructed her nephews. "Stay here."

She met Rand at the other side of the room. "Hello," she said evenly.

He showed no surprise, his face a proud mask. "Karen." He nodded in recognition.

"I didn't know if you'd remember me." She was being untruthful. He may not have contacted her, but he darn well hadn't forgotten her. She would have staked her life's savings on the fact.

"I remember you."

"I realize this is slightly out of the ordinary," she

began haltingly, "but I'd like to know what I did wrong."

His brows drew together in a frown of confusion. "Wrong?" He repeated the word. "You did nothing wrong."

Of their own volition, her eyes were drawn to his face. It was unfair that he should have this much effect on her after all this time. For a moment, Karen thought he wanted to reach out and touch her, but he clenched his fist and held it stiffly at his side.

"Is it Cora?" At least she thought that was the name her godfather had mentioned.

Surprise flickered briefly over his expression.

"Uncle Evan mentioned her the night of the party," Karen explained shakily. "He said you usually attend social functions with her, and I thought there…there may be some romantic involvement."

His mouth thinned with impatience. "No, this has nothing to do with Cora."

"If I didn't do anything to offend you and…and if there's not another woman involved, I'd like to know what I did wrong."

He paused long enough to take his coat from the rack and slip it on. Pulling the gloves from the pocket, he clenched them tightly in one hand.

"My godfather also said you were a professor."

"What did you think I did? Sold pencils on street corners?" The tightening muscles of his jaw were the only evidence of anger.

"No, of course not." Oh dear, she was making a horrible mess of this. She inhaled deeply, hoping to calm herself and clear her thinking. "Listen, I'm going about this in the worst possible way. Could we start again?"

Ignoring her plea, he stepped outside, allowing the door to close before she could follow.

As childish as it seemed, Karen was tempted to stomp her foot and scream. Instead, she swallowed her anger and opened the door, stepping into the dark afternoon.

He had gone only a couple of feet. Karen allowed the door to shut before approaching him. "Rand," she said softly, "it doesn't matter to me that you're blind."

His posture remained rigid and uncompromising until Karen could tolerate it no longer. Without questioning the wisdom of her action, she placed a hand on his arm.

"Randall Prescott, would you kindly listen to me? If you had perfect twenty-twenty vision or if you were as blind as a bat, I'd still find you the most captivating man I've ever met."

His mouth twisted into a cynical smile that told her he didn't believe a word she'd said.

"It doesn't make any difference," she stressed again, quickly losing patience.

"Of course it makes a difference," he shouted angrily, startling Karen. He caught her shoulder in a tight grip. "Blast you, Karen. Blast you for being here. Blast you for—what the hell?"

Icy water hit Karen in the face. She gasped before being hit again. "James… Carter…stop it right now."

The two boys magically appeared and lowered their weapons. "I told you we'd get in trouble," Carter said righteously.

James ignored him. "I'm sorry, Aunt Karen. I didn't mean to squirt you. I was aiming at him." He pointed a finger at Rand. "You moved in my way."

Rand handed his handkerchief to Karen. "You didn't mention you were related to the Dalton Brothers." A mere hint of a smile lifted the corners of his mouth.

Karen accepted the cloth and wiped the water from her face. "These are my nephews, James and Carter Turner."

"He was holding your shoulder real mean," James explained, hoping to vindicate his actions. "He looked like he was mad at you." Rand's imposing figure was enough to give the stoutest of men second thoughts. As far as Karen was concerned, the boys deserved a medal for bravery.

"You both owe Dr. Prescott an apology." Her voice was stern, but she worked hard to suppress a smile. Rand's face and shirt were soaked, and, feeling guilty, she returned his handkerchief.

"You're the one who got Aunt Karen in the face," Carter shouted angrily at his brother. "Now I bet we don't get dinner in the restaurant."

"It's all right, boys." A smile relaxed Rand's taut features. "You were right to protect your aunt."

"You're not mad?" James asked hesitatingly.

Rand allayed his fears. "No, but I want you to know I'd never do anything to hurt Karen."

Carter was obviously pleased with the turn of events and was quick to make peace. "I like her real well. She took us to the movie and let us eat all the popcorn we wanted and—"

"If you'd never hurt my aunt Karen, how come you were holding her shoulder like that?" James was not as easily appeased as his younger brother.

Rand didn't get the opportunity to answer, for Matthew burst upon the scene and demanded, "Where have ye been? I've been ready for five minutes. If it hadn't been for your purse, Karen, I wouldn't have known ye were even here."

"My purse!" Karen cried in dismay. She'd completely forgotten it in her eagerness to speak to Rand.

Her father handed the leather bag to Karen, who distractedly checked its contents for anything missing.

"I took the keys, so the boys and me will be leaving ye now."

"Dad?" she asked, her face a puzzled frown. What was he talking about? She was having dinner with him and the boys; it was what they'd planned. "I thought all of us were having dinner."

"Ye need to be discussing things with Rand," he said, dismissing her lightly. "Are ye hungry, boys?" he asked, grinning devilishly at Karen.

The boys gave a chorus of cheers, and with a hearty shout ran to Karen's car.

"Damn good game, Prescott. I demand a rematch."

Karen's attention swiveled to Rand, searching his face. "Did you have a match with my father this afternoon?" Karen could only imagine the things Matthew had been telling Rand. Indignantly, she turned her attention to Matthew to discover he had already left. Her small car purred as the engine came to life.

"Dad," she shouted angrily. "What about me?" Her full mouth compressed angrily as Matthew passed her in the street and gave her a friendly wave goodbye.

"I think he's abandoned you to my care." Rand's frown showed her he was none too pleased with her company.

"Well, don't look so thrilled," she snapped.

Silence followed until Rand began to chuckle, but

the sound of his amusement did little to soothe Karen's ruffled feelings.

"This isn't funny," she insisted.

"Yes, it is." Rand broke into full rumbling laughter that shook his shoulders.

He continued laughing. "The fact is, I haven't found anything this funny in years." He contained himself somewhat. "Is it always like this with your family?"

"Sometimes it's worse," Karen stated dryly.

His amusement relaxed to soft chuckles. "Since Matthew's seen fit to throw us together, let's find someplace to talk."

Karen's spirits soared. This was what she'd originally wanted, to be with Rand. All at once, she wanted to kiss her interfering, meddling father.

They discovered a café several blocks from the chess club, and Rand ordered them coffee.

The silence stretched between them until Karen found her hands were trembling. Nervously, she clenched them together in her lap.

"Coffee hits the spot," she said with a false cheerfulness that sounded awkward even to her own ears.

Rand looked away. "Listen, Karen," he breathed forcefully, "I don't need to tell you I enjoyed meeting you and the Forsyths' party." He paused, his jaw tightening. "I thought you got my message when I didn't contact you afterward."

Karen gave a short, sarcastic laugh. "I got it, all right. I just don't happen to like it."

Rand placed his coffee cup on the table, and Karen noted how tightly he was clenching it. "Do you always get what you like?"

"No," she said lightly, "but not from lack of trying."

"I find this all flattering, but—"

"Flattering?" she interrupted.

"Very flattering," he said firmly. "But, Karen, you're young and pretty, and I won't have you wasting your time—"

"On a blind man?" she interrupted him again. "Squandering my youth and beauty—is that it?"

"Yes," he retorted angrily.

"Honestly, Rand, the next thing you'll be telling me is that I deserve a whole man or something equally stupid."

"That's exactly what I'm saying."

Karen nearly choked on her coffee. "I can't believe this," she said, keeping her voice level. "And even with this ridiculous attitude, don't you think I should be the one to decide? It's my life. I can squander it if I want." She ended with a short, nervous laugh.

"Not necessarily," Rand replied with a twinge of bitterness. "If you aren't going to use common sense, I must."

"What do you mean?" she demanded. "I've got terrific common sense."

Rand leaned against the back of the red booth. "You seem to be disregarding the fact that I don't want you, nor do I need you."

"I know that," she countered swiftly. She glanced down at her coffee, relieved he couldn't see the hurt in her eyes. "All I know is that I've never experienced anything more beautiful than that night with you. I don't even know how to explain myself. But you can't deny it, Rand. You felt it, too." She paused and waited for him to comment, but he didn't. "It might have been some crazy kind of magic that touched us that night—

the Christmas spirit of love and goodwill. I can only guess." She hesitated. His mouth had become the thin, hard line she recognized. Her back stiffened. Rand could say what he liked; instinct told her he would lie. She'd backed him into a defensive corner, and he'd say anything to block her from his life. She simply wasn't going to let him.

Suddenly, something changed in his posture. He relaxed somewhat; his mouth softened enough for her to realize he was remembering. The enchantment of the party touched him again, or perhaps he was as weary of the argument as she.

With his resolve weakening, Karen quickly seized the opportunity. "I remember you once told me you wished to be treated like a sighted person. Well, I think you should know that if you could see me, you'd notice I'm half starved."

His mouth twisted into a fleeting smile. "Is that a hint?"

"No, it's a blatant attempt to con you into taking me to dinner." A full smile wrinkling the corners of his eyes told her she'd succeeded. "But before we do anything, I think we need to make an agreement."

A dark brow lifted itself expressively. "Such as?"

"We need a trial period to test our feelings. Everything was so crazy that night—the stars, the music, the moonlight."

"The champagne," Rand added dryly.

She nodded before realizing he couldn't see her acknowledgment.

"I guess I need to know if what I felt was real or some romantic dream." She hesitated before adding,

"There would be no obligation on either side. Are you willing to do that?"

A veiled look came over him, one so transient and brief that Karen wondered if she'd imagined it. Then Karen knew. In that fleeting second, she knew. For all his resolve, for all his determination, he wanted her. He desired her more than she dreamed possible. At the same time, he hesitated; the flint hardness of his will and years of hard-wrought self-control warred with the tumult of his desires.

"No obligation on either side?" he questioned.

"None."

He ran a weary hand over his face, then slouched forward. "All right, Karen."

Three

"I've never known you to be particularly proper about this sort of thing," Judy said with straight pins between her teeth. "If I were you, I'd contact *him*. Turn," she directed.

Karen was standing atop her coffee table while Judy secured pins in the hem of the wild-rose-colored dress. "I think with any other man I would. But not Rand... I've done as much as I dare." It'd been two long weeks since their meeting at the chess club. Two of the longest weeks of Karen's life. A hundred times she was convinced she'd never hear from Rand again. Not even the gentle caress of his hand against her cheek when he'd dropped her off at her apartment or the promise he'd phone had been enough to dispel her insecurities. Karen had been so confident after that night. They'd eaten sandwiches at the café and drunk several more cups of coffee. They'd talked for what seemed only a short time but was actually hours. Karen told him of her childhood and friends, the pain of her mother's death—things she'd never shared with anyone else. Rand could not see her with his eyes, perhaps, but he could read her as if they'd known each other for years. Several times he paused and asked, "That's not all, is it?" or, "What were your feelings?" Karen had bared her soul to him as she hadn't with any other human. He listened intently when she spoke of her worries over Matthew and the changes in him since Madeline's death. He didn't offer advice, only listened with a knowing look that engendered confidence.

That evening, Karen learned bits and pieces of Rand's life, too. His mother lived in New York and worked for the state insurance commissioner's office. His father had died when he was eleven; Rand was an only child.

"Okay, let me stand back and see if this is even." Judy broke into Karen's thoughts. A warm smile formed. "This dress is going to be lovely. I'm proud of it." The vibrant jacquard material was being hand-crafted for Karen as a birthday gift from her sister. "I'm sure if Rand could see you now, he'd be knocking the phone off the hook."

Karen didn't bother to correct Judy by saying Rand would never "see" her or the dress.

Judy's hand went to her chin as she continued to study Karen. "I don't think I've ever realized how much you resemble Mom. You've got her tilted nose and those warm, dark eyes. You're as beautiful as she was."

Karen had always been referred to as the "pretty" McAlister daughter. Judy was far from ugly, but her nose was a trifle too large, her mouth too full. But in the things that mattered, Judy Turner was the most beautiful woman Karen knew. "A lot of good a cute nose does me!" She smiled gently. "You've got the talent, while I'm stuck with two left hands. I could never sew anything this lovely."

"Sure you could." Judy dismissed her lack of confidence with a short shake of her head. "You'd better change. I imagine Dad's thoroughly tired of showing my boys chess moves."

Karen was in the bedroom when the phone rang. "I'll get it," Judy called. Karen stopped dressing, her pants zipper half-closed. Her heart beat expectantly, as it always did when the phone rang.

"No, this is her sister, Judy," Karen heard her sister say. "Yes, I am," Judy added. "I heard you three had quite an introduction. Let me apologize again for the boys." She laughed. "Just a minute. I'll get Karen."

Judy burst through the bedroom door. "It's him… It's him."

Karen released the breath she'd unconsciously been holding. A flooding sense of relief came over her until her knees trembled.

"Well, aren't you going to answer it?" Judy whispered fiercely.

"Yes…yes," she said again, hoping her voice sounded composed and confident, knowing it didn't. Slowly, to calm her nerves, Karen walked into the living room and picked up the phone. "Hello, Rand," she said softly.

"Karen"—his voice was curt—"how are you?"

"Fine, thank you." She was, now that he'd phoned. "And you?"

"Good." An awkward silence followed. "The Tacoma Actors Guild is putting on a play at the Pantages Thursday night. Would you like to go?"

"Yes, I would," she said with an eagerness that betrayed her.

"Wouldn't you like to know the name of the play?" he chided softly.

Karen silently berated herself. Why did she have to appear so anxious? "All right, if you feel it's important." Suddenly, she wanted to laugh. What did it matter if he knew how eager she was to see him? If she'd answered him in a completely monotone voice, he would have guessed her feelings, anyway. "What time should I be ready?"

Rand paused. "I'll be coming directly from the school and will probably be at your place around seven-fifteen. The play's at eight; that should give us plenty of time."

"I'll be ready." Karen felt like singing; she wanted to laugh and dance all at the same moment.

When he spoke, she could hear the smile in his voice. "I'll see you then. Bye for now."

"Bye." Karen replaced the receiver and glanced at her sister's curious face. Driven by a happiness she couldn't contain, Karen flung her arms around Judy. "How soon did you say my new dress would be ready?"

For the second time, Karen smoothed a wrinkle from her skirt. Nervous fingers toyed with the deeply veed neckline of the bodice, examining again the velvet ribbon, lace, and pearls of the ornate trim. The skill and patience it had taken to string each pearl between the delicate lace and ribbon brought a sense of awe to Karen. The dress was far more than a simple birthday gift; it was a labor of love.

Karen was ready early, absurdly so. Rand wasn't

due for another twenty minutes, and already she had checked her appearance ten times in the hallway mirror. Careful attention had been paid to her makeup, although she seldom wore much, preferring the natural look. Styling her hair had taken the major part of an hour. If anyone had known she was going to such trouble for someone who could never see her, they would have thought she was crazy.

When Rand's knock came, Karen nearly jumped from her chair. Releasing a deep sigh of tension, she paused long enough to calm herself.

"Hello, Rand," she greeted cheerfully.

He moved into her apartment, and again Karen was struck by his basic masculine appeal. His face possessed character and strength.

"Karen," he said, his voice formal, "are you ready, or do you need a few extra minutes?"

"I'm ready." They were acting like awkward strangers meeting for the first time on a blind date. The analogy nearly sent her into nervous giggles. "Would... would you like something to drink before we go?"

Rand shifted; everything about him seemed controlled. "Thank you, no. The taxi's waiting."

Their conversation in the cab was so polite and stilted that Karen wanted to scream in frustration. This evening would never work with Rand's attitude. His formal greeting, the stiff conversation, indicated that although he was complying with his part of the agreement, he regretted it.

The seats for the play were among the best. The oppressive silence stretched between them while the theater began filling. Suddenly, Karen turned toward Rand and said the most ridiculous thing that came to mind.

"The rain in Spain stays mainly in the plain."

He relaxed. "The rain?" He arched a curious brow.

"That's right," she assured him coolly. "It stays mainly in the plain."

Against his will, Karen noted his eyes deepened into smiling grooves. "What makes you say that?" He was completely earnest.

"I could see what was coming. First you'd ask me if I was comfortable, and then we'd discuss the weather. It was either say something totally ridiculous or scream."

Amusement softened his expression. "I'm eternally grateful you didn't scream."

"You're most welcome. Now, are you going to enjoy the evening, or do I have to create a scene?"

For a moment, Karen thought Rand was going to laugh. "My mother warned me about women like you."

"I'm sure she did," she said resolutely after a pause. She shifted forward slightly. "Would you mind helping me with my coat? If I don't take it off now, I'll roast later."

His hand lingered as it cupped her shoulder in the briefest of contacts before following the sleeve and holding it stationary while she withdrew her arm.

"Thank you," she said softly.

His mouth moved into a lazy smile as he relaxed against the plush seat. "You're welcome." Tentatively, his hand sought hers, gently folding her slim one in his.

Karen settled into her seat, too. It was almost impossible to describe what a simple thing like holding hands with Rand did to her. Even a dictionary, Karen decided, couldn't define the pleasure she found in his company.

"Tell me about the play. It has the most curious

title—*Deadly Vintage*." An aura of anticipation and excitement touched Karen, who enjoyed live performances above all else.

"A friend of mine wrote it," Rand began. "I think you'll find the plot intriguing. I won't spoil it for you by discussing details." He finished just as the curtain rose.

Rand was right; the plot was excellent, and the cast held the audience's full attention. The story revolved around a young man facing financial ruin, struggling against all odds to keep his business and family together. Karen felt herself tense as one complication after another fell upon the young man's shoulders. Right before the intermission, a second, older man was introduced, who promised to help the young man.

Karen sighed gratefully. "Things were beginning to look a little bleak there for a minute," she said to Rand.

He squeezed her hand and murmured cryptically, "Things aren't always what they appear."

"Oh, no?" She slouched against the back of her seat. "I thought you said you wouldn't ruin the story for me."

Amusement glittered from his dark eyes. "I wouldn't dream of it."

A sick feeling knotted Karen's stomach as the second part of the play unfolded. The older man agreed to pay all the younger man's debts on one condition. The young man must agree to have dinner with the older man. Sometime during the course of the meal, the young man would be offered wine. But the wine contained a deadly poison. No physical pressure would be applied to the man to drink the wine. If he chose to drink, it would be of his own free will. The man hesitantly agreed, but told the rich man he had much to live for and had no intention of drinking the wine.

The older man amicably agreed that that was exactly as he wished it. Later, the young man learned this same agreement had been made many times over with others in the same financial difficulties. They, too, had agreed to the dinner with no intention of drinking the deadly vintage. In every instance, the men drank the wine and died.

The characterization of the rich man was portrayed superbly. The overwhelming force of his personality, his power of persuasion, had Karen sitting on the edge of her seat, wishing there was some way she could intervene and help the younger man. The play ended just as the wine was offered.

"That's it?" Karen gasped as the final curtain closed. "It can't possibly end there. What happened?" She turned anxiously to Rand. "What happened?" she demanded again.

"My dear Karen, I have no more idea than you."

The cast was called for three curtain calls, after which the theater began emptying. "Are you ready?" Rand questioned.

"No...not yet," Karen said stubbornly. Again and again, certain phrases and scenes played in her mind.

Rand shifted impatiently. "Karen," he said finally, "no one's coming to add a postscript. This is it."

"He didn't accept the wine," she said more forcefully than she meant. She stood and reached for her coat.

"Is that so?" He was mocking her.

"Yes. If you examined the evidence, you'd realize it, too," she defended herself.

"It seems to me you're searching for a satisfactory conclusion. That sensitive female nature of yours insists upon a happy ending."

"Honestly, Rand, my sensitive female nature, as you call it, has nothing to do with this. What do you think he did?"

Karen had the curious sensation Rand was watching her, not with his eyes, of course, but with his other senses.

"I'm not sure," he said thoughtfully. "Why don't we go somewhere and discuss it? Have you had dinner?"

Karen hadn't; her nerves had been a jumbled mess most of the day, and although she hadn't eaten since lunch, she wasn't the least bit hungry.

"No, as a matter of fact, I haven't." Karen smiled to herself. She may not have much of an appetite, but she wasn't about to refuse an invitation from Rand.

Karen ordered a shrimp salad and coffee while Rand had apple pie. "Are you sure you wouldn't care for a glass of wine?" he teased after the waiter had taken the menu.

"Hardly!" She didn't bother to disguise her amusement. This was how she'd prayed their evening would be—a teasing banter between them without the steel-wall façade Rand had erected earlier. They discussed the play in detail; Karen argued her view while Rand, with clearheaded logic, proved exactly the opposite, that the younger man had drunk the wine.

"Now I don't know what to believe." Irrationally, she was almost angry with him. The matter had been settled in her own mind, and he had completely shattered her confidence. "I was perfectly content before."

Rand grinned that crooked little smile she'd seen only at rare times when he was especially pleased about something. Using some of the same rationale she'd used, Rand proceeded to prove that indeed the man had not drunk the wine.

Karen was astonished as she listened to him. Everything he said seemed perfectly sensible, sound, and reasonable, yet only a few minutes before he'd taken the opposing viewpoint.

"Remind me never to argue with you," she muttered.

"I've had more time to think about it, is all. And if past evidence is anything to go by, you hold your own in any argument. I certainly never intended to see you again, and look at us now."

Karen's eyes widened in hurt astonishment.

"I'd better phone Carl," Rand added after checking his watch. It was one made specially for the blind, and Karen was curious as to how it worked. "It's nearly midnight, and you're a working girl."

"Not tomorrow I'm not," she answered absently, trying to catch a glimpse of his wrist again.

"Is there some holiday I don't know about?" he asked, a teasing glint in his eye.

"Not a holiday, exactly." She placed her coffee cup on the china saucer. "It's my birthday, and the cable company gives their employees the day off with pay. Rather a nice gesture, I think."

"Your birthday?" His expression turned serious, as if he'd made a social blunder. "You should have said something."

Karen gave a tiny laugh. "I just did."

"You're twenty-four?" It wasn't really a question, and Karen didn't bother to answer. "There are twelve years between us. I'm far too old for you, Karen."

"My goodness, at thirty-six you must be sitting

around just waiting to collect Social Security," she said with a mocking laugh.

She watched as he rubbed a weary hand across his forehead. "See what I mean? You effectively smash any argument I have against the two of us. Rather well, I might add."

While he phoned Carl, Karen excused herself to go to the ladies' room. She took longer than necessary, checking her appearance and applying fresh lip gloss and combing her hair. She felt so different with Rand and wondered if that tingling awareness between them affected her looks. Although she studied her reflection for several moments, she decided she looked exactly the same. Repressing a sigh of disappointment, she joined him.

"Carl is meeting me at your place in about twenty minutes," he told her in the foyer of the restaurant. "I have a cab waiting."

"That's fine," she agreed. "We'll have time for coffee."

Karen rested her head against his shoulder as they rode to her apartment. She could feel the roughness of his breath against her hair.

Once inside her apartment, Karen had no more desire for coffee than she had had for dinner. She hung up both their coats, suddenly feeling uneasy. "Make yourself at home. I'll get the coffee going."

As she turned toward the kitchen, Rand's arm caught hers, drawing her back. "I don't want coffee," he murmured, pulling her close to him.

Without hesitation, Karen accepted his embrace, lifting her face to meet his kiss. It began sweet and gentle but deepened as he parted her mouth. The surge of passion that sprang between them was like a wind-driven wildfire. Her arms slid around his neck, her fingers wending through his hair.

His own hands were molding her hips and back against the contours of his body. It was a devastating kiss that left Karen as powerless as a newborn baby. It was very much like coming home after a long absence. They hadn't kissed since the night of the Christmas party, and Karen discovered that the magnetic attraction between them had only been enhanced by lapsed time.

Ripples of desire continued as Rand nibbled the sensitive cord of her neck. "Happy birthday, my lovely Andromeda," he whispered huskily.

"When I was a little girl," she began, her voice soft and trembling, "my mother insisted upon giving me kisses to count my birthday instead of spankings."

Karen could feel Rand's smile against her temple. "I'm afraid I haven't the restraint to kiss you twenty-four times without falling prey to other temptations."

Their lips met again in a fiery kiss that fused them together. Karen clung to him as the only solid form in a reeling world. When the kiss ended, she buried her face against his chest while he continued to rain soft kisses on her hair.

"Are you busy tomorrow?" he questioned, his voice no more even than her breathing.

"No," she lied skillfully. Evan Forsyth had invited her and her sister to lunch. Judy and the boys were preparing a birthday dinner for her that evening with Matthew. But nothing mattered, not friends, not family. Nothing save Rand.

"Can I see you, then?"

"Yes." She gloried in the eagerness of his request.

"Could you come to the campus—say, around eleven? I've got a class at nine-thirty."

Karen was too full of happiness to speak. He wanted to see her again soon. They wouldn't be separated for weeks, as had been the past pattern. "Yes, fine," she murmured, seeking the intimate taste of his mouth upon hers again.

A light tap, then the doorbell, interrupted them. "That'll be Carl," Rand murmured thickly, continuing to hold her shoulders.

Involuntarily, Karen swayed toward him, not wishing to break the contact. Gently, he kissed her lightly one last time. "Until tomorrow," he said, and paused. "My coat?"

"Oh, sorry." She fumbled awkwardly and withdrew it from the closet. Before she could add another word, he was gone.

The doorbell chimed impatiently several times the next morning at about nine-thirty. Karen rushed to answer it, her bathrobe knotted tightly about her waist.

"Dad," she exclaimed, letting him in. "What are you doing here? You're supposed to be working."

"'Tis a fine greeting for the man responsible for ye being here," he scolded her lovingly. "I've come to wish ye a happy birthday." He sauntered through the apartment to the kitchen and poured himself a cup of coffee.

"Did ye notice I rang the bell?" he said as he pulled a chair from the kitchen table and sat.

"I'm real proud of you, Dad, real proud." Her voice hinted sarcasm, but her smile negated any scorn by curving upward in a gentle smile. "Why aren't you at work?" she quizzed again.

Matthew deposited a second spoonful of sugar into his mug before answering. "I didn't feel like working," he told her indifferently. "A man needs an excuse to take a day off every now and then. And what better excuse than my lass's birthday?"

Karen poured herself a cup and sat opposite him at the tiny round table. She would have argued, but Matthew looked pale and drawn; perhaps a day's vacation was a good idea.

"Twenty-four years," he said with the glazed look that crossed his face when he was thinking of her mother. "Ye realize, when your mother was twenty-four, she was married, had Judy, and was pregnant with you."

Karen sighed heavily. She'd hoped to avoid another one of her father's tirades about her single status. "I know that, Dad."

"You're far behind her, lass. Even Judy had James and Carter before she was twenty-four."

Karen stood abruptly and emptied her coffee in the kitchen sink. "I know that, too," she said with a tight rein on her temper.

"There's not much time remaining before people will begin thinking of you as unmarriageable. I'd hate to see ye an old maid."

Karen's eyes ballooned angrily. "That's ridiculous," she spat impatiently. With storm clouds gathering, hands on her hips, Karen squarely faced her father. "Why is it you and I can't have a decent conversation anymore? You're constantly bugging me about getting married, and I'm not about to jump into a relationship to satisfy your whims. It's getting to the point I don't even like being around you anymore. Would you kindly lay off?" she said forcefully.

Her father's sad eyes met Karen's fiery gaze, and once again she noted that her father looked like a man well past his prime, a man without purpose. Taking deep breaths to control her temper, she offered him a weak smile. "I love you, Dad. Let's not argue, especially today. Okay?"

"Okay, lass." He responded to her smile with one of his own. "How was the date with Rand last night?"

Telltale emotions flickered across her face. "Wonderful. In fact, I'm meeting him this morning." Pointedly, she checked her wristwatch.

"I thought you were having lunch with Evan. He seems to have invited the whole family except me." If Matthew was hinting for an invitation, Karen wasn't going to issue one. Both girls were aware that although the lunch had been planned to correspond with Karen's birthday, the purpose was to discuss Matthew. The change in his personality over the past months had not gone unnoticed by his friends, and Evan was as worried as Karen and Judy.

"I am having lunch with Evan, but I'm meeting Rand first. That's why I've got to get moving."

"All right, lass, I'll see you tonight."

After surveying her wardrobe carefully, Karen chose designer jeans and a forest-green velour top. Since it was raining, she chose fashionable knee-high leather boots.

At precisely eleven, she entered Rand's office building.

"May I help you?" his assistant, an elderly gray-haired woman, inquired politely.

"I'm Karen McAlister. I have an appointment with Dr. Prescott."

The woman scanned the appointment schedule. "Yes, Dr. Prescott mentioned you this morning." There was a hint of censure in her tone, and Karen wondered what inconvenience their meeting was causing.

"Follow me, please." The cool smile displayed an efficient assistant's welcome. She paused outside the door. "Dr. Prescott's on the phone, but he's asked that you be shown in immediately. Would you like a cup of coffee while you're waiting?"

Politely, Karen declined. With her jittery nerves, she wasn't beyond dumping the contents across Rand's desk. She entered the office quietly so as not to disturb him. He gave no indication that he noticed her arrival, his full concentration directed at the person on the other end of the line. From the conversation, Karen assumed it was either his agent or his publisher.

She stood awkwardly in the middle of his office for several minutes, not wishing to sit, yet equally unwilling to feel like a child being disciplined. Her gaze swept the walls, resting on the degrees and certificates decorating the office. As she read their contents, her discomfort grew. On further investigation, she found Rand was the recipient of several prestigious awards. There was even a picture of him with the president of the United States. Nothing could have made her more aware of how separate their worlds were. A knot grew in the pit of her stomach as she read the contents of each framed accomplishment.

His achievements were astonishing, and Karen experienced a budding respect for the obstacles he'd overcome. She doubted there was any situation or crisis

Rand couldn't surmount with patience and persistence. But her admiration did little to quell her uneasiness.

No wonder Rand questioned their relationship.

Depression, heavier than any yoke, weighted her shoulders. She actually felt her body droop under its burden. There could be no basis for a meaningful relationship between them.

Dismally, she moved to the picture window overlooking Commencement Bay. Oyster-gray clouds met murky waters in a thin overcast. Only a few brave souls weathered the promise of rain, their sailboats slicing through the water. Yet Karen was blind to the picturesque beauty that lay before her.

"I'm sorry, Karen." Rand stood. "I didn't mean to be so long."

"No problem," she murmured abjectly, refusing to face him.

As soon as she spoke, Rand came to stand behind her. His hands rested lightly on her shoulders, drawing her against him. Gently, his lips touched her hair.

Karen suppressed an overwhelming urge to turn and bury herself in his arms. Instead, she stared at the world outside the window, feeling wretched and small.

"You're angry?" he asked, his tone suggesting surprise.

"I'm not," she murmured unhappily.

"Obviously something is troubling you."

Inhaling deeply, she faltered over the words. "I... I know why you asked me here today. It's shown me without words why you haven't wanted to see me again. I don't blame you. I understand now."

The grasp on her shoulders tightened, and, using

his strength, he turned her to face him. "Just what are you implying?"

"I'm saying that I've never fully realized how important you are. You're a respected professor, a noted author…a man of unquestionable financial insight. Do you realize I'm not so very different from the woman who ushered me into your office? Basically, I'm a nobody."

"A nobody?" He openly scoffed. "If that's the case, you've managed to wreak havoc on my life in short order." His expression didn't alter. "Do you really believe I invited you here to impress you with our differences?"

A lump rose in her throat, and she swallowed hard. It was ironic that she would argue with him without relenting a whit and then accept defeat after ten minutes in his office without a spoken word.

"Yes." Her voice trembled slightly.

"It was never my intention to see you after the Christmas party," he said deliberately.

"I'm aware of that."

"I said goodbye to you that night, and I meant it. But no woman has ever affected me the way you have, Karen. I'm not a romantic. The relationships I've had with women have been for the express purpose of satisfying a basic human need. That night with you shattered every preconceived idea I have regarding love and romance. You were gentle, sweet, and warm, more like the mythological Andromeda than a mere human. I knew then what could never be."

"I'm hardly a goddess," she interrupted with dry sarcasm.

He began again, his voice fervent. "I'm almost totally blind. I have no intention of maintaining a personal relationship with any woman. Not now, not ever. Even the attraction I feel for you will not convince me differently. You're special, Karen, and you deserve the best…certainly not a blind man."

Immediately, she bristled, but before she could say anything, Rand continued, "Maybe it's best we end this testing time now. That choice is yours, but I won't have you believing you're not good enough for me."

"Then why did you ask me here?" Her voice nearly failed her.

His features softened as the intensity left his face. "For this." He withdrew a jeweler's box from his pocket.

Hesitantly, Karen accepted the small case.

"It's not wrapped, but happy birthday, anyway."

Karen almost gasped when she lifted the lid. A lovely gold locket rested on a bed of purple velvet. It was old, but not an antique; the jeweler's box and style were outdated, but the locket was obviously new.

"It's beautiful," she whispered, lifting the heart-shaped locket from the case to examine it more fully.

"Can you get it on okay? I doubt that I'll be much use."

"I think so." The chain clasped effortlessly as the locket fell naturally into place between her breasts. Karen longed to ask if the jewelry had been his mother's, but if it had any special significance, he wasn't telling her.

"Thank you, Rand. I'll treasure it always."

Softly, his hand caressed her cheek. As if it were suddenly too much restraint to keep her from his arms, he pulled her to him, hugging her fiercely. "Happy birthday," he whispered huskily.

His assistant's buzzer interrupted them, and Rand responded to the intrusion with a clear, crisp voice. The words were in a cloud as Karen gradually returned to the present.

"I've got to leave for a meeting," Rand told her reluctantly. "I'll phone you at the end of the week."

Karen smiled, her eyes dancing. "It seems I'm doomed to sit by my phone waiting for you to call."

Chuckling at her teasing sarcasm, he reached for his coat. "All right, how about dinner on Saturday? I'd like you to meet Cora Dibner. I believe Evan Forsyth's mentioned her."

Karen's spirits descended rapidly; she had no desire to meet the woman, but wondered what claim Cora had on Rand.

They walked from the building together, exchanging the teasing banter they both enjoyed. Halfway down the wide cement walkway, Rand stopped abruptly. "My book," he said with a shock. "I've left it in the office." He chuckled. "I've left my office a thousand times in the past seven years, and this is the first time I've forgotten my book. See what you do to me?"

Karen smiled, and her heartbeat raced with a new happiness.

"I'll have to go back. Karen McAlister, you'll be the downfall of me yet."

She watched as Rand progressed through the throng of students. "I hope I am," she said to no one in particular.

Four

Karen enjoyed her birthday lunch. The fettuccine complemented a lighthearted celebration, but it didn't take Evan long to come to the point of their meeting. He noted the changes in Matthew's personality, voiced his concern, and suggested the root of the problem was loneliness. Matthew needed to remarry, Evan concluded. Karen could feel the tiny hairs at the back of her neck bristle. No woman, however wonderful, could ever replace her mother. Selfishly, she did not wish to see her father marry someone else.

But the more they discussed the situation, the more both Judy and Karen were forced to acknowledge that perhaps Evan was right. It would take a readjustment in their thinking, but both were willing to make the effort as long as it helped Matthew—anything to change his present attitude.

Anxiously, Karen longed for the weekend and the dinner date with Rand. Her curiosity regarding Cora Dibner was keen; only when she had met Rand's associate could she evaluate the extent of their relationship.

With each passing day, Karen discovered that Rand

was coming to occupy more and more of her thoughts. Even the little things in life like shopping and cooking brought him to mind. While preparing a meal, she found herself questioning his likes and dislikes. When dressing, she wondered how he'd feel about a certain outfit she was planning to wear. Seldom did Karen consciously think of him as blind. Accepting his lack of sight was very much like accepting Judy's too-large nose. After a while, it became unnoticeable, a part of her person that was unconsciously overlooked.

When Rand phoned late and unexpectedly Wednesday night, Karen was reading and ready for bed.

"Karen?" A hint of doubt entered his husky voice.

"Were you expecting someone else to answer?" she teased.

He chuckled, his voice rich and low; the sound of his amusement contained an element of music. "No. I'm sorry to be phoning so late."

"That's fine. I was reading." He could phone any time he wanted, Karen yearned to tell him, but to admit that would be revealing too much.

"I'm afraid I'm going to have to cancel our dinner date Saturday night." The regret in his voice communicated his own disappointment.

"Oh…" She sighed in frustration and absently fingered the gold locket he'd given her. Karen wore it continually, as if wearing it would result in some wonderful magic. She'd been so impatient to see Rand again, and the throbbing happiness she experienced just hearing his voice vanished with his announcement. It seemed their whole relationship was a series of setbacks.

"Karen, I'm phoning from Washington, D.C. I won't be back before Sunday."

"Washington, D.C." she gasped, and quickly glanced at the kitchen clock. "It must be two a.m."

"After two," he murmured tightly. "I've been tied up in one of those dreadful meetings that last forever and solve nothing." He sounded both tired and frustrated. "I suppose I should have phoned tomorrow night, but I needed to hear your voice."

Karen's spirits soared. The need to talk to her was something he admitted grudgingly, as if she were becoming a weakness he couldn't overcome.

"I'm glad you did call," she whispered softly. "I like to hear your voice, too, but I'm sorry to miss meeting Cora." Karen flushed guiltily; her curiosity regarding his business associate had little to do with friendly overtures.

"You'll meet her," Rand assured her, then paused for a moment. "I've been invited to a wedding reception sometime next week. Would you like to attend with me? Cora will be there," he added, as if she needed an incentive.

"Yes, I'd enjoy that." Rand could issue an invitation to a funeral and she'd still experience a thrill of anticipation.

"I'll let you know what day and time later."

"That'll be fine. I don't have anything special planned for next week." She paused, then began hesitantly, "Would you like a kitten?"

"A what?" he asked in disbelief.

"A cat." She giggled. "My two crazy nephews brought home six kittens yesterday. Judy sent them to the store for a loaf of bread, and some lady was sitting outside the store with a box of kittens. The boys couldn't believe the cats were *free* and took all six. After all, they considered six free cats to be quite a bargain. By the time Judy returned to the store with the boys and the cats, the lady was long gone. In fact, Judy and I spent the evening posting 'free kitten' signs around the neighborhood."

"Those two rascals," Rand said, chuckling. "I suppose all six are females?"

"Do you have anything against females?" Karen asked with mock indignation.

"Not of late," he murmured with a chuckle. "All right, I'll take one regardless of sex."

"Judy thanks you, kind sir."

"Go ahead and choose one for me; I'll have Carl contact you to make the arrangements to pick it up. You can name it for me if you want."

"I'd like that." Already her mind was buzzing with several possibilities.

"I suppose I'd better let you get some sleep." His voice was warm and husky, creating in Karen anything but the desire to slumber.

"I suppose," she whispered on a sigh.

"Good night, my sweet Andromeda."

"Good night, Rand." She replaced the receiver and leaned back in the chair to savor every word of their conversation.

Karen met Carl Friday afternoon at Judy's. By the time he arrived, Karen still hadn't decided among the three remaining kittens. All were equally adorable, with feisty personalities and soft, cuddly fur. Carl stood by silently, refusing to be drawn into the decision making. In the end, James helped her choose the calico.

"The reason no one wants her is because she's female," James declared, "but I think she's the best one."

"Well, that settles it," Karen said matter-of-factly. "Little calico, you're the one." She lifted the multicolored kitten from the box, examining her face carefully. "She's lovely. Thank you, James."

A hint of a smile touched Carl's wrinkled features. "Mr. Rand said you'd be choosing a female. Have you picked out the name?"

"Not yet," she said, frowning thoughtfully, "but I'm working on it."

"I like Super Pooper, because she's the one…"

"Carter, that's quite enough," Judy snapped, looking a bit abashed.

"Yes, Mom." The youngster's enthusiasm was immediately quelled, but his eyes sparked mischief.

Carl happened to catch Karen's eye, and she noted the difficulty with which he restrained his laughter.

The boys enthusiastically helped Carl load the kitten into the carrier he'd brought. Both made their farewells as if they were seeing their only sister depart to an unknown world.

"Such dramatics," Judy whispered with a sigh.

"Is Tuesday evening at seven convenient?" Carl questioned as Judy and Karen walked him to the car, obviously referring to the wedding reception Rand had mentioned.

"That'll be fine. Thanks, Carl…for everything." She gave him a pleasant smile and waved as he pulled from the driveway.

On Tuesday evening, Karen was once again meticulous with every detail of her appearance. She chose a white taffeta puffed-sleeve blouse with a coordinating burgundy tiered skirt. The striking contrast of the two colors highlighted the dark, rich tones of her hair and winter complexion. Her face glowed radiantly with a light application of cosmetics, and her eyes were clear and sparkling. Although an emerald brooch was pinned to the neck of her blouse and she wore matching earrings, Rand's locket remained in place beneath the taffeta.

She looked and felt lovely, but again discovered her confidence slipping. Her stomach twisted with butterflies as she waited for Rand, not knowing how he would greet her. The gruff exterior he'd displayed at their first two meetings after the Christmas party was gradually wearing away. After her visit to his office and their telephone conversation, she knew he was mellowing. Intuitively, she recognized Rand was withholding part of himself, the part she'd witnessed the night of the party. Unexplainably, the barriers had been lowered that wonderful evening, and, with a heavy sigh, she wondered how long it would take to bring them to that point again.

Aside from the brief visit to his office, she recognized his game. Rand had purposely planned that all their times together involved others: the play, the wedding reception—even the dinner date he'd been forced to cancel had been arranged with Cora Dibner. It didn't matter; he could avoid being alone with her for only so long.

As before, Rand arrived promptly, and Karen was surprised to note that he came by taxi and Carl hadn't driven. Her heart raced with excitement. He was tall, strong, and handsome enough to be any maiden's dream.

"I'm early," he explained as Karen took his coat. "The reception isn't until eight."

"I don't mind. Would you like something while we're waiting?" She took the hanger from the closet.

"You wouldn't believe what I want," he murmured almost inaudibly, rubbing a weary hand across his face.

"Pardon?" She stopped, her hand suspended in midair.

"Nothing...it wasn't important." He stood awkwardly in her tiny entryway, suddenly looking unsure.

"The most comfortable chair is to your left," she said lightly, hoping he wouldn't find her directions a form of rescue.

He smiled gratefully. "Thanks." He located the large overstuffed chair and sat down.

"Would you like something to drink?" Nervously, she placed a strand of hair behind her ear. She didn't keep a large supply of beverages on hand and could only hope she had what he wanted.

"Coffee, if you have it."

"I do."

"Why the sigh of relief?"

"What?" Although halfway to her kitchen, Karen turned back toward him.

"You sighed like you were afraid I'd ask for a Smith and Currens."

"I did?" she asked blankly. "I didn't even realize it."

"Don't worry. Blind men rarely drink anything stronger than coffee," he remarked.

Waving her hands excitedly, Karen marched to his chair and sat on the ottoman. "There, you did it again."

Her voice was high-spirited. "I was trying to explain to Dad about your ability to listen."

"I don't have any unusual listening ability," he contradicted her.

"Of course you do," she said dramatically. "Do you remember when I bumped into you on the balcony the night of the party?"

"I'm unlikely to forget it." He smiled rakishly.

"You knew right away I didn't have my coat because my voice trembled."

Rand straightened, his posture suddenly defensive and stiff. "In case you weren't aware of it, nature often compensates for the lack of one sense by enhancing another. I've been told my hearing is extraordinary."

"Honestly, Rand." She shifted irritably. "That's what Dad said. One would think you of all people would know the difference between hearing and listening."

A frown creased his brow. "I don't understand what you're saying."

Exasperated, Karen expelled her breath unevenly. "Okay. The other day in your office you apologized for being on the phone so long. I told you I didn't mind, but immediately you detected there was something wrong—"

"My dear Karen, it was obvious you were upset; your voice was low and tight—"

"But that's it," she interrupted. "I've used that same tone of voice a hundred times, and no one has ever guessed my feelings. You did because you *listen*. I mean really *listen*. That's so rare, Rand. It's probably the most appealing thing about you."

"You mean my dashing good looks don't faze you?" he teased.

"Well, not entirely." Her long, thick lashes fluttered downward in a disconcerted movement. "The other day, I invited Dad to dinner. He gets home earlier than me, so I asked him to come to my apartment, take the casserole from the fridge at five o'clock, and put it in a three-fifty-degree oven. Dad put it in at five hundred degrees at three-thirty. Needless to say, we went out for hamburgers. If I'd given you the same instructions, I have no doubt they would've been followed explicitly."

Again, he dismissed her theory. "People misunderstand one another all the time. My ability to hear or listen or whatever," he said a little impatiently, "is a figment of your imagination."

Karen studied him, the tiny crow's-feet that appeared at the corners of his eyes, the salting of gray hairs at his temple. The deep-colored eyes stared back at her, but how much he could see, Karen could only guess.

"All right, Randall Prescott"—she gave in graciously—"you're right. The whole thing is a wild, unreasonable assumption." She should have known better. With his defensive attitude, it was unlikely he'd admit to anything that set him apart or made him different.

"Did you say something about coffee?" he reminded her gently.

"Oh, sorry." She apologized quickly and stood, returning to the kitchen.

Both cups were full and steaming when she returned and sat opposite Rand.

"By the way, have you come up with a name for the cat?"

"Yes," she told him uncertainly, "but I'm not sure you'll like it."

He arched a curious brow. "Well?"

"Everyone knows a cat is supposed to have nine lives, but did you also know there are said to be nine heavens, nine regions of hell, nine heads of the hydra, nine muses, nine crosses, nine orders of angels, nine worthies…and…"

"A cat-o'-nine-tails," Rand injected smoothly.

"Right"—she laughed nervously—"and seeing how there are so many nines in the world and all, I thought I'd name her Number Nine." She shifted in an anxious movement. "What do you think?"

"My birthday is October ninth."

"See, all the more reason," she said, laughing lightly.

"I don't suppose this decision has anything to do with the fact that we met December the ninth?"

"Absolutely nothing," she lied smoothly, then giggled because it was so obvious she was lying. She should have known better than to try to outwit Rand. He was too perceptive, too astute.

He gave her a full smile that did crazy things to her heartbeat. "I knew you'd come up with some connection to our first meeting."

Suddenly, they were both quiet, each entangled in the memories of that night. Perhaps it was a time Rand would as soon forget. Perhaps it was even an embarrassment to him now. But for Karen it was more an assignment with destiny. She smiled secretly to herself; Rand would laugh if he could hear her thoughts. Yet more and more she had come to think of their meeting as preordained and as irrevocable as uttered vows.

Rand spoke first. "I think Number Nine, although a bit unusual, will be a fine name."

They talked for a while longer, laughing over the

antics of James and Carter with the comfortable ease of friends. More than once Karen found herself thinking that Rand would make a wonderful father. Picturing Rand with children did funny things to her stomach. The mental image of him holding a child, their child, was more intoxicating than any wine. Karen quickly reined in her imagination. Taking their relationship any further than the moment was a dangerous pitfall she was going to avoid.

The taxi delivered them to the Elks Lodge, where the reception was being held. With Rand's arm placed gently around her waist, they entered the crowded room. At Rand's request, Karen signed the guest book for them both.

Seeing so many people put Karen on edge; meeting a roomful of strangers wasn't her idea of a romantic evening.

"Why so tense?" Rand whispered after the first couple of introductions.

"I'm sorry," she said, surprised at how tight her voice sounded. "I'm a little ill at ease when I don't know anyone. Does it show that much?"

"Only to me." A suggestion of a smile touched his eyes, as if he were suddenly aware he'd almost admitted his listening ability was more astute than others. "I'm not particularly fond of these affairs myself."

"Rand!" A tall, attractive blonde propelled her way through several people to greet him with an affectionate hug. "You made it, after all."

Hastily, Karen removed her hand from Rand's arm as the woman stepped forward.

"Aren't you going to introduce us?" she questioned, eyeing Karen resentfully. She was older than Karen, perhaps thirty, and carried herself proudly, confidently. Her metallic-blue eyes were piercing.

"Cora"—Rand's voice was warm and friendly— "I'd like you to meet Karen McAlister. Karen, this is Cora Dibner."

"Pleased, I'm sure," Cora said, but her look belied any pleasure.

Karen's heart beat painfully; she had hoped to be friends with Rand's associate. He spoke of Cora so often—often enough for her to suspect their relationship went beyond business interests. Now that they'd met, there was no denying the jealousy in Cora's eyes. Or that she was in love with Rand.

"I'm pleased, too." Karen smiled in return and nodded, as worthy opponents often do when facing each other.

A glimmer of respect entered Cora's eyes. "Are you one of Rand's students?" Her voice remained friendly, but the whiplike flicker of her gaze cut into Karen.

Involuntarily, Karen stiffened. This woman was after blood in their first round. Cora must have known Rand was uneasy with their age difference. She laughed lightly, giving the impression such a question was ridiculous.

"Hardly. Are you?"

"You wouldn't believe the things he's taught me."

The mocking words hit Karen with the impact of a hammer pounding a nail. Were Rand and Cora lovers? A sickening knot twisted her stomach until she thought she might be sick.

Rand cleared his throat in embarrassment. "Yes… well, I think it's probably time Karen and I went through the reception line. If you'll excuse us, Cora."

"Of course." Cora's smile, directed at Karen, was full of malice. "Nice meeting you, *Carol.*" She purposely used the wrong name as a means of telling Karen she wasn't worried. Her grip on Rand was secure; she had nothing to fear from Karen.

"You, too, *Nora,*" Karen said in kind, her eyes narrowing. "I hope we meet again."

Rand frowned. "Cora seems to be out of sorts tonight." He dismissed his associate's behavior. Karen wanted to cry because making excuses for Cora's behavior showed he cared.

"We all have off days." She swallowed tightly. "Would you mind if we had something to drink before going through the reception line?"

"I think we could both use something," Rand said.

Two glasses of champagne clouded the encounter with Cora. Another glass and Karen saw the whole incident as comical. Rand was distracted by friends and didn't notice how many times her glass was refilled. But Karen, held protectively to his side, was always introduced and included in the conversation. Another half glass and her former nervousness dissipated; her smile was friendly, her laughter quick, and her eyes sparkled.

"We better do the honors while we can," Rand suggested after a while. "Are there many people left in the reception line?"

"Hardly any," she told him, and had the crazy desire to giggle. Rand honestly believed people really listened. She'd show him.

Rand introduced her to the first person in the reception line, one of the ushers, a brother-in-law of the groom's. Bravely, Karen looked him directly in the eye and smiled sweetly. "I'm very pleased to meet you," she said, shaking his hand. Although her eyes never left his face, she added impishly, "The elephants are loose."

Rand's arm stiffened its hold around her waist, biting into her tender flesh.

"How do you do?" the usher responded politely to her warm smile. "I'm so glad you could come."

"I am, too." Her eyes sparked with mischief. "I am, too," she repeated.

Before proceeding farther, Rand's low voice growled in warning, "Karen, what are you doing?"

She laughed saucily. "I thought you said people listen," she whispered back. "I'm just proving a point."

Undaunted by Rand's tight grip around her waist, she made the same obscure announcement to the next member of the wedding party. Again, nothing was said or noticed. Apparently, wild elephants on the loose were not of interest to the entire wedding party. The only one to add anything to Karen's ridiculous statement was the last woman in the line, who proudly boasted she was the one who introduced the wedding couple.

They'd gone no more than three paces from the line, just out of earshot, when Rand demanded in a low snarl, "Just how many glasses of champagne have you had?"

Karen had to stop abruptly in order to think, causing Rand to bump into her. She would have stumbled forward if not for his grip. "Three." She hiccuped loudly. "Oops, sorry. No, I think it was four." *Could it have been five?* she mused; she'd lost count.

"I'm getting you out of here." The words were

muted, and for a moment Karen wondered if she'd heard him correctly.

"Gee, I was just beginning to have some fun." She hiccupped again.

"Karen, don't say another word," he warned.

Her lips moved to protest, but somehow the words couldn't get past her tongue.

"Promise me you won't say a word to anyone."

She hiccupped again. "How can I promise you that when I'm not supposed to talk?" She shot a quick glance at Rand. Why was he so interested in leaving all of a sudden?

The cold air outside the lodge stunned Karen, although she felt flushed and warm. The street was deserted, the sidewalk bathed in shimmering moonlight. It reminded Karen of the night she and Rand had met. The stars were shining, but to gaze at them did funny things to her equilibrium.

Suddenly, Karen had the overpowering desire to dance.

"Rand," she whispered seductively, waltzing a few steps ahead of him, "may I have the pleasure of this dance?" She curtsied politely.

"Karen."

Was it impatience she heard in his voice? It must be the hiccupping; it was driving her crazy, too. "Then for heaven's sake, kiss me," she demanded. "That'll stop them."

"Stop what?"

Rand was definitely on a different wavelength, Karen mused, and giggled on another hiccup.

"The taxi's here," he told her, his hand gripping her upper arm firmly.

"But, Rand, I want to dance," she pleaded. Her lashes fluttered downward suggestively.

Rand ignored her and directed his attention to the driver. "I need to get some strong coffee into her."

The driver laughed as Karen hiccupped again. "Drive-through or restaurant?" he queried.

"Drive-through…definitely a drive-through."

Again, the driver laughed.

"But, Rand, I don't want any coffee." She forced herself to concentrate on him. His eyes were anxious, disturbed. That worried Karen. Was he angry? One arm cupped her shoulder protectively, as if she needed his strength to sit upright. The fingers on his other hand drummed a nervous tempo against the seat.

Her eyes narrowed. "You think I'm drunk," she said in an accusing, high-pitched voice that suggested absurdity.

"My dear Karen, another glass of champagne and I'd have had to carry you from the reception."

Karen giggled. "Honestly, Rand, I'm as sober as a"—she couldn't think of anyone sober—"a judge." She waved her finger wildly, as if to prove her point.

Rand snorted, but his mouth deepened into grooves as he suppressed a smile.

Karen's fingers crept to his face, caressing his jaw, outlining his mouth with the tips of her fingers. "Please kiss me," she whispered softly as her hands moved up and over his shoulders, meeting behind his neck, urging his mouth to hers.

At first, his kiss was slow and gentle, but Karen moaned, seeking deeper contact. She wasn't disappointed when his lips hardened and parted hers. Desire seared through her blood until Karen thought she would drown in the pleasure of it.

As he released her, she felt the cold air come between them and rested her head against his shoulder.

"Either your kisses are more potent than I remember," she said, smiling lazily, "or else I shouldn't be closing my eyes, because the whole world goes into a tailspin."

She could feel Rand's smile against her hair. "Then by all means protect Mother Earth and keep your eyes open."

Karen groaned when her alarm rang early the next morning. The shrill ring triggered a burst of pain in her head. When she sluggishly sat upright to turn off the offending noise, she thought her head would burst.

Slouching against the pillow, she groaned again, holding her head. Looking around her, she found her normally neat bedroom in a shambles; clothes littered the floor, and one shoe sat on the windowsill, while the other remained hidden from view. She could vaguely recall singing and dancing around the apartment as she undressed. Taking deep breaths, she calculated the consequences of staying in bed, but the call of responsibility soon moved her into action.

Once fortified with a cup of strong coffee and two aspirin, Karen showered and dressed. She lifted her eyebrows expressively when she located her second shoe in the bathroom sink.

Fifteen minutes before she was due to leave for work, Rand phoned.

"How are you feeling?" His tone was laced with concern.

"Don't ask." She tested her voice for the first time and found her tongue thick and her words husky. "I think I'll live if my head quits pounding." Memories of the night remained hazy; she could recall Rand saying something about coffee and a beautiful, sensuous kiss in the back of the taxi, but beyond that, the evening was veiled in her mind.

"I'm almost afraid to ask, but did I do anything out of the ordinary last night?"

She could hear his soft chuckle. "My dear, I've got enough information to blackmail you for life."

Her breath was forced from her lungs; things were worse than she imagined. "I was afraid of that."

"Just remind me never to argue with you again. I didn't know what lengths you were willing to go to to prove a point. From now on, if you insist most people don't really listen, I won't question the fact."

Karen laughed, wondering where she got the courage to pull anything so crazy. "I think everyone in the whole wedding party probably heard me but was too shocked to respond."

Rand did little to relieve her anxiety. "I think you've made your mark among my friends."

Karen's face remained tight and strained when the smile died. "I believe," she began awkwardly, "that I owe you an apology. I'm so sorry, Rand. I don't know what got into me."

"I'd say it was several glasses of excellent champagne," he interrupted smoothly.

Karen closed her eyes for a moment. "I feel terrible about the whole thing."

"Honey"—Rand's chuckle was warm and sincere—"I can't remember when I've enjoyed a wedding reception more."

Five

Thursday afternoon, the sky was thick with threatening gray clouds that promised rain. Karen rushed out one door, down half a block to the restaurant, and in another, where Judy was waiting.

Her sister waved as soon as Karen entered. "Hi." Judy smiled in greeting as Karen sat opposite her in the small booth. "I've got our order in; it should be here any minute."

Karen sighed appreciatively. "Thanks, Jude. It works out great when you can get here early and order for me. It's been a madhouse this morning. I didn't even think I'd get here at all for a while."

"It's a darn good thing you did." Judy laughed, her eyes sparkling. "You should have seen the look the waitress gave me when I ordered *two* chef salads."

Karen laughed, a natural release from the tension of a hectic morning. "What have you heard from Mike?" she asked just as the waitress brought their salads.

"Not much. He's miserable, counting the days till he can come home, but he loves his job and the challenge. Sometimes I wish he was like a normal husband with a nine-to-five job, but he isn't. It's something I learned to accept long ago."

Judy and Mike had been right for each other from the time they started dating in high school. Karen was almost envious that her sister had been so fortunate to have found her husband as a teenager. It was a fact Matthew had often used to convince Karen she was being overly choosy. But since Karen had been seeing Rand regularly, Matthew had all but ceased his demands.

"You're seeing quite a bit of Rand, aren't you?" Judy questioned unexpectedly. Her voice held a worried note, and she watched Karen closely.

"Not as much as I'd like." Karen was surprised by her sister's attitude. "Does it bother you that Rand is blind?"

Judy shook her head, quickly denying the implications. "Of course not."

"Then why the censure?"

"Karen"—Judy hesitated, looking uncertain and more than a little uncomfortable—"I know you like Rand, but I don't want to see you hurt. I think you should tread carefully with this relationship."

Karen studied her sister thoughtfully. *Liking Rand.* That was the understatement of the year. Judy and Karen had always been close, even as children. Almost five years separated them—a big difference when Judy was a sensitive teenager and Karen was a pesky younger sister. Even then, they had shared a special relationship. Yet, in all her years, Karen couldn't remember her sister acting in quite this manner.

"Things between Rand and me are going even better than I'd hoped," Karen told her sister, but Judy avoided eye contact, paying inordinate attention to her salad.

"Rand's just beginning to be comfortable with me; the defensiveness over his blindness is almost gone. More important, I sense he is accepting me into his life. It's more than I'd hoped to accomplish in such a short time. Although"—she smiled before continuing, as if she'd overcome an important hurdle in their relationship—"tonight is the first time we'll be alone together. His reader is sick, so I'm going to the school after work and read his students' papers to him. He's promised me dinner. More than a fair trade, I think."

Judy didn't mince words. "Do you love him?"

Karen didn't even hesitate. "More than I thought it was possible to love any man."

"Does he know it?" Judy still hadn't touched her salad.

Karen sighed heavily. "I'm sure he does." A hundred times, Karen had longed to speak freely of her feelings, but this was a sensitive area, and she knew she must be patient. Not that she doubted his feelings.

"If you love him, why don't you tell him?" An odd expression crossed Judy's face.

"I can't, Jude. Rand doesn't want to hear it. I know that's difficult for you to understand, but for now that's the way things have got to be."

Judy shifted uneasily, again giving the impression something was weighing heavily on her mind. "Are you sure of his feelings?"

Karen's soft mouth curved into a smile. "All right, sis, what is it?"

Judy looked all the more uncomfortable. "What's what?"

"Obviously, you've seen or heard something about Rand, and you're worrying yourself sick over it."

Judy sent her a sidelong glance, and her shoulders drooped forward in defeat. "Am I really so easy to read?"

Karen smiled with sudden humor. "My heavens, I've seen James and Carter less obvious."

Judy laughed, too, her smile more relaxed. "I was on campus the other day and saw Rand," she began, her fingers nervously twisting her napkin. "I knew who he was the minute I saw him. I mean, you've talked about him enough."

Karen knew Judy was taking a couple of classes at the university, and it didn't surprise her that she'd seen Rand.

"Only Rand wasn't alone." Her eyes met Karen's briefly. "There was a woman, a tall blonde, with him, and Karen, I may be an old married lady, but I know a come-on when I see one. This woman was definitely on the make, and Rand was eating it up."

"That's Cora Dibner," Karen interjected on a long breath. "You don't need to tell me she's after Rand. The lady and I have met."

Judy sighed, visibly relieved. "I've been so worried. I don't think I've ever seen any woman that smooth. What gets me is that Rand seemed oblivious to what was happening."

Karen smiled ruefully. "As far as Cora is concerned, I think Rand is more aware than he lets on. I don't doubt that he can see through that layer of cool sophistication. Rand's no fool."

Judy studied her sister pensively. "For your sake, I hope you're right."

Karen went directly to Rand's office after work. She stopped only once at the ladies' room to check her appearance. Her lipstick had faded, and she freshened the honeysuckle-rose color and ran a quick comb through her hair. Impishly, she sprayed her favorite fragrance to the pulse points of her neck. Rand had commented once on the delicate white ginger scent she wore. He was sure to detect it again and smile at her womanly wiles.

"Karen?" Rand's welcome was both a question and statement.

She let herself into his office; the door between his office and his assistant's was open, anticipating her arrival.

"Yes, it's me." Her heart beat a little quicker each time she saw Rand; he was everything she'd ever wanted in a man, more than she dared dream she'd find. "I hope you're not one of those slave drivers who won't allow coffee breaks? I'm dying for a cup."

"Now, just a minute," Rand teased. "There's nothing in our contract about coffee breaks." His expression altered. "Hmm, you smell good."

Excitement churned inside her. "Good enough to kiss?"

"Definitely." His voice was both low and hoarse.

Karen floated into his open arms with the sense that this was where she belonged. The whole world could be at war, but as long as she was loved by Rand, there was nothing that could touch her. She wound her arms around his neck, marveling at the strength of his muscular shoulders. His mouth took possession of hers. It was a demanding kiss that parted her lips. Rand kissed her cheek, her ear, her eyelids, and when she groaned, he returned to her mouth. Again, Karen was trapped in a whirlpool—the warmth, the taste, the feel of him—until it didn't matter if she ever surfaced.

With her head resting against his chest, she could hear the erradic tempo of his heart and knew he was as affected by their kiss as she. His breathing was hoarse and uneven; his arm gently caressed her back as if he couldn't bear to let her go.

"I have the feeling that either we start work now or we'll spend the entire evening exactly like this." The reluctance in his voice thrilled Karen.

She agreed, knowing she'd have a difficult time speaking, almost regretting the need to pull herself away from the hazy fog of pleasure that blurred her mind.

Reluctantly, Rand withdrew his arms and sat on the corner of his desk, giving Karen his chair, the most comfortable in the office.

When Karen began reading, her voice was shaky and a bit awkward, but gradually she gained confidence, and her tone became steady and sure.

Rand's transformation from lover to professor was accomplished with an ease Karen envied. Could it be he wasn't as affected by their lovemaking as she? Quickly, she dismissed the thought. Rand had lived with rigid self-control all his life. He was as affected as she; it just didn't show.

After reading each paper, Karen wrote Rand's comments on top of the page. She found his grading system to be stringent and uncompromising, but she was impressed by his fairness and judgment. His comments to the students included some form of encouragement, but he didn't offer praise unless it was warranted.

At the end of the first stack of papers, Karen's throat felt dry and scratchy.

"You need a cup of coffee," Rand commented before she began reading the next pile. "There's usually a pot of coffee in the kitchen."

Karen stood, stretching her tired muscles. "Do you want a cup while I'm at it?"

"I never drink and grade papers," he admonished her jokingly.

Karen laughed and suddenly couldn't resist kissing him. Rand's reaction was immediate, pulling her into his arms and deepening the contact. "Karen," he groaned in warning, "you're not making this any easier."

She straightened. "Sorry." Even now her voice sounded faintly raw from the lingering effects of his kiss.

"Karen"—he stopped her—"bring me a cup, after all. I'm going to need something to clear my head." His eyes were warm and loving. "You don't exactly encourage the sensible side of my nature. You know that, don't you?"

"Yes, sire," she answered saucily.

The next hour and a half were interrupted only by coffee breaks or when Karen had a question about something Rand needed to explain. They found they worked well together. Everything about them was right, Karen mused on a happy note.

"Didn't you say something about buying me dinner?" she asked quietly after marking Rand's comments on the last paper.

Rand walked across the office, flexing his shoulder muscles as if he were stiff. "I had Dorothy pack us a dinner. I hope you don't mind." His back was turned toward her.

"Dorothy?" Was there someone besides Cora she needed to contend with?

"Dorothy is Carl's wife." Rand paused, taking a deep breath before raking his hand through his thick hair. "The thing is, Karen, I don't like to eat in restaurants. Most blind people don't. It presents an unfamiliar environment."

Karen could have bit her tongue. How could she have been so thoughtless, so insensitive? She had made it necessary for Rand to admit something he considered a fault. It was a humbling experience that set him aside and made him appear different.

Karen was appalled at her own insensitivity. "You know, I thought I smelled something delicious when I came in this afternoon. But I couldn't very well accuse you of hiding prime rib in your desk drawer."

The tension faded from Rand's face. She'd done right by making light of his admission; apologizing would only have made the situation worse.

"Dorothy did pack roast beef. Between the ginger scent you're wearing and the aroma of beef, I've been like a man on the rack for the last two hours."

Karen drew a deep, troubled breath. "Well, which one of us would you like to devour first?"

Rand groaned and reached for her, pressing a hard kiss upon her lips. But before he allowed it to develop into something deeper, he straightened. "I think you'd better unpack the picnic basket before you find out. Carl put it in the coat closet against the wall."

Whoever Dorothy was, she certainly knew how to cook. The meal couldn't have been prepared or packed more efficiently. Karen spread the tablecloth on the thick carpet of Rand's office and unpacked their meal of French dip sandwiches made on crusty French bread. The beef, sliced thin, was piled on so high Karen doubted she would be able to fit the sandwich in her mouth. She poured steaming au jus into the bowls while Rand removed the cork from the bottle of wine.

"Fresh strawberries!" Karen exclaimed enthusiastically. "Where in heaven's name did she ever find strawberries this time of year?"

Rand chuckled, the sound of his laughter brightening the evening. "I never ask. The woman's a wonder."

As they ate, Karen's admiration for Dorothy grew. Everything was perfect, beautifully done.

"Ready for a strawberry?" Karen questioned, but when Rand reached for one, she restrained his hand and instead carried it to his mouth. Hesitantly, Rand accepted it, rubbing the juice from his chin as he bit into the tender pulp.

"Your turn," he insisted. Her lips trembled as his fingers touched her mouth, awakening within her a whole range of sensual sensations. When they kissed, the taste of fresh strawberries, mingled with the wine, was more potent than anything Karen had ever experienced.

His hands fell away from her shoulders as Rand took a deep, uneven breath. "I think we'd both benefit from some cold air."

Karen's breath wasn't any less jagged. "Yes," she said, finding her voice barely audible against the tightening in her throat. She was so intoxicated with her love for Rand that tears stung her eyes.

The night was cold and dark; the wind bit into Karen as they walked hand in hand across the campus. They needed the cold to put things into perspective, to re-move them from the passion of the moment.

By mutual agreement, they chose the paved path-way leading to Commencement Bay. Lovers of all ages had used the path leading to the beautiful waters of Puget Sound. There was a freshness in the air, and Karen inhaled deeply, finding the faint odor of salt water pleasant. The wind whipped her hair across her face, but she ignored the cold, taking delight in the simple pleasure of walking along the beach with the man she loved. There was no need for words; it was their spirits that communicated. Rand needn't voice his love; his arm, pressing her possessively against his side, warding off the brunt of the wind, said it far more effectively than words.

Karen was too full of pleasure to speak. When Rand paused, stopping to gaze into the dark, cold night, the only sound was the pounding of the surf against the smooth beach. Somehow Karen found herself in his arms; their lips met in a fiery kiss that fused them to-gether. Karen clung to him. He was her love, her life for all eternity. Nothing could ever make her happier than what she was at this moment.

"Oh, Karen," he groaned, his voice deep and pained.

"No." Her fingers hushed his lips. "Don't talk." She buried her face against his coat, feeling the roughness of his breath against her hair.

He walked Karen to the parking lot where she had left her car. Again, he kissed her, a featherlight kiss that teased and promised.

"I'll be out of town this weekend," he whispered into her hair. His finger gently circled the small of her back in a sensuous movement that melted her bones. "Meet me at the airport Sunday afternoon."

Karen seemed incapable of speech; his physical impact on her was complete.

"I'd like to show you my home." Gently, he released her from his embrace.

"I'd like that," she managed, extracting herself from his arms.

He opened the car door for her. "Drive carefully," he cautioned, and Karen watched him from the rear-view mirror as he stood in the lot until she was safely on her way.

Sunday afternoon, Karen chose a dark chestnut-colored wool skirt and a cream cashmere sweater with a single gold strand woven in a delicate pattern to wear to the airport. She debated between boots or her heels, finally deciding on the knee-high leather boots because it was raining. She was adding the final touches to her makeup when Matthew spoke.

"Ye seeing Rand again?" His eyes showed appreciation for Karen's natural good looks.

She turned sharply at the unexpected intrusion, her eyes angry. "Dad, you did it again. When will you learn to knock?" It was more a statement of indignation than a question.

"Lass"—Matthew gestured helplessly, showing impatience with himself—"I keep forgetting."

It was impossible to be angry with her father when she was in such high spirits. "Well, try, won't you?"

Karen knew he was just as likely to walk in unannounced the next time.

"Ye seeing Rand again?"

Karen knew he wouldn't be satisfied until she'd told him about their dinner date. "Yes, I'm meeting him at the airport. We're having dinner at his home near Graham."

"You love him, don't ye, lass?" The question was more of an announcement, and Karen couldn't deny the obvious. Besides, Matthew was a master in the art of inquisition and would have dragged the words from her one way or another.

"Yes, I do…very much." Self-consciously, she lowered her eyes.

Matthew flashed her a proud smile. "Randall Prescott will make me a fine son-in-law. You've chosen well."

"Dad," Karen said with indignation, "you're rushing things. There's been no talk of marriage."

"Aye, but there will be," he said confidently.

Karen laughed impishly. "If I have anything to say about it, there will be." It was impossible to imagine life without Rand now.

"Ye know, the course of true love between your mother and me wasn't smooth. I had my problems getting her to agree to marriage."

Karen was shocked. As far as she knew, her mother and father had been madly in love from the time they'd met.

Her eyes must have shown her surprise. "Your mother was the most beautiful girl I've ever seen. I took one look at her sweet face and knew I wanted her for my wife. But I was thirteen years older than Madeline, and her parents didn't take kindly to a thirty-one-year-old man courting their teenage daughter."

"Little wonder." Karen knew, of course, that thirteen

years separated her parents, but she'd never thought of it in terms of eighteen and thirty-one. Nor had she been aware that her grandparents had voiced any objection to her father.

"Not only did Madeline's parents not trust me, but yer mother had more beaux than a movie star. For a while I became discouraged, but in time I was able to win her over."

"But, Dad, what did you do?"

Matthew followed Karen into the kitchen and bent close to whisper: "I've never told another living soul this, but I tricked your mother into marrying me. But not for a day did she regret it."

"You didn't," Karen said with a gasp.

"Aye, but I did."

Karen could hardly believe what she was hearing. "How did you trick Mom?"

His whole face broke into a wide, mischievous grin. "I whisked her away. By the time we arrived in Idaho, she'd agreed to be me wife."

Karen felt the sudden need to sit down. "You mean to tell me you kidnapped Mom?"

Matthew laughed boyishly. "It was hardly a kidnapping. I was just helping her make up her mind."

For a moment, Karen was dumbfounded. "Honestly, Dad, you astonish me."

"Aye, it was a brave thing, but your mother never regretted it. I knew she loved me."

Karen would have said more, but her doorbell rang. When she introduced Carl to her father, the two men shook hands respectfully. Karen slipped on her full-length leather coat, and the three left together. Matthew was invited to Evan and Milly Forsyth's for Sunday dinner and promised to give them Karen's love.

The drive to Sea-Tac Airport was accomplished in a companionable silence. Carl seemed to be a quiet, gentle man about the same age as Matthew. His loyalty to Rand was unquestionable. They parked with relative ease and waited in baggage claim.

Rand was the last passenger to arrive, and again the sight of this virile man sent her heartbeat racing. She experienced the urge to rush to him and hug him fiercely; instead, she walked forward almost hesitantly and whispered his name.

Smiling, Rand immediately held his arms open for her. Karen was there in a second, as if it were the most natural place in the world for her to be.

"Welcome home." Carl greeted him with a smile.

"Thanks, Carl. It's good to be home." He smiled at Karen, his look tender and warm. Slipping his arm around her waist, he added, "Very good indeed."

After a thirty-minute drive, Carl turned off the road and into a long driveway. Karen watched with growing anticipation for the first view of Rand's home. Having him invite her to his home held a special significance; Karen felt it was almost symbolic. The final defense was being lowered.

She tensed slightly as they drove down the winding driveway. The first view of the house left Karen awe-struck. The house was magnificent, a long, sprawling, contemporary rambler. The large grounds were land-scaped meticulously. Another smaller home stood in the distance and roused her interest.

Carl answered her unspoken curiosity. "The smaller

house is for me and the missus." His voice was filled with pride.

Holding her hand, Rand led her into his home. He was confident and sure in the familiar surroundings; his movements were precise and made with ease. They stood in the elegantly tiled entryway that led to a sunken living room. The fireplace was lit, the flames reflecting a warm, welcoming glow. A solid-oak dining-room table was set in the formal dining room off the spacious kitchen. The candles flickering from the table's centerpiece cast dancing shadows across the bone china and crystal glassware.

"It's beautiful…everything's beautiful." Karen spoke with a sense of awe. Rand's personality was stamped in every piece of furniture, every room. He had allowed her into the inner sanctum of his life; this home was his pride. Shown a hundred different locales, Karen would have immediately known this house belonged to Rand.

Carl brought in the luggage with the instruction to call when Karen was ready to leave.

The door had no sooner closed behind him when Rand turned to her. Very gently, he took her face between his hands. "I've missed you." He bent forward and kissed her with a fierceness that spoke of longing and frustration. Karen responded with an urgency that matched his own. It had always been like this between them; that jolt of charged electricity that sparked the fire of awareness until every nerve sang with life.

He whispered her name, and then slowly released her. With her eyes still closed, Karen swayed toward him. Rand chuckled and kissed her again fleetingly before placing an arm around her shoulders and leading her to the dining room.

"Let's eat," he murmured, "while I'm still in control of my senses."

Karen would have willingly forgone the meal to have remained in his arms.

As before, Dorothy's cooking was superb. Karen couldn't remember ever tasting chicken tetrazzini with such exquisite flavor.

After the meal, they decided to have their coffee in front of the fireplace in the living room. Karen cleared the table and brought in the coffee on a tray already prepared by the efficient Dorothy.

Enjoying the warmth of the fire, they talked for a long time. With her head resting against Rand's shoulder, his arm around her, Karen discovered they shared several interests. They enjoyed the same authors, and both played chess and were addicted to mellow music.

While Karen returned the coffee tray to the kitchen, Rand placed a CD featuring Rimsky-Korsakov's *Scheherazade* into his CD player. The melodious sounds filled the air as Karen returned.

"May I have the pleasure of this dance, kind sir?" She curtsied before him, her wool skirt brushing the cream pile carpeting. "As I recall, the last time I did this I was rudely rejected."

"The last time you wanted to dance, we were on a downtown sidewalk with half of Tacoma looking on," he remarked, his voice full of humor.

Karen giggled, lifting her arm in entreaty, her body already swaying to the music. "You have no sense of adventure," she chided him softly.

He gathered her in his arms, his body moving rhythmically with hers. "Every time I'm with you, it's an adventure." His hand arched her spine closer, pressing her body intimately against the hard length of his.

Karen closed her eyes and nestled against Rand, glorying in the dizzy emotions he could arouse within her.

They danced, although they barely moved, content to be in each other's arms, lost in a world created only for them.

When the CD finished, they didn't move. The pressure of Rand's fingers at the base of her neck lifted her face upward to meet his descending mouth. Obediently, Karen's lips parted as she molded herself against him, responding with all her love to his deepening kiss. Her hands around his neck were winding a path through his hair, pulling him closer, igniting a slow-burning fire of passion between them until Karen ached.

The fierceness of his lovemaking awoke yearnings Karen had never experienced, and she moaned in surrender as Rand lowered her onto the couch. His hungry mouth claimed hers again and again while his hand slid intimately over her body, seeking the satin contours of her breasts. Caught in the powerful undertow of her love, Karen felt herself drowning in an ocean of sensations.

Suddenly, Rand raised his head, holding himself away from her. "No...no," he uttered harshly, his voice hoarse and barely distinct.

Suddenly bereft, Karen tried unsuccessfully to bring his mouth back to hers, struggling against him, holding him as if her life depended on his.

Angrily, his hand closed over her wrists, firmly pushing her away. He stood and strode across the room, his fingers raking his hair.

Bewildered, Karen sat upright. She was shocked by her wanton behavior, but equally disturbed by Rand's rejection. Her cheeks flamed red from embarrassment and the lingering effects of desire.

"Rand?" It was a muffled cry from her heart.

Rand sat down slowly beside her, gripping her shoulders, forcing her against him.

"Karen, oh, Karen…" His jagged breath was rough against her ear. "It would be the most natural thing in the world to carry you to my bed and love the very life from you. But there would be the reality to face in the morning. Heavens knows I want you. And right now you think you want me, too, but someday you'll thank me for this."

"Oh, Rand…" Her voice wobbled, and she clung to him as if being in his arms would prevent the new day rising. Let there be no tomorrow if she couldn't have him.

Gradually, the desire ebbed, leaving her confused.

Six

"Thank you, I had a wonderful evening," Karen lied with an ease that amazed her.

The elderly hostess gave her a sympathetic smile. "Do come again."

Karen smiled weakly in return; the lump in her throat had grown so thick she could barely swallow. She slipped into her coat and stepped outside, where Carl was waiting. Rand remained inside for several minutes. Why had he stayed? He couldn't possibly be enjoying this. Did he wish to humiliate her further?

Carl glanced at her quizzically. The strain about her mouth and the hurt in her eyes were impossible to hide; she looked away, not wanting anyone else to witness her pain.

Rand joined them.

The ride to Karen's apartment was completed in a wearisome silence that crowded the large vehicle.

Pride held Karen stiff. What had happened? Why was Rand doing this? Things had been strained between them ever since the night he'd invited her to his home. They had been together several times since, and on each occasion he'd grown less civil, less courteous. He was erecting the granite wall between them again, and Karen didn't know if she could stand it.

This evening's party had brought to a climax everything that was wrong between them. Perhaps it wouldn't have been such a disaster if Cora hadn't been there, but Rand had made every effort to make Karen uncomfortable. His attitude from the very beginning had been chilling, but once they'd arrived at the party, it was almost as if he'd forgotten her. He sat with Cora, rarely leaving her side, making excuses to touch her, attentive in a way he had never been with Karen.

Karen chatted with several people, attempting to ignore his behavior, but there could be no pretending when Cora flashed her a look of triumph. A look as loud and clear as if she'd shouted it across the room: Rand was hers, had always been hers, and would forever be hers.

"I suppose you're waiting for an apology?" Rand asked stiffly.

They sat as far apart from each other as possible. "Not unless you feel like making one."

His laugh was short and humorless. "I don't."

"Then it would be pointless, don't you think?"

He shrugged as if an apology were of little consequence either way.

When Carl stopped in front of her apartment building, Rand straightened. "Would you escort the lady to her door, Carl?" The command was issued as if he couldn't bear to even say her name.

Carl muttered something unintelligible under his breath. Karen didn't wait for him to open her car door, jerking it open with a violence that demonstrated the pain of this final humiliation. Had she come to mean so little to Rand that even the courtesy of taking her to her door was beyond him?

Her lips trembled, and she avoided Carl's probing gaze. "Don't bother, Carl," she spoke in a tight, shaky voice. "I'll let myself in."

"It's no problem, miss."

As he inserted the key into her lock, Karen looked back to the car. The streetlight illuminated the dejected, solitary figure inside. Rand had slouched forward, his hands covering his eyes, portraying the picture of a man weighted by an intolerable sadness.

Carl's eyes followed Karen's. "He's been under heavy pressure lately. I'm sure he didn't mean anything."

Tears welled in Karen's eyes; she blinked with the effort to hold them back. Gently, she placed her hand on the older man's arm.

"Thank you," she said softly.

"Well, you certainly look in better spirits than you did the other day." Judy took a slice of carrot from the tray; James and Carter quickly followed suit.

"Hey, you guys, cut it out. There won't be anything left for Rand." She slapped their hands playfully, her eyes laughing. "I feel a whole lot better." Her eyes met Judy's briefly, knowingly. "I don't know what's up with Rand, but you can darn well bet I'm going to find out."

Judy laughed at the spark in Karen's eye. "You know, I almost pity him."

"How do I look? Do you think I'm overdoing things a bit?" She was wearing the birthday dress Judy had made for her. Not only was it one of the loveliest things she owned, but it boosted her confidence, reminding her of the support and love of her family.

"You're lovely," Judy assured her quickly.

"Aunt Karen, can I light the candles?" James questioned enthusiastically.

"Not yet; I don't want to light them until right before Rand gets here."

Both boys gave a disappointed sigh. "All right, I'll tell you what." She playfully tousled the tops of their heads. "The next time you're over, I'll have a candlelight dinner just for you."

"Can I light the candles?" James asked again.

"Naturally."

"But I'd rather have hot dogs than the smelly stuff." Carter wrinkled his nose at the odor of marinating steak.

"I'll have you know that smelly stuff cost me a week's allotment for meat," Karen informed them indignantly. "But don't worry, if you want hot dogs, then we'll have hot dogs."

The boys gave their approval with a loud cheer.

"I think we'd better go. I don't want to be here when Rand arrives," Judy said after checking her wristwatch.

Karen was grateful. "Remember to keep Dad occupied and out of my hair. It would be just like him to drop by for a visit, and I don't want any interruptions."

Judy winked dramatically. "Gotcha."

Suddenly, Karen was unsure of herself. Was she doing the right thing by forcing the issue? "Are you sure everything is right? The wine goes with the meal? The candles aren't too much? I'm not overdressed?" she asked all in one giant breath.

Judy shook her head dismissively. "Settle down. Everything is perfect; you have nothing to worry about."

"You're sure?" Karen glanced around nervously.

"I'm sure. All right, boys, let's visit grandpa." The boys ran ahead. Impulsively, Judy gave Karen a hug. "Good luck. Everything will work out beautifully; wait and see."

Karen wished she possessed the same confidence. Her fingers toyed with the gold locket Rand had given her as if she could draw solace and courage from its presence.

She was placing the finishing touches on the salad when the doorbell chimed. Karen hurriedly wiped her hands on the apron, then carelessly tossed it aside. Pausing for a moment, she closed her eyes to compose herself.

It had been only a few days since she'd last seen Rand, and yet her nerves raced at the physical impact of his presence.

"Hello." She greeted him with false cheerfulness and slid her hands up the lapels of his coat, anticipating his kiss. He hesitated before claiming her mouth. The kiss lacked tenderness or warmth, and Karen avoided another.

"I hope you like marinated steak," she said casually as she hung up his coat. His face looked tight and a little pale. "How about a glass of wine?"

Rand smiled faintly. "Do you have anything stronger?"

"Do you think you're going to need it?" she challenged.

He ignored the question and sat in the overstuffed chair Karen had purchased for its deep-cushioned comfort. But Rand didn't relax; his posture remained tense and straight. "I'll take the wine."

While Karen poured for both of them, her gaze rested briefly on Rand. His facial features, which suggested strength and pride, seemed more pronounced. She watched as he wearily rubbed the back of his neck.

When he accepted the wine, his eyes held a dark, unreadable light. As she sat opposite him, he withdrew a neatly wrapped package from his pocket.

"This is for you," he said tightly.

Karen took the package, her eyes widening with surprise. Was the gift a means of apologizing for his rude behavior these past weeks? Karen relaxed against the back of her seat, suddenly wanting to sing.

Her fingers fumbled as she removed the ribbon and paper. It was a jeweler's case; the name of an exclusive and expensive store was stamped in gold across the top. She hesitated for only a moment before opening the lid.

On a bed of red velvet lay a shimmering gold bracelet, one more beautiful than anything she'd ever hoped to own. She longed to go to him, touch him, thank him as only a lover could. Instead, she whispered softly, "I've never seen anything this beautiful. Thank you."

When she glanced at him, she was surprised to note his wineglass was empty and she'd yet to taste hers. She was reaching for her glass when Rand spoke.

"The bracelet is my way of saying goodbye." The words, savage and tender all at once, were spoken softly.

Karen was so shocked she nearly dropped her glass; part of the wine emptied into her lap.

"What did you say?" She was so stunned she hardly noticed the sudden wetness.

"I said," he began coldly, deliberately, "this is good-bye."

Karen searched his face, praying she'd find some evidence that would tell her he was joking. "You don't mean that."

He gave one of those abrupt, mirthless laughs she had come to hate. "I mean it. We're both adults, and I believe we can do this in an adult manner. I won't be coming here again, and I don't want you to make an effort to see me."

"Why?" The lone word was wrenched from her.

"Damn it, Karen, I'm tired of playing your romantic games. I think it's time you grew up." His body was stiff with determination, his face expressionless, a tight mask.

"I can't understand why you're doing this." Her eyes pleaded with him, implored him.

"Why did you *make* me do it like this? The things I've done to you in the last two weeks couldn't have driven the message home more forcefully. Why do you have to be so damn stubborn? Why did you keep coming back for more hurt, more humiliation?" Although his voice was forceful and steady, it contained an element of pain, as if he found it as difficult to say the words as it was for her to hear them. "I don't want you. Can I make it any plainer than that?" He was shouting at her, then paused and began again, more controlled. "I don't like myself when I'm around you."

Karen's throat muscles were so tight she didn't know if she could breathe much longer. "Please, Rand, don't do this to us." Where was her pride? She choked on a sob but swallowed it before it could escape and humiliate her further.

"*You* did this to us," he accused her harshly. "You and your trial relationship. Why in the hell couldn't you leave things alone? I didn't want you then, and I don't want you now. Do you understand?"

Hurt and anger flashed from the depth of her dark eyes. "I understand, all right. You're only half a man, a blind coward, and I've discovered I want a whole man. Would you just leave?" she screamed, but her heart was begging him to stay.

He stood abruptly. "I've heard enough."

"While you're at it, take the bracelet with you." She threw it at him, box and all; it hit his chest and bounced onto the floor, spilling onto the carpet.

"And this." She jerked the locket from her throat, snapping the delicate gold chain, and threw it at him with all her strength. Rand flinched as it hit him in the face.

"Now, will you get out of my life?"

She ran to her room; she'd be damned before she'd let him see her tears. She sat on her bed, her hands twisting nervously in her lap, noticing for the first time the stain of the spilled wine. The dress, the lovely dress Judy had spent so many hours sewing, would be ruined. In a panicked rush, she unzipped it, allowing it to fall to the floor. She needed to soak it, or the stain would never come out.

She turned blindly and crashed into the open closet door with a sickening thud. Pain stunned her for several seconds before she slumped to the floor, releasing a cry of anguish and pain. The tormented cry of a wounded animal.

"Karen, Karen…" Suddenly, Rand was there, rushing toward her. To her horror, he caught his foot on the edge of the carpet and stumbled into the room. Karen reached out to help him regain his balance, but her action sent him crashing to the floor. Rand grabbed her bare waist and twisted his body so he would absorb the full brunt of the fall. They lay on the floor, their arms and legs entwined, catching their breath.

Rand spoke first. "Are you all right?"

Her tears became sobbing hiccups. "No."

He shifted their position so he was above her. "Where's the pain?" The tender concern in his voice made her weep all the harder.

"My heart."

He groaned as his arms curved around her, gathering her against him while his lips unerringly located her eyes, kissing away each salty tear. He began at the corner of her face, kissing her forehead, her chin, her neck, her ears, before claiming her mouth in a kiss that was as fierce as it was devouring. Karen lifted her mouth to meet his, her trembling lips parting in anticipation.

They clung to each other, their hearts beating wildly as one. His lips followed a slow path down her neck and bare shoulder while his hand wandered over her back, over her hip, molding her soft, womanly body to the hardness of his. Their mouths met, slanting across each other with hungry impatience.

Karen's mind reeled, and she couldn't convince herself this was reality. A whispering sigh escaped her as Rand buried his face along the side of her neck, his mouth spreading hot kisses over her naked flesh. Karen caught her breath at the flood of pleasure, her fingers gripping his head, drawing him back to her lips. His open mouth sought hers in an urgent kiss that sent her world careening. His hands, sensuously caressing her hip, slipped upward, capturing the ripe fullness of her upturned breast, and she was swept along in a violent whirlpool of desire. Winding her arms around his back and pressing her full length to him, she answered his passion with her own.

Suddenly, Rand tensed, his muscles rigid with attention. Lifting his head, he listened attentively to the stillness, leaving her naked and bereft as he stood in anticipation.

"Rand?" Karen whispered, sitting upright.

"I thought I heard a noise." Wearily, he rubbed his hands over his face. He lowered himself onto the bed; leaning forward, he buried his face in his hands.

"I thought you'd gone." She covered herself with the housecoat from the end of the bed.

He smiled wryly. "I couldn't find my coat. What happened in here?"

She gestured weakly with her hand. "I was crying and didn't see where I was going."

He nodded, his face weary and pinched.

"Please, Rand," she pleaded, her voice wobbling dangerously, "don't do this to us."

He stiffened at the sound of her voice. "Don't... it's over."

"There will never be anyone who will love you as much as I do." Bitterness was etched in her pain-ridden eyes.

He stood abruptly, hurrying from her room. "I've got to get out of here. Damn it, Karen, my coat."

Tying the sash of her housecoat, she followed him into the living room and to the closet.

"Here." She handed it to him. "I'm going to let you

go, and I'm not even going to say goodbye. We'll probably never meet again. You'll live your life, and I'll live mine. But I love you, Rand. I'll love you as long as I live, and someday, maybe not for a long time, you'll regret this."

The hand closed over the door handle was clenched so tight it became stark white. He didn't pause or acknowledge her words. Instead, he yanked open the door and left.

Karen jerked as the door slammed, crying as she had never cried, her breath coming in desperate gasps, the tears from her soul.

Hugging her arms protectively against her stomach, she sat in the chair Rand had vacated, curling into its softness like a hurt child seeking comfort from a parent. The gold locket and bracelet remained on the floor, and Karen stared at the glimmering gold for a long time before bending down to retrieve the pair. Clenching them to her breast, she rocked back and forth with an anguish too deep for tears.

She remained in the chair the entire night, her gaze watching the candles while they burned themselves out. First one, then the other, the last desperate flicker before extinction. The room went dark. Karen stared with sightless eyes into a moonlit, shadow-filled room, realizing the throbbing pain in her head would diminish, but not the pain in her heart.

The sun, gradually rising to announce a new day, spurred her into sluggish action. It took a careful application of makeup to camouflage the red swollen eyes as she dressed for work. "I'll make it through this day, and then I'll be all right," she told herself, knowing she was lying. It would be a very long time before she was all right again.

Until that day, Karen had had no idea how good she was at lying, how automatic certain responses became in one's life.

Late afternoon, she sat at her desk, examining the final details of a day's work, knowing she'd never find solace in her job, wondering if she'd ever find comfort.

Matthew's cheerful face was waiting for her outside her apartment. Karen avoided his eyes, praying he wouldn't mention Rand.

"Evening, lass."

"Hi, Dad. I'm kinda busy…" She didn't have the heart to tell him he couldn't come inside.

"'Tis fine. I'll only stay a minute." He followed her and sat at the kitchen table while she put on coffee to brew. When she gave him a sidelong glance, she found he was watching her with an odd expression.

"When will ye be seeing Rand again?"

Karen turned back to the countertop, closing her eyes for a moment at the searing pain. "I won't," she said flatly.

She could sense the shock that rocked him. "I'm sure I must not be hearing ye right," he said after a few minutes of stunned shock.

"Look, Dad"—her voice shook violently—"I don't feel much like discussing it right now."

"But ye love him," he cried indignantly.

"Of course I love him," she whispered through the pain.

"And he loves you?" This time, Matthew's voice was quiet and probing.

Karen couldn't keep her bottom lip from trembling.

"Yes, he loves me…but love doesn't make everything right," she uttered in a hoarse whisper, blinking wildly to restrain the tears.

"But why?" her father asked in confusion. It was a question that had haunted Karen half the night.

"Because he's proud; he thinks he's only half a man and if I love him now, that love will eventually die when he loses his eyesight completely." She inhaled a shaky breath. "He wants me so much it's eating a hole in him; he had to push me away before it was too late." Karen grimaced with the memory that she had accused Rand of being half a man, lashing back where it would hurt him the most because he was hurting her so desperately.

Gently, a pair of hands settled on her shoulders and turned her around.

"Don't," she told him tautly, shrugging off his hands. "I'm a grown woman now. I'm not your little girl anymore."

Matthew ignored her, turning her into his arms, holding her close, his cheek resting gently against her head. "Even big girls require a father's comfort every now and then," he whispered.

Karen buried her head against his chest, the tension draining from her as she allowed the tears to come. "Oh, Dad, I love him so much."

"I know you do, lass," Matthew crooned. "Let it all out, darlin'. Let it all out."

A week passed. Matthew and Judy enfolded Karen in their love and support, trying to make sure she was busy, not letting her stay alone for any long length of time. Karen lost weight she could ill afford to lose, and her eyes developed dark shadows that cosmetics were unable to hide. When she wasn't working or with her family, she sat in the big overstuffed chair, looking pensive and lost.

Matthew seemed to feel talking about Rand would make things easier. Her father felt certain that once Rand had come to his senses, he would be back. Karen didn't bother to correct him.

Another week slipped by, and Karen knew she couldn't live like this much longer. Friday afternoon, she gave Tacoma Cable a two-week notice, drove home, and handed a similar notice to the apartment manager.

"Lass." Her father let himself into her apartment, his face hurt and confused. "What have ye done?"

Karen didn't pause. "I'm leaving Tacoma," she announced without emotion. Dark curls escaped the scarf she'd tied around her head. She was standing on the kitchen counter, cleaning out her top cupboards. Boxes littered both the kitchen and the living-room floor. "I should have done this two weeks ago." She dipped the cleaning rag in the bucket of hot, steaming water and wrung it out.

"But, lass, when Rand comes back…"

"Dad," she protested angrily, "when will you get it into your thick skull? Rand isn't going to come back. It's over between us."

Matthew grew visibly pale and sat down.

"Dad"—concern laced her voice, and she jumped down from the counter—"are you all right?"

He nodded weakly. "I'm fine." His eyes searched hers, holding a desperate appeal. "I don't want you doing something rash. You've been hurt, and seeking a geographical cure would be the worst possible thing for you. I told you before, things have a way of working out for the best. Just where are ye planning to go?"

Karen had expected an argument, and squared her shoulders defiantly. "Away... I don't know yet."

Matthew shook his head sadly. "I don't like this, lass."

Karen had known he wouldn't and that she hadn't heard the last of it. "I'm twenty-four years old, and I've barely left the state of Washington. I think it's time I learned to live a little, let my hair down, travel." Her enthusiasm was as phony as that of a used-car salesman. There was only one thing she wanted in life, and that was impossible. She couldn't chance meeting Rand. She couldn't stay. Not in the same city, not in the same state. Not in the same world.

Judy arrived an hour later; her eyes held an accusing, disbelieving look. "You've pulled some good ones in your life, little sister, but this takes the cake."

"Oh? What have I done now?"

"Do you realize you've got Dad worried sick?"

Karen flushed guiltily, dropping the pretense. "I know, but I've got to leave. I wish I could make you understand. Do you realize what it does to me every time I'm near the university or see Uncle Evan or even drive in downtown Tacoma? Someday it's going to happen. By fate or design, I don't know, but someday I'm going to run into Rand. I won't be able to take it." Her voice rose, and she took a moment to compose herself. "I'll fall into a thousand pieces. I know I will. If you and Dad think I'm running away, then all right, I'll admit it."

Judy sighed, her eyes filled with compassion. "I wish I had some magic formula that would take away the hurt, but I don't." She gave a weak gesture of help-lessness. "I'm not convinced you're doing the wrong thing, like Dad is. But I do know we all love you. Let our love support you; let us be your strength." She paused for a minute and withdrew something from her purse. "Maybe if you read this, it'll help."

Karen accepted the letter, grown yellow with age.

"When Mom died," Judy continued, "Mike and I were stationed back East. Both boys were little, and I was stuck home alone most of the time. I had no family, no close friends, or anyone I could talk to about my feelings. I didn't know how to handle my grief. For weeks, I walked around in a haze of emotional pain."

Karen understood; her life had been a haze of pain since that last night with Rand.

"All I seemed capable of doing was crying. I know Mike was worried about me. He must have written Dad because I received this letter. It's the most beautiful thing Dad has ever given me."

Karen opened the letter and was greeted by Matthew's familiar scrawl. The date was exactly three months after her mother's death. It was a vivid memory. Madeline had suffered from a chronic kidney disorder, and when she contracted an infection, it didn't overly concern Karen or her father. She'd had several infections over the years. Karen had even felt her mother was getting better. Then one day she was in the hospital, insisting she should be home, and two days later she was dead.

Karen had loved and sorely missed her mother, too, but her concern had been for Matthew and the changes that had come over him after Madeline's death.

The letter showed the wear of many readings; the stain of Judy's tears marked the pages.

It read:

My darling Judy,

It hurts so terribly, doesn't it? But, my darling lass, we must learn to accept the pain. It is the price we must pay for having loved. I hold this ache of loneliness inside, and although I have loved and lost my beloved Madeline, I accept and gladly pay the cost. It is but a small price for the love we shared those many years. They have been good years, the best of my life. Sometimes I am overcome by my agony. I weep with you, my daughter. I pray God will surround you with His love.

Mike is worried about you. He loves you just as I loved my Madeline. Drink of his love; let it be your strength.

We must go on, just as life does. James and Carter need you just as Karen yet needs me. Accept the pain with joy...it was worth the cost.

Your loving father

Tears blurred Karen's eyes and spilled down her face. The end of her relationship with Rand was very much like her mother's death to Judy. She smiled through her tears, grateful for her sister's love. She, too, would pay the price for loving Rand, but now, because of a letter full of love and wisdom, she would pay the price with joy.

Judy may have accepted Karen's decision to leave, but Matthew made repeated efforts to dissuade her.

Karen listened politely to his logic, sometimes doubting the wisdom of her actions, but never wavering from the decision.

Selling her furniture and packing her things filled her last remaining days in Tacoma. It was the nights that continued to haunt her. She'd lay awake for hours in a reflective mood, wondering what she might have done differently to have won Rand. The sharp pain remained, and Karen pondered how long it would take for it to lessen. Sometimes, if she lay very still and closed her eyes, she could almost feel the warmth of his breath against her cheek. She'd shake herself, realizing she was doing the right thing by leaving. She couldn't bear the struggle to be free of him for much longer. All the memories were right here to torment her.

Only three days remained of Karen's two-week notice. Most of the things from her apartment had been sold. Only her bed and the large, overstuffed chair remained.

Because she couldn't sleep, she sat reading, finding it hard to concentrate and equally difficult to answer the doubts that bobbed to the surface of her mind. Karen realized, perhaps for the first time, how much she would miss her home, her city. If she were honest with herself, she'd admit that she didn't really want to leave Tacoma, but the alternative was just as unacceptable.

When the doorbell rang, it caught Karen by surprise. She glanced at her watch, curious who would be visiting so late.

"Who is it?" she questioned before unlocking the door.

"Rand," came the muffled reply.

Was it some cruel joke? Her fingers were trembling so badly she could barely open the door.

When he entered, Karen was as shocked by his appearance as his presence. He looked as if he hadn't shaved in days; the dark growth did little to disguise his haggard features. Gaunt lines of fatigue were etched about his eyes and mouth, as if he hadn't seen a bed in days. If he had slept, it was in the wrinkled mass of clothes he wore. His hair, normally so neat and well groomed, looked like he'd raked his fingers through it several times over.

"Rand?" His name was twisted from her in shock. She longed to touch him, to comfort him. He was in as much hell as she had been these past weeks.

His mouth twisted cynically. "All right, Karen, you win."

Seven

Karen walked into his arms, gently resting her head against his chest. His hold tightened until it was difficult for her to breathe. But it didn't matter, not as long as she was in his arms. Rand's face moved against her hair, as if he couldn't yet believe the feel of her. They stood entwined for a long time, not talking, hardly breathing, savoring the tender moment.

When Karen placed her arms around his neck, urging his mouth to hers, she felt his reluctance. The kiss began hard, as if he wanted to punish her; then, with a groan, his lips softened into a warm possession, and what followed was anything but punishment.

"Hold me, please, hold me." Tears blurred her vision, her voice betraying the anguish of the past month without him.

"I love you." His voice was thick with emotion as if he were confessing a guilt. "I could have withstood anything if I didn't love you so much."

"I know, I know," she whispered in soothing tones, remembering how hard he had tried to convince her otherwise. Tenderly, his hand brushed her tears aside.

"I think I would have died if you hadn't come," Karen murmured. Already she had gone cold inside, withdrawing from her family and life.

Rand breathed heavily. "I'm here now." The words were clipped, almost angry.

His pride made him so defensive, Karen thought sadly. Knowing and loving Rand made her realize how much it had cost him to come to her.

"There's only one chair left in the apartment." She gave a tiny laugh and wiped the last happy tears from her face. "I'll have to sit on your lap."

The quizzical look on his face prompted her to add, "Everything else has been sold. I'm packed and ready to leave." Her arms automatically went around his neck as she positioned herself on his knees.

His hands tightened around her upper arms. "Were you so sure of me?" His look was weary, and there was a grimness in him.

"I wasn't sure of anything," she said, defending herself. Her eyes narrowed questioningly. Certainly he couldn't believe she had expected his return. In truth, she had never been more shocked in her life.

"I want the wedding to be small." The demand startled Karen. She hadn't expected him to mention marriage, not yet. Not that it mattered how many guests attended.

"Wedding?" Karen breathed in wonder as her heart soared with a new happiness. She began spreading kisses over his face, and fresh tears misted her eyes.

"Your father wouldn't accept anything less," Rand murmured caustically. "Nor would you."

Karen was too happy to question his decision.

* * *

They were married nine days later in Evan and Milly Forsyth's home. The preceding days were a whirlwind of activity as Judy, Karen, and her godmother rushed to have everything ready. Karen saw Rand only once, when they applied for their wedding license, and if he was curt and taciturn, she attributed it to nerves and the pressures of teaching. Because Rand had a speaking engagement in New York scheduled for the weekend of their wedding, it was decided that Karen would travel with him on a working honeymoon. Rand's mother lived in New York, and Karen was eager to meet her.

As Rand wished, the wedding was unpretentious, with only family and a few intimate friends attending. The Forsyth home was decorated with garlands and several bouquets of fresh flowers. Their sweet fragrance lingered in the air, their colors vivid. Karen felt she couldn't have asked for a more lovely wedding.

As Randall Franklin Prescott and Karen Madeline McAlister exchanged their vows, Rand's voice was firm and unfaltering. Karen's voice trembled slightly as she repeated hers. Her heart swelled with a burning love. Marrying Rand was the culmination of every romantic dream she'd ever had.

The wedding meal was served in the Forsyths' huge dining room. If Rand was somber and unusually quiet, no one noticed, for Karen was so obviously happy. Her spirits soared with an unrestrained freedom, yet she had just uttered vows that bound her for life.

It was late by the time they arrived at Rand's home. The stars were out in an ostentatious show, their brilliance lighting up the black velvet sky.

As Carl carried in her cases, Karen looped her arm

in Rand's, savoring the beauty of the evening. "This reminds me of the night we met." She smiled dreamily, placing her head against his upper arm. "Oh, Rand, I'm so happy... I love you so much." She longed to have him take her in his arms and whisk her over the threshold, but he paused, holding himself stiff and unyielding against her.

"My mother had a homemade sampler in the living room when I was a little girl. I've thought about it so often these past few days. I'd like to make one for our home."

Rand remained unresponsive, and Karen hugged herself to him. "Aren't you interested in what it said?" she asked with a gentle smile.

"I have the feeling you're going to tell me whether I want to hear it or not," he murmured.

Karen laughed. "It said, 'If you love something, set it free. If it doesn't return, it was never meant to be. But if it does, love it forever.'" She gave a long sigh. "I let you go that night. It nearly killed me to let you walk out of my life, but you've come back, and now I'll love you forever."

Rand jerked her arm from his. "That's just the point," he retorted angrily. "I didn't come back. You forced me into this farce."

"Forced you?" Karen asked in confusion. "I *didn't* show up on *your* doorstep. You were the one who came to me."

Rand gave a short, derisive laugh. "That I did, two hours before the deadline." He stormed into the house, leaving Karen standing alone and baffled. When she followed him, Rand had already poured himself a tall drink from a decanter of whiskey.

"I thought you said you rarely drink?" she asked accusingly.

He snickered. "I find I can't stand to be in your presence without something to dull my sense of decency."

"That's a rotten thing to say." What was happening to him? Why was he acting like this? Karen searched his face, hoping to find some clue of what was wrong. All she could read was contempt.

"That'll be all, Carl." Rand broke into her thoughts. "I'll call you when we're ready to leave for the airport."

Carl's eyes avoided Karen's, although she silently pleaded with him; for what, she didn't know.

As soon as the front door closed behind her husband's driver, Karen asked, "What...what did you mean when you said you came to me two hours before the deadline? What deadline?"

His face twisted malevolently. "Drop the charade, Karen. You're not going to fool me by playing dumb. I'd guessed you'd try something like this."

"Something like what? Rand, please, I don't know what you're talking about."

He emitted another sadistic laugh. "I walked into the whole thing like a lamb going to the slaughter. I have to admire you, Karen. You were more cunning than I thought possible."

"Rand?" she pleaded urgently. "I don't know what you're talking about."

"Sure you don't." He tipped his head back and drained the glass. "I needed that." Wiping his mouth with the back of his hand, he sat, leaning his head against the back of the couch. "Like a lamb to the slaughter," he repeated. "You must have been frantic when you saw your little ploy wouldn't work that night. You hadn't counted on me handing you your walking papers so soon, did you? It was quick thinking on your part to pretend you'd hurt yourself. It got me into that bedroom." He ran his hand over his eyes. "I should have known something was up when you were practically naked."

"I'd spilled wine on my dress," she cried.

"Sure you did." His words were uttered in a harsh whisper.

Karen paced the living-room floor, her mind racing, her thoughts confused. Nothing made sense, least of all the things he was saying. "Rand," she whispered imploringly, "I'm going to ask you one last time. Please tell me what's going on."

He sat upright, flexing his shoulders as if he were going to ignore her. "What did you expect me to do? Welcome you with open arms? I don't take kindly to blackmail; I could hate you and your father for what you've done to me."

"Blackmail? Dad?" She glared at him, her face tightening with shock. Walking the full length of the floor, Karen poured herself a drink from the same decanter Rand had used, then choked and coughed after the first gulp. "Good grief, how do you drink this stuff?" Her eyes were watering, and she shook her head; her mouth felt as if she'd been sucking lemons. She moved back to Rand. "All right," she murmured tightly, "let's start at the beginning. I invited you to dinner—"

"Like a black widow to her web," Rand interrupted mockingly.

Karen clenched her hands together, fighting the urge to scream. "I invited you to dinner because…because I had to know what was happening with us."

"Ha!" Rand laughed sarcastically. "More likely to lure me to your bed so your father could find us."

"So my father could find us?" She echoed one of the short, bitter laughs he'd given her. "Really, Rand, if I'd gotten you into my bed, the last person I'd want to see is my father."

"So you say," he remarked flippantly.

Karen studied him closely again, feeling hurt and bewildered.

"I have to admit your duplicity worked well. I wasn't given much choice, was I? Since Evan Forsyth is your godfather, who do you think he'd believe?" His mouth twisted bitterly. "I haven't got ten years in at the university; you knew that. I'd stand a snowball's chance in hell of finding another decent position after Forsyth was through with me."

Even as understanding came, Karen refused to believe what she was hearing. Matthew had seen them together that night and was using what he'd witnessed against Rand, forcing him to marry her. She inhaled sharply. "The noise that night was Dad," she said incredulously, her voice tight with embarrassment.

"My contempt would be less if you'd admit your part in this."

"Damn it, Rand," she shouted, "I *am* telling you the truth." Suddenly, her knees became so weak she had to sit down. She sat tense and stiff in the chair opposite Rand as she pleaded with him. "Please listen to me." She spoke softly, enunciating each word. "I swear by everything I hold sacred that I had nothing to do with this."

Uncertainty flashed across his face, wrinkling his brow. "I could almost believe you…almost." His fingers twisted the wedding band, so recently placed on his finger, tying him to her. "But everything falls into place so neatly. You set up this trap for me…"

"I didn't, I swear," she cried.

"All right, you didn't, but why was it when I came to your room, thinking you were hurt, that I found you half-naked?"

"I already explained that," she pleaded. "I spilled wine on my dress. I had to take it off and soak it, or it would have been ruined. After I removed the dress, I bumped into the closet door."

"Your father just happened to walk in and witness that sordid little scene with us on the floor?"

Karen felt sick. "Dad… Dad has a terrible habit of walking into my apartment unannounced."

Rand's face turned sour. "Sure he does. You were so confident you had me trapped that you quit your job and packed your things."

"No! I'd decided to leave Tacoma…to move away." Karen could see it was useless; she couldn't argue or reason with him. Rand had already tried her and found her guilty. "Nothing I can say will make a difference, will it?"

"That's right," he jeered. "I have to admit you play the innocent well, but I've fallen for your deceit once. I won't be such easy prey next time."

A sick sensation churned her stomach; they could never build a marriage under the circumstances. "I realize you believe I was involved in this. I think I can even understand that." She spoke softly, her voice barely audible. "The evidence certainly points in that direction."

"What takes the cake is that you even had the marriage performed at the Forsyth home," he accused her again. "That was like rubbing salt in an open wound, my dear."

"That's the point, isn't it?" she asked, with pain-filled eyes. "I'm not your dear. You must hate me." Karen didn't know how she could sound so calm when she wanted to scream.

Rand's fingers tightened around the whiskey glass until Karen was sure the tumbler would be crushed into a thousand pieces. "I wish I could hate you," he whispered in a tone that reminded her of the night he'd returned and admitted his love almost as if it were a guilty secret.

"You once reminded me that we are two adults," she began shakily, gathering her resolve, "and that we should be able to handle things in an adult manner."

Rand nodded curtly.

"I can only apologize for my father's behavior. I don't know why he would do something so under-handed…"

"Karen…" Rand's voice rose threateningly.

Despondently, Karen realized Rand thought she was placing the blame entirely on Matthew's head.

"Please, let me finish," she asked, her voice stiff, polite. "I can only hope that someday you'll find it in your heart to forgive Dad…and to think kindly of me." She slipped the exquisite diamond from her long, slender finger and watched it slide off with a sadness she had never known. The ring had been on her finger for only a few hours, and Karen thought she'd rather have lost her finger than part with this symbol of their love. "I'm… I'm giving you the wedding ring back. I'll begin annulment proceedings first thing Monday morning."

Rand smiled stiffly as he accepted the diamond. "Maybe an annulment would be best."

"I'll have my things moved out before you return from New York," she said weakly, fighting back the first shock waves.

Rand's look became intent. "Where will you go?"

She turned away from him, tilting her head back and blinking wildly to keep the tears from spilling. "I… I don't know yet, but it won't matter. Once the annulment is final…" She left the rest unsaid, the words stuck in her throat.

Rand slouched forward, running his fingers through his hair. "You don't need to leave immediately. I'll be gone for the next three days. We both need time to think, to decide what we're going to do. By the time I return, I'll have the situation in perspective and a better grip on my emotions. I think you should do the same thing. We'll talk then. Is that agreeable?"

"All right," she murmured tightly. "I'll stay here for now and let my family assume I've left for New York with you. Maybe while you're gone, I'll come up with a solution to this mess."

"Until we decide, I'd like for you to keep the ring."

Miserably, Karen shook her head. "No… I don't think I should. Marriage is something very binding as far as I'm concerned. My parents were married for twenty-seven years, and if I place a wedding ring on my finger, I think my intention should be for a life-time…not a three-day weekend."

Rand frowned slightly. "Whether we stay married or not, the ring is yours."

"I'd prefer it if you kept it for now." The ring would become very much like the bracelet he'd given her.

Unless they stayed married, it could be only a painful reminder of what could have been.

Carl drove Rand to the airport an hour later. If he was surprised that Karen was staying behind, he didn't show it. Sadly, Karen stood in the open doorway as the car drove into the distance, watching until the lights faded and the car turned onto the main road. Rand's farewell had been cool, but the open hostility was gone. For that, at least, Karen could be grateful. Rand's face was drawn and tired as he'd stepped into the car, and Karen yearned to go to him and erase the finely strung tension between them. But she'd stayed where she was, watching him go.

Her suitcase remained in the master bedroom, a room indelibly marked by Rand's presence, and Karen avoided it as long as possible. Instead, she sat in the sunken living room, feeling lost and very much alone. Suddenly, she remembered this was her wedding night and could have wept with bitterness and disappointment.

Shortly after midnight, it began to rain, a steady torrent with mounting fury that pounded sheets of rain against the windows. Thunder rolled closer and closer; lightning flashed in jagged arcs across the sky. How quickly the storm had come; only a few hours before, Karen had been staring at clear skies and brilliant stars. The storm was like the day. It had begun with such promise; she had entered Rand's home as his wife, determined to do her best. Now, only a few hours later, her marriage was threatened, her life in turmoil.

When the phone rang, Karen was surprised. "Hello," she answered hesitantly. Surely Rand didn't receive many calls after midnight. More than likely it was a prank call.

"Miss Karen?"

The voice was familiar, and Karen recognized it immediately. "Yes, Carl, it's me."

He sounded awkward, as if he didn't often use the telephone. "I was phoning to see if you are all right… the storm and all."

"I'm fine, thank you. I'm not frightened by thunder and lightning. Did…did Rand get off okay?"

"I assume he and Miss Dibner were not delayed. I didn't stay to see the flight off."

Cora was with Rand. A sick feeling came over Karen's stomach. She had endured so much this day, the whole gauntlet of emotions from utter happiness to abject misery. Knowing Cora was traveling with Rand was almost more than she could bear.

"No, of course you wouldn't wait to see him off," Karen murmured, the lump in her throat building. "Thank you for your concern, Carl, but I'm fine."

"Let me know if you need anything," he offered soberly.

"I will." Her voice suddenly sounded frail and wobbly.

There was a pause on the other end of the line. "Good night, then."

"Good night." She replaced the receiver, looking around her helplessly. Rand and Cora. The picture of them traveling together when it was her and Rand's wedding night was almost more than she could bear. When the sobs came, she roughly jerked her hand across her face. If this was what love does, Karen decided, she wanted no part of it.

Stiffening her back, she turned out the living-room lights and walked determinedly into the master bedroom. Ignoring Rand's dominating presence, marked in every corner, she lifted her suitcase onto the king-size bed and took out her nightgown. It was a lovely full-length satin of pale blue that Judy had given her before the wedding. Karen took one look at it, stuffed it back inside the suitcase, and slammed the lid closed. Randall Prescott could fly across the country with another woman on their wedding night, but she…but she… The anger drained as quickly as it had flared.

Karen sat on the bed and lightly ran her fingers along the pattern of the multi-brown-colored bedspread. For an instant, she'd been ready to run, to surrender without so much as a confrontation. She couldn't stay, yet she couldn't leave. Releasing her breath slowly, Karen wandered from the room and found two other large-size bedrooms and a den that Rand obviously used as an office. She moved her suitcase into one of the other bedrooms; sleeping in the master bedroom was an agony she couldn't bear tonight.

Karen woke early the next morning, her heart heavy. She sat up, deciding to get away from the house for a while and sort through her thoughts. Evidence of the night's storm littered the yard; short branches of fir and pine from the trees that surrounded the property were scattered everywhere. Karen kicked them aside, her irritation so strong she failed to appreciate the freshness of the early-morning air. Heavy gray clouds continued to darken the sky, rain ready to pelt the earth at any time. Yet Karen noticed none of this.

"Just wait till I get my hands on you, Dad," she

said aloud, letting the branches receive the brunt of her anger.

Did her father realize the impossible position he had put her in? What could he possibly have been thinking? Blackmailing Rand was an underhanded trick that went against the very core of honesty she had always known from her father. Karen wanted to shout at him every rotten name she knew. How could he have possibly done anything so unscrupulous? Rand had every reason to detest the backhanded methods Matthew had used to get them married. And yet as much as she disagreed with her father's schemes, she could understand why he did it. Against the flint hardness of his will, against his better judgment, Rand loved her. But that love was doomed almost from the beginning. Without Matthew's intervention, there would never have been a marriage. Now it was up to Karen to see that they remained married. With a new resolve, she walked back to the house.

A movement out of the corner of her eyes caught her attention, and she found Carl watching her from the kitchen of his home. Impulsively, she gave him a friendly wave and watched the smile grow on his face before he returned her greeting.

"Miss Karen."

She turned to find Carl's long strides eliminating the space between them. The calico kitten James and Carter had given Rand was under his arm.

"Hello, Number Nine," she greeted the kitten softly. She was more cat than kitten, and Karen was surprised how much she had grown. "I wondered what had become of you."

"Mr. Rand asked the missus and me to keep the kitty while he was away, but…"

"I'll take her," Karen offered, interrupting him to avoid explanations of why she was here and Rand in New York.

Carl handed her the cat. "With Mr. Rand gone so much of the time, the kitty seems to think of my place as home. The missus has tried to discourage her, but she stands outside the kitchen door and cries until we let her inside. My missus has a soft heart," he added.

Karen concealed a smile. No doubt Dorothy was a warmhearted soul, but it didn't take Karen long to realize Carl had a soft touch where animals were concerned. She'd found hay, food, and a salt block by the creek and knew he'd hauled it down the narrow path to feed the wild creatures in the woods.

"Now that I'm here, Number Nine will know her home," Karen said, her voice conveying the confidence of her newly formed resolve. "She's had her shots and everything?" Rand was sure to want her spayed as soon as possible.

"Oh, yes. First thing Mr. Rand had me do was take her to the vet."

"Thank you, Carl." The older man was fast becoming both ally and friend. Karen was grateful for both.

Without hesitation, Karen entered her new home, walking straight to the master bedroom. The cat followed her, jumped on the king-size bed, and curled into a little ball as if that were exactly where she belonged. *I'll do the same,* Karen decided.

One side of Rand's walk-in closet had been cleared for her things, and Karen spent the rest of the morning unpacking. She found herself singing, her confidence building. As she placed her things around the room, a sense of rightness replaced her insecurities. If her father could convince her mother to marry him, certainly she should be able to persuade Rand, who she knew loved her, that they should stay married. She'd face him with that quiet, unshakable McAlister resolve, she decided. Feeling as if a weight had been lifted from her, Karen slept in the master bedroom that night, finding courage in the fact that she was acting like a wife, waiting for her husband's return.

Rand's flight was due late Sunday afternoon. Karen waited impatiently as each minute passed with an incredible slowness. After pacing the floor innumerable times and checking the dinner she'd cooked, Karen decided she needed to vent some of her anxiety by walking.

She followed the same path she'd discovered the day before, a winding trail that led into tall trees alive with a natural beauty. When she returned, strolling leisurely into the clearing beside the house, she saw Carl's car had returned and was parked in front. Her footsteps hastened, her long strides filled with purpose.

"Hello, Carl," she called happily.

He gave her a frown that confused her and stepped into the entryway carrying Rand's suitcase. "I'll be heading home to *my missus,*" Carl quipped, his tone showing obvious displeasure.

He tipped his cap to Karen, his eyes avoiding hers. As Karen watched him go, her eyes clouded with confusion. Stopping to take a deep breath, she entered the house, but the welcoming smile died on her lips as soon as she moved through the door.

"Darling," Cora purred, her arms entwined around Rand's neck. "She must have left."

house as her welcoming smile darted to Rand's wife
as she moved through the door.

"Rand," Cora purred, her gaze only on the ground
Randi as she crossed the foyer. She leaned over, kissing him firmly on the lips.

Eight

"But I haven't," Karen interrupted, fighting to keep
her voice even and to hide her shock.

Gripping Cora's wrists, Rand forcefully removed
her hands, which continued to cling to him. "Karen,
I..." He sounded unsure and disconcerted.

"You must be exhausted from the flight, Cora,"
Karen interrupted again. If Rand wanted to give her
an explanation, he could do it later, privately. "I'll have
Carl drive you home." She returned Cora's cold glare
with one of her own. Cora may have found encouragement in the fact that Rand had left her on their wedding
night, but the woman had yet to discover the lengths
Karen was willing to go to keep her husband.

Carl must have been waiting outside, because the
minute his name was mentioned, he entered the house.
"I'm ready to leave, Miss Dibner." He gave Karen a
conspiratorial wink that did little to please Cora.

"Rand," she purred, giving the impression her feelings had been crushed by such a lack of welcome. But
if she'd hoped for his support, she was again disappointed.

"As Karen says, you must be tired from the flight. I know I am."

"You will phone me?" Cora's attitude immediately changed from a feline on the prowl to the business-woman she was. Professionally, Cora was Rand's equal, her list of credentials as impressive as Rand's. The look she flashed Karen let her know she had yet to concede the battle.

"I'll contact you in the morning," Rand murmured without enthusiasm.

Her eyes filled with resentment; she gave Karen an almost imperceptible nod.

Karen returned with a slight dip of her head. "We'll meet again. Goodbye, Cora."

With a cool sophistication Karen envied, Cora gave her a meaningful sidelong glare on her way out the door. "You can count on it," she murmured for Karen's ears alone.

As soon as the door was closed, Rand crossed the living room and poured himself a stiff drink from the whiskey decanter. "I didn't mean for that to happen," he began, but his voice contained no apology, his posture defensive.

"I'm sure you didn't," Karen murmured.

"Where were you?" he demanded. "I walked in the door expecting you to be here."

For the first time since his arrival, Karen began to relax. "I went for a walk in the woods out back. I wasn't exactly sure what time you planned on being here."

His face showed fatigue. "Did you discover the creek?" he questioned, then took a sip of his drink.

"Yes, I did." She was still standing in the same spot as when she'd come in.

"Carl has seen several deer drinking from it. I believe he's put some hay and a salt block out for them."

"I wondered about that," Karen said stiffly. Why did they have to talk to each other like polite strangers? Why couldn't they come to the matter that was uppermost in both their minds?

"Would you like something to eat?"

He shook his head dismissively. "I ate on the plane."

"Yes…of course you would." She glanced at the meal simmering in the kitchen, feeling chagrined. He was three hours ahead of the West Coast, and by his clock it was nearly eight. He would have eaten long ago.

Rand lifted his head and turned his face toward the kitchen. "You've cooked dinner?"

"I didn't go to any trouble; it's nothing special." She dismissed his concern and walked into the kitchen to turn off the oven. She had no appetite, and wouldn't until things were cleared between them.

He followed her, wrinkling his nose appreciatively. "What's this nothing special you're cooking?"

Placing a rebelling curl of soft brown hair around her ear, she turned her back to the stove. "Cornish game hens in orange sauce."

The beginnings of a smile threatened his stiff mouth. "If you consider this nothing, I'll look forward to your fancy meals."

She gave a small, nervous laugh. "Actually, I'm not a very good cook. I thought I'd ask Dorothy if she'd share some of her recipes."

"It was a very wifely thing to have dinner waiting for me."

Did she imagine an inquiry in his voice? If so, she wasn't likely to ignore it. "Yes, it was," she said as matter-of-factly as possible. "I... I am your wife, for the present, at least."

Rand scowled, and Karen's heart sank. She couldn't stand it for another minute. If he wasn't going to say something, she would. "I think the question remains of exactly how long I am to be your wife."

A muscle flexed in his jaw, and Karen could see the pride that narrowed his eyes. "Yes, that does seem to be the question. What have you decided?"

For a moment, Karen's stomach pitched unsteadily. Her hands twisted together, and she looked around, wondering why she had to have the most important discussion of her life in a kitchen with her back supported by an oven door because she was too nervous to stand upright.

"I've decided that my father played a dirty trick on the both of us. I know you believe I had a hand in this scheme, but I didn't."

Rand's mouth twisted.

"I know you don't believe me," she continued, her voice shaky. "Someday, I pray, you'll trust me enough to accept what I'm telling you as the truth. I do know"—she hesitated, her voice dipping slightly—"that I'm glad Dad did what he did. Admittedly, it was an underhanded trick, unworthy of my father, but you would never have married me otherwise, and Dad knew it."

"You knew that, too," he said tightly, accusingly.

"I only know you love me and that it hurt you just as much as it did me to walk away that night. I know that you'll never hold another woman in your arms without pretending it's me. I know that if you send me away, you'll always wonder about the life we could have had together."

"I never said I loved you." His upper lip curled into a defensive smile.

Karen's response was gentle. "You did the night you came back, the night of the deadline. But it doesn't matter if you spoke the words or not. I would have known, anyway. I've known for a long time. Do you imagine you could have hidden it from me the night we walked along Commencement Bay? Or any number of times since when you've held me in your arms?"

Ominously, Rand's jaw tightened. His fingers raked his hair in a savage motion. "All right, I love you, but it doesn't change things." The words were hardly an admission of tenderness, but more a biting accusation.

She met his fury calmly. "The only thing left to decide is the status of our relationship. Are we going to stay married, or are you going to allow that arrogant pride of yours to ruin both our lives?"

Karen could actually witness the inner turmoil etched so painfully on his profile. "No, we're married now. God knows it's not what I wanted for either of us, but the deed is done, and I haven't the strength to undo it."

"Okay," she whispered on a lengthy, drawn-out breath. Her love-filled eyes searched his face.

"All I know is I can't bear to face life without you now. I can't let you go again. It hurt too damn much the first time."

"I know," she said, assuring him of her own pain. Still, they remained apart at opposite ends of the kitchen. "Will you meet me halfway, Rand?"

His face relaxed, his look almost tender.

They walked into each other's arms, their grip tightening as if they never wanted to part again. When his mouth found hers, it was a gentle kiss that soon deepened. Karen's body flooded with warm excitement, and she moved against him sensuously, her arms locked around his neck.

No matter how deep their desire had run before, Karen had always tasted Rand's restraint. Now he returned his love and physical appetite in full. Their needs rose to a fever pitch; his kisses left her panting and breathless.

"I find I'm hungry," he whispered huskily against her ear. "I'm starving to death, but my want is not for food."

Karen gave a demure laugh, his words touching a spark of urgency within her. Tears of happiness glistened in her dark eyes as she spread happy kisses over his face. "Then let us wait no longer to dine."

Gathering her close, he kissed her brow and then her lips longingly, smiling down on her. "Yes, let us wait no longer to dine." He kissed her again, and her mouth parted in welcome. Again and again, their mouths met, each kiss more ardent, more rousing.

A soft sigh escaped Karen as she laid her head on his chest. His fingers brushed the soft curls from her neck, clearing the way for his lips.

Karen nestled against him, curving her womanly figure all the closer. "Will you carry me over the threshold?"

She could feel the smile against the satin smoothness of her neck. "It's raining outside."

"I meant the threshold of our bedroom," she whispered.

Rand groaned; their lips met again, rousing Karen until she gave a deep, heaving sigh of longing.

His hands caressed her back, sliding over her hips and buttocks, pressing her softness against his solid length. Bending slightly, he placed his arm behind her knees and lifted her from the floor. Her arms automatically went around his neck, and she rested her head on his shoulder. The tip of her tongue found the sensitive area behind his ear. When he gave a muted groan, she turned her attention to the thick column of his neck, spreading delicate kisses there until he shuddered.

A whisper of a sigh escaped her as Rand placed her with infinite care on their bed.

"Wait," she pleaded breathlessly.

"Wait?"

She thrilled to the impatience in his voice. "I'll be right back," she promised in a gentle whisper.

He released her reluctantly, his fingers never quite loosening their hold as she slipped from his embrace. The lovely silk gown her sister had given her was at the foot of the bed. Karen undressed, almost wishing Rand could watch her as she removed each item of clothing and placed it aside.

Wordlessly, she went to him and slipped her arms around his neck, urging his mouth to hers. They were locked in a frantic embrace, an all-consuming desire. Trembling, she buried her face in his shirt, her body shuddering with the effort to breathe. Their kisses were now wild and fierce; his hands loosened her gown and leisurely caressed her.

Unbuttoning his shirt, she placed her hands on his hard ribs, gliding them upward over the hair of his chest, her fingers caressing and stroking as his heart thundered beneath her palm.

"Karen, Karen," he rasped, his mouth seizing hers in a passionate kiss. Deftly, his fingers released the tie of her gown and slipped it away. Her soft breasts seemed to sear his chest, and he groaned before kissing her lips, then descended lower, spreading a molten path of desire that left Karen quivering with anticipation. She clung to him, eager to give herself to his passion. It was a tender, intimate moment, and Rand hoarsely whispered his love as he parted her thighs and gently entered her trembling body. Karen's eyes widened at the sudden influx of pleasure; she arched against him, murmuring her love, and surrendered to the swirling excitement.

Afterward, they lay together, Rand's arms protectively holding her as she rested her head against the cushion of his chest. Each was spent by the fierceness of their lovemaking.

When they spoke, it was whispered phrases of love, their emotions too strong to express with mere words what their bodies had said for them. Soon they slept in a deep, untroubled slumber.

Karen woke around ten, the room dark and still. A surge of love for the man sleeping beside her overcame her, and she nestled closer in the haven of his arms. Rand loved her as she loved him; together, they would build a good life. With a languid sigh, she rested her head in the crook of his arm. Playfully, her fingers ran through the hair on his chest. When he stirred, she asked him softly, "Are you awake?"

Karen could hear the amusement in his voice. "How

do you expect me to sleep with your fingers driving me insane?"

Karen laughed, her arms tightening around him. "I'm hungry."

Rand turned so his body lay above hers, his mouth parting her lips with an urgency that almost startled Karen.

"Rand." She pressed her face against his throat. "I'm hungry for food."

He paused, although his hands enjoyed the freedom of her pliant, soft body. A low protesting moan followed her words as she slid out of his arms and climbed from the bed.

"Do you want something?" she asked while tying the sash of her robe.

Rand raised his brows and sat upright. "Yes, but I think it'll have to wait."

With a smile of contentment, Karen wandered into the kitchen and fixed herself a sandwich. Her stomach growled, reminding her she hadn't eaten since breakfast.

Rand was on the phone when she entered the bedroom. She sat on the bed, waiting for him to finish, her eyes studying the man she loved. There was a tenderness about him she hadn't seen before. The lines of fatigue were gone, and his eyes held a warm light.

"I've canceled my classes for tomorrow," he said, breaking into her thoughts. "It seems I have an urgent business matter that needs attending to at home." His eyes grew intense. "Come here, urgent matter."

A soft sigh slipped from her as she slid her arms around his neck. The thin piece of silk that was wrapped around her fell aimlessly to the floor.

"Karen," he groaned as his lips searched and found hers. She yielded to the urgency and clung to him, her smooth skin pressing against his muscular body. His touch was capable of drawing her strength as she responded to the intensity of his lovemaking. She was surprised by her abandonment as they came together again. They were caught in a whirlwind of spiraling sensations that hurled them upward to unscalable heights, then released them gently until they floated back to the reality of being in each other's arms.

They didn't speak; words would only diminish the wonder. Karen rested against him, and her cheek lay on his chest while he smoothed the tangles from her hair.

"I love you, Karen Prescott," he murmured softly; his voice contained a reverent note, as if he understood a love as deep as theirs could have been ordained only from above.

A loud ring roused Karen from the depths of sleep, but instead of reacting to the persistent peals, she incorporated them into her dream. Drawn naturally to the warmth beside her, she snuggled against Rand, folding her arms over his lean ribs. It was Rand's groggy "Hello" that brought her into reality.

Morning. Sunlight streamed into the window between a small crack in the drapery. With something akin to wonder, Karen marveled that she should be here with Rand, that they were man and wife, and that their love was secure and complete.

Unable to resist, she ran her fingers teasingly over his back. Rand shifted positions and sat upright. The telephone conversation continued, but it was distinctly a one-sided dialogue. All Rand murmured was "Yes," "good," "fine," "okay."

It must be Cora, Karen mused, and stiffened when Rand issued an invitation for dinner that evening. The woman wouldn't accept defeat easily, and an uncomfortable chill ran through Karen.

When Rand replaced the receiver, Karen slid her arms around his middle. "Good morning, Mr. Prescott," she whispered tenderly.

Rand turned, looping his arms around her, his face buried in the softness of her hair. "Good morning, Mrs. Prescott."

Tipping her head back, she gently stroked his chin and guided his mouth to hers to kiss him with a lingering warmth.

The hall clock chimed, reminding them it was well into morning.

"It would be easy to spend the whole day making love to my wife, but we're expecting company for dinner."

"Yes, I heard. What time is she coming?" A heavy sigh slipped from Karen. She didn't want this wonderful day to be ruined by Cora.

"She?" Rand's brow twisted dubiously.

"Wasn't that Cora on the phone?"

His mouth compressed into a taut line. "No, that was your father. He's coming to make sure his little girl is a happy bride. Believe me, the invitation for dinner was issued grudgingly."

"Dad?" Karen's thoughts raced furiously. "You mean that was my father on the phone?" she asked again in disbelief.

"Matthew McAlister, the blackmailer himself, is entering the lion's den."

Karen's face grew serious as she studied Rand sitting on the end of the bed. The initial rush of pleasure at waking with Rand at her side quickly faded. She went to him, holding his head against her abdomen, stroking the hair from his face. "I want us to talk to Dad tonight." Her voice was sober. "Perhaps then you will believe me. Your trust is important to me."

Gently, he pushed her away as if her nearness disturbed his resolve. When he stood, his back was facing her. The silence hung heavy between them until Rand spoke, his voice somber, quiet. "No, there's no need to discuss our situation with your father. He would naturally deny you had any part in the marriage trap. Trying to make me believe your innocence is all part of the game. I'm not a fool, nor am I stupid. You're my wife now, but I think it would be better if we never mentioned how we came into this marriage. Doing so would only bring bitterness between us. Is that understood, Karen?" He turned around, his face proud and strong.

She searched but could find no words to answer him. "But, Rand, please…"

"Karen"—his tone was stern—"you do yourself more harm than good by insisting you're innocent. Now, I said I don't want to talk about it."

"All right," she murmured tightly. "We won't speak of it again."

Rand didn't want to argue; Karen could see it in his face as it relaxed, his look almost gentle. "Now, how about fixing me breakfast? I'm starved."

Karen swallowed the tightness lodged in her throat. "Starved?" she returned, forcing herself to shrug off the hurt. "My dear husband, you've been feasting all night." She tried to sound gay and lighthearted, but the word *husband* nearly stuck in her throat.

As their relationship stood now, she was little more than a glorified mistress. She yearned to satisfy far more than his physical desires; she wanted to share his joys, his burdens, the everyday rituals of life that make a wife a wife. Rand wouldn't accept that from her yet. Not until she'd proven herself, had earned his faith and trust. There was little he would accept from her other than the delights her body could give him. For now, she must be content with that. Did her father have any conception of the hellish situation he had cast her into? she wondered wearily.

"I *have* been feasting all night." Rand's words broke into her thoughts. "But I fear having you once is like drinking salt water. I'll never be satisfied." His arms slid around her waist, his mouth seeking the gentle curve of her neck. "But for right now," he murmured thickly, "I was referring to something more basic, like bacon and eggs."

Karen snuggled against him, resting her head on his shoulder. If Rand's desire for her was only physical, she would accept that. In time, she would be able to tear down the bitter walls he'd erected against her. Eventually, under the determined onslaught of her love, he would be her husband, and she would be his trusted, cherished wife.

"Bacon and eggs?" She sighed, feigning disappointment. "And I was prepared to satisfy another hearty appetite…" She wasn't allowed to finish the sentence.

With a laugh, Rand lifted her from the carpet and placed her on the bed, his fingers eagerly searching for the opening of her gown. The unexpected action took her breath away. Before she could object, his mouth greedily claimed hers. When his head lifted from hers, Karen gave a weak protest. "Rand, I was only teasing."

"Don't act so outraged, my love. You did offer to satisfy my appetites," he murmured before planting another hungry kiss on her open mouth.

Karen responded fully to his passion, moving her body against him provocatively...

It was a long time before either of them entered the kitchen.

They spent a portion of the day arranging Karen's things around the house so Rand knew their whereabouts. He had a complicated system regarding the placement of his clothes and personal items. It showed Karen again the difficulties he encountered with partial eyesight and reminded her never to leave her things lying around. In his home, it was difficult to remember that he had limited vision. His knowledge of the house and everything in it was complete. The old saying "a place for everything and everything in its place" certainly applied to the system Rand employed.

Karen was arranging her small collection of ballerina figures on the living-room bookcase when Rand spoke. "Karen," he said with a faint huskiness.

Her cheeks were flushed with a warm glow of satisfaction as she turned around. "Yes?"

"We forgot something last night."

"Impossible." She laughed lightly and circled her arms around his middle, tipping her head back to study his face. His smile was warm and sensuous; his eyes glowed with a happiness she knew came from her love.

It was a heady realization that the love they shared could change so much in each of them.

Because of Rand, Karen saw life with clear, more revealing eyes. She found herself ready to listen to others the way Rand listened. She was willing to look beyond pretense with business associates and acquaintances.

With Rand, there had been a definite softening. He was more relaxed and not as apt to erect the angry facade he had worn when they first met. Even his iron-clad will had shown signs of a willingness to compromise.

"We forgot your wedding ring." Rand withdrew it from his pocket. It lay in the palm of his hand. The solitaire diamond slid to his fingertips, and he manipulated it as if his hands were familiar with its feel.

Karen glanced at her naked left hand. She didn't need a wedding band to say she was his wife. Ring or no ring, she would always belong to him.

"Karen." His voice was low and earnest. "I want more than a weekend marriage. I want you for a lifetime." He took her hand, his fingers caressing hers until he singled out the ring finger. With a tenderness that was almost reverent, he slid the ring on.

"I'll love you all my life, Karen Prescott," he whispered, as if it was a vow.

Instinctively, Karen's arms slid over his shoulders as she brought his mouth to hers. As their lips met, Karen felt him shudder as he buried his face in the dark curls that fell over her shoulder.

Later, they sauntered hand in hand over the grounds, talking and teasing. Following the trail, they strolled to the creek and back.

"Would you mind if I went back to work?" she

quizzed, watching Rand's face. It was a question that had troubled Karen. Her own feelings were mixed; her mother had never worked outside the home, but Karen was sure she'd quickly find herself growing bored without the challenge of a job. Being a housewife would mean a drastic change in her lifestyle, and she wasn't sure she wanted to make the adjustment.

Rand shrugged. "That's entirely up to you. In my opinion, you were foolish to quit. Did you think I would demand your presence day and night?"

Karen stiffened defensively. "I quit because I was leaving Tacoma. I know you don't believe that, but it happens to be the truth."

His hand squeezed hers as if he wanted to punish her. "I thought we'd agreed to leave well enough alone? As for you returning to your job, I really don't care. My hours are long, and I'm often not home until late. You might do well to have some outside interests."

Karen bit back the hurt, wishing she'd never asked Rand's opinion.

The sun was setting, leaving a red glow on the horizon, when Matthew arrived, bringing flowers and a bottle of wine. Karen answered the door hesitantly, unsure how she'd greet her father; her feelings were mixed and ambivalent. She was grateful Rand was still in the shower.

"'Tis a sad day when a father is forced to beg an invitation to his own daughter's," he announced gruffly, handing her his gifts.

"'Tis a sadder day when said daughter's honeymoon is interrupted," Karen chided in return.

He hugged her close, and when he spoke again, there was an odd ring in his voice.

"I've missed you, lass." He studied her intently for a long, sober minute.

Two days before, Karen would have ranted at her father, called him an interfering old fool. His impudence had cast her into a sea of misunderstandings, creating an almost insurmountable lack of trust between husband and wife. Instead, she gently kissed his weathered cheek. "I've missed you too, Dad."

Matthew watched his daughter closely. "Are you happy, lass?" he asked with concern. His eyes held a troubled light, as if he were seeking far more than his words implied. Approval? Forgiveness? Praise? Condemnation?

Matthew's face looked wan and drawn, as if he'd been under a great deal of stress, as he well might have been, wondering about Rand and Karen. Seeing the question in his eyes, she couldn't berate him. "I'm happy, Dad."

"Rand?" His eyes wavered from hers.

"In time," she offered gently.

Matthew grinned as if relieved of a burdensome load. "Didn't I tell you things had a way of working out for the best?" he said, chuckling.

"I think you should repeat that for Rand's benefit," she teased lovingly.

"Did I hear my name mentioned?" Rand entered the kitchen, his hair still wet from the shower, his smile welcoming.

Karen gave a grateful sigh. She wasn't sure how Rand would react to her father. That morning, he'd made it clear he didn't wish to confront Matthew with the details of the marriage, but Karen feared he might harbor some resentment against her father.

"Welcome to our home, Matthew," Rand greeted, and the two men shook hands, an unspoken understanding between them.

Matthew relaxed and started checking under the lids of the pots bubbling on the stove top. "When's dinner?"

"Not until our other guest arrives," Karen said, trying to keep a straight face.

"Other guest?" Matthew quizzed.

Rand's brow wrinkled in question, but he didn't say anything.

"Yes, Dad. Rand invited the Widow Jackson."

Matthew's grin was wry until all three broke into hearty laughter.

While Karen placed the serving dishes on the table, she could hear Rand and her father laughing and joking together in the living room. She paused, watching them; her heart swelled with love for these two men. It was a relief beyond words that Rand showed no open hostility toward her father.

The lighthearted banter continued through dinner, and afterward, Rand challenged Matthew to a game of chess. Nothing could have pleased Karen's father more, and the board was soon set.

As before, Rand played the game entirely from memory. Karen moved the figures on his command, amazed how he could keep track of every move in his mind.

Matthew was an excellent player, and Rand a worthy opponent; the game dragged on, the skill of the two men evenly matched. Karen wasn't surprised when Rand won.

Matthew shook his head disbelievingly, moving the figures around the board, studying Rand's strategy.

Her eyes gleaming with pride, Karen turned and gave her husband a congratulatory hug.

"Well done, Prescott," Matthew said, but his eyes continued to study the board. "I accept defeat from you a second time, but want the chance to redeem myself."

With a lazy smile, Rand promised a rematch at a later date. Matthew left a short time later, and with a yawn, Karen closed and locked the front door behind him. Rand welcomed her into his arms with a smile.

"It's getting late," she whispered invitingly. Her fingers unbuttoned his shirt and teased his chest with light strokes before she wound her arms around his neck and drew his mouth down to hers.

Rand's lips moved hungrily over hers as he pressed her tightly against him until he shuddered with desire. "What is it about you?" he whispered thickly. "I'll never get enough of you, will I? Fifty years from now, I'll still be panting with desire for you." He led her purposefully toward their bedroom. Karen followed willingly but stopped at the doorway of one of the spare bedrooms, examining the room.

"This room will make a lovely nursery. What do you think, Rand?"

He stopped and became suddenly very still, his mouth drawn in a taut line. "I think there's something you'd better understand right now. There will be no children as a result of our marriage."

A shocked silence followed his announcement. Karen stared at him disbelievingly. "No children? But why?"

"For heaven's sake, Karen, think about it," he said bitterly. "I'm in no position to be any kind of father.

Nor do I want children; they're an encumbrance I can live without."

"You're being unfair."

"Unfair?" He gave a short, derisive laugh. "You're a fine one to talk. If it had been up to me, I wouldn't have had a wife, either. If you want to talk about unfair, then we can talk about you and your father."

The cruel words struck her harder than any blow. "But, Rand…" she pleaded, then halted. A brooding scowl darkened his face, and Karen knew him well enough to recognize that arguing was useless.

"You got what you wanted, Karen. We're married, but from here on, I make the decisions, and there will be no children. I don't ever want to discuss the subject again. The matter is closed." His tone was emphatic and hard as he strode away angrily, leaving her standing speechless in the hall.

An ache began to grow within her heart. She was married to Rand, a dream she believed would fulfill her every desire. But the deep womanly need to bear his child would be denied her. How easy it was to picture a dark-haired baby boy; Karen shook her head to cast the picture from her mind. Silently, she walked into their bedroom.

Rand was sitting at the end of their bed, bent forward, his face in his hands. He straightened when he heard her enter. "Karen, listen, it's bad enough having a wife I'll never see. I won't endure the same agony with a child." A hand moved wearily across his face. "Trust me in this. I know what you're feeling, but give us a chance. Together we'll build a good life; we don't need anything else."

Pictures of James and Carter flashed through her

mind; she knew the love she felt for her two nephews was only a fraction of the emotion she would experience for her own child. She looked away; the searing, raw disappointment left an aching void in her heart. Gently, she went to him and traced the determined line of his jaw.

"Shall I take the precautions, or will you?" she asked in a tortured whisper.

Nine

"Karen?"

Faintly, she could hear Rand's call and carefully rolled from the bed. But when she attempted to straighten, her muscles knotted in protest.

"I'm coming," she called, stopping to rub the small of her back. When she limped down the hall from their bedroom, she could hear Carl's worried voice.

"All day she was out there. Wouldn't let me help; said I had enough to do without adding a garden to the list. Your missus is going to be real sore, mark my words. Real sore."

"Hi, honey. How was your day?" She greeted Rand cheerfully, belying the discomfort of her aching muscles. Her eyes narrowed as they fell on Carl. She could tell Rand of her foolishness herself; Carl didn't need to do it for her.

"I'm fine," Rand answered shortly. "What's this Carl is telling me about you working outside all day?"

"It wasn't all day," she denied, and winced from a shooting pain in her back. "It seems certain people are cursed with loose tongues around here. Isn't that right, Carl?"

The older man shuffled his feet, avoiding her eyes. "I'll be going home now." He turned to leave, but not before Karen saw the smile that crinkled the crow's-feet about his eyes.

Karen moved closer to Rand, wrapping her arms around his waist, then groaned softly. "Kiss me if you must, but please be gentle."

Rand scowled. "You crazy little fool. What were you doing, shoveling hard dirt?" He was both bemused and angry. He released her, and instantly Karen missed the warmth of his touch.

"I thought I'd plant a garden," she explained, flexing her overworked muscles, then flinching because even the slightest movement hurt. "My mother had a big garden every year. I don't think I ever realized how much work she put into it. The most I did was pull weeds. Believe me, I appreciate her efforts more fully now."

"If you wanted a garden, why didn't you say something?" he questioned, the irritation leaving his face. "I could have had someone come and rototill for you." He brought her back into the circle of his arms, his fingers gently rubbing the back of her neck.

His touch did insane things to her equilibrium, and she swayed against him. "I don't know," she responded huskily, her eyes closed, savoring the gentle caress of his hands. "I forgot, I guess." Clear thinking was almost impossible when Rand was holding her like this. His hands molded over her buttocks, lifting her pliant body against him. "Don't stop," she pleaded.

Rand's voice was low and husky as he murmured against her skin. "I have no intention of stopping."

Karen gave a sighing laugh. "I was referring to the massage. I could use a good rubdown."

With soft kisses, Rand closed her eyes. Again, the pressure of his arms increased as he lifted and carried her into the bedroom.

His fingers were soothing and gentle as he manipulated the sore muscles. Her flesh responded to the overwhelming comfort of his touch. She was encompassed in warmth; a fury of sensation assaulted her, and she yearned to roll over and bring his mouth to hers. Anything to satisfy this aching void he was creating within her. A small cry of pleasure slipped from her parted lips. But if Rand knew what he was doing to her, he ignored her plea until she released another soft moan.

His hand settled over her shoulder to gently turn her. Karen stared for a moment at the intensity that burned from his eyes. "You know what I want," he murmured thickly before lowering his mouth to hers.

A long time later, they rested, Karen's head nestled in the crook of Rand's arm. His fingers continued to explore her body by leisurely tracing an imaginary line around her breasts. The rounded flesh seemed to swell at his caress.

The meandering pattern followed down her abdomen. "I believe you're gaining weight."

"I know." She smiled, leisurely reveling in the power of his touch to arouse her. "It's Dorothy's recipes, but if you notice it, too, then it's time to go on a diet."

"Just as long as you only abstain from food," he whispered, claiming her mouth in a searing kiss that left her breathless.

Rand's breathing wasn't any more even, and when

he spoke, there was a hoarse quality to his voice. "I have some news."

"Good or bad?"

A smile lifted the corners of his full mouth. "I'll let you decide. I've been asked to participate in a lecture series across the country. The schedule isn't completed yet, but I imagine I'll be gone two, possibly three weeks."

The smile died on Karen's face, and she closed her eyes to block the loneliness a long separation would bring. Tears burned for release, and she brushed them away, angry with herself for being so emotional. "Will Cora be with you?" she questioned after a while.

"Of course Cora will be with me." His voice held a mocking note. "We are partners, you know."

"I thought we were partners, too? Remember me? I'm the wife you promised to love and cherish. I don't exactly relish twiddling my thumbs for several weeks while you go gallivanting across the country with another woman."

A scowl darkened Rand's face. "Karen, this isn't like you. Cora isn't another woman in the sense you're implying."

"Not from lack of trying, I bet," she snapped childishly, pulling herself from his arms and sitting upright.

"Karen?" Rand's voice held a puzzled note. His hands slipped over her shoulders to bring her back. "As for us being partners, if you recall…"

Abruptly, Karen twisted away. "Are you going to throw the fact you didn't want to marry me in my face every time we have an argument? You don't need to tell me your feelings on the matter. Believe me, actions speak louder than words."

"Karen, would you kindly listen to me?" he demanded, his mouth thinning angrily.

With her back facing him, she responded stiffly, "I'm listening."

"You could have fooled me," Rand murmured under his breath. Then he began again slowly. "Now, what I've been trying to say is this: Cora and I have been invited to participate in a lecture series. We have accepted the invitation. But there is no reason why you should stay here without me. I want you to accompany me on this trip."

"Oh." The anger drained from her all in one breath. "Oh," she said again, feeling chagrined and stupid. What was the matter with her? Why was she acting like such a shrew? "In that case, I'd like to do two things," she said softly, swallowing her pride. "First, I want to apologize for being so hotheaded, and second, I want you to know how very pleased I'd be to travel with you."

"Good," Rand said simply, holding her again.

Suddenly Karen came to the realization that Rand was trusting her now as he'd never done before.

Karen woke the next morning stiff and more than a little sore. When she started to get out of bed, she moaned as her stomach heaved unsteadily. Lying back against the pillow, she took deep breaths, afraid she would be sick.

"Rand," she murmured tightly, "I think I really must have done too much yesterday. I feel awful."

Tenderly, he brushed the hair from her face and kissed her forehead. "Stay in bed. I'll phone later and see how you're feeling."

"I'll be fine. Don't worry about me. Oh, if I'm not

here, don't worry. Judy and I are taking the boys to Point Defiance Zoo. I'd hate to disappoint them."

"They can make the trip without you," Rand said, tucking in his shirt. His brow was knit with concern.

"I won't go unless I feel better," she promised.

Rand's kiss was gentle as he tucked the blankets over her shoulders.

Karen watched him go, her heart full of love. After several weeks of married life, she was beginning to discover the joys and benefits of being Rand's wife. As he claimed, his hours were often long as he worked with Cora on a textbook they were compiling. Karen often waited up for him on the sofa, sometimes falling asleep. She'd been so tired lately. Rand woke her, rousing her by spreading tender kisses over her face. Drowsily, Karen would loop her arms around his neck and direct him to her moist lips. The evenings he was home, Karen would read aloud while they sat together, Rand's arms securely wrapped around her. Their taste in literature was surprisingly similar, and they explored everything from Kipling to Tolkien. In bed, she desired him as much as he desired her. Rand was the perfect lover, patient, tender, coaxing. They never spoke of the reasons for their marriage, but it was almost as if their love and need for each other had brought them together.

After a two-hour tour of the zoo and park, they were all hungry and tired. Dark clouds began rolling in to threaten the picnic that had been planned and packed so carefully.

"I wanna stay," Carter objected, ignoring the first drops of rain.

"We aren't going to let a little rain stop us, are we?" James echoed his dissatisfaction.

A few intermittent drops quickly became a fierce downpour, and the four ran to the parking lot without further discussion.

"I still want to have a picnic." Carter's voice dripped with disappointment as he climbed into the backseat of the car.

"Let's wait a few minutes; maybe it'll stop," Karen offered encouragingly. "If not, we'll have a special picnic at my house."

"All right!" both boys chimed.

"If we're going to wait here, I'll pour us some coffee." Judy opened the top of the thermos, and Karen's stomach pitched at the aroma.

She shook her head dismissively. "None for me, thanks. I don't know what it is, but coffee doesn't agree with my stomach lately."

Judy jerked her head up, and the liquid sloshed over the side of the cup and onto the seat. "Karen," she whispered in disbelief, eyeing her sister intently, "the first few months I was pregnant with James, I couldn't tolerate the taste or smell of coffee. I knew almost immediately when I was going to have Carter because the same thing happened. Even before the doctor confirmed my condition."

Karen gave a low laugh. "Well, I'm not pregnant. In fact, I'm sure I'm not," she said, more to assure herself than Judy. "Oh, heavens! Rand would be furious."

"What's pregnant?" Carter questioned, leaning over from the backseat.

"I'll explain later," Judy promised, studying Karen's worried expression.

A half hour later, the four were positioned under Karen's dining-room table, eating their lunch, when Rand entered through the front door.

"Karen, I'm home," he announced, shaking the rain off his umbrella.

Normally, Karen was there to greet Rand, but James and Carter were intent on playing a game of hide-and-seek.

"I'm here," squeaked James in an attempt to imitate Karen.

"James? Carter? Okay, boys, what tricks are you up to now? I suppose you've got your aunt tied up outside somewhere." He arched an amused brow toward the sound of their voices.

"Rand's certainly got my boys pegged," Judy whispered.

"We're under the table." Karen laughed as she watched his dark-trousered leg walk toward her.

"Under the what?"

"Come and join us; we're having a picnic," Judy explained, stifling her own laughter.

"It's times like these that make me wonder just exactly what kind of a family I married into." His face was smiling as he knelt down. "Just what will be required of me before I can talk to my wife?" he quizzed suspiciously.

"I'm here, Rand." Karen edged her way between bodies, sandwiches, and Number Nine to meet her husband. "Sit down and make yourself at home," she invited, and placed a welcoming kiss on his puzzled brow.

"May I remind you, I am home!" Humor glinted

briefly in his expression. "I'm almost afraid to ask this, but just why are you eating your lunch under the table?"

"Because it's raining," the boys explained simultaneously.

"True," he reasoned, "but not inside the house."

"Well, it wouldn't be a picnic on top of the table, would it?" Karen asked him with an impatient sigh.

"There's logic in this someplace, but I swear it's beyond me." The humor in his smile held a wealth of love and warmth.

Karen regarded him curiously. "You're home awfully early. Is anything wrong?"

"Can't a husband come home early? May I remind you we've only been married a short while." His husky voice held a suggestive note, and Karen flushed.

"Finish your lunch, boys." Judy tipped her head back and winked knowingly at her sister. "It's time we left."

"There's no need to rush," Karen said, but she didn't insist they stay. Rand was rarely home early, and she selfishly wanted him to herself.

The picnic items were quickly packed while the boys protested. Judy ushered them out the door, and it suddenly became very quiet without the chatter of the two boys.

"Would you like some lunch? Are you hungry?" Rand stood beside her, and she turned, sliding her arms around his middle. Tilting her head back, she watched his expression alter.

"Starving." His mouth explored the side of her neck and sent shivers of delight shooting down her body.

"What would you like?" She melted against him, her heart thundering wildly.

"Don't ask silly questions," he whispered before

claiming her mouth in a flaming kiss that left her weak and clinging. When he led her into their bedroom, Karen had no intention of protesting.

The nagging suspicion Karen was pregnant became a reality as the days passed. She'd refused to acknowledge the early signs, but there could be no denying the slight thickening of her waist or the added fullness of her breasts. Now it wasn't only coffee that upset her stomach; the smell of certain foods, especially bacon, would cause her to wretch. She found herself irritable, and it didn't seem to matter how much sleep she got, for she was constantly tired.

The first morning she lost her breakfast was the day Karen accepted the truth. Deathly pale and still nauseated, she staggered back to the bedroom and lay down.

With her arms cradling her stomach, she closed her eyes and let out a low moan of despair. "No, please, God, no." Rand would never believe she hadn't purposely gotten pregnant. The knowledge was sure to destroy the budding trust between them. She had worked so hard to gain his confidence in her integrity. How would she ever tell him? No possible explanation would make things right. And his reaction would defy comprehension.

Forcing herself to dress, she brushed her teeth, still feeling wretched and miserable. Her reflection in the bathroom mirror told her she looked as rotten as she felt.

Her sister had advised her to make an appointment with the doctor as soon as possible. But Karen had delayed, hoping against Las Vegas odds that she had some weird, unexplainable virus. *Some virus,* she mused. Her fingers trembled when she made the call. She wouldn't say anything to Rand until she was sure. His mother was coming for a visit, and she couldn't tell him before then.

Depression as heavy as Karen had ever experienced weighed on her. A baby. She found her hands resting on her abdomen while a myriad of emotions filled her all at once. A gentle smile touched her lips. A baby. This should be one of the most glorious days of her life, knowing that the love they shared had created this life growing within her.

Love. What a strange emotion, but not really an emotion at all; more an act of the will. Certainly it wasn't anything she could define. Did Rand really love her? Could she be totally secure in his love? He desired her physically. Was that love? He had accused and doubted her regarding their marriage. Was that love? As sure as the sun would rise on the morrow, he would doubt her again when he learned of this pregnancy. Was that love?

Hiding her symptoms from Rand became a worrisome game. The mornings she was especially ill, she would complain of being overly tired and stay in bed. Rand would lovingly accuse her of being lazy. Karen watched him dress, praying he'd hurry while she took deep breaths to delay the inevitable. The minute he was out the door, Karen would rush to the bathroom to empty her stomach.

Judy recommended eating soda crackers before rising in the morning to relieve the nausea. But when Rand complained of crumbs between the sheets and accused her of cheating on her diet, Karen laughed and promised not to eat in bed again.

A hundred times, she was grateful Rand couldn't see her. One look at her pale, bloodless cheeks and he would have guessed her condition immediately. That he hadn't put the facts together knotted Karen's stomach with guilt. His trust in her had become so complete that he didn't even suspect.

Karen was sure Carl knew. More than once she found his eyes following her, his look concerned and worried. She wasn't sure if he was anxious because she was obviously having such a bad time with the morning sickness or if he realized what this child would do to her and Rand's relationship. Either way, her eyes silently pleaded with him not to say anything. The look he returned assured her that he would not betray a confidence.

There was another problem Karen had yet to resolve. Number Nine was obviously pregnant.

"But Carl," Karen had protested, "I thought you said you'd taken her to the vet and everything had been taken care of."

"All her shots." Carl looked away nervously. "Number Nine was just a kitten then, and the vet wanted to wait a few weeks before having her spayed. I assumed you realized that. I'm sorry, Miss Karen."

She sighed in defeat. She couldn't be angry with Carl; it hadn't been his fault. If she hadn't been so wrapped up in her own problems, she would have known something was wrong when all the male cats started prowling around.

"Don't worry, Carl," she reassured him with a weak smile. "I'm sure Rand will understand."

"I'm sure he will, too," Carl told her, and Karen had the funny feeling he wasn't referring to the cat.

"But I don't understand how it could have happened." Karen's eyes pleaded with the doctor.

"It's not unusual for a pregnancy to occur even with the appropriate precautions, but judging from the look of things, I'd say you were already pregnant when you came for your first visit." Dr. Marshall offered Karen a reassuring smile. Since she was obviously so upset with her condition, he took the time to talk with her and answer her questions in a gentle, reassuring manner.

"Already pregnant?" Karen stared back in disbelief.

"I'm afraid so. I'd guess you were close to three months pregnant."

"Three months?" she whispered incredulously. Had she been so obtuse that she had not recognized even the most obvious signs? Dazed and unsure, Karen responded to the remainder of the appointment with little more than feeble nods.

Judy was waiting for her in the reception area. "Well?" She rose expectantly as Karen entered the larger room.

Karen stared at her sister with sightless eyes. "The doctor thinks I may be as much as three months along—"

"Karen." Although she shared her sister's anxiety, Judy didn't bother to disguise her pleasure. "Good grief, you won't be hiding this from Rand much longer. When do you plan on telling him?"

"I don't think it's a matter of when but how I'm going to tell him," Karen answered.

"But, Karen, the longer you delay, the more likely he is to guess."

"I know." Karen expelled her breath and looked to her sister helplessly. "I'll tell him soon."

After his mother's visit, Karen promised herself. Judy's look was skeptical.

Each day, Karen answered her sister's inquiring gaze with a negative shake of her head.

Rand had described his mother perfectly, and when she stepped off the plane, Karen spotted her instantly.

Eileen Prescott was tall and slender. Her blue business suit, smart and stylish, was a pleasant contrast to her hair, which was completely gray, cut fashionably short. There wasn't a striking resemblance between mother and son, but it wasn't difficult to tell the two were related.

"I see her," Karen said nervously.

"Relax, Karen. My mother's going to love you." His hand, resting on her shoulder, gave her an encouraging squeeze.

With swift, bold strides, Eileen Prescott walked directly to Rand. Karen stepped aside as mother embraced son.

She gave him a surly look. "Well, introduce me. I didn't fly two thousand miles to look at your dour face."

There was an affectionate smile in Rand's eyes as he held his arms open for Karen's return. "Mother, this is my wife, Karen."

Karen moved forward, still in awe of this overpowering woman. "Welcome to Tacoma, Mrs. Prescott." Her senses were clamoring under the woman's cold, unfriendly gaze.

Eileen ignored Karen's welcome. "Why, Rand, she's barely more than a teenager." It was the same gruff tone as before.

Karen eased herself closer to Rand, embarrassed and uncomfortable. The welcoming smile died on Rand's face, and he spoke sharply. "Woman enough, Mother."

Eileen ignored his tone and returned her attention to Karen. "I understand your father was an immigrant. The Prescotts can trace their family tree back to the sixteen hundreds. I expected Rand to marry within his own class," she stated stiffly, as if she doubted Karen's legitimacy.

The assertion stung. The McAlisters were of proud Scottish descent, and what they lacked in heritage was compensated for in pride. Karen bit back angry words, but Rand felt no such restraint and snapped angrily.

"Are you sure you wouldn't like to check out her teeth?"

There was dead silence. Eileen's severe expression altered to a twinkling smile, and she laughed, smiling at Karen with satisfaction. "Welcome to the family, Karen, such as it is." She stepped forward and gave her daughter-in-law a vivacious squeeze.

Astonished at the extreme change in mood, Karen was at a loss for words but managed a tremulous smile. "Thank you."

In the days that followed, Karen came to respect her unpretentious mother-in-law. Her manner was sometimes surly and forward, but it didn't take long for Karen to discover her warm and sincere heart.

Eileen discovered Karen's secret the first morning of her visit. As soon as Rand was out the door to school, Karen slumped in the chair, feeling wretched.

Eileen was waiting for her with a damp washcloth. "Are you going to be sick?" she asked abruptly.

Karen shook her head, closing her eyes to ward off the nausea. She was used to the gruff tone of her voice. Eileen spoke with a brusque affection that couldn't offend.

"I'm fine." Karen looked away.

Her mother-in-law's smile was tender and knowing. "Does Rand know?"

Miserably, she gave a negative shake. "Rand has made it very clear he doesn't want children. I don't know how I'm going to tell him."

"Doesn't seem to me he has much choice in the matter. He's going to be a father, like it or not." She made it sound so simple and matter-of-fact.

"I wish it were that easy."

"He can't place the blame entirely on you…it does take two. That son of mine can be such a fool sometimes. Leave him to me. I'll set him straight."

"No, don't. It's important that I be the one to tell him," Karen pleaded, and sat down as another wave of nausea threatened.

"Well, you'll have to tell him soon. I've been here less than a day and guessed almost immediately. Don't be a ninny about it. He's bound to be unhappy for a while, but he loves you." She paused and chuckled. "Rand surprised the heck out of me at the airport the way he stepped in to protect you. I didn't know he had it in him. First time he's raised his voice to me in twenty years." She laughed again, as if finding the whole situation amusing.

"He's my husband; it was only natural—" Karen began.

"Not so," Eileen interrupted quickly. "Rand and I have a special mother-son relationship. His father died when Rand was eleven. George was working in Alaska; we were desperately in need of extra money for Rand's medical expenses. We traveled from doctor to doctor, seeking the latest professional skill for his deteriorating eyesight, but no one could offer us hope. The public schools weren't equipped to teach the boy, and it meant sending him to expensive boarding schools for the blind. All this took money, so George accepted this high-risk, high-paying job in Alaska. He was there two years before being killed in a mining accident. The only frivolous thing he ever sent home was that locket you're wearing. It arrived after we received word George had been killed. I never could wear the thing; too many sad memories."

Karen fingered the locket that hung around her neck. It did hold special significance to Rand, perhaps because he assumed their love would end with the same bittersweet memories.

"Rand seemed to blame himself for George's death. Nothing I could say would lessen his guilt." Eileen continued speaking; even after all this time, reliving the memory proved painful. "In all the years since, Rand has been a model son. He's cared for my every need, given me every consideration. When he stood up to me the way he did at the airport, I knew he loved you. I needed to be assured of that. Things were mighty fishy when he arrived for his so-called honeymoon with that other woman. I've been wanting him to marry for years. He needs a wife, and selfishly, I wouldn't be opposed to a few grandchildren, but Rand would laugh and quickly change the subject. He mentioned you first thing off the plane, but I wondered what he was doing bringing me Cora when I wanted to meet you."

"Eileen?" Karen's fingers clenched tightly together in a nervous action.

"Speak up; I can't be expected to hear you if you insist on talking to the floor."

"Rand... Rand didn't exactly want to marry me." Karen flushed as she related the events leading up to their wedding.

"Lordy me, your daddy's one sly devil." She laughed brusquely. "I can well imagine Rand's reaction to that," she said, laughing all the more.

Karen looked away.

"Don't look so put out. Rand wasn't totally opposed to this marriage, or nothing on God's good earth would have persuaded him to marry you. Being pressured was sure to ruffle a few of his proud feathers, but I know my son well enough to tell you he would have rotted in hell rather than marry someone he didn't want."

"But don't you see?" Karen murmured dismally. "He's sure to believe I tricked him with this pregnancy."

"No doubt he'll be as angry as a wounded bear, but given time, he'll come around. Now, don't be a quitter; give him time to sort through his feelings. If he said he was opposed to a family, it's not because he doesn't like children. Rand will make an excellent father. My only advice to you is to tell him soon. It's bound to go better for you if he hears it from your lips than if he discovers it on his own."

Acknowledging the wisdom of her mother-in-law, Karen had to agree.

Eileen returned to New York four days later, leaving with Karen's promise that she'd tell Rand about the baby soon.

Karen mentally prepared herself all the next day, determined to tell Rand about the baby right after dinner.

"It was nice having my mother for a visit, but quite frankly, I'm glad she's gone. I like having you to myself." Rand sat on the sofa, pulling Karen onto his lap; his fingers wasted no time unbuttoning her blouse.

Abruptly, Karen twisted away and stood. "Rand, no, don't touch me, please."

"Karen?" He sounded surprised by her sudden rejection.

She stood across the room from him, rigid with apprehension. Her hand rested protectively on the slight swelling of her stomach. "Rand," she told him boldly, her voice tight, "I'm going to have a baby."

Ten

The room crackled with a stunned silence; Rand expelled an uneven, disbelieving breath before his jaw tightened ominously. Despair flickered over his face, and he paused to run his fingers through his hair wearily. He was silent for so long, Karen didn't know how much more tension she could endure.

"Yell, scream, do what you need to do. But please, don't just sit there." She felt far more capable of dealing with his anger than the tormented ache in his eyes.

"All my life I've had to deal with people who feel that because I'm handicapped, I must also be mentally retarded. I expected more from you, Karen."

His words stabbed at her heart. She yearned to go to him, hold him, reassure him, anything but this intolerable, tortured look. He resembled a man defeated and friendless. He slouched forward, burying his face in his hands.

"I realize this is of little comfort to either of us at the moment, but I want you to know the doctor says I was already pregnant when I went to see him about birth control." Her voice faltered slightly.

Rand's head snapped up, his eyes blazing. The short, abrupt laugh was full of malice. "Get out."

Karen stared at him with disbelieving eyes.

"I said get out," he raged in white fury.

She choked back a sob, her voice raw as she spoke. "Just how far do you want me to go? Out of the room? Out of the house? Out of your life?"

Violently, Rand swung around, his hand slamming against the lamp, sending it crashing into the coffee table. The ceramic base shattered into a thousand pieces as his anger exploded.

Karen backed away from him fearfully as he stumbled from the living room. The picture windows vibrated as he slammed the front door.

Where would he go? Karen looked around her with the most helpless feeling in the world. A knot in her throat was so tight she could barely swallow. Her first inclination was to run after him, plead with him to understand. But it was useless, and she knew it. Miserably, she picked up the larger pieces of the broken lamp.

There was no use attempting to sleep; she couldn't until Rand was home. The car was gone; apparently, he had gotten Carl to drive him someplace. Possibly Cora's? She quickly cast the pain-inducing thought from her mind. A long time later, she heard the soft purr of the car engine as it died, and she sighed with relief. But Rand didn't come into the house. The time grew so long that Karen nervously stared out the window, hoping to see him. The yard—everywhere she could see—was deserted. Why did she have to love him so much? Why couldn't she just go to bed and let him work out the problem his own way? She'd been shocked, too, when she'd first realized she wasn't suffering from some obscure virus.

Was he walking in the woods? It was dark; he could hurt himself. Another half hour passed, each second interminable. Karen couldn't stand it anymore and carelessly threw a sweater over her shoulders.

"Rand?" she called, venturing down the path leading to the woods. "Please answer me."

The night was so clear and still. She stopped to listen, but everything was deadly quiet until Karen wanted to cry with frustration.

"Miss Karen," Carl spoke from behind her, and Karen swiveled around.

"Where's Rand?" Her eyes pleaded with him.

"I don't know." The older man's eyes avoided hers. "He had me take him to a bar, said he didn't want me to wait. But he was in a bad way; real angry, he was. I sat outside for a long time, wondering what to do. When I went back inside, Mr. Rand was gone."

Karen's hand squeezed Carl's arm. "I told Rand about the baby."

Carl's smile was wry. "I figured as much. Give him time; he'll come around. It won't be long before he'll be handing me a cigar as proud as any father; you wait and see."

Tears shimmered in Karen's eyes, tears of hope. "Thank you. I needed to hear that."

Carl patted her shoulder gently. "Do you want me to wait up with you? Neither of us is going to sleep until he's home."

"Dorothy?" Karen's gaze flickered back to Carl's house.

"Been asleep for hours." He chuckled softly.

With a slight nod, Karen accepted the man's kind offer. They walked to the house together.

Several hours later, the sound of a door closing and someone singing told them Rand was home. The words of the song were slurred and barely discernible.

"WHATCHA GONNA DO WITH A DRUNKEN BLIND MAN? WHATCHA GONNA DO WITH A DRUNKEN BLIND MAN? EARL-LIE IN THE MORNING."

Carl was immediately at Rand's side while Karen paid the taxi driver. The man gave her a sympathetic smile and drove into the night.

Rand's weight was giving Carl trouble as they weaved toward the bedroom. Karen hurried to help, slipping her arm around Rand's waist, accepting a portion of his weight as his arm fell haphazardly across her shoulders.

Rand staggered slightly, then paused as if suddenly realizing Karen was there.

"Karen, my sweet Karen." A haunted, tortured look came over his masculine features. His mouth twisted into a dark, foreboding glower. Angrily, he pushed her aside.

"Trick the blind man. Hurt the blind man. Fool the blind man," he shouted, madly waving his arms.

No one was more surprised than Karen when Carl unexpectedly lifted Rand, placing his bulk over his shoulder like a fireman. When Carl laid him on the bed, Rand was either asleep or dead drunk.

"He'll be all right until morning," Carl assured Karen as he stopped to remove Rand's shoes.

Numbly, Karen took a blanket from the hall closet, and laid it over his still body. A few minutes later, she walked Carl to the door. When she returned to the bedroom, Rand was making sleeping noises, lost to the world. Gently, she touched his face, the weight of unhappiness bearing hard upon her shoulders.

She slept in the spare bedroom, the room she thought would make a lovely nursery. It seemed fitting somehow. When she woke, Rand had already left for school. She looked at the unkempt bed and experienced a bittersweet agony. Trailing her fingers across the pillow that had held his head, she was hoping to draw some solace. Instead, she experienced an acute loneliness.

Rand wasn't home for dinner. Carl phoned to say Rand was working late with Cora, but she guessed the call had been made on his own initiative. It was after midnight before she went to bed, lying awake until she heard Rand enter. He undressed in the dark, pulled back the covers on his side, and climbed into bed. Their bodies were only a few inches apart, yet a whole world lay between them. Karen was completely still, willing Rand to say something, anything. After a while, she abandoned the hope and with an agonizing sigh drifted into sleep.

First thing the next morning, she woke again, experiencing the now-familiar waves of nausea. Deep breaths didn't help, and she rushed into the bathroom. When she straightened, she found Rand's large frame blocking the doorway.

"Are you all right?" he questioned tightly.

"I'm fine." Rand looked as drawn and pale as she did.

"Does this happen often?" he asked again, gruffly.

Karen's voice sounded choked and small. "Sometimes two or three times a week."

His face twisted into a vicious smile, almost as if he was pleased she was experiencing some discomfort with this pregnancy. "Next time, close the bathroom door. The sound of you vomiting isn't a pleasant way to wake up."

"All right," Karen agreed, hoping to hide the hurt in her voice.

Leaving early and coming home later and later was a pattern Rand followed rigidly the next few days. Karen rarely saw him, and if she did, he didn't speak to her unless it was in gruff, impatient tones.

He was obviously overworking himself, skipping meals and not getting enough sleep. Karen's tortured gaze followed him.

Rand had told her to get out, but seemed unwilling to tell her how far he wanted her to go. The temptation was strong to pack her things, but Karen had never been a quitter, and this marriage was worth saving. If anything, her resolve to work things out grew stronger as the days passed.

Saturday morning, Karen woke with a queasy stomach but held her own until after breakfast; then she was sick again.

"Isn't there anything you can do about this?" Rand asked her impatiently after she reappeared in the kitchen.

"I'm usually okay if I can force down some soda crackers first thing. I try to keep some on the nightstand..." She paused at the look of disgust that came over Rand's face.

His upper lip curled into a snarl. "Those were the crumbs I felt in bed, weren't they?"

"Yes." She wouldn't lie to him even if it meant condemning herself.

Karen had never seen anyone's look turn as cold or hard.

"You're a deceitful bitch, Karen."

"Can't you understand?" she snapped. "I didn't plan this pregnancy."

"Just like you didn't plan our marriage?"

Karen dropped her eyes, her hands clenched tightly at her sides. It was no use trying to reason with Rand, nor would she again. If he loved her, truly loved her, then his faith in her integrity would eventually overcome his doubts. She couldn't force the issue.

Perhaps his irritation wouldn't have been so explosive if he hadn't gone to stroke the cat and discovered she was pregnant.

"Karen." His voice had vibrated through the house. When she didn't respond immediately, he shouted again.

She'd gone to the bedroom, taking her time. She wouldn't rush to him; she wasn't a servant who responded to threats and yelling. "What is it?" she asked calmly, ignoring his scowl.

"The cat." Anger furrowed his brow, and his mouth curved in a taut line. "Number Nine is pregnant, isn't she?" It wasn't a question, but an accusation, as if this, too, were something Karen had purposely done to thwart and undermine his authority.

"Yes," she responded simply, without explanation.

"Why wasn't I warned of the blessed event?" he demanded sarcastically.

She replied in mocking tones, "I would have been more than pleased to tell you, but I haven't seen you in nearly a week. And, shall we say, the timing was wrong."

Karen had never seen anyone angrier. His hands were knotted into tight fists; his dark eyes became as hard as steel, his jawline white and tense. "Get rid of the cat." The softly spoken words were more menacing than if he'd raged at her.

Karen gasped in disbelief; all attempts at impudence collapsed with his words. "You don't mean that."

His lip curled sardonically as he moved past her and into the den, his message clear.

Later, Karen went for a walk. Tears stung her eyes, and she tilted her head back to prevent their spilling. She followed the worn path leading into the woods and heard Carl's approach before she saw him. Hurriedly, she wiped the tears from her eyes and put on a bright smile.

"Good morning, Miss Karen." He greeted her with a broad grin.

"Been leaving little tidbits around for the animals again, I see." She responded in a teasing banter, belying the hurt that lay just below the surface of her smile.

He chuckled, and the sound of his amusement lifted her soul from the mire of self-pity. Likable, lovable, understanding Carl. Why did life have to be so complicated? Why couldn't she be more like this man, who wore a ready smile and looked as if he'd never known trouble or discouragement?

"Carl?"

"Yes'm."

"Rand found out about Number Nine."

The older man chuckled again. "I've been wondering about that bellow that came from your house this morning. Was he angry?"

Karen couldn't prevent a smiling response to his humor. Rand had sounded like a bull elk in his irritation. "He wasn't exactly pleased. I have to find another home for Number Nine."

The smile faded from Carl's weathered face. "I don't think he means that, Miss Karen. He seems to be saying a lot of things he doesn't mean lately." The dark eyes grew intense. "Me and the missus will take Number Nine. If Mr. Rand doesn't want her back, that's fine, 'cause we've been needing a mouser."

"But she's going to deliver the litter soon."

"Not to worry." Again, Karen was reassured with a grin. "We have several friends who need mousers."

Karen was afraid that if she spoke, her voice would crack and Carl would know how much his generosity had affected her.

Eyes dancing, he touched the tip of his cap and sauntered down the path.

"Carl?" she called after he'd gone several feet.

He spun around.

"Thank you." She couldn't hide the choke in her voice.

As she continued walking along the well-worn path, she could think, sort through her own feelings. For all the unhappiness she was experiencing, there was also a budding excitement beginning to blossom. A child was growing within her, a child created in love.

Rand and Karen were scheduled to leave for the lecture series next week. The thought of time alone together brought a surge of hope. Rand had purposely made separate flight plans so they wouldn't be traveling with Cora. He'd promised to make this trip the honeymoon they'd never had. Karen believed that only when they were separated from the pressures around them would Rand begin to accept the child. Six days; she could last another six days. The lecture series offered hope and promise.

When she returned to the house feeling refreshed and invigorated, she found Rand asleep on the davenport. The Braille book he'd been reading lay twisted on the carpet where it had fallen. As Karen picked up the book and placed it on the end table, an encompassing warmth filled her. In sleep, the gaunt lines of fatigue in Rand's face were relaxed. She brought him a pillow and blanket and impulsively brushed her lips softly over his cheek.

Baking chocolate-chip cookies gave her an excuse to stay in the kitchen and have a full view of her husband. It was obvious he was exhausted, and she guarded his sleep jealously.

The phone rang, jerking her attention to the kitchen wall. Karen raced across the floor to answer it before a second ring could sound.

"Hello," she greeted softly.

"Let me speak to Rand." It was the brisk business voice of his associate.

"He's sleeping, Cora," Karen said with a glance toward Rand to be sure the phone hadn't awakened him. "Unless it's important, I'd hate to disturb him."

A heavy sigh followed. "No, it can wait."

"I'll tell him you phoned."

"Do that," Cora said sharply, then added. "By the way, I'm sorry to hear you won't be traveling with us next week." Her tone suggested just the opposite.

"Rand said you're much too ill with morning sickness to travel. I've had my flight plans rearranged so Rand and I can fly together. You'll tell him that for me, won't you?"

"Yes…yes, I will." Confused and hurt, Karen could only make a feeble response. "I'll tell him you phoned. Goodbye." She heard the click as the other end of the line was disconnected.

She stood there, the phone still in her hand, staring at Rand while tears brimmed in her eyes. Rand knew how much she'd been looking forward to traveling with him. How much she'd been counting on this trip. He hadn't even bothered to inform her of his change of plans. He was going to leave her behind, just walk out the door without her, without a word of explanation.

Replacing the receiver, Karen leaned her head back and closed her eyes. Instinctively, she wrapped her arms around her middle as a protective buffer to shield her unborn child. As if the baby could feel her hurt, her ache.

Perhaps she was being too optimistic regarding their marriage. Perhaps Rand would never accept her condition, never love or cherish their child. Perhaps he felt the necessity of being away from her to decide exactly what he wanted to do. Perhaps send her away. He had shouted for her to leave. Certainly the tension between them hadn't lessened.

Doubts, uncertainties, and questions pounded her from all sides, until her hands flew to her face as if to ward them off.

She needed to escape, too, but Rand had discounted any of her needs. He had been so angry with her because she'd hidden the pregnancy from him as long as she could. Yet he hadn't told her he'd changed their travel plans. Did that make him any less guilty? Rand had hoped to hurt her and had succeeded.

She waited until the cookies finished baking, then took a suitcase to the bedroom to pack her things. Where she'd go remained unclear—just away, she reasoned, to set order to her thoughts, decide what she wanted to do.

Carl was weeding the flower beds in the front of the house and glanced up when Karen quietly closed the front door. She jerked around when he spoke.

"Miss Karen, where are you going?" His eyes fell pointedly on the suitcase.

Karen looked away self-consciously, feeling like a cat burglar trapped in a bedroom. It was wrong to leave without saying a word. Everyone would worry, and she didn't want that.

"I'm not exactly sure where I'll go." Her eyes studied the tops of her shoes.

"Are you leaving Mr. Rand?"

"Oh, no," she denied instantly. "I just need to get away for a couple of days."

"Are you going to your family?"

"No." She couldn't put Judy and her dad in the middle of this. It would be unfair to all concerned; she hadn't even told her father she was pregnant yet. "I think I'll go down the Oregon coast. There was a little inn my parents loved, and they often vacationed there. It's someplace outside of Tillamook on the ocean. I think I'll head that way. Tell Rand where I am and not to worry. I'll be back in three days, four at the most. If you need to get ahold of me, Dad can tell you the name of the inn." She hesitated. "Take care of Rand for me, won't you, Carl?"

The older man gave her a toothy grin. "All right, Miss Karen, I will."

The drive down the rugged coastline was exhilarating, the scenery breathtakingly beautiful. Karen stopped at several scenic viewpoints to watch the waves explode against the huge, jagged rocks in majestic harmony. Several times she found herself wishing Rand was with her so she could describe the vivid colors and the brilliant beauty of the coast. Narrating a scene for him was one of the simple pleasures she enjoyed; it gave her a greater appreciation for the beauty of God's world. Rand had once told her after they'd made love that when he was holding her in his arms, it didn't matter that he couldn't see. For the first time in his life, he didn't hate being blind.

Now Karen wondered if he'd ever hold her again. The thought brought so much pain that she instantly rejected it.

The white shuttered inn her parents often visited was still there, but it was older and much smaller than Karen remembered. The family-owned enterprise had changed hands, but the new family was friendly and welcoming. Their teenage son carried Karen's lone suitcase upstairs, chatting the whole distance, offering advice about the best dinner spots, as it was nearing that time.

The room was small but adequate and had a panoramic view overlooking the ocean. Karen stood staring at it for a long time, watching the tide ebb away. The ocean mesmerized her; it was like watching sand sift through a bottle, wondering what would happen when all the sand was gone. The ocean was turbulent as the waves crashed along the beach, yet Karen found it soothing and relaxing after the long drive. She fell asleep without venturing from her room. She woke refreshed and hungry the next morning. In fact, she felt wonderful, better than any morning for three long months. A smile softened her mouth. Judy had claimed that if they were alike, the morning sickness would pass almost as quickly as it came—after about three months.

Karen was more like her sister than she realized. Anxious to enjoy the ocean air, Karen dressed in faded jeans, which fit snugly around her waist, and a pale purple short-sleeved sweatshirt.

"Good morning." She smiled at the boy who'd carried her suitcase the night before.

The returning smile was instantaneous. "Good morning."

"Want to recommend someplace for breakfast?"

It was the most enjoyable breakfast Karen had eaten in months. Without even a hint of morning upset, she took a long stroll along the undisturbed beach. It had rained during the night, hardening the sand, but as the sun appeared, drying the beach, it became impossible to walk in her tennis shoes. She paused long enough to remove them and flex her toes in the sand. She walked for so long that she lost sight of the inn. Her shoes were now used to store little treasures she discovered along the way, mostly small shells.

Pausing, she decided to rest before venturing back. The soft sand welcomed her weight, and she laid back, waving her arms to make a pattern of angel wings in the soft surface, then laughed at her childishness. How simple life would be if only she was a little girl again. Closing her eyes, she could almost hear her mother's worried voice telling her, "Karen, move back; the tide's coming in." But Karen had refused to leave her project, thinking her stubbornness would prevent the waters from sweeping away an afternoon's work.

"Matthew, do something. She'll be drenched," her mother had pleaded.

Helplessly, Karen had cried as her father had carried her onto the beach and she witnessed the sand castle washed away in minutes. Karen now felt much the same as she had then, the ache within her almost identical. That helpless feeling of holding on to something, then watching it disintegrate after having spent a part of herself in constructing it. Only this time it wasn't a simple sand castle; it was the love and marriage she had built with Rand.

Jerking herself upright, she brushed the sand from her pants. She'd come here to meditate, re-collect her thoughts; now she found them too painful and forced them from her mind.

For all her wanderings along the beach and the unaccustomed exercise, sleep remained elusive that night. After fighting herself and her thoughts, Karen rose and dressed, slipping outside into the moonlight. It had rained again that afternoon, but the skies were clear now, alive with glittering jewels that seemed to smile down on her. The wind was strong as it whipped her hair across her face. It felt good and right to be exactly where she was and who she was.

Karen found herself talking to the child, her hand placed over her stomach as if to communicate her thoughts. The baby had barely begun to form within her, yet the overwhelming love Karen felt for this tiny being was beyond description. Recognizing and accepting this overpowering emotion had a very calming effect on her.

Never again would she apologize to Rand for this pregnancy. This child had been created in love, her love for Rand, if not his love for her. That didn't matter anymore. Releasing a sigh from deep within, she strolled back to the room and fell into a deep, restful sleep.

The next morning fell into the pattern of the day before. Karen walked along the beach, her bare feet leaving imprints in the wet sand. Today, she would settle, if only in her own mind, the problems that existed between her and Rand.

A conversation she'd had with Judy at the zoo played again in her mind.

"I think I'd die if Rand and I had to be separated for a year. I love him so much it almost frightens me; Rand has become my whole life."

Judy had laughed. The wise, knowing, older-sister look had come over her. "It's amazing the things a woman can endure when it's necessary. I didn't think I'd ever survive without Mike, but I have, and I will."

Recalling their conversation, Karen realized that although she deeply loved her husband, she could make a life for herself and their child without him.

Symbolically, she built another sand castle, far from the water's edge. It was hard work, carrying buckets of wet sand onto the beach, but now the tide wouldn't steal it away. Perspiration wetted her brow when she finished; a dull ache throbbed in the small of her back. She waited until the tide came in, proud that her castle stood serene and secure. Tears misted her eyes; she was ready to face what awaited her in Tacoma.

The drive home was made with a sense of impatience. Karen left early the next morning and didn't stop for either breakfast or lunch. The instinct of a migrating bird seemed to be driving her home.

Home, she sighed, turning into the long driveway five hours later. She'd lived in the apartment for a number of months, and it had never produced in her the feelings this long rambler did.

Everything looked so peaceful, calm. Nothing had changed, yet everything looked different. She parked around back and glanced at her garden on the way past. After three days without hoeing, it was difficult to distinguish between plant and weed. The kitchen door was unlocked, and with dauntless courage she walked inside.

Karen stifled a gasp at the mess that lay before her. Dirty dishes, food, and utensils littered the table, countertop, and sink. It resembled the kitchen after James and Carter had prepared a meal.

Clothes and books were carelessly tossed about the living room; the drapes were closed, blocking out the afternoon sunlight.

Karen put her suitcase down and immediately opened the drapes, stooping to pick up several items along the way. The house smelled strange, as if no one had opened the windows and allowed fresh air to circulate in days.

"Damn it, Carl, I said leave me alone." The angry words were shouted and cutting.

Karen paused as a dejected figure moved down the hall. The sight of Rand shocked Karen, and she stared at him with disbelieving eyes. It looked as though he hadn't shaved since she'd gone. His clothes were wrinkled as if he'd been sleeping in them; his hair was a mass of tangles.

"It isn't Carl," she said quietly.

A flicker of pain touched his face as he stopped. "Karen?" he questioned as if he wasn't sure of the sound of her voice.

"What's happened?" The whole house possessed a sense of unreality; Rand would never live in such disorganization. "Have you been ill?" she questioned, gazing at him anxiously.

"Karen, Karen." He repeated her name incredulously, his voice raw and barely above a whisper. "Where the hell did you go?" he demanded, his back stiffening, ramrod straight.

A bewildered frown narrowed her brow as she went to him. "Where have I been?" she asked. "I told Carl where I was going. You were asleep when I left. I didn't want to wake you. Carl was supposed to tell you."

"He didn't." Rand's smile was contemptuous. "I suppose he thought letting me suffer was poetic justice." His hand ran wearily over his face and eyes. "It doesn't matter." Slowly, he turned, retreating to his den. Halfway down the hall, he paused, his back facing her. "Why did you go?" It was as if the question had been wrenched from him, had cost him more than she would ever know.

"Cora must have tried again to reach you. I apologize for not giving you the message."

"Damn it, Karen," Rand bit out savagely. "You disappear for three days and apologize for not giving me a telephone message? I don't give a damn hell about

Cora right now. I want to know why you found it so sam-hell important to run out on me?" His hands were clenched so tightly the knuckles appeared white. He turned around, his face twisted, like a man pushed beyond his limit.

Karen watched him with a sad, almost pleading expression. His agony...hers. "Cora phoned to say she's had her flight reservations changed, so she'll be traveling with you since...since I won't be going with you, after all."

Her response angered Rand all the more. "Do you mean to tell me this whole disappearing act of yours was nothing more than a fit of jealousy?" he questioned between clenched teeth.

"Apparently so," she told him flippantly. "If it's jealousy to have the man I married take two honeymoon trips with another woman, then that's what I am. I won't question if it's reasonable or unreasonable; it's just the way I happen to feel."

Rand swore harshly under his breath.

"Well, what did you expect?" Karen asked. "More important, when did you plan on telling me I wouldn't be going? At the airport? We're supposed to leave in three days. Excuse me," she corrected herself with a bitter smile. "*You're* leaving in three days."

"You couldn't come," he shouted, his face red and angry. Then he paused, taking several deep breaths as if to calm himself. Gesturing with his hand, he added with a helpless, frustrated note, "You're sick every morning."

"If you'd bothered to ask, you'd have learned most of the morning sickness has gone." She looked away guiltily. It had only been the last couple of mornings that she'd felt like her old self. "It doesn't matter." She felt tired and defeated. Holding a conversation while ten feet of hall separated them seemed utterly useless. She returned to the living room, stopping to pick up clothes along the way. She deposited the pile on the sofa.

"Did you want to come?" Rand asked quietly.

"Of course I did. You could have asked me, Rand."

She heard his uneven sigh. "The lines of communication weren't exactly open last week, and as far as I'm concerned, you're angry over nothing." His voice was raised as he fought for control.

"That's what the baby and I are to you…nothing," she intoned sadly, and turned to witness the hard mask that slipped over his face.

"I don't want that baby," Rand shouted.

"You didn't want a wife, either," she reminded him.

Rand bit off another caustic reply and paced the floor, saying nothing.

"It's obvious I expect more from your love than you're capable of giving. Somewhere along the road, I got the twisted notion love implies trust and faith. You've accused and doubted me twice." She took a shaky breath, gathering her resolve. "You once told me to get out, but you didn't say how far you wanted me to go. I think that time has come."

Rand's expression remained impassive and stoic. If it hadn't been for the nerve that jerked in his jaw, she wouldn't have known the effect of her demand.

When the telephone rang, she ignored it. "Undoubtedly, it's for you," she uttered sarcastically. "Probably Cora wanting to confirm your plans."

Rand jerked himself around and strode toward his

den. The phone went silent. Either Rand had answered it, or the caller had hung up; Karen didn't know.

She drew in a deep, calming breath and leaned her head back to quell the emotion. She hadn't meant to say those things; her anger was hurting them both.

When Rand returned, his face was strangely troubled, the smoldering anger extinguished. "Karen, that was the hospital. Your father's had a massive heart attack. We must hurry."

Eleven

The blood drained from Karen's face, her hand flying to her mouth in shocked reaction. "Dear God, no," she gasped. "Rand, tell me he's all right, please."

"Carl's coming; we must hurry." Her husband's voice was tight with concern.

Later, Karen could hardly recall the tense drive to the hospital. She sat rigid with apprehension, her eyes closed. Matthew, her sweet, scheming, Scottish rogue of a father. Her lips moved in silent prayer, her spirit soothed by Rand's fingers tightly clenching hers, offering his support, his love.

Their shoes sounded loudly against the polished floors of the hospital as they hurried down the winding corridors.

Evan, Milly, and Judy were already there, sitting silent and frightened. It was as though they were in a stupor; no one reacted to Karen until Judy gave a feeble cry and stood.

"He's dying; surgery is his only chance."

Evan remained seated, his look despondent, his face

buried in his hands. When Karen entered the waiting area, he raised his hopeless, weary eyes to hers.

Milly, tears glistening in her eyes, could offer no encouragement.

"What happened?" Karen asked as if searching for some plausible reason for such a thing to happen to her father.

"I've known about his heart condition for a year now," Evan answered her, "but I had no idea it was this serious."

"Dad knew he needed the surgery but refused," Judy added, shaking her head as if she couldn't comprehend what was happening around her. "He was waiting to die," she mumbled incredulously.

"To die?" Karen echoed her disbelief. She looked quizzically to Evan for an explanation.

The events of the evening were exacting their toll. Evan stared back, his face white and drawn. "I didn't know. I swear to God I would have forced him to have the surgery if I'd known."

Karen still didn't understand; her gaze moved to Milly, helplessly searching for answers.

"Matthew learned his heart was bad, but decided he'd rather die and be with Madeline than prolong his life. He told us tonight before the aid car arrived that it was all right now that you and Rand were married. He needn't worry about you anymore."

Her father's strange behavior this past year suddenly became clear. All the dates he'd begun arranging for her, the pressure for her to marry and produce grandchildren. His heart condition was the reason he'd coerced Rand into marrying her. Matthew had known she loved Rand, and when things didn't look as though they were going to work out between them, he took matters into his own hands.

No wonder Matthew had looked so wan and pale at times. She knew that he missed her mother, but not to the extent that he would rather die than go on living. How stupid she'd been. It was as if the weight of the whole world had come crashing down on her. She had been closest to her father; she should have guessed what was happening, should have recognized the symptoms. Her father had been biding his time all along, hoping she would marry, forcing men upon her so she would be secure before his heart gave out.

"We were playing chess," Evan began, interrupting Karen's thoughts. "He just fell over. I thought he was dead."

"The doctor says that unless Dad has the surgery, he won't last the night. They're prepping him now. It doesn't look good, not good at all." Judy's voice cracked on a sob.

For the first time, Rand spoke: "It seems to me the lot of you have given Matthew up for dead. Matthew McAlister is a cursed old bulldog; once he's faced death, I doubt that he'll go without a gallant fight."

The doctor appeared, his face grim. Matthew was ready for surgery. Again, the older man explained the procedure, making it sound very routine, yet didn't minimize the risks involved. Karen and Judy could see their father for only a few minutes.

The sight of tubes and IVs brought reality to the seriousness of Matthew's condition. Slow tears wound their way down Karen's cheeks and chin as she stooped to kiss Matthew's brow tenderly. Judy remained at the foot of the hospital bed, her hand over her mouth to hold back her distress.

Matthew's eyes flickered open; he appeared drugged and woozy. Nurses were keeping a constant watch on his vital signs and hovered around the bed.

"Dad," Karen whispered, leaning close to his ear. "The granddaughter you've been wanting so long is due in five short months. She'd very much like to know her grandfather. Please live, Dad. Fight this."

Gently, the arms of a nurse comforted Karen, pulling her back from the bed. "We're ready to take him to surgery," she whispered soothingly. "Don't worry, honey. We'll take good care of your father."

Judy collapsed into tears, returning to Evan and Milly, while Karen stood alone in the hall until her father had been wheeled from sight.

When Karen entered the waiting area, she'd never felt so alone or so afraid. As if by instinct, Rand met her, wrapping her tightly against him, lending her his strength, his faith. Karen clung to her husband, desperately needing his support.

The night seemed endless, each second, each minute interminable. The small group huddled together, as if their presence would aid Matthew's battle for life. By dawn, the thin thread of hope remained taut and capable of snapping at any time. Yet Matthew clung to it obstinately.

Sometime during the long night, each one fell victim to despair and discouragement. Only Rand remained confident during the endless vigil. His gentle assurance lent strength, encouragement, and hope; all four leaned heavily on him.

When Dr. Phillips reappeared, clothed in a green

surgical gown, the family, watching his approach, remained paralyzed, afraid of what he would say, yet equally fearing the unknown.

Matthew had survived the surgery. He remained a critically ill man, and the next few days would hold the highest risk. Dr. Phillips advised them to go home and get some rest; there was nothing any of them could do to help Matthew's condition.

Rand, Milly, and Evan rose to leave, but Karen and Judy glanced at each other in unspoken agreement. They would stay, confident their love for Matthew was stronger than the power of death.

"Judy and I are staying," Karen told Rand.

"Karen," Rand coaxed softly, "come home. You won't be able to help your father any more here than you could at home. You need your rest. You'll only make yourself ill."

Stubbornly, Karen shook her head. "No," she whispered on a fervent note. "Judy and I are staying."

Rand didn't attempt to pressure her further. He left a few minutes later with the promise to return later that afternoon.

The hours merged together. Nothing mattered. There were no stars, no sun, no universe; nothing was of consequence while her father's life hung in a delicate balance.

The two sisters rarely spoke; the communication between them didn't require words.

The doctor had left word that Karen and Judy could visit Matthew for five minutes every hour, but only one at a time. When Karen went, she stroked his brow lovingly and murmured soothing phrases. Sometimes Matthew's eyes would drift open to gaze at her sightlessly, but his lashes lowered slowly, as if sleep had lured him back into her arms.

Seeing her father for only those few minutes wrenched at Karen's heart. He was so pitifully weak, so vulnerable. The picture of her physically strong, active father was far removed from the man who lay in the intensive care unit fighting for his life.

Rand returned and again attempted to persuade the women to go home and rest. Just as adamantly, Karen and Judy refused, fearing Matthew would wake, wanting them, believing with all their being they would instill in their father their own strength.

For a second time, Rand accepted their decision, remaining until late that night, having meals sent and ordering pillows and blankets when it became obvious neither of them would leave. Rand's quiet strength fueled Karen with desperately needed hope. She sat with his arms supporting her and relaxed for the first time in twenty-four hours. She was dimly aware of being lowered upon a soft cushion and covered with a blanket. A faint shadow stood above her, but the magnetic allure of sleep, sweet, blissful slumber, called, and she slipped into unconsciousness.

The next day followed the pattern of the first. Matthew's condition remained unchanged. Friends and relatives continued to visit, but there was no word, no hope to offer as Matthew clung to the delicate thread of life.

Rand was with them as much as possible, concerning himself with their basic needs of food and rest. He held Karen again until she fell asleep; she faintly recalled a caressing kiss on her cheek as she slipped into sleep on the third night of their vigil.

Early the next evening, the doctor appeared and for the first time greeted Karen and Judy with an encouraging smile.

"Your father has made definite improvement today. He's awake and already giving the nurses a bad time." He seemed to find amusement in this and chuckled over some private joke. "Although the immediate danger has passed, Matthew must remain in the coronary care unit for several days, depending on his progress. From there he'll be transferred to the progressive care unit." Dr. Phillips took care to explain the details of Matthew's recovery and left with an optimistic smile a few minutes later.

After the unbearable wait, the news of Matthew's improvement was like a refreshing, life-giving rain after a summer drought. Karen and Judy hugged each other, the tension broken as happy tears blurred their eyes.

When Judy gave a small, strangled sound, Karen looked up, confused and unsure, to find her sister hurrying down the corridor. Walking toward them was Rand and her brother-in-law, Mike Turner.

Judy floated into her husband's arms and was enfolded in an embrace that spoke of worry, concern, and months of longing.

"How…when?" She didn't seem capable of forming a complete sentence.

Mike laughed. "Rand contacted the air force, and I was given emergency leave. I can see I'm going to appreciate my new brother-in-law." His smile was broad; then he sobered as if remembering the reason for his being there. "How's Matt now?"

"Better, much better," Judy supplied the information. "The doctor was just here. There's a long uphill road to recovery for Dad, but Dr. Phillips feels optimistic."

Rand rested his hand lightly across Karen's shoulder, and she slipped her arm around his waist. The simple contact brought a ray of hope to the problems they had yet to face regarding her pregnancy. When she glanced at Rand, she found him smiling smugly.

"What did I tell you? I knew that crusty old devil was going to make it." His expression altered. "It's time to come home. Evan and Milly are coming later. They'll phone if there's any change."

After three restless nights, catching what sleep they could on a lumpy davenport, both daughters were ready to agree.

The two couples left the hospital, and for the first time in three days Karen breathed in fresh air and looked toward the sun. Her eyes were lambent, her relief almost translucent.

Carl greeted her with anxious eyes but relaxed after she gave him a reassuring smile. "I don't need to ask how your father's doing, Miss Karen," he said. "The smile on your face answers all doubts."

"Dad's better, much better. Thank you for your concern."

The older man looked pleased. "The missus has dinner waiting. She'll be glad to hear your father is improving."

Everyone was being so wonderful. Karen felt a knot building in her throat, never having realized before how the loving support of friends could mean so much.

"Thank her for me," Karen murmured, holding back the tears.

Home held the comfort of familiarity, and Karen looked around her as if seeing it with new eyes. Flowers decorated the table; her collection of figurines on the mahogany bookcase stared back at her, providing solace that would have been difficult to describe with words.

The aroma of the meal warming in the oven couldn't deter Karen from the thought of a hot shower and washing her hair. As she entered the bedroom, she halted in midstep; the open suitcase on the bed caused her to stop and stare.

"Oh, Rand, the trip...the lecture series. I'd forgotten. You were supposed to leave today," she said, horrified. Everything was so confused in her mind; time had lost meaning as the days blended together. The trip, their argument, seemed so far removed, so distant. Not since the phone call from the hospital had Rand's leaving with Cora crossed her mind.

"I'm flying out early tomorrow morning. There's no question of you accompanying me," he said flatly, pulling his tie free and unfastening the top buttons of his shirt.

Was he referring to the pregnancy or her father? Karen was too weary to question him. "No, I suppose not," she mumbled, feeling dejected and sad. Rand was leaving with Cora, and all the things Karen had so desperately wanted to have clear between them remained to trouble her. All her efforts to normalize their relationship had been thwarted.

Rand was waiting for her in the living room, relaxing, his head leaning back against the chair, listening to the classical music they both enjoyed.

She sat opposite him, wishing he was on the davenport so she could be closer. "I want to thank you for all you did to help my family," she began, feeling awkward. "You were wonderful. None of us will ever forget it."

Rand frowned; his mouth twisted in a taut line as if her words had displeased him. "I didn't do anything anyone else wouldn't have done," he told her flatly.

Karen looked around her; the welcome of her home had faded from the lack of warmth in her husband.

Rand was leaving in the morning. Nothing had been settled between them, and already the cold mask was slipping over her husband's face. A knot tightened the tender muscles of her stomach.

"If you don't mind, I… I think I'll skip dinner and go to bed," she added, hoping to hide the despair in her voice.

Rand shrugged noncommittally. "As you wish."

Karen returned to the bedroom, feeling depressed and weary.

The gentle caress of Rand's mouth woke her the next morning. The alarm had rung, sounding as if it'd come from a far-off distance, but that had seemed so long ago. Karen welcomed the warm touch as he rolled her over, his mouth seeking hers. Automatically, her lips parted, savoring his ardent kiss. Her silken arms wound around his neck as his hand slipped under her night-gown, capturing the rounded fullness of her breast.

Karen gave a muted groan; Rand hadn't touched her like this since she'd told him about the baby. She was starving for his love and responded with all the hunger of weeks without him.

"I've got to go or miss the flight," he murmured low in her ear as his other hand stroked her exposed thigh.

"Can't you stay a bit longer?" she questioned, drugged with desire. Unfastening his suit coat, her arms circled the broad expanse of his back, stroking, caressing, drawing him to her.

Rand's mouth parted hers hungrily, and she clung to him, arching her back.

He groaned hoarsely. "I'll catch another flight."

Matthew was awake for Karen's visit later that morning. He was pale and so weak that his smile was no more than a slight quiver at the corners of his mouth. He struggled to speak, frustrated until he managed one word.

"Bairn?"

Karen flashed him a proud smile, her eyes sparkling with happiness as she nodded. "A granddaughter, we're hoping. Who told you?" He was unlikely to have remembered her frantic whisper that night.

Matthew rolled his head, indicating the nurse near his bed.

Mrs. Thomas looked away guiltily. "I hope you don't mind my telling him, dear. He needed a bit of good news."

Karen assured her it didn't matter; she'd liked Mrs. Thomas immediately. The kind eyes and reassuring manner had done much to relieve Judy and Karen during the bleakest hours.

"I hope this dirty old man isn't giving you problems," the nurse said with a wink as she connected another IV bottle to the stand above Matthew's head.

For an instant, angry fire sparked in her father's eyes, and Karen smiled at the sight, strangely comforted by this small display of anger.

Rand phoned that evening to assure Karen he'd caught his flight and had arrived in Chicago safely. He sounded relaxed and less tense than she could remember since finding out about the baby. It was a little thing that showed her Rand was beginning to come to terms with her pregnancy. Their conversation lasted only a few minutes, but when Karen replaced the phone, she closed her eyes, confident for the first time things would work out between them.

Matthew was much more alert the next two days as his strength gradually returned. Karen's visits remained short, and on several occasions she enjoyed the banter between her father and Mrs. Thomas. Their quick wits were well matched, and Matthew appeared to find solace from the tedious days in the good-humored teasing.

His first words to Karen the next morning were a plea for food. "Karen, lass, I'm starving to death. Will you see what you can do to get me off this sugar water and on to some real food?"

Even before Karen could assure him she would, Mrs. Thomas moved to his bedside.

"Feisty this morning, aren't you?" she said, hands on her hips, her flashing blue eyes glaring at Matthew.

He lowered his brows disapprovingly. "How can a man be anything else when he's near fainting from hunger? If you were any kind of a nurse, you'd see about getting me some food."

"Listen here, you meager-witted, croaking toad. If you had any brains in that buffooned head of yours, you'd know none of the patients in the intensive care unit are allowed solid food. Be patient for once."

"Meager-witted toad, is it? Well, you're nothing more than a domineering battle-axe."

"Dad!" Karen's gaze bounced from one to the other. Mrs. Thomas's eyes were sparkling with delight; she loved this teasing raillery. Her father's mouth quivered with the effort to suppress a smile.

"Go tend your patients, nurse, but let it be known ye sorely task my temper."

"Thirty years of nursing and I've yet to meet a more ill-mannered, ill-tempered man." She continued to make busywork around Matthew's bed, and meeting Karen's eye, gave a girlish wink.

Karen's gaze followed the older woman as she moved around in the large, open area. Catherine Thomas's hair was completely white, and Karen guessed her age to be close to Matthew's. The woman's deep-blue eyes seemed to dance with mischief, and her smile was ready and warm. It was easy to picture this woman with her father; somehow it seemed right.

Rand telephoned from Kansas City the next evening and laughed as she related the scene between Matthew and Mrs. Thomas.

"It sounds to me like a little romance is brewing between those two."

"I was thinking the same thing myself," Karen confessed. "I've often wondered how I'd feel if Dad showed interest in another woman. I loved my mother so much, and Dad loving someone else is almost painful. But I like Catherine Thomas immensely. I wouldn't feel bad at all if they got to know each other better." The picture of the couple together brought a charmed smile to Karen's face. "What a pair they'd be. Mrs.

Thomas is barely five feet tall, and Dad's well over six feet."

"Karen, I don't want you interfering with those two."

"Randall Prescott, I wouldn't!" She was surprised he would even make such a suggestion. Her back stiffened with resentment.

"Of all the couples in the world, you and I know what it's like to have someone intrude."

You and I, he'd said. Did Rand finally accept her innocence in the contrived marriage? So much had been said the night of her father's open-heart surgery to help her understand his strange behavior; Karen had wondered if Rand had understood the implications. Matthew was aware that Rand and Karen were in love, but he also knew his time was limited with a bad heart. Forcing the marriage had been a desperate act by a desperate man.

"Yes, I guess *we* do," she said evenly.

"How are you feeling?"

In the past, Karen had always responded with a flat "fine." Now that Rand possibly accepted that she hadn't tricked him the first time, maybe he would be willing to accept the truth about her pregnancy. Perhaps it was time to begin talking about the baby.

"I'm doing much better now that the morning sickness has passed."

"Good." The one word came out abrupt and clipped. They hadn't spoken about the pregnancy since the night of Matthew's heart attack. Rand's response didn't encourage her to continue, but she ignored the unspoken warning. "I've had to buy some new clothes," she added, forcing herself to sound bright and cheerful.

"You'd hardly believe how rounded I've become since you left."

"I'm pleased you're feeling better." He didn't attempt to disguise his displeasure or the chill in his voice. "I'll phone tomorrow night. Good-bye."

"Good-bye." The line had already been disconnected; the buzz continued to drone for several moments before Karen replaced the receiver.

When Rand phoned again, they talked briefly, but he didn't inquire about her health. It was as though he were purposely avoiding the slightest reference to the baby.

Most of the discomforts of the early months of the pregnancy had passed, but her emotions remained sensitive and fragile. For several nights afterward, Karen had a difficult time sleeping, continuing to mull the problem in her mind.

It was a day for rejoicing when Matthew was transferred to the progressive care unit. His condition had improved so rapidly that even Dr. Phillips was surprised.

Catherine Thomas followed the small party down the corridor to the new ward, beaming a proud smile. Her delight at his improvement was apparent as she joked and laughed along the way.

Catherine stopped at the nurses' station and said, loud enough for Matthew to hear, "Keep your eyes on this ole buzzard, girls. He can be more trouble than a nursery full of newborn babies."

"Ha," Matthew emitted harshly, but his eyes followed Catherine without even a hint of anger.

Karen and Judy exchanged meaningful glances.

"How long before I get any decent food?" Matthew asked eagerly.

"Patience, my dear man, patience." Catherine grinned sheepishly at the girls on her way out the door.

"Dad"—Judy glanced out the window as if finding the street below an intriguing sight—"is there a Mr. Thomas?"

"Of course there's a Mr. Thomas," he boomed, his voice angry. "There must be a thousand Mr. Thomases in the world, but if ye're referring to Catherine, she's a widow."

Color rose in Judy's cheeks, but she managed a weak "Oh."

When Catherine reentered the room, Matthew's eyes widened appreciatively. His gaze fastened on the large serving of chocolate pudding. "Grand, pudding is one of my favorite—"

He didn't get to finish his thought. "But, Matt, this isn't pudding." She gave Judy and Karen a wicked smile. "This is strained liver."

A disgusted sound came from Matthew. "It seems I'm beset by a cruel woman who delights in punishing a sick man." But his laughter joined theirs.

Rand had been away for almost two weeks, and Karen was miserable. She wasn't sleeping well; so much had been left unsaid between them. Karen discovered the pleasure she enjoyed in simple things diminishing because he wasn't there to share them with her. She worked in the garden, listened to mellow music, and eagerly awaited his daily phone calls. These were mostly a disappointment. Their conversations remained stilted and formal because neither would speak openly of what was uppermost in their minds.

With Rand gone, the baby was becoming more and more the focal point of Karen's world. The forming child moved often now; the first light fluttering, as delicate as a butterfly testing its wings, had confused Karen. She wasn't sure if it was something she ate or the baby. Gradually, the movements grew stronger, more pronounced, and Karen didn't doubt the source.

Rand phoned early one morning, early for Karen, midmorning for him in Cleveland. She was still in bed, her hands pressing against her abdomen, feeling the baby's movement.

"I know you don't want to hear this," she told him, her voice high with enthusiasm, "but I'm lying here feeling the baby kick. I mean a good solid kick."

"You're right. I don't want to hear it," he said dryly.

The balloon of happiness burst, leaving Karen speechless and unbelievably hurt. "Whether you face the fact or not"—her low voice wavered—"I'm going to have a child, your child. I did not create this child on my own. The baby is part you, part me. This should be one of the happiest times in our marriage, yet I'm afraid even to mention the baby. What am I supposed to do, Rand? What do you want from me?"

He sighed heavily. "I've told you repeatedly I don't want that baby," he said bitterly. "You seem to be living under the misconception that given time, my feelings will change. They won't. I'll have nothing to do with that baby. You've chosen to become pregnant against my wishes; as far as I'm concerned, the baby is yours, not mine. Don't expect me to touch it, hold it, or in any way have anything to do with it."

The baby was an *it* to Rand, a nonentity, unworthy of importance.

"Maybe you don't want me, either," she whispered through the agony.

"Maybe I don't," he returned.

His rejection knotted her stomach into a tight ball of pain. "That doesn't leave much to be said, does it?"

A long pause followed. "No, I guess it doesn't."

Fifteen minutes after the phone call, Karen remained in bed, the enormity of their conversation crushing against her heart like a huge boulder.

In effect, Rand was saying it was him or the baby. How could she possibly choose between the two? The image of a child the father refused to touch or acknowledge ripped at her soul. Loving them both so much would tear her in two. Rand was asking the impossible.

If this was the way he wanted things, forcing her to decide, then the decision would be an easy one. They had no marriage. Rand was selfish, hurtful, and totally unreasonable; he had been almost from the beginning of their marriage. They had made a mistake by not getting an annulment.

Karen jerked the suitcase from the closet and set it on the bed, throwing her clothes from the drawers into it without thought or organization. Her vision was blurred with unshed tears, her lips pressed tightly closed to restrain the sobs.

How naive she'd been to believe their love would conquer all their differences. Rand didn't need her; he'd just told her he didn't want her, either. Maybe it was time to prove she was perfectly capable of making a life without him.

She'd leave him this time, really leave him, not another three-day jaunt down the Oregon coast. A small, hurt laugh came from deep inside; three days without her and Rand had fallen apart. How did he expect to live without her, and for that matter, how would she ever make it without him?

She paused, sitting on the end of the bed, her tortured gaze moving around the room and sensing all the love represented there.

How could they ever settle anything when separated by hundreds of miles? Their telephone conversations frustrated them more than settled anything. They needed to sit across from each other and talk out their problems. Other than never being able to see the baby, Karen had no idea why Rand objected so violently to the child. There could be no more running, no more telephone conversations, when it was too easy simply to hang up the phone rather than talk things out. She needed to know his feelings, his thoughts; she needed to explain hers.

Tilting her head back, she closed her eyes as waves of depression rippled over her. Rand wasn't due home for another ten days. He was in Cleveland; she was in Tacoma. It couldn't wait; they'd delayed discussing it for too long. She'd simply have to go to him…the sooner the better.

The flight touched down at nine o'clock Cleveland time. Karen was tired and hungry. The conviction she was doing the right thing was reinforced by every mile of the journey. As the hours passed, Karen recalled Rand's mother telling her she need only be patient. Rand would make a good father; would accept the child. Carl had told her that Rand would be handing out cigars, proud as any father. Karen need only believe this herself, trust in his love.

By the time she'd collected her luggage, gotten a taxi, and arrived at Rand's hotel, it was after ten. The clerk gave her Rand's room number and kindly offered to keep her suitcase, since she hadn't been able to locate him. Rand didn't respond to either the telephone call or the knock when they tried his room. Discouraged, Karen went into the restaurant for something to eat while she waited.

Where would he be this late? Cora hadn't answered her telephone, either. Were they together? With so many other things on her mind, Karen didn't want to think about Cora.

Seated in the dimly lit restaurant, Karen read over the menu. She hadn't eaten in hours, but nothing sounded appetizing. Where was Rand? She almost asked the question aloud.

As she laid the menu aside, the sound of a laugh, Cora's laugh, caught her attention from across the room. The lighting was low. At first, Karen was sure it wasn't them; it couldn't be. A bubble of hysteria rose in her throat. Rand and Cora were sitting together across the room, their heads close together like lovers sharing intimate secrets.

Numbly, she stood. Her heart hammered irrationally as she approached their table.

"Hello, Rand, Cora," she said in a complete monotone. A sick feeling rose in her throat as she saw Cora's hand holding Rand's.

"I'd advise you to remove your hand from my husband's, Cora. Otherwise, I'll have to create a scene in this very nice restaurant."

Twelve

"Please excuse us, Cora." Rand offered the other woman an apologetic smile and stood.

"You don't need to make apologies for me, Randall Prescott." Karen's gaze narrowed menacingly on Cora and was surprised by the lack of challenge. Was she so confident of her hold over Rand that she needn't show the least concern? Karen was studying the other woman so intently she didn't hear the parting words Cora issued Rand.

Rand held Karen's upper arm. "Thanks, we're going to need it."

Neither of them said a word until they entered the elevator.

"Let go of my arm," Karen demanded coldly.

Rand's mouth twisted, his look hard and resolute. "Like hell!" But his hold relaxed.

Karen didn't struggle; it would have been useless, anyway.

Once inside his room, Rand leaned against the closed door. "Just what kind of game are you playing?" he questioned, his voice hoarse.

Karen was trembling fiercely. She didn't trust her voice.

"Karen," he demanded again.

Turning her back to him, her arms cradled her chest to ward off the cold, the ache, the hurt. Tears coursed a haphazard route down her face, the strength of her will unable to abate their fall. Every breath became a sob, wrenched from her heart.

He clasped her shoulder to turn her toward him. "Karen, please don't cry," he pleaded.

Closing her eyes, she averted her face, burying her chin into her shoulder, her body shaking with uncontrollable sobs.

Rand brought her head against him, supplying the loving support she needed so desperately.

"I can't stand it when you cry," he said.

She gave a short, almost hysterical laugh. Almost from the time they'd met, all she'd done was cry. The power Rand had to hurt her was so sharp it was incomprehensible.

"Don't, please." Gently, his lips moved against her hair. His hands, which had been holding her, now began a caressing provocation over her shoulders, back, and hips.

His mouth sought the gentle curve of her neck. Just as powerful as his ability to hurt was his power to comfort, to love. His mouth found hers, claiming the trembling softness with a gentleness that caused her knees to quiver. His lips hardened in possession, and Karen could taste the salt from her tears on his mouth.

"No," she mumbled imploringly, breaking the contact and burying her face in his chest.

"Karen."

She could hear the rawness in his voice and knew he was as affected by their kissing as she. His chin moved against her hair as if he couldn't bear to release her from his arms.

"We need to talk." She was surprised by the strength in her voice.

"I know." His hold relaxed slightly, but she remained in the protective circle of his arms. "I've tried to contact you all day. Even Carl wouldn't answer. I've been sick with worry. I thought you'd left me for sure this time."

Lifting her face, she watched his reaction. "Would you care if I'd left you, really left you?"

Almost angrily, he broke the embrace and strode to the other side of the room, clenching his hands at his sides as he paced the floor. "Yes, I'd care." He ground out each word as if it were a weakness he was confessing. "I need you." He turned around, and his face shone with the intensity of his feelings.

"What about the baby?" she asked, her voice shaking violently.

Karen thought she glimpsed pain in his eyes. "I never wanted the child."

Her shoulders hunched forward in defeat until the baby kicked, almost as if the child were saying she must fight for her father's love. Approaching Rand, she took her husband's hand and placed it against the budding roundness of her abdomen. Rand resisted at first until he felt the activity. A sense of wonder came over his face, and for a second, Karen was sure she witnessed a flicker of pride move across it.

"That's the baby?" he asked incredulously. "He's so strong."

Karen smiled. Rand had referred to the baby as *he*, not as *it*.

"The doctor says I'm carrying the baby high; that's why I'm showing as much as I am."

Karen was sure he hadn't even heard her as his hand moved over her stomach in a gentle caress, his eyes proud but tortured.

"How can I be any kind of father?" The raw pain in his voice shocked Karen. "I'll never see this child. More than that, I'll never be the kind of father a child needs."

"Rand"—her voice shook with her own pain— "that's not true."

He emitted a dry, bitter laugh. "You know what's going to happen, don't you? It's inevitable. One day that child is going to be embarrassed to have me as his father. I'll never be able to do the things other fathers do." His voice trembled with emotion as he strode across the carpet like a man pushed to the limit. "I don't want that baby, Karen, but I'm trying. At least give me credit for that."

She watched him with a sense of unreality. "Rand?" She had once stood in his office reading over his accomplishments, with the realization that there wasn't anything this man couldn't do. He'd overcome obstacles and prejudices she could only imagine, but the thought of this new life they'd created frightened him beyond all else. "You're afraid, aren't you?"

He didn't bother to deny her accusation. "I'm scared to death," he bit out savagely, his face white and drawn.

"Rand..."

"No, let me finish. It's always been important to me to be completely independent. I've struggled for that.

Now, within the space of a few short months, I find myself responsible not only for myself but first a wife and now a child."

"I entered your life with the subtlety of a racing locomotive, didn't I?" she asked with a tender smile.

His returning one appeared involuntary. "Now the baby is doing the same thing to the both of us."

Karen's smile relaxed, and she watched Rand with questioning eyes. "You believe me now, don't you? I didn't purposely get pregnant."

Rand's mouth thinned. "Yes, I realized that almost immediately, but I was confused and hurt. I lashed out in anger. I wanted you to suffer, and yet every time I purposely hurt you, I suffered, too. I created my own hell. Then you were gone for those three days, and I nearly went insane. I couldn't imagine what my life would be like without you now. Your love has affected every facet of my existence. I almost ruined what we have, didn't I?"

"No." Her voice wavered slightly, a lump of happiness choking off her words. "I could never leave you."

"Then, this morning, when I phoned and you started talking about the baby, I went cold inside. My stomach knotted into a ball of pain, and I knew I'd lost. I was going to love the baby. Perhaps I was even subconsciously happy you were pregnant. I got scared. All I could think of was all the things a father should do… things I'll never be able to do."

"But, Rand"—her hand gripped his arm—"don't you realize what you have to offer is far more valuable than shooting baskets or tossing a baseball? Why is it you feel that being a good father is synonymous with being a jock?" She sighed, her voice husky with emotion. "Just being the person you are is more important than any physical feat you could ever accomplish."

"But, Karen…"

"No, let me finish." She stopped to kiss his throat softly but found the temptation too strong; fearing it would lead to other things, she broke the contact. "I fell in love with you almost from the time we met. It didn't take me long to see past the angry facade you wore. I was sick with disappointment when I didn't hear from you after the Christmas party. I knew then that I'd never meet anyone who would be more of a man than you. When we started seeing each other on a regular basis, it was like every dream I'd ever hoped to fulfill." She gave a small, nervous laugh. "Every woman has a picture of what she'd like in the perfect man. Some see him as tall, dark, and handsome. You're all of those, but I've known lots of men who fit that description. It was your sensitivity, your intelligence, your strength, both physical and emotional, that attracted me. When you decided to break off our relationship, it was like dying. I knew that although someday I would probably love and marry another, I'd never love anyone as much as I loved you. It was a dreadful thing Dad did to us. Such trickery goes against everything I've ever known from my father. I understand why he did it now. But even before I knew his reasoning, I was glad he'd forced your hand."

Gathering her close in the haven of his arms, he gently parted her moist lips in a kiss that kindled a fire of warmth and need that quickly spread through her body. But Rand also showed restraint, as if what they must say to each other was more important than the desire between them.

"As much as I resented your father's interference in my life, I realize he acted in the only way he could. I would never have married you otherwise, for the same reasons I didn't want the baby. I left New York alone after the wedding with a harrowing ache eating at me. Your wedding ring was in my pocket, and every time I touched it, the ring felt like it had seared my skin. I kept remembering how you said you wanted a marriage that would last a lifetime and you weren't interested in a three-day weekend. You'd been so shocked, so genuinely surprised, when I told you about being forced into the marriage. It was like being pulled apart. I was caught in the middle of a tug-of-war between my intellect, my will, and my desire for you." He paused for a moment as if the memory continued to haunt him. "I wanted to hate you, make you suffer for all the agony I was enduring. At the same time, I desperately wanted to believe you. I yearned to hold my wife in my arms and love you as any husband. But most of all, I realized it didn't matter what you'd done or how deceitful you'd been. I couldn't deny myself any longer. I desired you as I've never wanted anything in my life. Do you remember when I replaced the wedding ring on your finger?"

Karen smiled softly. "I'm not likely to forget."

"Your wedding ring burned my pocket the whole trip. I couldn't keep myself from fingering it, as if touching it would ease the ache of not having you with me. I couldn't return to Tacoma fast enough to place it where it belonged. And then you weren't there."

"But I was," she reminded him mockingly. "When I hurried into the house, Cora had her arms wrapped around you."

"I could have choked her for that, but I'll explain the situation with Cora in a minute." Gently, his hand caressed her cheek. "I hurried back to put the ring on your finger. Suddenly, you were there, and I realized, ring or no ring, you were my wife."

"About Cora?" Karen questioned.

"Yes, Cora." Rand expelled his breath in a long, drawn-out sigh. "At one time, she may have harbored some hope of the two of us getting together. But she realized such expectations are useless. I'm very much in love with my beautiful wife."

Karen held herself stiff. "That wasn't exactly the impression I got tonight when I saw you in the restaurant."

Rand's returning grin was wry. "I've behaved like a madman most of the day. I tried repeatedly to get ahold of you and couldn't. I was positive I'd really done it this time. I'd lost you, driven you away. I booked a flight home for tomorrow morning. It was the soonest I could get out. Cora was, I guess you'd say, comforting me, assuring me that things would work out between you and me."

The unyielding stiffness ebbed from Karen. "From now on, if you need any comfort, come to me."

"Don't worry, honey. Cora knows where she stands."

Rand wasn't explaining the complete situation to her. A lot had been left unsaid, perhaps for the better. This was her husband; she trusted his judgment.

"And the baby?"

"My attitudes aren't going to change overnight. I'd rather you weren't pregnant. The thought of this child terrifies me more than anything I've ever faced. I'm trying to accept the fact we're going to have a family, but I'll need time."

Karen swallowed tightly. "I can't ask for anything more than that. The baby and I need you. We're willing to do whatever it takes, to wait as long as you need. Your daughter and I will simply have to learn to be patient."

Rand's arms tightened their grip around her, and he buried his face in her hair. "A daughter?" He looked surprised. "From the time you first told me you were pregnant, I've assumed the baby would be a boy."

"My dad has wanted a little granddaughter for years, and I've promised him a girl. Would you be unhappy with a daughter?" Karen questioned in afterthought.

"In truth, I'd rather you weren't pregnant at all. But as long as you and the baby are healthy, it doesn't matter what you have."

His words of indifference still had the power to hurt, but she disguised their effect. "Good, because I'm hoping for a girl." Unable to resist him much longer, she gave Rand a kiss.

Rand's laughter held a musical note. "I swear you're still more McAlister than Prescott."

With a warm smile, Karen cupped his face and drew him down invitingly to her waiting lips. "I'm feeling very much like a Prescott right now."

Rand sucked in his breath and groaned before his mouth hungrily claimed hers.

Her response was automatic as she wrapped her arms around his waist and pressed her face to his shirt. Rand smoothed her hair; then his hands ran through it, tangling it between his fingers, and his mouth descended to the slim column of her throat. Nestled in the comfort of his arms, Karen yawned. Their emotional talk that morning, the hurried flight to Cleveland, the time difference between Cleveland and Tacoma, were all demanding their due, and before she could prevent another, she yawned again.

Rand sighed and gave a soft chuckle. "Come to bed, my love. You're exhausted."

"I am." Karen was too tired to argue.

They undressed, and a few minutes later, she was again securely settled in her husband's arms. A pang of hunger reminded her she'd hardly eaten all day.

"Rand," she whispered, "I'm starving—" She wasn't allowed to finish. Rand's mouth claimed hers again as his hands began a gentle exploration of her breasts.

"Me, too," he whispered huskily before claiming her mouth in a rousing, twisting kiss that left Karen weak with longing. This wasn't exactly what she had in mind, but she didn't bother to correct him.

When Karen and Rand returned to Tacoma almost two weeks later, Karen was amazed at the rate of Matthew's recovery. Although she'd spoken to him daily, she was unprepared for the healthy flush in his cheeks or the smile in his eyes. Karen was convinced Catherine was responsible for the renewed vitality.

"Karen, lass." Matthew flashed her a happy smile as they sauntered into the hospital room. "Rand, welcome. How was the trip?"

"Good," he responded simply, but the hand holding Karen's tightened. The trip had been the honeymoon they'd never had. It was a time of reassurances, settling doubts and misunderstandings, and days of wondering at the strength of their love for each other.

They rarely spoke of the baby. One morning, Karen had awakened to the feel of Rand's fingers traveling lightly over her abdomen in a gentle caress. They had both felt the baby's kick. Quickly, Rand jerked his hand away as though unprepared to touch this child or begin the simplest form of communication. Rand had told her he needed time; she must learn to be patient. Rushing things would do more harm than good.

"Dad, you look wonderful." Karen hugged him, her eyes aglow with a warm light. "Catherine," she greeted, and impulsively gave the older woman a hug. It was the first time Karen had seen the other woman out of a nurse's uniform and she was pleasantly surprised by her attractiveness.

"I should be going," Catherine offered, reaching for her purse. "Your family's here to visit now."

"I'd like you to stay." The unspoken message in his eyes was clear.

A smile widened Catherine's mouth, and she conceded.

"How are you feeling, lass?" Matthew's grin widened as his gaze rested on Karen's rounding stomach.

"Fine, Dad." She looked away self-consciously, praying he wouldn't go on about the baby in front of Rand. She wanted to warn him, plead with him to drop the subject, for she could already sense Rand's withdrawal.

"I guess I should have warned you, Rand. The McAlister women are a fertile group. I no more than hung my pants over the bed with Madeline and we had two girls before I knew what had happened. And as I recall, Judy had no trouble getting caught with James and Carter, either."

Karen stiffened, her smile frozen on taut lips.

"I could have done with a warning," Rand replied stiffly, but if Matthew noticed anything was wrong, he didn't show it, laughing off Rand's remark.

Karen continued her daily visits to the hospital, but as the days passed, Matthew's attitude became withdrawn. He was often melancholy, although he attempted a cheerful facade.

Several days later, Karen asked, "Where's Catherine? I haven't seen her in a while."

"She's busy, lass," he explained stiffly, "too busy for an old man."

"I know you asked me to stay out of this," Karen told Rand that night, "but I know something is wrong. Dad's miserable, and other than a few brief visits, I don't think Catherine's been to see him at all."

Rand's expression tightened. "Karen, your father is old enough to handle his own affairs. What's between him and Catherine is none of our business."

She gave him a determined glance. "I'm going to visit Catherine."

"Karen," Rand said with a note of warning.

"I'm only going to say hello," she assured him, her eyes glinting with mischief.

Forced to wait for several minutes, Karen sat in the waiting room that had been a prison of anxiety the first days following Matthew's surgery.

"Karen!" Catherine joined her; a smile of welcome didn't reach her eyes. "Your father's not worse, is he?"

There was no disguising the note of anxiety in her voice.

"No, Dad's doing fine. How have you been? We've missed you. We *all* have." She hoped the inflection in her voice conveyed the message.

Catherine glanced nervously at her hands. "I've been busy."

"That's what Dad said."

Catherine avoided eye contact, her face slightly drawn.

"All right," Karen demanded, "what is it with you and Dad?"

"There's nothing between your father and me," Catherine responded tightly, and stood.

"Catherine!" Karen murmured in frustration.

With an exasperated sigh, she turned around. "You're more stubborn than your father. I don't know what's wrong, but every time I've been to see him lately, I get the impression he'd rather I didn't come anymore. I think it's obvious that he's recovering and doesn't want me around. I'm nothing but a bossy old woman. I do wish him the best."

Karen watched Catherine return to her ward. What was wrong with her father? Why would he behave in such a way?

"I don't understand it, Rand," she told him later that evening. "Why would Dad act like that toward Catherine?"

Rand arched an exaggerated brow. "Karen, I want your promise you won't interfere in this. What goes on between Matthew and Catherine is none of your business."

"But, Rand—"

"One Minute" Survey

You get up to **FOUR** books <u>and</u> Mystery Gifts...

ABSOLUTELY FREE!

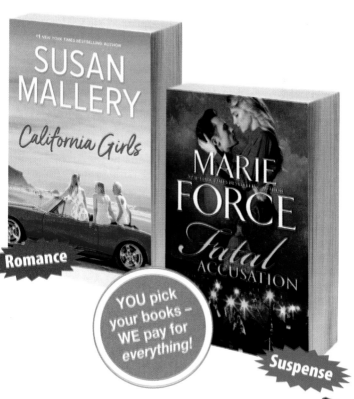

Romance

Suspense

YOU pick your books – WE pay for everything!

See inside for details.

YOU pick your books –
WE pay for everything.
You get up to FOUR new books and TWO Mystery Gifts..
absolutely FREE!
Total retail value: Over $20!

Dear Reader,

Your opinions are important to us. So if you'll participate in our fast and free "One Minute" Survey, **YOU** can pick up to four wonderful books that **WE** pay for!

As a leading publisher of women's fiction, we'd love to hear from you. That's why we promise to reward you for completing our survey.

IMPORTANT: Please complete the survey and return it. We'll send your Free Books and Free Mystery Gifts right away. **And we pay for shipping and handling too!** *We pay for EVERYTHING!*

Try **Essential Suspense** featuring spine-tingling suspense and psychological thrillers with many written by today's best-selling authors.

Try **Essential Romance** featuring compelling romance stories with many written by today's best-selling authors.

Or TRY BOTH!

Thank you again for participating in our "One Minute" Survey. It really takes just a minute (or less) to complete the survey… and your free books and gifts will be well worth it!

Sincerely,

Pam Powers

Pam Powers
for Reader Service

www.ReaderService.com

"One Minute" Survey

GET YOUR FREE BOOKS AND FREE GIFTS!

✓ Complete this Survey   ✓ Return this survey

◄ DETACH AND MAIL CARD TODAY! ◄

1 Do you try to find time to read every day?
☐ YES   ☐ NO

2 Do you prefer stories with happy endings?
☐ YES   ☐ NO

3 Do you enjoy having books delivered to your home?
☐ YES   ☐ NO

4 Do you share your favorite books with friends?
☐ YES   ☐ NO

YES! I have completed the above "One Minute" Survey. Please send me my Free Books and Free Mystery Gifts (worth over $20 retail). I understand that I am under no obligation to buy anything, as explained on the back of this card.

☐ I prefer Essential Suspense 191/391 MDL GNRG

☐ I prefer Essential Romance 194/394 MDL GNRG

☐ I prefer BOTH 191/391 & 194/394 MDL GNRS

FIRST NAME _____   LAST NAME _____

ADDRESS _____

APT.# _____   CITY _____

STATE/PROV. _____   ZIP/POSTAL CODE _____

ST-220-OMLR20

© 2019 HARLEQUIN ENTERPRISES ULC and ® are trademarks owned by Harlequin Enterprises ULC. Printed in the U.S.A.

READER SERVICE—Here's how it works:

"No buts," he insisted. "Your father's behavior isn't so difficult to understand. He's going through a period of readjustment. He may love Catherine, but he wants to be sure he can offer her a healthy man. Let him work this out himself."

As the days progressed, Matthew showed renewed strength; his discharge date was set for the end of the week. When Rand and Karen visited the next night, they found Matthew out of bed, sitting in a chair waiting for them.

"Rand, Karen, I need to be talking to ye."

His tone was so serious, Karen wondered if the doctors had found a complication to his heart condition.

"Sit down," Matthew ordered.

Karen complied, her hand reaching for Rand's. She'd never seen her father act so nervously.

"Lass, I've already spoken to Judy and received her blessing; now I'm seeking yours. If ye have no objection, I plan on asking Catherine Thomas to be my wife. I love her," he told them simply, directly.

Karen could have cried with relief. "Dad, of course. I love her, too."

"Congratulations, Matthew," Rand added.

It wasn't until they were alone that Rand chided Karen affectionately. "Now, didn't I tell you things have a way of working out themselves without your meddling?"

Karen gave a happy laugh. "I knew you couldn't resist that, but I didn't know you were the kind of husband who would stoop to saying 'I told you so.'"

Rand's mouth twisted humorously. "Sure I am."

Matthew and Catherine were married at the end of

October and left almost immediately afterward for a two-week honeymoon in Scotland and England.

Rand and Karen drove to the airport with them, excitedly waving them off. Rand was unusually quiet as Karen drove home.

Later, as Karen sat on top of their bed, brushing her hair before changing into her pajamas, Rand asked, "Now that all the rush has passed, how do you feel?"

She paused, her hands resting lightly on her stomach. "Tired." As the pregnancy had progressed, Karen had lost the ability to move gracefully. The baby's first gentle movements now resembled the activity of a soccer team.

"I don't want you driving the car any longer," Rand declared casually.

Her look was puzzled. "Why ever not?"

He walked away from her, hanging his clothes in the closet, as if reluctant to let her know his reasons. "Because."

A faint smile quivered at the corner of her mouth. "All right, if you insist." Rand was worried about her, about the baby, but was unwilling to admit as much.

"I do." His words were abrupt. "Either Carl will take you where you need to go, or if he can't, perhaps your sister"—he hesitated—"and, Karen, please wear your safety belt."

"I promise," she said gently.

Another month passed, the longest month of her life. Rand didn't mention the baby or her pregnancy. He touched her, held her in his arms, loved her with a tenderness that was beyond description, but he never spoke of the child. A hundred times, Karen wanted to cry out that her time was drawing near, that he'd have to hurry. She couldn't bear it if the baby was born and Rand refused to have anything to do with their baby or couldn't love him or her. Somehow Karen felt the infant would know, would sense Rand's reluctance, and the thought of that rejection brought a harrowing ache within her heart.

With only a couple of months remaining, Karen didn't think she could grow much larger. Even getting up from a sitting position proved to be a difficult task. Judy reminded her that large babies ran in the family and that James and Carter both weighed more than eight pounds at birth. But even she looked upon Karen with worried eyes.

Following her regular visit to the doctor in December, Karen sat in her living room with brooding thoughtfulness. As she stared into the distance, a lump began to form in her throat.

"Do you think Rand will be angry?" Judy sat opposite Karen; her eyes sparkled in excitement.

"Of course he's going to be angry. I suppose I shouldn't be so shocked, but how was I to know anything was unusual? I've never had a baby before."

Judy chuckled softly. "To be truthful, I suspected something. I could understand it when you looked down and couldn't see your shoes, but when you lost sight of the floor, I knew something was up."

Karen's voice wobbled uncontrollably. "How can you joke? Rand will be here in a few minutes. He didn't want one baby. How am I supposed to tell him it's a multiple birth?"

"You've really done it this time, little sister." Judy

chuckled. "If I wasn't so delighted, I'd sympathize with you. But I think twins are wonderful."

The beginnings of a small smile formed. "I think I could be happy about it, too, if only I could be sure of Rand's reaction."

After Judy left, Karen entered the bedroom that had been transformed into a nursery. Running the tips of her fingers over the pink-and-blue-plaid wallpaper, she glanced around the room with mixed emotions. Rand had given her a free hand to do as she wished, never asking what she had done, not listening when she told him. She had tried to discuss names for the baby with him. Rand had cut her off, telling her she could choose any name she wanted. Little by little, she could see a softening in him, but it was so infinitesimal. How would he react to the news she was having twins?

The doctor had been so reassuring, so kind. When he had first suggested the ultrasound, Karen had been surprised. The results confirmed his suspicions, and Karen didn't know if she should laugh or burst into tears. She chose the latter. Of course, the doctor had no way of knowing Rand's attitude regarding the pregnancy.

"Karen." The front door opened, and Rand called for her, his voice eager.

"I'm in here." She walked out to meet him.

"How did things go with the doctor today?"

She stiffened slightly. "Fine."

Rand kissed her softly, his lips teasing hers, but his hold tightened as the possession of his mouth hardened.

"My childbirth classes begin next week. I can't wait any longer if I'm going to take them at all." Her eyes studied his face. "Will you come with me?"

His face darkened, and a scowl narrowed his eyes. "No, I'm not ready, Karen."

A lump of painful hoarseness tightened her throat. "That's okay. I understand." She broke from his embrace and moved into the kitchen. "I... I better start dinner."

Rand nodded, and Karen saw the flicker of sadness that passed over him.

Karen couldn't sleep that night. There didn't seem to be a comfortable position, and turning over was a difficult task. She lay on her back, staring at the ceiling in the moonlight, wondering how she could even broach the subject of a multiple birth when Rand couldn't accept or love even one child.

"Are you awake?" Rand whispered.

"I'm sorry. Am I keeping you up?"

"No." He rolled over, cradling her head on his shoulder. "I can't sleep, either." His fingers gently caressed the length of her arm. "I love you, Karen."

"I know," she whispered, the lump in her throat constricting.

"Honey, I'm trying as hard as I can. I know you're upset about me not attending those birth classes with you, but I can't force this. It's got to come naturally."

Rand believed the reason she had been so quiet and withdrawn that night was because of his reluctance regarding the classes. She hadn't the courage to tell him otherwise. Perhaps when he was more comfortable with her pregnancy, was closer to accepting the baby, then she'd tell him.

"Did you tell him?" Judy asked the next day.

Abjectly, Karen shook her head. "I couldn't."

"Honestly, Karen, when are you planning to tell the poor guy? On the delivery table?"

"If I have to. What do you suggest?" she questioned sharply. "He's trying to come to terms with his feelings for one child. I can't suddenly announce there's more."

"He's been so good to you."

"I know, Rand's been wonderful. But it's all me, not the baby."

"I don't understand."

Karen inhaled deeply. "He follows me around like a lost puppy. The other night, I found him standing outside the shower listening in case I fell. He calls two and three times a day and canceled his speaking engagements close to my due date. He's even hired Dorothy to do the housework for me. I'm barely allowed to lift a finger around my own home."

Judy chuckled, dimples forming in her pink cheeks. "It's a good thing. I don't imagine you're able to do much."

She laughed. "It takes me an hour to get dressed. I've only got a few weeks left before the baby comes. And as far as I can see, Rand's no closer to accepting this child than he was in the beginning."

"Chin up, kid. Things will work out," Judy spoke reassuringly.

The first glimmer of hope came a week after the break of the new year. Rand arrived home with a large box under his arm.

"Hi, honey. I'm home."

"I'm in the kitchen," she called, drying her hands on a terry-cloth towel. Her back had been aching most of the day. Finally, in an effort to take her mind from the dull pain, she'd baked Rand's favorite cookies.

"What are you doing?"

"Dishes," she replied weakly. The ache seemed to be moving slowly from her back to her stomach.

He paused behind her, slipping his arms around her swollen stomach, caressing her roundness. "Leave them for Dorothy. I've got something for you—a present."

"For me?" She brightened, noticing the large box on the table for the first time.

"Go ahead; open it."

Lifting the lid, Karen stifled a cry, tears shimmering in her eyes. "Oh, Rand," she murmured tightly. "Oh, Rand." Inside the box, wrapped in tissue, lay a giant teddy bear. He had said the present was for her, but he had gotten it for the baby.

His hug was warm and gentle. "Hey, why the tears? If I'd known you were going to cry, I wouldn't have gotten it."

"I'm just so surprised," she said, sniffling, before he brought his mouth down to hers.

Sitting through dinner was an uncomfortable task. The pain in her back and abdomen seemed to grow more intense as the night progressed.

"Karen, are you feeling okay?" Rand asked as they got ready for bed.

Rubbing her hands over her stomach, she hesitated. "I don't know... I feel funny."

"Funny?" he straightened. "How do you mean 'funny'?"

"I've had a backache all day, and now it seems to be traveling around to my stomach. I think it might be a good idea if we started timing these pains."

The blood drained from his face. "Pain? You said you felt funny. You didn't say anything about pain."

Her hand traveled down his tense jaw. "Relax, Rand. I'm sure it must be false labor. It's almost three weeks too early."

"I'll call the doctor."

"Don't do that. It's much too soon even if this is the real thing."

An hour later, there could be no denying the pain that constricted her abdomen.

"I'm sorry, Rand, but I think we should call the doctor. This pain is too intense to be anything but real."

"Dear God." For a moment, Rand remained frozen, as if in his own silent terror. "You're sure?" he questioned.

Again, Karen was seized with another contraction, taking deep heaving breaths before she could respond. "Yes," she groaned softly, "the baby's coming."

"Carl." The name was wrenched from Rand as panic seemed to fill him. "I have to phone Carl...then the doctor."

"Honey, settle down. I'm all right; everything is fine." For the first time, Karen saw that Rand was troubled, unsure. "Rand...if you'd prefer it, I could go to the hospital alone."

"No." He nearly shouted the word. "I'd go insane sitting at home worrying about you. I want to be there when...the...our baby is born."

A minute later, Carl was knocking on the door, his face tight and anxious. "Miss Karen, are you okay?"

"It's too early," Rand repeated, as if hoping against hope she was teasing.

"It is too early," she agreed with a soft smile, "but I'm afraid no one bothered to tell the baby that."

"Oh, God."

The drive to the hospital was a bad dream. Rand kept telling her it was weeks too soon—she must be mistaken—and then shouting at Carl to hurry.

Karen was met at the hospital door by one of the nursing staff, who took her into the obstetrics ward. It was more than an hour later before she saw Rand.

He looked pale, drawn, his hair a mess, as if he'd jerked his hands through it several times.

"Karen." He caught her fingers, holding them tightly to his mouth.

She bit into her bottom lip to keep from groaning as she was wrenched by another pain. "Rand." Her hand smoothed his hair away from his face. "Listen, there's something I must tell you."

"No, you listen. I love you... I've done so little to deserve your love. The thought of my life without you is unbearable."

Tears blurred her eyes, and she drew a ragged breath. "Oh, Rand, I love you, too." Again, her stomach hardened and contracted. Against her will, she whimpered softly as the pain ebbed.

"Nurse," Rand cried, "my wife is in pain. Do something."

"Rand, you must listen to me...it's about the baby."

The white-capped nurse rushed into the room. "Mr. Prescott, there's nothing we can do now to ease your wife's discomfort. The doctor's on his way." The woman sounded so calm and sane against the frantic cries of her husband.

Karen smiled tenderly at this man she loved.

"Rand"—she placed his hand on her stomach—"please listen, because I want to be the one to tell you." She paused as the grinding agony ripped through her once again.

"Tell me what?" he asked as she relaxed.

"Rand." She kept her eyes shut, afraid to look into his eyes, then couldn't help herself. "We're having twins."

"Twins," he bellowed, then repeated it incredulously. "Twins?" He shook his head as if stunned. "I should have known to expect something like this."

"Are you angry?"

"No," he denied instantly.

Again, Karen was gripped by the tormenting pain. Rand kissed her hand several times. "My love," he whispered as if the pain was his own, "let us work together to bring these new lives into the world. Show me what I can do to help you."

Her eyes shining with an infinite tenderness, Karen smiled softly.

Several hours later, after the delivery, Rand joined Karen in her hospital room. She was exhausted but radiant, content and happy as her husband sat beside her and kissed her.

"How are they?" she questioned softly.

A look came over him, unreadable at first, myriad emotions. There was pride, satisfaction, and a wealth of love. "They're perfect, Karen. The nurses let me hold Jody and then Jenny. It was incredible to touch and feel our daughters. For the first time, I realize that you and I are bound together by far more than vows. The whole while you were in labor, I was experiencing this terrible guilt because I hadn't wanted a family. Then suddenly they were there, and I knew I would love these little girls beyond reason, as I love their mother."

Karen held his hand against her breast. "I love you."

"My wife, my lover, the mother of my children. You hold my life and everything important in the palm of your hand." Tenderly, he took her hand, lifted it to his lips, and very gently kissed her palm.

* * * * *

THE SOLDIER'S SECRET CHILD

Lee Tobin McClain

To my daughter, Grace,
who shows me every day that families
aren't about bloodlines; they're about heart.

Also available from Lee Tobin McClain

HQN

Safe Haven

Low Country Hero
Low Country Dreams
Low Country Christmas

Love Inspired

Rescue Haven

The Secret Christmas Child

Redemption Ranch

The Soldier's Redemption
The Twins' Family Christmas
The Nanny's Secret Baby

Rescue River

Engaged to the Single Mom
His Secret Child
Small-Town Nanny
The Soldier and the Single Mom
The Soldier's Secret Child
A Family for Easter

Visit the Author Profile page
at Harlequin.com for more titles.

One

Lacey McPherson leaned back, propped her hands on the low white picket fence and surveyed the wedding reception before her with satisfaction. She'd pulled it off.

She'd given her beloved brother and his bride a wedding reception to remember, not letting her own antiromance attitude show. But she had to admit she'd be glad when her half-remodeled guesthouse stopped being a nest for lovebirds.

"Nothing like a spring wedding, eh, Lacey?"

She jumped, startled at the sound of the gruff, familiar voice right behind her. She spun around. "Vito D'Angelo, you scared me!" And then her eyes widened and she gasped. "What happened?"

His warm brown eyes took her back to her teen years. She'd been such a dreamer then, not good at navigating high school drama, and her brother's friend had stepped in more than once to defend her from girls who wanted to gossip or boys who tried to take advantage. She and her brother had welcomed invitations to the D'Angelo family's big, loud Italian dinners.

But now the most noticeable thing about his face wasn't his eyes, but the double scar that ran from his forehead to his jawline. A smaller scar slashed from his lower lip to his chin.

Instinctively she reached out toward his face.

He caught her hand, held it. "I know. I look bad. But you should see the other guy."

His attempt at a joke made her hurt more than it made her laugh. "You don't look bad. It's just…wow, they barely missed your eye." Awkwardly, she tried to hug him with the fence in between.

He broke away and came inside through the open gate. "How're you doing, Lace? At least *you're* still gorgeous, huh? But you're too thin."

"You sound just like your grandma. And you're late for the wedding." Her heart was still racing from the surprise, both of seeing him and of how he looked.

She wanted to find out what had happened. But this wasn't the time or the place.

"Buck won't mind my being late. He looks busy." Vito looked past the wedding guests toward Lacey's brother, laughing and talking in the summer sun, his arm slung around his new bride. "Looks happy, too. Glad he found someone."

A slightly wistful quality in Vito's words made Lacey study her old friend. She hadn't seen him in almost ten years, not since he'd brought his army buddy home on a furlough and Lacey had fallen hard for the handsome stranger who'd quickly become her husband. Back then, after one very stormy conversation, Vito had faded into the background. He'd been in the firestorm that had killed Gerry, had tried to save him and had written to Lacey after Gerry's death. But he'd continued on with another Iraq tour and then another. She'd heard he'd been injured, had undergone a lot of surgery and rehab.

Looking at him now, she saw that he'd filled out from slim to brawny, and his hair curled over his ears, odd for a career military man. "How long are you home?"

"For good. I'm out of the army."

"Out?" She stared. "Why? That was all you ever wanted to do!" She paused. "Just like Gerry."

"I felt awful I didn't make his funeral." He put an arm around her shoulders and tugged her to his side. "Aw, Lace, I'm sorry about all of it."

Her throat tightened and she nodded. Gerry had been dead for a year and a half, but the loss still ached.

A shout went up from the crowd and something came hurtling toward her. Instinctively she put her hands up, but Vito stepped in front of her, catching the missile.

Immediately, he turned and handed it to her.

A bouquet of flowers? Why would someone...

Oh. *The* bouquet. Gina's.

She looked across the crowd at her friend, glowing in her pearl-colored gown. Gina kept encouraging Lacey to date again. Happily in love, she wanted everyone to share in the same kind of joy.

The crowd's noise had quieted, and some of the guests frowned and murmured. Probably because Gina had obviously targeted Lacey, who'd been widowed less than two years ago. One of the older guests shook her head. "Completely inappropriate," she said, loud enough for most of those nearby to hear.

Well, that wouldn't do. Gina was a Californian, relatively new to Ohio and still finding her way through the unspoken rules and rituals of the Midwest. She hadn't meant to do anything wrong.

Lacey forced a laugh and shook the bouquet threateningly at Gina. "You're not going to get away with this, you know," she said, keeping her tone light. "I'm passing it on to…" She looked around. "To my friend Daisy."

"Too late." Daisy waved a finger in front of her face and backed away. "You caught it."

"Actually, Vito caught it," old Gramps Camden said. "Not sure what happens when a man catches the bouquet."

As the crowd went back to general talk, Lacey tried to hand off the bouquet to all the females near her, but they all laughingly refused.

Curious about Vito's reaction, she turned to joke with him, but he was gone.

Later, after Gina and Buck had run out to Buck's shaving-cream-decorated truck, heads down against a hail of birdseed, Lacey gave cleanup instructions to the two high school girls who were helping her with the reception. Then, after making sure that the remaining guests were well fed and happy, she went into the guesthouse. She needed to check on Nonna D'Angelo.

Having Nonna stay here was working out great. The light nursing care she needed was right up Lacey's alley, and she enjoyed the older woman's company. And the extra bit of income Nonna insisted on paying had enabled Lacey to quit her job at the regional hospital. Now that the wedding was over, she could dive into the final stages of readying the guesthouse for its fall opening.

Nonna D'Angelo had mingled during the early part of the reception, but she'd gone inside to rest more than an hour ago. Now Lacey heard the older woman crying and hastened her step, but then a reassuring male voice rumbled and the crying stopped.

Vito.

Of course, he'd come in to see his grandma first thing. He hadn't been home in over a year, and they'd always been close.

She'd just take a quick peek to make sure Nonna wasn't getting overexcited, and then leave them to their reunion.

Slowly, she strolled down the hall to the room she'd made up for Nonna D, keeping her ears open, giving them time. She surveyed the glossy wood floors with satisfaction. The place was coming along. She'd redo this wallpaper sometime, but the faded roses weren't half-bad for now. Gave the place its historical character.

She ran her hand along the long, thin table she'd just bought for the entryway, straightened her favorite, goofy ceramic rooster and a vase of flowers. Mr. Whiskers jumped up onto the table, and Lacey stopped to rub his face and ears, evoking a purr. "Where's the Missus, huh?" she cooed quietly. "Is she hiding?"

Hearing another weepy sniffle from Nonna D, Lacey quickened her step and stopped in the doorway of Nonna's room.

"My beautiful boy," Nonna was saying with a catch in her voice. "You were always the good-looking one."

Vito sat on the edge of the bed, looking distinctly

uncomfortable as Nonna sat up in bed to inspect his cheek and brush his hair back behind his ears.

She felt a quick defensiveness on Vito's behalf. Sure, the scars were noticeable. But to Lacey, they added to his rugged appeal.

Nonna saw her and her weathered face broke into a smile, her eyes sparkling behind large glasses. "There's my sweet girl. Come in and see my boy Vito."

"We talked already, Nonna." Vito was rubbing the back of his neck. "Lacey, I didn't realize you were taking care of my grandma to this extent. I'll take her home tomorrow."

"Oh, no!" Lacey said. "I'm so happy to do it!"

"I can't go home!" Nonna said at the same time.

"Why not?" Vito looked from Nonna to Lacey and back again.

"I need my nursing help," Nonna explained. "Lacey, here, is a wonderful nurse. She's practically saved my life!"

Lacey's cheeks burned. "I'm really a Certified Nursing Assistant, not a nurse," she explained. "And I haven't done anything special, just helped with medications and such." In truth, she knew she'd helped Nonna D'Angelo with the mental side as well as the physical, calming her anxiety and making sure she ate well, arranging some outings and visits so the woman didn't sink into the depression so common among people with her health issues.

"Medications? What's wrong?"

"It's my heart," Nonna started to explain.

Vito had the nerve to chuckle. "Oh, now, Nonna. You've been talking about your heart for twenty years, and you never needed a nurse before."

"Things are different now." The older woman's chin quivered.

He reached out and patted her arm. "You'll be fine."

Lacey drew in a breath. Should she intervene? Families were sometimes in denial about the seriousness of a beloved relative's health problems, and patients sometimes shielded their families from the truth.

"If you want to move your grandma, that's fine," she said, "but I'd recommend waiting a couple more weeks."

"That's right." Nonna looked relieved. "Lacey needs the money and I need the help."

Vito frowned. "Can we afford this?" He looked down at his grandma and seemed to realize that the woman was getting distressed. "Tell you what, Grandma, Lacey and I will talk about this and figure some things out. I won't leave without saying goodbye."

"All right, dear." She shot a concerned glance at Lacey.

She leaned down in the guise of straightening a pillow for Nonna. "I'll explain everything," she reassured her.

She led the way to the front room, out of earshot from Nonna D'Angelo. Then she turned to Vito, frowning. "You don't think I'm taking advantage of your grandma, do you?"

"No!" He reached for her, but when she took a step back, he crossed his arms instead. "I would never think that, Lacey. I know you. I just don't know if you've thought this through."

She restrained an eye roll. "You always did like to interfere when your help wasn't needed."

"Look, if this is about that talk we had years back…"
He waved a dismissive hand. "Let's just forget that."

She knew exactly what he meant. As soon as Vito
had found out Gerry had proposed, he'd come storm-
ing over to her house and pulled her out onto the front
porch to try and talk her out of it. "You were wrong,"
she said now.

"I wasn't wrong." When she opened her mouth to
protest, he held up a hand. "But I was wrong to interfere."

That wasn't exactly what she'd said, but whatever.

"But back to my grandma. I don't know what her
insurance is like, but I know it hardly ever covers in-
home nursing care. I'm living on limited means and
until I get back on my feet—"

"It's handled. It's fine."

He ran a hand through his thick, dark hair. "She's
always tended to be a hypochondriac—"

"A heart attack is nothing to take lightly."

"A *heart attack*?" Vito's jaw dropped. "Nonna had
a heart attack?"

His surprise was so genuine that her annoyance
about what she'd thought was neglect faded away.
"About two weeks ago. She didn't tell you?"

"No, she didn't tell me. Do you think I'd have stayed
away if I'd known?" His square jaw tightened. "Not a
word. How bad was it?"

Lacey spread her hands. "Look, I'm just a CNA.
You should definitely talk to her doctor."

"But from what you've seen, give me a guess."

Outside, she could hear people talking quietly.
Dishes rattled in the kitchen, the girls cleaning up.
She blew out a breath. "It was moderate severity. She

had some damage, and there are some restrictions on what she can do. Changes she needs to make."

"What kind of changes?" He thrust his hands in his pockets and paced. "I can't believe she had a heart attack and I didn't know. Why didn't you call me?"

"It's her business what she tells people."

His mouth twisted to one side. "C'mon, Lace."

"I'm serious. Patients have the right to confidentiality. I couldn't breach that. In fact," she said, stricken, "I probably shouldn't have told you even now."

"You're my friend. You can tell me as a friend. Now, what kind of changes? What does she need to do to get back on her feet?"

She perched on the arm of an overstuffed chair. "You can probably guess. It's a lot about diet. She needs to start a gentle exercise program. I have her walking around the block twice a day."

He stared. "Nonna's walking? Like, for exercise?"

"I know, right?" She smiled a little. "It wasn't easy to talk her into it. I make sure we have an interesting destination."

"How did you get so involved?"

She let her forehead sink down into her hand for just a second, then looked back up. Vito. He'd never take her seriously. He'd always been a big brother to her, and he always would be.

He held up a hand. "I'm not questioning it, Lacey. I'm grateful. And I feel awful having been out of the loop, not helping her. I've had lots of personal stuff going on, but that's no excuse."

His words flicked on a switch of interest in her, but she ignored it. "I worked her hall at the hospital, and since she knew me, we talked. She was worried about coming home alone, but she didn't want to bother you, and your brother's far away. I was looking to make a change, anyway, moving toward freelance home care so I could have time to finish renovating this place." She waved an arm toward the unfinished breakfast area, currently walled off with sheets of plastic.

"So you made a deal with her." He still sounded a little skeptical.

"Yes, if that's what you want to call it." She stood, full of restless energy, and paced over to the fireplace, rearranging the collection of colored glass bottles on the mantel. "She's had a lot of anxiety, which is common in people recovering from a heart attack. She's on several new medications, and one of them causes fatigue and dizziness. The social worker was going to insist on having her go to a nursing home for proper care, which she couldn't afford, so this was a good arrangement." She looked over at him, mentally daring him to question her.

He rubbed a hand over the back of his neck. "A nursing home. Wow."

"It wouldn't have suited her."

"For how long? How long do you think she'll need the extra care?"

Lacey shrugged, moved an amber bottle to better catch the sun. "I don't know. Usually people take a couple of months to get back up to speed. And your brother's happy to pay for as long as we need."

Vito's dark eyebrows shot up. "She told him and not me?"

"She said you'd find out soon enough, when you came back home."

"And he's paying for everything?"

"He felt bad, being so far away, and apparently he

begged her to let him help. Look, if you want to make a change in her care, I totally understand." It would mess up her own plans, of course; she'd given notice at the hospital only when she had this job to see her through, so if Nonna left, she'd have to apply for a part-time job right away. But Nonna was improving daily. If she had Vito with her, and he could focus on her needs, she'd probably be fine. A lot of her anxiety and depression stemmed from loneliness and fear.

Truth was, Lacey had found the older woman a hedge against her own loneliness, as her brother had gotten more and more involved in his wedding plans.

Now Buck and Gina and their dogs would be living in a little cottage on the other side of town. She'd see them a lot, but it wouldn't be the same as having Buck living here. "Whatever you decide," she said. "For now, we'd better go reassure your grandma, and then I need to attend to the rest of my guests."

Vito followed Lacey back into his grandmother's room, his mind reeling. Nonna had mostly raised him and his brother, Eugene, after their parents' accident, and she was one of the few family members he had left. More to the point, he was one of *her* only family members, and he should have been here for her.

Everyone treated him like he was made of glass, but the fact was, he was perfectly healthy on the inside. His surgeries had been a success, and his hearing loss was corrected with state-of-the-art hearing aids, courtesy of the VA.

He just *looked* bad.

And while the scars that slashed across his face, the worse ones on his chest, made it even more unlikely that he'd achieve his dream of marriage and a large family, he couldn't blame his bachelorhood entirely on the war. Women had always liked him, yes—as a friend. And nothing but a friend. He lacked the cool charisma that most women seemed to want in a boyfriend or husband.

Entering his grandmother's room, he pulled up a chair for Lacey, and then sat down on the edge of Nonna's bed, carefully, trying not to jolt her out of her light doze. He was newly conscious that she was pale, and thinner than she'd been. A glance around the attractive bedroom revealed a stash of pill bottles he hadn't noticed before.

Nonna's eyes fluttered open and she reached out.

He caught her hand in his. "Hey, how're you feeling?"

She pursed her lips and glared at Lacey. "You told him about my heart."

"Yes, I told him! Of course I told him!" Lacey's voice had a fond but scolding tone. "You should have let him know yourself, Nonna. I thought you had."

He squeezed his grandmother's hand. "Don't you know I would've dropped everything and come?"

Nonna made a disgusted noise. "That's exactly why I didn't tell you. You and your brother have your own lives to lead. And I was able to find a very good arrangement on my own." She smiled at Lacey.

"It *is* a good arrangement, and I'm glad for it." Vito glanced over at Lacey, who had gotten up to pour water into a small vase of flowers.

With its blue-patterned wallpaper, lamp-lit bedside table and a handmade quilt on the bed, the room was cozy. Through the door of the small private bathroom, he glimpsed handicapped-accessible rails and a shower seat.

Yes, this was a good situation for her. "Look, I want to take you back to the house, but we'll wait until you're a little better."

Nonna started to say something, and then broke off, picking restlessly at the blanket.

"I haven't even been over to see the place yet," he continued, making plans as he thought it through. "I just got into town. But I'll check it out, make sure you've got everything you need."

"About that, dear…" Nonna's voice sounded uncharacteristically subdued.

"I hope you don't mind, but I'm planning to live there with you for a while." He smiled. It was true comfort, knowing he could come back to Rescue River anytime and find a welcome, a place to stay and a home-cooked meal.

Lacey nodded approvingly, and for some reason it warmed Vito to see it.

"Neither one of us will be able to live there," Nonna said, her voice small.

Lacey's eyebrows rose in surprise, and he could feel the same expression on his own face. "What do you mean?"

"Now, don't be angry, either of you," she said, grasping his hand, "but I rented out the house."

"You *what?*"

"When did you do that?" Lacey sounded bewildered.

"We signed the papers yesterday when you were out grocery shopping," Nonna said, looking everywhere but at Vito and Lacey.

"Who'd you rent it to?" If it had just been finalized yesterday, surely everything could be revoked once the situation was explained. Lacey hadn't said anything about cognitive problems, but Nonna *was* in her early eighties. Maybe she wasn't thinking clearly.

Nonna smiled and clasped her hands together. "The most lovely migrant family," she said. "Three children and another on the way, and they're hoping to find a way to settle here. I gave them a good price, and they're going to keep the place up and do some repairs for me."

"Nonna…" Vito didn't know where to begin. He knew that this was the way things worked in his hometown—a lot of bartering, a lot of helping out those in need. "You aren't planning to stay here at the guesthouse indefinitely, right? How long of a lease did you sign?"

"Just a year." She folded her hands on top of her blanket and smiled.

"A year?" Not wanting to yell at his aged grandma, Vito stood and ran his hands through his hair. "Either you're going to have to revoke it, or I'm going to have to find another place for you and me to live." Never mind how he'd afford the rent. Or the fact that he'd named Nonna's house as his permanent residence in all the social services paperwork.

"No, dear. I have it all figured out." She took Lacey's hand in hers, and then reached toward him with her other hand. Once she had ahold of each of them, she smiled from one to the other. "Vito, if Lacey agrees, you can stay here."

No. She wasn't thinking clearly. "Nonna, that's not going to work. Lacey made this arrangement with you, not with me." And certainly not with the other guest he had in tow. No way could Lacey find out the truth about Charlie.

"But Lacey was thinking of getting another boarder for this period while she's remodeling. It's hard to find the right one, because of all the noise." Lacey started to speak, but Nonna held up a hand. "The noise doesn't bother me. I can just turn down my hearing aid."

Vito knew what was coming and he felt his face heat. "Nonna..."

"Vito's perfect," she said, looking at Lacey, "because he can do the same thing."

Lacey's eyebrows lifted as she looked at him.

No point in trying to hide his less visible disability now. "It's true," he said, brushing back his hair to show his behind-the-ear hearing aids. "But that doesn't mean you have to take us in." In fact, staying here was the last thing that would work for him.

He'd promised Gerry he'd take care of his son, conceived during the affair Gerry had while married to Lacey. And he'd promised to keep Charlie's parentage a secret from Lacey.

He was glad he could help his friend, sinner though Gerry had been. Charlie needed a reliable father figure, and Lacey needed to maintain her illusions about her husband. It would serve no purpose for her to find out the truth now; it would only hurt her.

Lacey frowned. "I *was* looking to take in another boarder. I was thinking of maybe somebody who worked the three-to-eleven shift at the pretzel factory. They could come home and sleep, and they wouldn't be bothered by my working on the house at all hours."

"That makes sense," he said, relieved. "That would be better."

"But the thing is," she said slowly, "I haven't found anyone, even though I've been advertising for a couple of weeks. If you wanted to…"

Anxiety clawed at him from inside. How was he supposed to handle this? He could throttle Gerry for putting him into this situation. "I… There are some complications. I need to give this some thought." He knew he was being cryptic, but he needed time to figure it all out.

Unfortunately, Nonna wasn't one to accept anything cryptic from her grandchildren. "What complications? What's going on?"

Vito stood, then sat back down again. Nonna was going to have to know about Charlie soon enough. Lacey, too, along with everyone else in town. It would seem weirder if he tried to hide it now. "The thing is," he said, "I'm not alone. I have someone with me."

"Girlfriend? Wife?" Lacey sounded extremely curious.

Nonna, on the other hand, looked disappointed. "You would never get married without letting your *nonna* know," she said, reaching up to pinch his cheek, and then pulling her hand back, looking apologetic. It took him a minute to realize that she'd hesitated because of his scars.

"One of my finished rooms is a double," Lacey said thoughtfully. "But I don't know what your…friend… would think of the mess and the noise."

This was going off the rails. "It's not a girlfriend or wife," he said.

"Then who?" Nonna smacked his arm in a way that reminded him of when he'd been small and misbehaving. "If not a woman, then who?"

Vito drew in a breath. "Actually," he said, "I've recently become certified as a foster parent."

Both women stared at him with wide, surprised eyes.

"So I'd be bringing along my eight-year-old foster son."

He was saved from further explanation by a crash, followed by the sound of shattering glass and running feet.

Two

Lacey raced out of Nonna's bedroom, leaving Vito to reassure the older woman. A quick scan of the hall revealed the breakage: her ceramic rooster lay in pieces on the floor.

One of the kids, probably; they were all sugared up on wedding cake and running around. She hurried to get a broom and dustpan, not wanting any of the remaining wedding guests to injure themselves. As she dropped the colorful pieces into the trash, she felt a moment's regret.

More important than the untimely demise of her admittedly tacky rooster, she wondered about Vito fostering a child. That, she hadn't expected.

"Miss Lacey!" It was little Mindy, Sam Hinton's daughter. "I saw who did that!"

"Did you? Stay back," she warned as she checked the area for any remaining ceramic pieces.

"Yes," Mindy said, "and he's hiding under the front porch right now!"

Behind her, Lacey heard Vito coming out of Nonna's bedroom, then pausing to talk some more, and a suspicion of who the young criminal might be came over her. "I'll go talk to him," she said. "It wasn't Xavier, was it?"

"No. It was a kid I don't know. Is he going to get in trouble?"

"I don't think so, honey. Not too much trouble, anyway. Why don't you go tell your dad what happened?"

"Yeah! He's gotta know!" As Mindy rushed off to her important task, Lacey walked out of the house and stood on the porch, looking around. The remaining guests were in the side yard, talking and laughing, so no one seemed to notice her.

She went down the steps and around to the side of the house where there was an opening in the lattice-work; she knew because she'd had to crawl under there when she'd first found Mrs. Whiskers, hiding with a couple of kittens. When she squatted down, she heard a little sniffling sound that touched her heart. Moving aside the branches of a lilac bush, breathing in the sweet fragrance of the fading purple flowers, she spoke into the darkness. "It's okay. I didn't like that rooster much, anyway."

There was silence, and then a stirring, but no voice. From the other side of the yard, she could hear conversations and laughter. But this shaded spot felt private.

"I remember one time I broke my grandma's favorite lamp," she said conversationally, settling into a sitting position on the cool grass. "I ran and hid in an apple tree."

"Did they find you?" a boy's voice asked. Not a familiar voice. Since she knew every kid at the wedding, her suspicion that the culprit was Vito's new foster son increased. "Yes, they found me. My brother told them where I was."

"Did you get in trouble?"

"I sure did." She remembered her grandma's reprimand, her father chiming in, her own teary apology.

"Did they hit you?" the boy asked, his voice low.

The plaintive question squeezed Lacey's heart. "No, I just got scolded a lot. And I had to give my grandma my allowance to help pay for a new lamp."

"I don't get an allowance. Did you…" There was a pause, a sniffle. "Did you have to go live somewhere else after that?"

Lacey's eyes widened as she put it all together. Vito had said he'd *recently* become certified as a foster parent. So this must be a new arrangement. It would make all the sense in the world that a boy who'd just been placed with a new foster father would feel insecure about whether he'd be allowed to stay.

But why had Vito, a single man with issues of his own, taken on this new challenge? "No, I didn't have to go live somewhere else," she said firmly, "and what's more, no kind adult would send a kid away for breaking a silly old lamp. Or a silly old rooster, either."

Branches rustled behind her, and then Vito came around the edge of the bushes. "There you are! What happened? Is everything okay?"

She pointed toward the latticed area where the boy was hiding, giving Vito a meaningful look. "I think the person who *accidentally*—" she emphasized the word "—broke the rooster is worried he'll get sent away."

"What?" Vito's thick dark eyebrows came down as understanding dawned in his eyes. He squatted beside her. "Charlie, is that you? Kids don't get sent away for stuff like that."

There was another shuffling under the porch, and then a head came into view. Messy, light brown hair, a sprinkling of freckles, worried-looking eyes. "But they might get sent away if they were keeping their dad from having a place to live."

Oh. The boy must have heard Vito say he couldn't live here because of having a foster son.

"We'll find a place to live," Vito said. "Come on out."

The boy looked at him steadily and didn't move.

"Charlie! I mean it!"

Lacey put a hand on Vito's arm. "Hey, Charlie," she said softly. "I grew up next door to this guy. I was three years younger and a lot smaller, and I did some annoying things. And he never, ever hit me." She felt Vito's arm tense beneath hers and squeezed. "And he wouldn't hurt you, either. Right, Vito?" She looked over at him.

His mouth twisted. "That's right." He went forward on one knee and held out a hand to the boy. "Come on out. We talked about this. Remember, I look meaner than I really am."

The boy hesitated, then crawled out without taking Vito's hand. Instead, he scuttled over to the other side of Lacey and crouched.

Vito drew in a breath and blew it out. His brow furrowed. "You're going to need to apologize to Miss Lacey, here, and then we'll find out how you can make up for what you did."

The boy wrapped his arms around upraised knees. A tear leaked out and he backhanded it away. "I can't make it up. Don't have any money."

"I might have some chores you could do," Lacey said, easing backward so she wasn't directly between Charlie and Vito. "Especially if you and your foster dad are going to be living here." As soon as she said it, she regretted the words. "Or living nearby," she amended hastily.

She liked Vito, always had. And she adored his grandmother, who clearly wanted her family gathered around her. But Lacey had been planning to have the next few months as a quiet, calm oasis before opening her guesthouse. She still had healing to do.

Having Vito and this boy here wasn't conducive to quiet serenity. On the other hand, young Charlie seemed to have thrown himself on her for protection, and that touched her.

"Can we live here? Really?" The boy jumped up and started hopping from one foot to the next. "'Cause this place is cool! You have a tire swing! And there's a basketball hoop right across the street!"

Vito stood, looking at her quizzically. "The grownups will be doing some talking," he said firmly. "For tonight, we're staying out at the motel like we planned. But before we go back there, I want you to apologize."

The boy looked at Lacey, then away, digging the toe of a well-worn sneaker into the dirt. "I'm real sorry I broke your rooster. It was an accident."

She nodded, getting to her feet. "That's all right. I think I can find another one kind of like it."

Her own soft feelings surprised her. Generally, she avoided little ones, especially babies; they were a reminder of all she couldn't have.

But this boy touched her heart. Maybe it was because his reaction to breaking the rooster was so similar to her own reaction when she'd broken the lamp. *Hide. Don't let the grown-ups know, because you never know what disaster will happen when grown-ups get upset.* She'd been fortunate, found by her grandma and father instead of her mom. Come to think of it, her brother had probably gone to them on purpose. He'd wanted her to get in trouble, but not from their volatile mother.

Lacey was beyond all that now, at least she thought so, but she still identified with the feeling of accidentally causing disasters and facing out-of-proportion consequences.

"And the other question you have to answer," Vito said, putting an arm around Charlie's shoulders lightly, ignoring the boy's automatic wince, "is how you got down here when you were supposed to be staying with Valencia."

Lacey moved to stand by Charlie, and her presence seemed to relax him.

"I asked her if we could take a walk," Charlie explained, a defensive tone coming into his voice. "When we came by here, she started talking to the people and I came inside. I just wanted to look around."

"You're not to do things like that without permission." Vito pinched the bridge of his nose. "You have another apology to make, to Valencia. And no dessert after dinner tonight."

The boy's lower lip came out, and Lacey felt the absurd impulse to slip him an extra piece of wedding cake.

An accented voice called from the other side of the yard. "Charlie! Charlie!"

"You run and tell Miss Valencia you're sorry you didn't stay close to her. And then wait for me on the porch."

As the boy ran toward the babysitter's anxious voice, Lacey looked up at Vito. "In over your head?"

"Totally." He blew out a breath. "What do I know about raising kids?"

"How'd you get into it, anyway?"

"It's complicated." He looked away, then back at her. "Listen, don't feel pressured into having us stay at your guesthouse. I don't expect that, no matter what Nonna says. And you can see that we'd be a handful."

She looked into his warm brown eyes. "I *can* see that. And I honestly don't know if it would work. But what are you going to do if you can't stay here?"

"That's the million-dollar question." He rubbed his chin. "We'll figure something out."

"Let me sleep on it. It's been a crazy day."

"Of course it has, and I'm sorry to add to that." They headed toward the rest of the guests, and he put an arm around her shoulders and squeezed. It was an innocent gesture, a friendly gesture, the same thing he'd done with Charlie.

But for some reason, it disconcerted her now, and she stepped away.

Something flashed in Vito's eyes and he cleared his throat. "Look, tomorrow Charlie has a visit with his birth mom up in Raystown. Let me take you to lunch. We can talk about Nonna and the possibility of Charlie and me staying here. Or more likely, how to break it to Nonna that we *won't* be staying here."

She'd planned to spend the next afternoon cleaning up and recovering from the wedding. "That'll work."

"The Chatterbox? Noon?" His voice was strictly businesslike.

"Where else?" She wondered why he'd gone chilly on her. "I'm looking forward to catching up."

And she was. Sort of.

The next morning, Vito pulled his truck into the parking lot at the Supervised Visitation Center and glanced into the backseat of the extended cab. Yes, a storm was brewing.

"Why do I have to do this?" Charlie mumbled. "Am I going back to live with her?"

"No." He twisted farther around to get more comfortable. "We talked about this. Your mom loves you, but she can't do a good job taking care of you, and you need to have a forever home." He'd practically memorized the words from the foster parenting handbook, and it was a good thing. Because apparently, Charlie needed to hear them a bunch of times.

"Then why do I have to visit? I wanted to play basketball with Xavier, that kid from the wedding yesterday. He said maybe I could come over."

Vito pulled up another memorized phrase and forced cheer into his voice. "It's important for you to have a relationship with your mom. Important for you and for her."

The whole situation was awful for a kid, and Krystal, Charlie's mother, wasn't easy to deal with. She'd neglected Charlie, and worse, exposed him to danger—mostly from her poorly chosen boyfriends—way too many times.

Someone who hurt a kid ought to be in prison, in

Vito's mind, at the very least. But he had to keep reminding himself that Krystal was sick.

"You'll have fun with your mom," he said. "I think you guys are going to go out for lunch in a little while and maybe over to the lake afterward."

"That doesn't sound fun." Charlie crossed his arms and looked out the window, making no move to get out of the car.

Vito looked that way, too, and saw Krystal getting out of the passenger side of a late-model SUV. Maybe things were looking up for her. He'd only met her a few times, but she'd been driving a car noticeably on its last legs.

The SUV roared off, passing them, with a balding, bearded, forty-something guy at the wheel. Vito looked back at Charlie in time to see the boy cringe. "What's wrong, buddy?" he asked. "Do you know that guy?"

Charlie nodded but didn't say anything.

Krystal strolled over to the back stoop of the Center, smoking a cigarette. Vito wished for a similarly easy way to calm his nerves.

He wished he knew how to be a father. He'd only had Charlie full-time for a month, most of which they'd spent in Cleveland, closing down Vito's previous life, getting ready to move home. Charlie had been well and truly welcomed by the Cleveland branch of Vito's family, though everyone had agreed on waiting to tell Nonna about Charlie until the foster care situation was definite. If everything went well, he'd be able to adopt Charlie after another six months and be the boy's permanent, real father.

Learning how to parent well would take a lifetime. Vito got out of the car. The small, wire-supported trees around the brand-new building were trying their best, sporting a few green leaves. A robin hopped along the bare ground, poking for worms, and more birds chirped overhead. It was a nice summer day, and Vito was half tempted to get back in the truck and drive away, take Charlie to the lake himself.

But that wasn't the agreement he'd made. He opened the passenger door and Charlie got out. His glance in his mother's direction was urgent and hungry.

Of course. This visit was important. No matter what parents did, kids always wanted to love them.

Vito forced a spring into his step as they approached the building and Krystal. "Hey," he greeted her, and tried the door.

"It's locked, genius." Krystal drew harder on her cigarette. She hadn't glanced at or touched Charlie, who'd stopped a few steps short of the little porch.

Looking at the two of them, Vito's heart about broke. He considered his big, extended family up in Cleveland, the hugs, the cheek pinches, the loud greetings. He had it good, always had. He squatted beside Charlie and cast about for conversation. "Charlie's been doing great," he said to Krystal, not that she'd asked. "Going to sign him up for summer softball."

"Nice for you. I never could afford it." She looked at Charlie then, and her face softened. "Hey, kid. You got tall in the past couple months."

Vito was so close to Charlie that he could sense the boy's urge to run to his mom as well as the fear that pinned him to Vito's side.

The fear worried him.

But Charlie would be safe. This was a supervised visit, if the caseworker ever got here.

"You were Gerry's buddy," Krystal said suddenly. "Did you know about me, or did he just talk about *her*?"

What was Vito supposed to say to that, especially in front of Charlie? The boy needed to think highly of his father, to remember that he'd died a hero's death, not that he'd lived a terribly flawed life. "It's better we focus on now," he said to Krystal, nodding his head sideways, subtly, at Charlie.

She snorted, but dropped the subject, turning away to respond to her buzzing phone.

Focus on now. He needed to take his own advice. Except he had to think about the future and make plans, to consider the possibility of him and Charlie staying with the *her*—Lacey—that Krystal was mad about. Which would be a really rotten idea, now that the ramifications of it all came to him.

He wasn't sure how much Krystal knew about Lacey and Gerry, what kind of promises Gerry might have made to her. From what he'd been able to figure out, Krystal hadn't known that Gerry was married, at least not at first. No wonder she was angry. Problem was, she'd likely pass that anger on to Charlie. She didn't seem like a person who had a very good filter.

And if she talked to Charlie about Lacey, and Charlie was living at Lacey's boardinghouse, the boy could get all mixed up inside.

If Gerry were still alive, Vito would strangle him. The jerk hadn't been married to Lacey for a year before he'd started stepping out on her.

Krystal put her phone away, lit another cigarette and sat down on the edge of the stoop. She beckoned to Charlie. "Come on, sit by me. You scared?"

Charlie hesitated, then walked over and sat gingerly beside her. When she put her arm around him, though, he turned into her and hugged her suddenly and hard, and grief tightened her face.

Vito stepped back to give them some space and covertly studied Krystal. He didn't understand Gerry. The man had had Lacey as a wife—gorgeous, sweet Lacey—and he'd cheated on her with Krystal. Who, admittedly, had a stellar figure and long black hair. She'd probably been beautiful back then. But now the hair was disheveled. Her eyes were heavy-lidded, her skin pitted with some kind of scars. Vito wasn't sure what all she was addicted to, but the drugs had obviously taken their toll.

It looked like she'd stayed sober to visit with Charlie today, knowing she'd have to submit to a drug test. Maybe she'd had to stay clean a couple of days. That would put any addict into a bad mood.

Even before she'd been an addict, Krystal couldn't have compared to Lacey.

A battered subcompact pulled into the parking lot and jolted to a halt, its muffler obviously failing. The driver-side door flew open and the short, curly-haired caseworker got out. After pulling an overstuffed briefcase and a couple of bags from her car, she bustled over to them.

"Sorry I'm late! These Sunday visits are crazy. Maybe we can switch to Mondays or Tuesdays?" She was fumbling for the key as she spoke. "Come on in, guys! Thanks so much, Vito!"

"Charlie." Vito got the boy's attention, held his eyes. "I'll be back at three, okay?"

Relief shone on Charlie's face. He ran to Vito, gave

him a short hug and whispered into his ear: "Come back for sure, okay?"

"You got it, buddy." Vito's voice choked up a little bit.

Charlie let go and looked at Vito. Then his eyes narrowed and he grinned purposefully. "And can we stay at that place instead of the motel?" he whispered. "With the cat and the nice lady?"

Vito knew manipulation when he saw it, but he also knew the boy needed both security and honesty.

"What's he begging for now?" Krystal grinned as she flicked her cigarette butt into the bare soil beside the building. "I recognize that look."

"I'm starting to recognize it, too," Vito said, meeting Krystal's eyes. Some kind of understanding arced between them, and he felt a moment of kinship and sorrow for the woman who'd given birth to Charlie but wouldn't get to raise him.

"Well, can we?" Charlie asked.

"We'll see. No promises." Vito squeezed the boy's shoulder. "You be good, and I'll see you right here at three o'clock."

In reality, he wished he could just sweep the boy up and take him home, and not just to protect him from an awkward day with his mom. Vito wasn't looking forward to the lunch date—no, *not* a date—he was facing in only a few hours. Whatever he and Lacey decided, it was going to make someone unhappy.

Three

"They left the two of us in charge of the nursery? Are they crazy?" Lacey's friend Susan put her purse up on a shelf and came over to where Lacey stood beside a crib, trying to coax a baby to sleep.

"I'm just glad it's you working with me." Lacey picked up the baby, who'd started to fuss, and swayed gently. "You won't freak out if I freak out."

Working in the church nursery was Lacey's counselor's idea, a way to help Lacey deal with her miscarriage and subsequent infertility. She needed to desensitize herself, find ways to be around babies without getting upset by them, especially if she was going to open a family-friendly guesthouse and make a success of it.

The desensitization had started accidentally, when Gina Patterson had showed up in town earlier this year with her son, Bobby, just ten months old at the time. With nowhere else to turn, she'd spent the early spring at the guesthouse, in the process falling in love with Lacey's brother, Buck. Being around little Bobby had made Lacey miserable at first, but she was learning. More than that, she was motivated; she wanted to serve others and get out of her own pain, build a well-rounded life for herself.

Which included being around babies. "I'm here to work through my issues," she told Susan, "but why are *you* here?"

Susan's tawny skin went pink. "Sam and I decided it would be a good idea for me to get comfortable with babies. I used to be terrified of even touching them, but... I guess I'd better learn."

Something in Susan's tone made Lacey take notice, and she mentally reviewed what Susan had just said. Then she stared at her friend. "Wait a minute. Are you expecting? Already?"

Susan looked down at the floor, and then met Lacey's eyes. "Yeah. We just found out."

Selfish tears sprang to Lacey's eyes as she looked down at the infant she held, feeling its weight in her arms. Something she'd never experience for herself, with her own child. A joy that Susan and many of Lacey's other friends would find effortlessly.

Susan would be a part of the circle of happy young mothers in town. Lacey wouldn't, not ever.

"I'm so sorry to cause you pain. News like this must be hard for you to hear."

Susan's kind words jolted Lacey out of her own self-centered heartache. Finding out you were having a baby was one of the most joyous times of a woman's life. She remembered when the two pink lines had shown up on her own pregnancy test. Remembered her video call to Gerry. She'd shown the test to him, and they'd both cried tears of joy.

Susan deserved to have that joy, too. She shouldn't have to focus on her friend's losses.

Lacey lifted the baby to her shoulder so she could reach out and put an arm around Susan. "It does hurt a little—I'm not going to lie. But what kind of friend would I be not to celebrate with you? I'm thrilled!"

"You're the best, Lace." Susan wrapped her arms around Lacey, the baby in between them, and Lacey let herself cry just a little more. Susan understood. She'd stayed a year at Lacey's guesthouse before the remodeling, the horrible year when Lacey had lost both Gerry and the baby. Susan had been an incredible comfort.

"Anyway," Susan added, "I'm going to need your help to fit in with the perfect mothers of Rescue River. You know I have a knack for saying the wrong thing."

"You'll be fine." And it was true. Susan was outspoken and blunt, but she gave everything she had to the kids she taught at the local elementary school, and people here loved her for it. "How's Sam handling the news?"

"Making a million plans and bossing me around, of course." But Susan smiled as she said it, and for just a moment, Lacey felt even more jealous of the happy-married-woman smile on Susan's face than of the tiny, growing baby in her belly.

"Hey, guys, can I leave Bobby here for a little while?" Lou Ann Miller, who was taking care of Gina's baby while she and Buck enjoyed a honeymoon at the shore, stood at the half door. "I want to go to adult Sunday school, but there's no way he'll sit through our book discussion."

"Sure." Lacey thrust the infant she'd been holding into Susan's arms. "Just hold her head steady. Yeah, like that." She walked over to the door and opened it. "Come on in, Bobby!"

"Laaasss," he said, walking right into her leg and hugging it. "Laaasss."

Lacey's heart warmed, and she reached down to pick Bobby up. "He'll be fine. Take your time," she said to Lou Ann. "Wave bye-bye to Miss Lou Ann, okay?"

Two more toddlers got dropped off, and then a diaper needed changing. Little Emmie Farmingham, who was almost three, twirled to show Lacey and Susan her new summer dress, patterned with garden vegetables and sporting a carrot for a pocket. Then she proceeded to pull the dress off.

Once they'd gotten Emmie dressed again, the infant sleeping and the other two toddlers playing side by side with plastic blocks, Susan and Lacey settled down into the tiny chairs around the low table. "Babies are great, I guess," Susan said doubtfully, "but I have to say, I like bigger kids better. I wish one could just land in my lap at age five, like Mindy did."

"Not me." Lacey looked over at the toddlers, another surge of regret piercing her heart. "I've always loved the little ones."

"I know you have." Susan's voice was gentle. "Hey, want to come over and have lunch with us after this? I think Sam's grilling. You could bring your swimsuit."

"You're sweet." The thought of lounging by Sam and Susan's pool was appealing. And Susan was a great friend; she'd stand by Lacey even as she was going through this huge transition of having a child. She wouldn't abandon Lacey, and that mattered.

Lacey shook her head with real disappointment. "Can't. I'm meeting Vito for lunch."

"Oh, *Vito*." Susan punched her arm, gently. "Is this a date?"

"It's not like that. We're old friends."

Susan ignored her words. "You should see where it leads. He seems like a great guy, from what I saw of him at the end of the reception. Good-looking, too. Even with the scars." Susan's hand flew to her mouth. "I shouldn't say things like that, should I?"

"Probably not." Lacey rolled her eyes at her friend, pretending exasperation. "But it's okay. You can't help but notice his scars. Anyway, we're just going to talk about this crazy idea his grandma dreamed up." She explained how Nonna had unexpectedly rented out her own house, and how Vito was newly a foster father. "Apparently, Vito had no idea that was her plan. He was counting on bringing his foster son, Charlie, to live in Nonna's big house out in the country. I actually got the feeling Nonna had kept it a secret on purpose, to make sure Vito ended up staying at the guesthouse."

"But that would be perfect!" Susan clapped her hands. "Vito could be with his *nonna*, and Charlie could get a sense of family, and they'd be right in town to get, like, reintegrated into the community."

"Yes, but—"

"And you wanted someone else to room in, right? He'd pay rent, which would help with your expenses. He and Charlie could have separate rooms, or those two connecting ones upstairs."

Lacey's response was cut off by the sound of crashing blocks and a wail, and they got busy playing with the babies. The subject of Vito moving into the guesthouse didn't come up again, but Lacey couldn't stop thinking about it.

Susan seemed to think it was a great idea, and Nonna had talked to Lacey over breakfast about how wonderful it would be to have Vito there and to get to know the newest member of the family. Her eyes had sparkled when she said that, and few enough things had brought a sparkle to Nonna's eyes since the heart attack.

There were all kinds of reasons to embrace the idea of Vito and Charlie moving in, but Lacey still felt uneasy about it.

She couldn't begin to articulate why, even to herself.

At lunchtime, Vito stood outside the Chatterbox Café, looking up at the town's outdoor clock, which clearly showed it was only eleven forty-five. He was early. Why had he come so early?

He loosened the itchy collar of his new button-down shirt. He shouldn't have worn a brand-new shirt today, should have at least washed it first, except that he was living out of a suitcase and he'd been rushing to get Charlie ready to go and there hadn't been the chance.

He could have just worn an old, comfortable shirt, but the fact was, he was trying to look good. Which was obviously a losing battle.

It wasn't about Lacey. It was about the fact that he'd probably see other people he knew here at the Chatterbox, and he needed to present a professional image. He had good benefits from the VA—they were paying for his online degree—but a man needed to work, and Vito would be looking for a part-time job just as soon as he'd found a place to live and gotten Charlie settled. Maybe something with kids, since he was looking to become a teacher.

No, it wasn't about Lacey. He'd had some feelings

for her once, but he'd turned those off when she'd married, of course. He'd been over her for years.

"Vito!" Lacey approached, a summery yellow dress swirling around her legs, the wind blowing her short hair into messiness.

She looked so beautiful that, for a moment, he couldn't breathe.

He crooked his arm for her to take it, an automatic gesture he'd learned at his *nonna's* knee. The way a gentleman treated a lady. And then he remembered how she'd stepped away when he'd done the Italian thing and thrown an arm around her yesterday. He put his arm back at his side.

People are disgusted by your scars, he reminded himself. *And she hasn't seen the half of them.*

As they turned toward the café—Vito carefully *not* touching her—he caught a whiff of something lemony and wondered if it was her shampoo, or if she'd worn perfume.

Inside, everything was familiar: the smell of meat loaf and fries, the red vinyl booths and vintage tables trimmed with aluminum, the sight of people he'd known since childhood. Even the counter waitress, Nora Jean, had been here since he was a kid and called a greeting.

"Sit anywhere, you two. Lindy'll wait on you, but I'm coming over to say hello just as soon as these guys give me a break." She waved at her full counter.

Dion Coleman, the police chief, swiveled in his chair and stood to pound Vito on the back. "I'm glad to see your ugly mug," he joked. Which didn't feel awkward, because it was the exact same thing Dion had always said when Vito came home, even before his injuries.

"Police business has been slow these past months, but with you home, it's sure to pick up."

Vito shook the man's hand with genuine pleasure. "I'll see what I can do about knocking down some mailboxes and shooting up signs, just to give you something to do. You're getting soft." He nodded down at Dion's flat belly and then at the grilled chicken salad on the counter in front of him. "Eating too much. Just like a cop."

"You never change." Dion was laughing as he sat back down. "Give me a call, you hear? We have some catching up to do."

Lacey had headed toward one of the few empty booths at the back of the café, and as he followed her it seemed to Vito that conversation stopped, then rose again when he'd passed. He rubbed a hand across his face, feeling the uneven ridges of his scars.

As soon as they sat down, they were mobbed. The young waitress could barely squeeze in to take their order. Everyone, friend or acquaintance, stopped by to say hello. They wanted to know where he was staying, how long he'd be in town, where he was stationed. Explaining that he wasn't in the army anymore felt embarrassing, since he'd always intended it to be his life's work. More embarrassing were the sympathetic nods and arm pats. People felt sorry for him.

But he kept it upbeat and answered questions patiently. Once people knew his story, they'd settle down some. And maybe someone would think of him when a job opening came up, so he made sure to let everyone know he was looking.

After people had drifted back to their tables and they'd managed to eat some of their lunch, Lacey wiped her mouth and smiled at him. "That got a little crazy. Are you wishing we'd gone somewhere else?"

He swallowed his massive bite of cheeseburger and shook his head. "Best to get it over fast. Let people get a good look."

She took a sip of soda. "You think they all came over to look at your scars?"

"That, and find out the latest news. But mostly to see how bad the damage is, up close and personal." His support group at the VA had warned him about people's reactions, how they might not be able to see anything but his scars at first.

"They're not looking at your scars in a bad way," Lacey said, frowning. "They're grateful for your service."

Of course, that was what most of the people who'd greeted them had said. And they weren't lying. It was just that initial cringe that got to him. He wasn't used to scaring people just by the way he looked.

His friend with severe facial burns had told Vito that you never really got used to it. "Older people do better, but young people like pretty," he'd said. "Makes it a challenge to get a date."

The waitress refilled his coffee cup and headed to a booth across the way. Vito gestured toward her. "You can't tell me someone like that, someone who doesn't know me, isn't disgusted when she first sees me."

Lacey looked at him for a long moment, her brown eyes steady. "Look over there," she said, pointing to a twenty-something man in an up-to-date wheelchair, sitting at a table with an older woman. "That's our waitress's brother," she said. "He served, too."

Vito blinked and looked more closely, seeing how

the man's head lolled to one side, held up by a special support. He wore a hoodie and sweats, and as Vito watched, the older woman put a bite of something into his mouth.

"Wounded in service?"

Lacey nodded. "I think he was a Marine."

"Is a Marine," Vito corrected. "And I'm sorry. You're right. I need to get out of my own head. I'm more fortunate than a lot of guys." He met her eyes. "Gerry included, and I'm a jerk to focus on myself."

She shrugged. "We all do that sometimes."

Had Lacey always had this steady maturity? He couldn't help but remember her as a younger girl, pestering him and her brother when they'd wanted to go out and do something fun. And he remembered how flightily she'd fallen for Gerry, swept away by love and unable to listen to anyone's warnings.

Now though, there was real thoughtfulness to her. She was quieter than she'd been, and more assertive.

He liked that. Liked a woman who'd call him on his dumb mistakes.

And he didn't need to be thinking about how much he liked the new Lacey. Best to get to the real reason for their lunch. "So, I was looking into options for Charlie and me," he said. "I talked to the family Nonna rented her house to."

"And? Did you ask if they'd let her out of the contract?"

"I couldn't even bring it up." He lifted his hands, shrugging. "They're thrilled with the house and the price Nonna gave them, and they need the space. And she's pregnant out to here." He held a hand in front of his stomach.

"Well, look who's back in town!" Old Mr. Love from the hardware store, who had to be in his eighties, stopped by their table and patted his shoulder. "I'd recognize that voice anywhere!"

Vito stood and greeted the man, and then looked at the gray-haired woman with him. "Miss Minnie Falcon? Is that you?"

"That's right, young man. You'd better not forget your old Sunday school teacher."

"I couldn't ever forget." He took her hand, gently. Unlike some of the other kids in Sunday school, he'd actually appreciated Miss Minnie's knowledge of the Old and New Testament, and the way she brought the stories to life, infusing them with a sense of biblical history.

Mr. Love was leaning toward Lacey. "I was hoping you'd find romance." His voice, meant to be low, carried clearly to Vito and Miss Minnie. "Now that Buck's out of your hair, it's your turn, young lady." He nodded toward Vito, raising an eyebrow.

"Harold!" Miss Minnie scolded. "Don't make assumptions. Come on. Let's get that corner table before someone else takes it." She patted Vito's arm. "It was nice to see you. Don't be a stranger. We like visitors over at the Senior Towers." She turned and headed across the restaurant at a brisk pace, pushing her wheeled walker.

"When a lady talks, you listen." Mr. Love gave Vito an apologetic shrug as he turned and followed Miss Minnie, putting a hand on her shoulder.

After they were out of earshot, Vito lifted an eyebrow at Lacey. "They're a couple?"

"It's anybody's guess. They both say they're just friends, but tongues are wagging. It *is* Rescue River."

"Gossip central," he agreed, sipping coffee.

"And speaking of wagging tongues," she said, "imagine what people will assume about us if you come and live in the guesthouse. Just like Mr. Love assumed when he saw us together here. They'll think *we're* a couple. And I'm not comfortable with that."

"I understand." He looked down at his hands, traced a scar that peeked out from his shirt cuff. "I'm not exactly a blue-ribbon bronco."

"Vito!" She sounded exasperated. "You haven't changed a bit since you had to try on six different shirts for the homecoming dance."

The memory made him chuckle. He'd gotten her to sit on the porch and judge while he tried on shirt after shirt, running back to his room to change each time she'd nixed his selection.

Little did she know that Buck had begged him to keep her busy while he tried to steal a few kisses from cheerleader Tiffany Townsend, ostensibly at their house for help with homework.

"That was a long time ago," he said now. "And the truth is, I *have* changed."

She rolled her eyes. "You're still good-looking, okay? Women don't mind scars." Then she pressed her lips together as her cheeks grew pink.

His heart rate accelerated, just a little. Why was she blushing? Did *she* think he was good-looking?

But of course, she hadn't seen the worst of his scars.

And even if there *was* a little spark between them, it couldn't go anywhere. Because he was living with a secret he couldn't let her discover.

"Look," she said, and then took a big gulp of soda. "Getting back to the idea of you and Charlie staying at the guesthouse. I'd be willing to consider it, for Nonna's sake, but…I'm trying to build a rich, full life as a single person, see, and I don't want everyone asking me questions or trying to match us up. I'm just getting over being Lacey, the pitiful widow. And now, if I have this good-looking man living in my guesthouse…" A flush crept up her cheeks again and she dropped her head, propping her forehead on her hand. "I'm just digging myself in deeper here, huh?"

She *did* think he was good-looking. All of a sudden, other people's curious stares didn't bother him half as much.

"Can I get you anything else?" The perky waitress was back, looking at Lacey with curiosity. "You okay, Lacey?"

"I need something chocolate," she said, looking up at the waitress but avoiding Vito's eyes.

"Right away! I totally understand!"

Vito didn't get women's obsession with chocolate, but he respected it. He waited until the server had brought Lacey a big slice of chocolate cream pie before blundering forward with their meeting's purpose. "I have an appointment tonight to talk to a woman who might want to rent me a couple of rooms in her farmhouse, out past the dog rescue. And there's the top floor of a house available over in Eastley."

"That's good, I guess." She toyed with the whipped cream on her pie. "But Nonna won't like having you so far away. And Charlie could make more friends in town, right?"

"He really took a shine to the place and to you, it's true."

"And Nonna wants you to live there. She pulled out all the stops at breakfast, trying to talk me into it again."

"She phoned me, too."

Lacey was absently fingering the chain around her neck, and when he looked more closely, he saw what hung on it.

A man's wedding ring. Undoubtedly Gerry's.

He wasn't worth it, Lace.

A shapely blonde in a tight-fitting dress approached their table. Tiffany Townsend. "Well, Vito D'Angelo. Aren't *you* a sight for sore eyes."

He snorted. "No." And then he thought about what Lacey had said: *Women don't mind scars.* And nobody, even a less-than-favorite classmate like Tiffany, deserved a rude response. He pasted on a smile. "Hey, Tiffany. It's been a long time."

"Where are you hiding yourself these days?" She bent over the table, and Vito leaned back in the booth, trying to look anywhere but down her low-cut dress. "We should get together sometime!" she gushed, putting a hand on his arm.

This was where a suave man would smile and flirt and make a date. But Vito had never been suave. He'd always been the one to console the girls whose boyfriends got caught on Tiffany's well-baited line. Always the friend, happy to take them out for coffee or a milk shake and to listen to them.

Unfortunately for his love life, it hadn't usually gone further than that.

Tiffany was looking at him expectantly. "Where did you say you're staying?"

"I'm not really..." He broke off. Did he really want to get into his personal business with Tiffany?

Lacey cleared her throat, grasped Vito's scarred hand and smiled up at Tiffany. "He's staying at my guesthouse," she said sweetly. "With me."

"Oh." There was a world of meaning in that word, backed up by Tiffany's raised eyebrows. "Well, then. It was good to see you." She spun on her high heels and walked over to the counter, where she leaned toward Nora Jean and started talking fast and hard.

Vito turned his hand over, palm to palm with Lacey. "Thanks," he said, "but you didn't have to do that."

"Tiffany hasn't changed a bit since high school," Lacey said. "She'd break your heart."

"It's not in the market."

"Mine, either."

They looked at each other and some electrical-like current materialized between them, running from their locked eyes to their intertwined hands.

No, Vito's heart wasn't in the market. He had enough to do to rebuild a life and raise a boy and keep a secret.

But if it *had* been in the market, it would run more toward someone like Lacey than toward someone like Tiffany.

Lacey glanced toward the counter. "Don't look now," she said, "but Tiffany and Nora Jean are staring at us."

"This is how rumors get started." He squeezed her hand a little, then could have kicked himself. Was he flirting? With the one woman he could never, ever get involved with?

"That's true," Lacey said briskly, looking away. "And we've obviously done a good job of starting a rumor today. So…"

"So what?" He squeezed her hand again, let go and thought of living at the guesthouse with Nonna and Charlie.

Charlie could walk to the park, or better yet, ride a bike. Vito was pretty sure there was one in Nonna's garage that he could fix up.

Vito could see Nonna every day. Do something good for the woman who'd done so much for him.

And he could get back on his feet, start his online classes. Maybe Nonna, as she got better, would watch Charlie for him some, giving him a chance to go out and find a decent job.

Soon enough, Nonna would be well and Charlie would be settled in school and Vito would have some money to spare. At which point he could find them another place to live.

He'd only have to keep his secret for the summer. After that, he and Charlie would live elsewhere and would drift naturally out of Lacey's circle of friends. At that point, it was doubtful that she'd learn about Charlie's parentage; there'd be no reason for it to come up.

How likely was it that Lacey would find out the truth over the summer?

"Maybe you could stay for a while," she said. "I'm opening the guesthouse this fall, officially, but until then, having a long-term guest who didn't mind noise would help out."

"How about a guest who makes noise? Charlie's not a quiet kid."

"I liked him."

"Well, then," Vito said, trying to ignore the feeling that he was making a huge mistake, "if you're seriously making the offer, it looks like you've got yourself a couple of tenants for the summer."

Four

The next Wednesday afternoon, Lacey looked out the kitchen window as Charlie and Vito brought a last load of boxes in from Vito's pickup. Pop music played loudly—Charlie's choice. She'd heard their good-natured argument earlier. The bang of the front screen door sent Mr. Whiskers flying from his favorite sunning spot on the floor. He disappeared into the basement, where his companion, Mrs. Whiskers, had already retreated.

Some part of Lacey liked the noise and life, but part of her worried. There went her peaceful summer—and Nonna's, too. This might be a really bad idea.

She glanced over at the older woman, relaxing in the rocking chair Lacey had put in a warm, sunny corner beside the stove. Maybe she'd leave the chair there. It gave the room a cozy feel. And Nonna didn't look any too disturbed by the ruckus Vito and Charlie were creating. Her eyes sparkled with more interest than she'd shown in the previous couple of weeks.

"I'd better get busy with dinner." Lacey opened the refrigerator door and studied the contents.

"I used to be such a good cook," Nonna commented. "Nowadays, I just don't have the energy."

"You will again." Lacey pulled mushrooms, sweet peppers and broccoli from the fridge. "You'd better. I don't think I could face the future without your lasagna in it."

"I could teach you to make it."

Lacey chuckled. "I'm really not much of a cook. And besides, we need to work on healthy meals. Maybe we can figure out a way to make some heart-healthy lasagna one of these days."

As she measured out brown rice and started it cooking, she looked over to see Nonna's frown. "What's wrong?"

"What are you making?"

"Stir-fried veggies on brown rice. It'll be good." Truthfully, it was one of Lacey's few staples, a quick, healthy meal she often whipped up for herself after work.

"No meat?" Nonna sounded scandalized. "You can't serve a meal to men without meat. At least a little, for flavor."

Lacey stopped in the middle of chopping the broccoli into small florets. "I'm cooking for men?"

"Aren't you fixing dinner for Vito and Charlie, too?" Nonna's eyebrows lifted.

"We didn't talk about sharing meals." Out the window, she saw Vito close the truck cab and wipe his forehead with the back of his hand before picking up one of the street side boxes to carry in. "They *are* working up a sweat out there, but where would I put them?" She nodded toward the small wooden table against the wall, where she and Nonna had been taking their meals.

Once again, she sensed their quiet, relaxing summer dissolving away.

At the same time, Nonna was an extrovert, so maybe having more people around would suit her. As for Lacey, she needed to get used to having people in the house, to ease into hosting a bed-and-breakfast gradually, rather than waiting until she had a houseful of paying guests to feed in her big dining room. And who better than good old Vito?

"There's always room for more around a happy home's table," Nonna said, rocking.

"I guess we *could* move it out from the wall."

Vito walked by carrying a double stack of boxes, and Lacey hurried to the kitchen door. "Are you okay with that? Do you need help?" Though from the way his biceps stretched the sleeves of his white T-shirt, he was most definitely okay.

"There's nothing wrong with me below the neck." He sounded uncharacteristically irritable. "I can carry a couple of boxes."

Where had *that* come from? She lifted her hands and took a step back. "Fine with me," she said sharply.

From above them on the stairs, Charlie crowed, "Ooo-eee, a fight!"

Vito ignored him and stomped up the stairs, still carrying both boxes.

"You come in here, son." Nonna stood behind Lacey, beckoning to Charlie.

Lacey bit her lip. She didn't want Nonna to overexert herself. And being from an earlier generation, she might have unreasonable expectations of how a kid like Charlie would behave.

But Nonna was whispering to Charlie, and they both

laughed, and then he helped her back to her rocking chair. That was good.

Lacey went back to her cutting board, looked at the stack of veggies and reluctantly acknowledged to herself that Nonna was probably right. If she could even get a red-blooded man and an eight-year-old boy to eat stir-fry, the least she could do was put some beef in it. She rummaged through her refrigerator and found a pack of round steak, already cut into strips. Lazy woman's meat. She drizzled oil into the wok, let it heat a minute, and then dumped in the beef strips.

"Hey, Lace." It was Vito's deep voice, coming from the kitchen doorway. "C'mere a minute."

She glanced around. The rice was cooking, Nonna and Charlie were still talking quietly and the beef was barely starting to brown. She wiped her hands on a kitchen towel. "What's up?" she asked as she crossed the kitchen toward him. "You're not going to bite my head off again, are you?"

"No." He beckoned her toward the front room, where they could talk without the others hearing. "Look, I'm sorry I snapped. Charlie's been a handful and…" He trailed off and rubbed the back of his neck.

"And what?"

"And…I hate being treated like there's something wrong with me. I'm still plenty strong."

"I noticed." But she remembered a similar feeling herself, after her miscarriage; people had tiptoed around her, offering to carry her groceries and help her to a seat in church. When really, she'd been just fine physically. "I'm sorry, too, then. I know how annoying it is to be treated like an invalid."

"So we're good?" He put an arm around her.

It was a gesture as natural as breathing to Vito as well as to the rest of his Italian family. She'd always liked that about them.

But now, something felt different about Vito's warm arm around her shoulders. Maybe it was that he was so much bigger and brawnier than he'd been as a younger man.

Disconcerted, she hunched her shoulders and stepped away.

Some emotion flickered in his eyes and was gone, so quickly she wasn't sure she'd seen it.

"Hi!" Charlie came out of the kitchen, smiling innocently. He sidestepped toward Nonna's room.

"Where you headed, buddy?" Vito asked.

"Lacey, dear," Nonna called from the kitchen. "I'd like to rest up a little before dinner."

"I'm glad she called me." Lacey heard herself talking a little faster than usual, heard a breathless sound in her own voice. "I try to walk with her, because I have so many area rugs and the house can be a bit of an obstacle course. But of course, she likes to be independent." Why was she blathering like she was nervous, around Vito?

"I'll help her." Vito went into the kitchen and Lacey trailed behind. "Come on, Nonna, I'll walk with you. Smells good," he added, glancing over to where the beef sizzled on the stove.

It *did* smell good, and the praise from Vito warmed her. She added in sliced mushrooms and onions.

For a moment, all she could hear was the slight sizzle of the food on the stove and the tick of the big kitchen clock on the wall. Peace and quiet. Maybe this was going to work out okay.

The quiet didn't last long. From Nonna's room, she could hear Charlie talking, telling some story. Vito's deeper voice chimed in. His comfortable, familiar laugh tickled her nerve endings in a most peculiar way. Then she heard his heavy step on the stairs. No doubt he was going up to do a little more unpacking while Charlie was occupied. Vito was a hard worker.

And just why was she so conscious of him? What was wrong with her?

She walked over to the sink and picked up the photo she kept on a built-in wooden shelf beside it. Gerry, in uniform, arriving home on one of his furloughs. Someone had snapped a photo of her hugging him, her hair, longer then, flying out behind her, joy in every muscle of her body.

She clasped the picture close to her chest. *That* was reality.

Reassured, she moved out the table and located some chairs for Charlie and Vito, almost wishing Buck hadn't taken her bigger kitchen table with him when he'd moved. She checked on the dinner. Just about done. She found grapes and peaches to put in a nice bowl, both a centerpiece and a healthy dessert.

"What's going on here?" She heard Vito's voice from Nonna's room a little later. He must have come back downstairs. She hadn't even noticed. Good.

Charlie's voice rose, then Nonna's. It sounded like an argument, and Lacey's patient shouldn't be arguing. She wiped her hands and hurried to check on Nonna.

When she looked into the room, both Nonna and Charlie had identical guilty expressions. And identical white smudges on their faces. Beside Nonna was a box from the bakery that someone had brought over yesterday. Cannoli.

"Dessert before dinner, Charlie?" Vito was shaking his head. "You know that's not allowed."

"Nonna!" Lacey scolded. "Rich, heavy pastries aren't on your diet. You know the doctor's worried about your blood sugar."

"She told me where they were and asked me to get them for her," Charlie protested. "And you told me I was supposed to treat older people with respect."

Vito blew out a sigh. "You just need to check with me first, buddy. And Nonna, you've got to stick to your eating plan. It's for your health!"

"What's life without cannoli?" Nonna said plaintively. "Do I have to give up all my treats?"

Vito knelt beside his grandmother. "I think you can have a few planned treats. But sneaking cannoli before dinner means you won't have an appetite for the healthy stuff."

"I didn't anyway," Nonna muttered.

"Me, either." Charlie went to stand beside Nonna on the other side. Obviously, he'd made a new friend in Nonna, and that was all to the good for both of them— as long as it didn't lead to Nonna falling off the diet bandwagon.

It was up to Lacey to be firm, so she marched over and picked up the bakery box. "Whatever you men don't eat for dessert is getting donated tonight," she said firmly. "Obviously, it's too much of a temptation to have things like this in the house."

An acrid smell tickled her nose.

"What's that burning?" Vito asked at the same moment.

"Dinner!" Lacey wailed and rushed into the kitchen, where smoke poured from the rice pan. In the wok, the beef and vegetables had shrunk down and appeared to be permanently attached to the wok's surface.

All her work to make dinner nice and healthy, gone to waste.

She turned off the burners and stared at the ruined food, tears gathering in her eyes. In her head she could hear her mother's criticism of the cookies she'd baked: *you'll never be much of a chef, will you?*

She remembered Gerry shoving away his dinner plate the first night they'd come back from their honeymoon, saying he wasn't hungry.

Nonna was calling questions from her room and Charlie shouted back: "Lacey burned up dinner!"

The acrid smoke stung her eyes, and then the smoke detector went off with an earsplitting series of beeps.

This was not the serene life she had been looking for. She was a failure as a cook.

She burst into tears.

Vito coughed from the smoke and winced from the alarm's relentless beeping. He turned down the volume on his hearing aids and moved toward Lacey, his arms lifting automatically to comfort her with a hug.

She clung on to him for one precious second, then let go and looked around like she didn't know what to do next.

He needed to take charge. He shut off the smoke detectors, one after the other. Then he opened all the windows in the kitchen, gulping in big breaths of fresh air.

Lacey flopped down at the kitchen table, wiping tears. He beckoned to Charlie. "Run and tell Nonna everything's fine, but dinner will be a little late." As Charlie left the room, Vito scraped the ruined food into the garbage and filled the two pans halfway with soapy water. They'd need some serious scrubbing later.

Lacey was sniffling now, blowing her nose and wiping her eyes.

He leaned back against the counter and studied her. "How come this got you so upset? You're not a crier."

She laughed. "I am, these days. And I'm also a loser in the kitchen, in case you didn't notice. My mom always told me that, and Gerry concurred."

"Gerry?" That was a surprise. The man had eaten enough MREs in the military that he should have been grateful for any home cooking, however simple.

She pushed herself to her feet. "What'll we eat now? Nonna needs dinner. We all do. I guess, maybe, pizza? But that's not the healthiest choice for your grandma."

"Do you have canned tomatoes?" Vito asked her. "Onions? Garlic? Pasta?"

She nodded and blew her nose again. "I think so."

"Great. You sit down and I'll give you stuff to chop. I'm going to make a spaghetti sauce." He might not know what words to say to comfort her, but he could definitely cook her a meal.

"Spaghetti!" Charlie yelled, pumping his fist as he ran into the kitchen.

"That's right." Vito stepped in front of the racing boy. "And you, young man, are going to do some chores. Starting with taking out this garbage."

Charlie started to protest, but Vito just pointed at the garbage can. Charlie yanked out the bag and stomped out of the house with it.

Lacey chopped and Vito opened cans of tomatoes

and set the sauce to cooking. As the onions sizzled in olive oil, the day's tension rolled off him. When Charlie came back in, he had Gramps Camden, a weathered-looking, gray-haired man, with him.

Lacey gave the older man a hug, then turned to Vito. "You remember Gramps Camden, don't you?"

Vito stood and greeted the older man, who'd been a part of the community as long as he could remember.

"Wanted to pay a visit," he said in his trademark grouchy way. "See what you've got going on over here."

"You'll stay for dinner, won't you?" Lacey asked.

"Twist my arm," the old man said. "Cooking's good over at the Senior Towers, but nothing beats home-made."

Lacey asked Charlie to take a couple of bills out to the mailbox, and he went happily enough.

A knock came on the back screen door, and there was Gina, the woman Lacey's brother, Buck, had married, holding a toddler by the hand. "Hey, Lace, are you in there?"

"C'mon in." Lacey got up and opened the door for the woman, a rueful smile on her face. "Welcome to the zoo."

"Hey," Gina greeted Vito and Gramps Camden, and then turned to Lacey, holding the little boy by his shoulders as he attempted to toddle away. "Can you watch Bobby for ten or fifteen minutes? I have to run over to the Senior Towers to check out a few facts."

Vito's curiosity must have shown on his face, because she explained. "I'm doing some research on the town and the guesthouse. This place was a stop on the Underground Railroad and has a really amazing history."

"Laaaaas," the little boy said, walking into Lacey's outstretched arms.

"Hey, how's my sweet boy?" Lacey wrapped the child in a giant hug, and then stood, lifting him to perch on her hip. Her bad mood was apparently gone. "Look, Bobby, this is Vito. And this is Mr. Camden. Can you say hi?"

Bobby buried his face in Lacey's neck.

"Taking off," Gina said, and hurried out the back door.

Lacey cuddled the little boy close, nuzzling his neck, and then brought him to the window. "Look at the birdies," she said, pointing toward a feeder outside the window where a couple of goldfinches fluttered.

"Birdie," Bobby agreed.

"You're a natural," Vito said, meaning it. Lacey looked right at home with a child in her arms, and the picture made a longing rise in him. He wanted a baby. More than one.

And Lacey probably needed to have another baby. It would help her get over the pain of her devastating miscarriage.

Lacey set the table, having Bobby bring napkins along to help, letting him place them haphazardly on the table and chairs.

Vito tasted the sauce and frowned. "It needs something."

"I have basil growing outside. At least, I *think* it's still alive. Want some?"

"Fresh basil? For sure."

"Come on, Bobby." She helped the little boy maneuver across the kitchen and through the back door.

Could Vito be blamed for looking out the window to

see where her herbs were planted? After all, he might do more cooking here. He was enjoying it.

And once he looked, and saw her kneeling in the golden late-afternoon sunlight, pointing and talking with Bobby, he found it hard to look away.

"Take a picture, it lasts longer," Gramps muttered. "Do I have to chaperone everyone around here?"

Vito blinked and went back to his cooking, but the image of Lacey, the curve of her neck, soft hair blowing in the breeze, stayed with him.

Who was he to think romantically about someone so beautiful, so perfect?

Half an hour later, they were about to sit down to a not-bad-looking dinner when Gina tapped on the back door.

"Mama!" Bobby cried and toddled toward the door.

She opened the door, scooped up her son and gave him a big loud kiss.

"You'll stay for dinner, won't you?" Lacey asked Gina.

"Oh…no. I would but…I need to get home." Her cheeks went pink and Vito put it together. She was a new bride, must have just gotten back from a brief honeymoon. She wanted to get home to her new husband.

Envy tugged at Vito's heart. Would he ever have a wife who was eager to return to him, or would he always remain just the best friend?

Dinner was fun. Nonna insisted they put on some Italian opera music—"the most romantic music on earth!"—and then got into a good-natured argument with Gramps Camden, who insisted that Frank Sinatra sang the best love songs. Her eyes sparkled with pleasure as everyone talked and joked and ate. Charlie enjoyed the company, too. Both of them would benefit from being part of a bigger family, Vito realized. He would, as well.

He just didn't know how to make it happen. But at least for the summer, it was something they could enjoy here at Lacey's. He would talk to her about having meals together as often as possible, splitting grocery bills and sharing cooking duties.

When he stood to clear the dishes, Lacey put a hand on his arm. "It's okay, Vito. You cooked, so I'll clean up."

"It's a lot," he protested, trying not to notice the delicate feel of her hand.

"I have an excellent helper," she said, letting go of Vito and patting Charlie's arm. "Right?"

"Sure," the boy said with surprising good cheer.

Of course. Lacey had that effect on every male of the species. Her charm wasn't meant specially for him.

"You can walk me back over to the Towers," Gramps said unexpectedly to Vito, so after a few minutes of parting conversation, the two of them headed down to the street. The Towers were almost next door to Lacey's guesthouse, and Gramps seemed plenty strong to get there on his own, but maybe he just wanted the company. Fine with Vito. He needed to get away from pretty Lacey, get some fresh air.

"How you handling those scars?" Gramps asked abruptly.

Vito felt the heat rise up his neck and was glad for the darkness and the cool breeze. "Apart from terrifying women and children, no big deal."

Gramps chuckled. "It's what's on the inside that

counts. Any woman worth her salt will know that. The kid over there seems like he gets it, too."

It was true; the few occasions Charlie still cringed away from Vito had more to do with leftover fears related to his mother's boyfriends than with Vito's looks.

They were almost to the front door of the Towers now, and Vito was ready to say goodbye when Gramps stopped and turned toward him. "Just what are your intentions toward Lacey?"

Vito pulled back to stare at the older man. "Intentions?"

"That's right. Some of us over at the Towers got to talking. Wondered whether you and she had more than a landlord-tenant friendship."

"Hey, hey now." Vito held up a hand. "Nobody needs to be gossiping about Lacey. She's had enough trouble in her life already."

Gramps propped a hand on the railing beside the door. "Don't you think we know that? For that matter, you have, too. The both of you have— What is it young folks call it?"

"Baggage," Vito said. "And we may be young compared to…some people, but we're not so young we need to be told what to do."

Gramps snorted. "Think you know everything, do you?"

"No. Not everything. Not much. But I do know my love life's my business, just as Lacey's love life is hers."

"Give it some thought before you mingle them together, that's all. I'd hate to see either Lacey or that boy hurt."

"I'd hate to see that, too." Vito lifted an eyebrow. "We done here?"

"We're done," Gramps said, "but have a care how you spend the rest of your evening over there."

And even though he found the warning annoying, Vito figured it was probably a wise one.

Five

When Vito walked back into the guesthouse, he heard dishes clattering in the kitchen. Lacey. Like a magnet, she drew him.

And maybe Gramps knew just what he was talking about. Being careful was the goal Vito needed to shoot for. A vulnerable woman and a vulnerable child were both somewhat under his protection, and Gramps didn't know the half of how any relationship between Lacey and Vito could cause damage to both of them.

He'd expected to see Charlie in the kitchen, but when he got there Lacey was alone, squatting to put away a pan.

"Hey," he said softly, not wanting to startle her. "Where's Charlie?"

She stood and turned toward him. "I told him he could watch TV. He was a good helper, but apparently, it's time for one of his favorite shows."

"Oh, right." Vito should go. He should go right upstairs, right now.

But in the soft lamplight, he couldn't look away from her.

She was looking at him, too, her eyes wide and confused.

He took a step toward her.

Leaning against the counter with one hip, she picked up a framed photo from the counter, studied it for a few seconds, and then placed it carefully on the shelf beside the sink.

"What's that?" He walked over but stopped a good three feet away from her. A safe distance.

She picked it back up and held it out for him to see. "It was Gerry's second time home on furlough. I'd missed him so much that when he came off the plane, I broke away from the other wives and ran screaming to hug him. Somebody caught it on film."

Vito studied the picture of Lacey and his friend, and his heart hurt. They *did* look happy, thrilled to see each other. "Could've been in the newspaper. Good picture."

"It was in the *Plain Dealer*," she said, smiling shyly. "That embarrassed Gerry. Me, too, a little. Everyone kept coming up to us to say they'd seen it."

"Gerry didn't like that, huh?" Vito felt sick inside, because he knew why.

Gerry had already been involved with Krystal at that point. Maybe she'd even been pregnant with Charlie. He thought about asking Lacey the year, and then didn't. He didn't even want to know.

How awkward for Gerry that his girlfriend might see his loving wife hugging on him.

Gerry had been such a jerk.

"He was everything I ever wanted," Lacey said dreamily, studying the picture. "Sometimes I don't think I'll ever get over him."

"Right. Look, I'd better go check on Charlie and

catch some sleep myself." He turned and walked out of the room. An abrupt departure might be a little rude, but it was better than staying there, listening to her express her adoration of a man who'd not been worth one ounce of it. Better than blurting out something that would destroy that idealized image she had of Gerry.

Don't speak ill of the dead. It was a common maxim, and valid.

Was he making a huge mistake to stay here, even though that was what Nonna and Charlie both wanted?

He scrubbed a hand across his face and headed up the stairs. He needed to focus on his professional goals and forget about his personal desire to have a wife and a large family. He needed to make sure that personal desire didn't settle on Lacey, like Gramps seemed to worry it would.

He and Charlie were living in the home of the one woman he could never, ever be involved with. He'd promised Gerry at the moment of his death, and that meant something. It meant a lot. The sooner he got that straight in his head, the better.

On Friday, Lacey strolled along the sidewalk with Vito and Charlie and tried to shake the odd feeling that they were a family, doing errands together. It was a strange thought, especially given that her goal was to get her guesthouse up and running so that she could dive into her self-sufficient, single-woman life and make it good.

She just needed to keep in mind the purpose of this trip: to create a cozy room at the guesthouse for any child who came to stay for a night or a weekend.

It was only midafternoon, but with the arrival of

summer, a lot of people seemed to be taking off work early on Fridays. A group of women clustered outside of the Chatterbox Café, talking. A young couple pushed their baby in a stroller. Several people she knew vaguely from the Senior Towers were taking their afternoon walk, and outside Chez la Ferme, Rescue River's only fancy restaurant, Sam Hinton stood with sleeves rolled up, talking to another man in a suit, smiling like he'd just tied up a deal.

"You're sure you don't mind focusing on Charlie's room right now?" Vito asked as Charlie ran ahead to examine a heavily chromed motorcycle in front of the Chatterbox. "It's not the project you were planning on, I'm sure."

"It's not, but it's a good change of plans. Having a room or two decorated for kids will only add to the guesthouse's appeal. And that little room off the big one is perfect for that."

"And you're being kind. Charlie's been in a mood, so maybe this will help." They reached Love's Hardware, and Vito held the door for her, then called for Charlie to come join them.

The front of the store was crowded with summer merchandise, garden tools and stacked bags of mulch and grass seed. A faint, pungent smell attested to the fertilizer and weed killer in stock. Farther back, bins of nails and screws and bolts occupied one wall while pipes and sinks and bathtubs dominated the other. Overhead, modern light fixtures, price tags hanging, intermixed with old-fashioned signs advertising long-gone brands of household appliances. The soft sound of R & B played in the background.

A string of small bells chimed on the door as it

closed behind them, and the store's owner, Mr. Love, came forward immediately, one weathered brown hand extended, subtly guiding him through the store aisle. His vision wasn't the best, but he still managed his hardware store almost entirely on his own.

"Hey, Mr. Love, it's Lacey. And you remember Vito D'Angelo, right?"

"I sure do, sure do. Glad to see you folks on such a fine day." Mr. Love fumbled for their hands, and then clasped each in a friendly greeting.

"And this is his foster son, Charlie."

"Say hello," Vito prompted the boy, urging him forward.

Charlie scowled as if he might refuse. But as he looked up at Mr. Love, he seemed impressed by the man's age and courtly dignity. "Hi, it's nice to meet you," he said, holding out his hand to shake in a surprising display of good manners.

After Lacey had explained their mission, Mr. Love led them over to the paint section, where Charlie's momentary sweetness vanished. "I want this blue," he said, selecting a bold cobalt paint chip and holding it out as if the decision was made.

Lacey bit her lip. She'd told Charlie he could help pick out the color, but she and her future guests were the ones who'd have to live with it. "How about something a little lighter, Charlie? It's an old-fashioned house, and this is a pretty modern color." She offered up a sample card featuring various shades of blue. "I was thinking of something in this range."

"That's boring. I want this one."

"It's Lacey's decision, buddy," Vito said, putting a

firm hand on Charlie's shoulder. "We're guests in her house, and she's nice to let you choose the color blue."

Charlie's lower lip stuck out a mile.

"Let's look at the cobalt in shades," Lacey suggested. "We could have that color, just a little lighter. Do you like this one?" She pointed at a shade halfway down the sample card.

"That one's okay." Charlie pointed at one toward the end, almost as bright as his original pick.

"Charlie. Lacey has the last word."

Lacey bent to see Charlie's downcast face. "I promise I'll take your ideas into consideration."

"Fine." Charlie gave Lacey a dirty look.

"Come on, let's go see the power tools," Vito suggested. "Guy stuff," he added, winking at Lacey.

Immediately, her distress about Charlie's attitude faded as her heart gave a funny little twist.

"I have to let my granddaughter mix the paint or she gets mad at me," Mr. Love said to Lacey. In a lower voice, he added, "I can't see the colors too well, but if you'd like, I can ask her to add in a little more white to whatever shade the boy picked."

"That would be fantastic," Lacey said gratefully. "Thank you."

"Don't you worry about young Charlie," Mr. Love said, patting her arm. "Kids usually come around."

That was true, and besides, Charlie wasn't her problem to worry about. But there was no point in explaining that to Mr. Love, so she let it go.

On the way home, they walked by a group of slightly older boys playing basketball in the park, and Charlie wanted to join in.

"No, buddy," Vito said. "We're painting today."

"I don't wanna paint! I wanna play outside!"

That made sense to Lacey, but Vito shook his head. "You can run ahead and play basketball outside the guesthouse for a while."

"That's no fun, playing by myself." But Charlie took off ahead of them, staying in sight, but kicking stones in an obvious display of bad temper.

Vito blew out a sigh. "Sure wish there was a manual on how to parent," he said.

"I think you're doing great," she said, reassuring him. "What's Charlie's background, anyway? Was it difficult?"

Vito looked away, then back at her. "Yeah. His mom's an addict. She loves him, but not as much as she loves to get high."

Poor Charlie. "What about his dad?"

Vito looked away again and didn't answer.

A sudden, surprising thought came into Lacey's head: was Charlie *Vito's* biological son?

But no. If Vito had fathered a child, he wouldn't deny it and pretend to just be the foster dad.

"His dad's passed," Vito said finally. "And Mom keeps getting involved with men who rough her up. It happened to Charlie a few times, too, which is why he originally went into foster care. His mom wasn't able to make a change, so Charlie's free for adoption. I hope we'll have that finalized within a few months."

"That's great, Vito." Even as she said it, she wondered how and why he'd gotten involved in foster care. It was so good of him, but not something most single men in their early thirties would consider. "Why did—"

"Charlie learned a rough style of play in some of

his old neighborhoods," Vito interrupted quickly, almost as if he wanted to avoid her questions. "And he doesn't have the best social skills. If he's going to play basketball in the park, I need to be there to supervise."

"You could stay with him now. You don't have to help me paint his room."

"Thanks, but no. It's only right that we help. And besides," he said, flashing her a smile, "it's what I want to do."

So they spent the afternoon painting as a team. Sun poured through the open windows, and birds sang outside. Stroking the brush, and then the roller, across the walls, soothed Lacey's heart. Again, more strongly this time, she got that weird feeling of being a family with Vito.

He was good around the house. He could fix things, he could paint, he could cook. And he liked to do those things with her.

Unlike Gerry, who'd always begged off family chores.

Charlie burst into the room, planted his feet wide and crossed his arms. He looked around the half-painted room, his lip curling. "That's not the color I wanted."

Something about his stance and his expression looked oddly familiar to Lacey, but she couldn't put her finger on what it was.

"The second coat'll make it brighter, buddy," Vito said. "Why don't you stay in here and I'll teach you to paint with the roller?"

"No way. That's boring." Charlie turned to stomp out and landed a foot directly in the tray of paint. When he saw what he'd done, he ran out of the room, tracking paint the whole way.

Vito leaped up and hurried after him, while Lacey raced to wipe up the paint before it dried on the hardwood floors, chuckling a little to herself. With Vito and Charlie around, there would never be a dull moment.

"Oh, man, I'm sorry," Vito said as he returned to see her scrubbing at a last footprint. "Charlie's in timeout in the kitchen, since I can't exactly send him to his room, and he'll be back up in a few minutes to help. Neatly. To make up for this mess."

"It's okay. It's part of having a kid."

Vito sighed. "I guess it is, but I wasn't ready for it. I never know if I'm doing the right thing or not."

"You're doing a good job. Really good." She smiled up at him.

"Thanks. I don't feel so sure."

Just like the other night, their eyes caught and held for a beat too long.

Charlie burst into the room in sock feet and stood, hands on hips. "I'm here, but I ain't apologizing and I ain't helping." He lifted his chin and glared at Vito as if daring him to exert his authority as a father.

Vito opened his mouth to speak, but Lacey's heart went out to the hurting little boy, and she held up a hand. "Let me talk to him," she said, and walked over to Charlie. "It's been a rough day, hasn't it? But that paint came right off and it won't be a problem."

"So?"

In every stiff line of his body she read a need for a mother's comfort. "Hey," she said, putting an arm around him, "I'm glad you're here and I think this is

going to be a great room for you. You can help deco-
rate it."

For a second Charlie relaxed against her, but then he
went stiff again and stepped away, his face red. "That's
what you said about the paint, and then I got this baby
color!" He waved a hand at the nearest wall.

"Oh, honey—"

"Don't call me that! Only my real mom can call
me that!"

"Charlie…" Vito said in a warning voice, approaching the two of them.

"She doesn't have any kids! She's not a mom, so
why is she acting like one?"

The words rang in Lacey's ears.

It was true. She wasn't a mom, and Charlie, with
a child's insight, had seen right into the dream inside
her head. On some barely conscious level she'd been
pretending that Charlie was her child and Vito was her
husband, and it had to stop.

Slowly, she backed away from Charlie just as Vito
reached him.

"I want you to apologize to Miss Lacey," Vito said
firmly.

"I'm not apologizing!" Tears ran down Charlie's
reddened face, but he ignored them, frowning fiercely
and thrusting his chest out.

"Charlie." Vito put a hand on the boy's shoulder.

"Don't you touch me! You're not my real dad. And
you're ugly, too!" Charlie ran from the room.

Vito's hand went to his scarred face for just a moment, and then he followed Charlie.

Even in the middle of her own hurt feelings, Lacey
wanted to comfort him, to tell him he *wasn't* ugly.

But that was exactly the problem. She wasn't the mom of the family. She wasn't the wife.

She never would play that role, and she needed to stop pretending and accept the truth.

Six

"Let's see if we can scare up a basketball game at the park," Vito said to Charlie the next day after lunch.

"Yeah!" Charlie dropped his handheld game and jumped up.

Vito laughed. He was still getting used to the time frame of an eight-year-old. "In ten minutes, okay? I have to clean up our dishes and make a phone call."

Vito had planned to spend Saturday setting up Charlie's room and looking for jobs online. But Charlie's behavior the previous day had changed his mind. Vito was no expert, but it seemed to him that Charlie needed structure, and chores, and attention. So they'd spent the morning weeding the gardens around the guesthouse, and with a little prodding Charlie had worked hard. He'd even taken a glass of lemonade to Lacey, who was sanding woodwork in the breakfast room, and Vito had heard her talk cheerfully to Charlie, which was a relief. Apparently, she wasn't holding a grudge against Charlie for yesterday's behavior.

So, amends made, Vito and Charlie half walked, half jogged to the park together, bouncing a basketball.

Lawn mowers and weed eaters roared, filling the air with the pungent fragrance of vegetation, and several people called greetings from flower beds and front yards. Things weren't much different than when Vito himself had been eight, growing up here.

The call he'd made had been to Troy Hinton, an old acquaintance whose son, Xavier, was just Charlie's age. Troy and Xavier met them by the basketball courts at the park, and immediately, the boys ran out onto the blacktop to play. Vito and Troy sat down on a bench to watch.

Xavier played well for an eight-year-old, making a few baskets, dribbling without too much traveling. Charlie, though, was on fire, making well more than half of the shots he took. Paternal pride warmed Vito's chest. He'd make sure Charlie tried out for the school team as soon as he got to sixth grade.

"That's a good thing you're doing, fostering him," Troy said, nodding toward Charlie. "He seems like he's settling in fine."

That reminded Vito of yesterday, and he shook his head. "A few bumps in the road."

"Yeah?" Troy bent down to flick a piece of dirt off his leg.

"I think he misses his mom. He sees her once a week, but that's hard on a kid."

"Any chance of her getting him back?"

Vito shook his head. "No. Supervised visits is all."

"Gotcha." Troy was watching the two boys play.

Even at eight, Charlie used his elbows and threw a few too many shoves.

"Charlie!" Vito called.

When Charlie looked over, Vito just shook his head. Charlie's mouth twisted, and then he nodded.

"We talked about sportsmanship this morning. I don't know why he thinks he can play street ball here, in the park."

Troy chuckled. "It's a process. And Xavier's holding his own." Indeed, the boy did some fancy footwork and stole the ball from Charlie.

Which was impressive, considering Xavier's background. "How's his health?"

"Almost two years cancer-free."

"That's great." Although Vito had been overseas, he'd heard from Nonna about the careworn single mom who'd come to town to work at Troy's dog rescue, bringing her son who was struggling with leukemia. Now Troy and Angelica were married, with another child, and it was great to know that Xavier was healthy and strong.

"He's doing so well that we can't keep up with him in the summer. So we've got him in a weekday program here at the park. Six hours a day, lots of activity. Charlie should join."

"Well…" Vito thought about it. "That's tempting, but Charlie has a few issues."

"People who run it are good with issues. And you should also bring him to the Kennel Kids." Troy explained the program for at-risk boys, helping once a week at the dog rescue farm Troy operated.

Vito had to thank God for how things were working out here in Rescue River. It was a great place to raise kids. "Sounds perfect, if you've got a space for him."

"Might have one for you, too. I could use a little help."

"Oh, so that's how it is," Vito joked, but truthfully, he was glad to be asked. Vito liked dogs, and Troy. And most of all, he wanted to do positive things for Charlie, and with him. "Sure thing. I can help out."

The boys came running over, panting, and grabbed water bottles to chug.

"You guys should come play!" Charlie said, looking from Vito to Troy.

"Aw, Dad's too tired." Xavier bounced the basketball hard so it went back up higher than his head.

"Who says?" Troy got to his feet and grinned at Vito. "Hintons against D'Angelos, what do you say?"

"I'm not a D'Angelo," Charlie protested.

"But you're going to be, pretty soon." Vito stood, too, and ruffled Charlie's hair. "Meanwhile, let's show these Hintons how it's done."

After an hour of play that left them all breathless and sweating, Troy and Xavier invited Charlie to come out to the farm for a few hours, and Vito agreed. It was good for Charlie to make friends.

But that left Vito with a hole in his day. He'd finished the preliminary work for his online courses, and the term didn't start for another week. Nonna was spending the day visiting at the Senior Towers.

He thought of Troy Hinton, married, raising two kids, the town veterinarian and dog rescue owner, volunteering with the Kennel Kids. What was Vito contributing by comparison? And Troy had a big property to handle, a place for kids to run, while Vito was living in two rooms.

He walked through the park, feeling uncharacteristically blue. There was a soccer game going on, a coed team of kids a little younger than Charlie, and

Vito stopped to watch. The game wasn't too serious. Parents chatted with each other in the bleachers while coaches hollered instructions, mostly encouraging rather than overly competitive. Nearby, a family with a new baby sat on a blanket, cheering on their kids who were playing while cuddling with toddlers who looked like twins.

Vito wanted that. Wanted a family, a large family. It was in his blood.

Suddenly, someone tapped his shoulder, and he turned to see Lacey and another woman, pretty, dark-haired, with Asian features.

"Hi!" the dark-haired woman said, holding out a hand. "I'm Susan Hinton. I've heard a lot about you."

What did that mean? He shook Susan's hand and shot a glance at Lacey. Her cheeks were pink. What had she been telling Susan?

"Vito D'Angelo," he supplied, since Lacey seemed to be tongue-tied. "It's a pleasure. Are you related to Troy?"

"Sure am. I'm married to his brother, Sam."

"I know Sam. Sorry to have missed the wedding." He'd been invited, but he'd been in the thick of his surgery at that point.

"Mindy could score," Lacey said, gesturing toward the soccer game. She looked like a teenager, dressed in cutoffs and a soft blue T-shirt. Her short blond hair lifted and tossed in the breeze, and Vito liked that she didn't glue it down with hair spray.

He felt an urge to brush back a strand that had fallen into her eyes, but that would be completely inappropriate. They weren't that kind of friends.

"C'mon, Mindy, go for it!" Susan yelled, and the little girl in question kicked the ball hard, making a goal. "Good job!"

"Susan's a teacher," Lacey said when the hubbub had died down. "She might have some good ideas about your career change."

"You're switching over to teaching?" Susan asked. "What age of kids?"

"I like the little ones," Vito admitted. "Seems like elementary teachers make a big difference."

"And we need more men in the profession," Susan said promptly. "Are you planning to stay local?"

"If I can find work."

Susan opened her mouth as if she were going to ask another question, but a shout interrupted her. Mindy, the child who'd scored a goal, ran over, accompanied by two little girls about the same age. "Did you see, Mama, did you see?"

"I saw." Susan hugged the little girl close. "You're getting better every day."

Vito was watching the pair, so it took a minute for him to become aware that the other two girls were staring up at him.

"What happened to the side of your face?" one of them asked.

"He looks *mean*," said the other little girl.

The remarks shouldn't have stung—he'd known that was how kids would feel, hadn't he?—but they did, anyway.

"Cheyenne! Shelby!" Susan spun and squatted right in front of the other two girls. "You know it's not polite to make personal remarks about someone's appearance."

"I'm sorry, Miss Hayashi," one of them said right away.

"It's Mrs. Hinton, dummy," the other said. "Don't you know she got married?"

Susan put a hand on each girl's shoulder. "First of all, it's more important to be… Do you remember what?"

"More important to be polite than right," the two and little Mindy chorused.

"And furthermore, Shelby," Susan said sternly, "this gentleman got those injuries serving our country, and you *will* show him the respect he deserves."

Vito didn't know which felt worse: being told how bad he looked by a second-gradeish little girl, or being defended by a woman approximately half his size. "Hey, it's okay," he said, squatting down, too, making sure his better half was turned toward the girls. "It can be a surprise to see somebody who looks different."

Mindy shoved in front of him. "I'm *glad* he looks different. Different is cool." She reached up and unhooked something from her back and then started fumbling with her arm.

"Don't take it off! Don't take it off!" the other two girls screamed, sounding more excited than upset.

At which point Vito realized that Mindy had a prosthetic arm, which she seemed set on removing.

Other kids ran in their direction, no doubt attracted by the screams. Vito stood and glanced at Lacey, who gave him a palms up that clearly said she had no idea how to handle the situation.

"Mindy!" Susan's voice was stern, all teacher. "Don't you dare take off that arm. You know the rules."

Mindy's forehead wrinkled, and she and Susan glared at each other. Then, slowly, Mindy twisted something back into place and let go of her prosthetic. "I just wanted to show them that everybody's different, and that's okay," she said sulkily.

Susan knelt and hugged her. "That was a very kind impulse. Now, why don't you girls get back on the field? I think the second half is starting."

Vito took a step back. "Hey, it was nice meeting you," he said to Susan.

"Vito—" Lacey sounded worried.

"Got to go. See you later." What he really needed to do was to be alone. Today's little scene had hammered the truth home to him: he couldn't work with kids in person. His appearance would create a ruckus that would interfere with their learning.

The trouble was he liked kids. And interacting with them through a computer screen just didn't have the same appeal.

Lacey looked from where Susan was ushering the little girls back into the soccer game, toward the path where Vito was walking away, shoulders slumped.

"I'm headed home," she called to Susan, and then took off after Vito. She couldn't stand what she'd just seen.

He was walking fast enough that she was out of breath by the time she got within earshot. "Vito, wait!"

He turned around to wait for her.

"Where are you going? Are you okay?" she asked breathlessly.

"I'm going for a walk, and I'm fine." His words were uncharacteristically clipped.

"Mind if I come?" She started walking beside him, sure of her welcome. After all, this was Vito. He was always glad to see her.

"Actually…" He walked slowly, glanced over at her. "Look, I'm not fit company. Go on back and hang out with Susan."

She gave him a mock glare. "No way! You hung out with me plenty when I wasn't fit company. I'm just returning the favor to an old friend."

He started to say something, then closed his mouth, and mortification sent heat up Lacey's neck. She was being intrusive. It was one of her flaws, according to Gerry, and she half expected Vito to bite her head off.

But he didn't speak and his face wasn't angry. They walked quietly for a few minutes, past the high school. The fragrance of new-mown grass tickled Lacey's nose. From somewhere, she smelled meat grilling, a summer barbecue.

"Where are you headed?" she repeated, because he hadn't answered. "Can I tag along?" Then she worried she'd pushed too far.

"I'm going to the river. To think." He gave her shoulders a quick squeeze. "And sure, you can come. Sorry to be such a bear."

So she followed him down a little path between the grasses and trees and they emerged on the riverbank. As if by agreement, they both stopped, looking at the sunlight glinting off the water, hearing the wind rustle through the weeping willow trees overhead.

"I'm sorry that happened back there," she said.

"That must be hard to deal with, especially…" She trailed off.

"Especially what?"

"Especially when you were always so handsome."

He laughed, shaking his head at the same time. "Oh, Lace. My biggest fan."

She had been, too. In fact, as a younger teen, she'd dreamed of a day when she'd be older, with clear skin and actual curves, and Vito would ask her out. A visceral memory flashed into her mind: lying on the floor of her bedroom, feet propped up on a footstool and CD player blasting out a sad love song, which in her fourteen-year-old brain she'd applied to herself and Vito's lost love.

"You were the best looking of all the guys in your class," she said. "Everyone said so."

He didn't deny it, exactly, but he waved a dismissive hand. "A lot of good it did me. I could barely get a date."

That had to be an exaggeration; she remembered plenty of girls noticing him. But it was true, he hadn't dated as much as you'd expect of a boy with his looks. "You were too nice. You weren't a player."

He laughed. "That's true, I never got that down." They turned and strolled along the river's grassy bank. "Now I look mean, like the little girl said. Maybe I should cultivate a mean persona to match. I'd get all the girls."

"As if that's going to happen." Lacey couldn't imagine Vito being mean. It just wasn't in his nature. "Is that what you want, Vito? All the girls?"

He gave her a look she couldn't read. "Not all. But

I'd like to get married, start a family, and I'm not getting any younger."

"Is that why you're adopting Charlie?"

He lifted a shoulder and looked away. "That's part of it."

"As far as getting married," she said, "you could have any woman you wanted."

A muscle contracted in his scarred cheek. "Don't, Lace."

"Don't what?" She stumbled on a root and he automatically caught her arm, steadied her.

"Don't lie to me. If I couldn't get the girls before, I'm not going to get them now."

"I'm not lying. You have a…" She paused, considering how to say it. "You have a rugged appeal."

"Is that so?" He looked over at her, his expression skeptical.

For some reason, her face heated, and she lifted it to cool in the breeze from the river. She focused on the birdcalls and blue sky, visible through a network of green leaves, while she tried to get her bearings.

When she looked back at him, he was still watching her. "Think of Tiffany Townsend," she said, trying to sound offhand. "She was all over you."

He rolled his eyes, just a little, making her remember him as a teen. "Tiffany Townsend isn't what I want."

"What do you want?"

Instead of answering, he walked a few paces to the right and lifted a streamer of honeysuckle growing against a thick strand of trees. Beyond it was a cave-like depression in a natural rock wall. "Wonder if kids are still carving their names in here?"

She laughed. "Lover's Cave. I'd forgotten about it."

She followed him inside, the temperature dropping a good few degrees, making a chill rise up on her arms.

Vito pinched off a vine of honeysuckle flowers, inhaled their scent, and then tucked them into Lacey's hair. "For a lovely lady."

Wow. Why wasn't Vito married by now? He was chivalrous, a natural romantic. Who *wouldn't* want to be with a man like that?

Inside the small enclosure, she turned to him, then stepped back, feeling overwhelmed by the closeness. *Make conversation; this is awkward.* "Did you ever kiss a girl in here?"

He laughed outright. "My *nonna* taught me better than to kiss and tell. Why? Were you kissed in here?"

"No." She remembered bringing Gerry down to the river, showing him the sights of her younger days. She'd hoped to finally get a kiss in Lover's Cave, but he hadn't wanted to follow her inside. Romantic gestures weren't his thing, but that was okay. He'd loved her; she was sure of that.

"What was wrong with the boys in your grade? Why didn't you get kissed here?"

"Guys didn't like my type." She turned away, catching a whiff of honeysuckle.

He touched her face, making her look at him. "What type is that?"

"Shy. Backward."

"Are you still?"

Lacey's heart was pounding. "I…I might be."

His fingers still rested on her cheek, featherlight. "Don't be nervous. It's just me."

A hysterical giggle bubbled up inside her, along with

a warm, melty breathlessness. She couldn't look away from him.

He cupped her face with both hands. Oh, wow, was he really going to kiss her? Her heart was about to fly out of her chest and she blurted out the first nervous thought she had. "You never answered my question."

"What was it? I'm getting distracted." He smiled a little, but his eyes were intense, serious.

He was *incredibly* attractive, scars and all.

"I asked you," she said breathlessly, "what *do* you want, if you don't want someone like Tiffany?"

"I want…" He paused, looked out through the veil of honeysuckle vines and let his hands fall away from her face. Breathed in, breathed out, audibly, and then eased out of the cave, holding the honeysuckle curtain for her, but careful not to touch her. "I want what I can't have."

Suddenly chilled, Lacey rubbed her bare arms, looking away from him. Whatever Vito wanted, it was obviously not her.

Seven

"Come on, Nonna, let's go sit on the porch." Vito was walking his grandmother out of the kitchen after dinner. Nonna hadn't eaten much of it despite his and Charlie's cajoling. Vito wished Lacey had stayed to eat with them, but she'd had something else urgent to do.

Most likely, urgently avoiding *him*. And rightly so. He was avoiding her, too, and kicking himself for that little romantic interlude in Lover's Cave.

"I'm a little tired for the porch, dear." Nonna held tightly on to his arm.

She sounded depressed, something Lacey had mentioned was common in patients recovering from a heart attack. Activity and socializing were part of the solution, so Vito pressed on. "But you've been in your room all day. A talk and a little air will do you good."

"Well…" She paused. "Will you sit with me?"

"Nothing I'd rather do." He kissed her soft cheek, noticing the fragrance of lavender that always clung to her, and his heart tightened with love.

He and Nonna walked slowly down the guesthouse hall. She still clung to his arm, and when they got to the bench beside the door, she stopped. "I'll just…rest here a minute. Could you get me another glass of that iced tea? I'm so thirsty."

"Sure." He settled her on the bench and went back to the kitchen to pour iced tea, looking out into the driveway to see if, by chance, Lacey had come in without his noticing. He'd feel better if she were here. Only because Nonna wasn't feeling well.

When he reached the guesthouse door with the tea, he saw that Nonna was already out on the porch. "Charlie helped me out," she said, gesturing to where the boy was shooting hoops across the street. "He's a good boy."

He set their tea on the table between the rocking chairs and sat down. The evening air was warm, but the humidity was down and the light breeze made for comfortable porch-sitting. In fact, several people were outside down the block, in front of the Senior Towers. A young couple walked by pushing a stroller, talking rapidly in Spanish. Marilyn Smith strolled past the basketball hoop with her Saint Bernard, and Charlie and his friend stopped playing to pet it and ask her excited questions.

Evening in a small town. He loved it here.

"Tell me about your course work, dear," Nonna said. "Is it going well?"

"Just finished a couple of modules today. It's interesting material."

"And you like taking a class on the computer?"

He shrugged. "Honestly, I'd rather be in a classroom where I could talk and listen, but we don't have a college here, and this is the easiest, cheapest option."

"That's just what Lou Ann Miller says. She's almost done with her degree. At her age!"

They chatted on about Vito's courses and Lou Ann and other people they knew in common, greeted a few neighbors walking by.

After a while, Vito noticed that Nonna had gotten quiet, and he looked over to see her eyes blinking closed. In the slanting evening sunlight, her skin looked wrinkled like thin cloth, and her coloring wasn't as robust as he'd have liked to see.

Lacey's little car drove into the driveway. She pulled behind the guesthouse, and moments later the back screen door slammed. Normally, she'd have come in by the front porch, stopping to pull a couple of weeds from the flower bed and say hello to Nonna. So she was still avoiding him, obviously, but at least she was home in case Nonna needed her.

Nonna started awake and looked around as if she was confused. "Tell me about your courses, dear," she said.

"We just talked about that." Vito studied her. "Are you feeling okay? Do you want to go inside?"

"I'm fine. I meant your job hunt. Tell me about your job hunt." She smiled reassuringly, looking like her old self.

"I keep seeing jobs that look interesting, but they're all in person." He paused, then added, "I want an online job."

As usual, Nonna read his mind. "You can't hide forever," she said, patting his hand.

"You're right, and I'm a coward for wanting to hide behind the computer. Except…would you want your kids to have a scary teacher?"

"I'd want them to have a smart, caring teacher. And besides, once people get to know you, they forget about those little scars. I have."

It was what Lacey had said, too. It was what Troy had said. It was even what his friends in the VA support group said. He didn't know why he was having such a hard time getting over his scarred face.

And okay, he was bummed for a number of reasons. If things had been different, if Charlie hadn't needed a home and if he hadn't been so scarred, then maybe he and Lacey could have made a go of things. She'd seemed a little interested, for a minute there.

But things weren't different, and he needed to focus on the here and now, and on those who needed him. He glanced over at Nonna.

She was slumped over in her chair at an odd angle, her eyes closed.

"Nonna!" He leaped up and tried a gentle shake of her shoulders that failed to wake her. "Charlie, come here!" he called over his shoulder.

He lifted his grandmother from the chair and carried her to the door just as Charlie arrived and opened it for him. "Is she okay?" Charlie asked.

"Not yet. Get Lacey, now!" Vito carried Nonna into her bedroom and set her gently on the bed. He should never have encouraged her to go out on the porch. On the other hand, what if she'd fainted in her room, alone? What had brought this on? Up until tonight she'd seemed to be improving daily.

Lacey burst into the room, stethoscope in hand, and bent over the bed, studying Nonna. "What happened?"

"She wasn't feeling well, and then she passed out."

Lacey took her pulse and listened. "It's rapid but…"

She stopped, listened again. "It's settling a bit." She opened Nonna's bedside drawer and pulled out a pen-like device, a test strip, and some kind of a meter. "I'm going to test her blood sugar."

Charlie hovered in the door of the room as Lacey pricked Nonna's finger, and Vito debated sending him away. But he and Nonna were developing a nice friendship, and Charlie deserved to be included in what was going on.

Nonna's eyes fluttered open. She was breathing fast, like she'd run a race.

Vito's throat constricted, looking at her. She was fragile. Why hadn't he realized how fragile she was?

Lacey frowned at the test strip, left the room and returned with a hypodermic needle. "Little pinch," she said to Nonna as she extracted clear liquid from a small bottle and injected her arm. "Your blood sugar is through the roof. What happened? It hasn't been this high in weeks!"

There was a snuffling sound from the doorway; Charlie was crying. Vito held out an arm, and Charlie ran and pressed beside him, looking at Nonna with open worry.

Lacey propped Nonna up and sat on the bed, holding her hand. "Are you feeling better? You passed out."

"Was it the cake?" Charlie blurted out.

Vito's head spun to look at the boy at the same time Lacey's did. "What cake?" they asked in unison.

Charlie pressed his lips together and looked at Nonna, whose expression was guilty.

"I…I gave him money…" Nonna broke off and leaned back against the pillow, her eyes closing.

"What happened?" Vito set Charlie in front of him,

put his hands on the boy's shoulders and studied him sternly. "Tell the truth."

"She gave me money and asked me to get her cake from the bakery. I didn't know what to do! I wanted her to have a treat. She said it would be our secret. And she gave me the rest of the money so I could get something, too." Charlie was crying openly now. "I'm sorry! I didn't know it would hurt her.'"

Vito shook his head and patted the boy's shoulder, not sure whether to comfort or punish him. "Remember, you're supposed to come ask me, not just go do something another adult tells you to do. Even if it's Nonna."

"Is she going to be okay?"

"She'll be okay." Lacey gave Charlie's hand a quick squeeze. "But your dad's right. Don't ever bring her something to eat again without asking one of us."

Even in the midst of his worries, Vito noticed that Lacey had automatically called him Charlie's dad. He liked the sound of that.

But he was second-guessing himself for bringing Charlie to live here at all. The kid was eight. He didn't know how to properly assist in the care of a very sick elderly woman, and he didn't have an idea of consequences.

Nonna said something, her voice weak, and Lacey put a hand on Charlie's arm. "Let's listen to Nonna."

"I...told him...to do it. Not his fault." She offered up a guilty smile that was a shadow of her usual bright one.

"Nonna! This is serious. We're going to have to take you to the emergency room to get you checked out."

"Oh, no," Nonna said as Charlie broke into fresh tears. "I just want to rest."

Lacey bit her lip and looked at Vito. "I might be able to talk Dr. Griffin into coming over to take a look at her," she said. "It would be exhausting for her to go to the ER, and I *think* she's going to be okay once her sugar comes down, but I'm not qualified to judge."

"If you could do that, I'd be very grateful." He knew that old Dr. Griffin lived right down the street.

"Okay. Charlie, would you like to come help me get the doctor?"

Charlie nodded, sniffling.

"Could you run upstairs and get my purse out of my bedroom?"

"Sure!" Charlie ran.

Vito was grateful. Lacey had every reason to be angry at the boy, but she was instead helping him to feel better by giving him a job. But that was how she was: forgiving, mature, wise beyond her years.

"Doc owes me a favor," Lacey said quietly to Vito. "I'm sure he'll come, if he's home. Just sit with her until we get back. It'll only be five minutes."

He nodded, gently stroking Nonna's arm, and Lacey and Charlie went out the door.

Beside Nonna's bed was a photo of him and his brother as children. She'd taken them in and raised them after their parents' accident, putting aside her bridge games and bus trips to rejoin the world of PTA meetings and kids' sporting events. And she'd done it with such good cheer that he'd never, until recently, understood the burden it must have been to her.

Now it was time for him to return the favor. To make sure that she was getting the very best care she could.

Which meant that later tonight if, God willing, Nonna was okay, Vito needed to have a very serious talk with Lacey.

After ushering Doc Griffin out the door with profuse thanks, Lacey walked back into the guesthouse as Vito emerged from Nonna's room, gently closing her door behind him.

"She's already asleep," he said. "She's exhausted, but she said to tell you again that she's sorry."

Lacey shook her head and paced the hall. "I'm the one who should be sorry. I should have been keeping closer track of her food."

"She's an adult," Vito said. "She made a choice." But something in his voice told her he didn't completely believe what he was saying, and what he said next confirmed it. "If you have a minute, could we talk?"

"Of course." She gestured for him to come into the front sitting room as her heart sank.

She'd been avoiding him hard all week, since that crazy moment in Lover's Cave. She'd thought he was going to kiss her, and she was sure that expectation had shone on her face. But instead of doing it, he'd gently pushed her away from him.

He was too kind to give her a real rejection, but even his careful one had made her feel like a loser.

He stood in the middle of the room, looking more masculine than ever amidst the delicate Victorian furnishings, and she realized he was waiting for her to sit down first. Who had those kind of manners these days?

Vito, that was who. And she was starting to care for him more than she should. Even though he didn't return the feelings, and nothing would come of it, she felt guilty. What would Gerry think if he knew that she was looking at his best friend in a way she'd once reserved for him?

Or, if the truth be told, in a different way but with the same end game? Because there weren't two men in the world more different than Vito and Gerry. And while Gerry's confidence and swagger had swept her away when she was young, Vito's warm and caring style appealed to her now.

He was still standing, waiting, so she sank down onto the chesterfield and pulled her feet up under her, leaving Vito to take the matching chair. It was a little small for him. Good. Maybe this conversation would be brief.

He cleared his throat. "I was wondering if you've been avoiding me."

Lacey felt her eyebrows shoot up, and against her will, heat rose into her cheeks. "Avoiding you?"

He nodded patiently. "After what happened last weekend. You know, at Lover's Cave."

She blew out a breath. She'd hoped to avoid that topic, but here he was bringing it out into the open to deal with. "I, um…" She wanted to lie, but couldn't bring herself to do it. "Maybe a little," she admitted.

"I thought so." He leaned forward, elbows on knees, and held her gaze. "You don't have to worry about a repeat. And you don't have to stay away from your own house to keep me at bay."

Keep *him* at bay? But of course, chivalrous to the core, Vito would put it like that. Make it seem like she was the one rejecting him, when in point of fact, it had been the other way around.

She swallowed and tore her eyes away from his. And for the life of her, she couldn't think of what to say.

How could she respond when she didn't even know what she felt, herself? When these feelings about Vito tugged at her loyalty to Gerry, even making her question some of her husband's behaviors? When Vito didn't seem to share her attraction at all?

"The thing is," he said, "I'm worried about Nonna's care. If Charlie and I are keeping you from focusing on that, then we should move out."

"She wouldn't like that."

"But if you hadn't come home tonight, and known just what to do, and given her that injection, something much worse could have happened, right?"

Miserably, Lacey twisted her hands together, staring at the floor. "I'm really sorry. I can see why you think I've been neglectful."

"That's not it. I don't think you and she ever had an arrangement where you had to be here with her 24/7. Did you?"

"No." Honesty compelled her to add, "But part of the appeal of living here was that she'd have me around a lot while I remodeled. Which I usually am. It's just been a week of running errands instead of remodeling."

He nodded. "I've been too focused on my own stuff, too, and apparently, it's given Nonna and Charlie too much time to get into trouble together."

"Does Charlie understand that he's not to do that anymore?"

"Yes. He was pretty upset when he saw Nonna passed out. He's grown very fond of her." He looked into her eyes again. "And of you. You've been very kind to him."

"He's a good kid."

He nodded. "So, this arrangement is working out well for Nonna, and well for Charlie. It's just you and me who need to manage our...interactions."

If he could be up front and honest, so could she. "I won't need to avoid you if you're serious about no repeat of that. I...I'm not over Gerry, you see." She fingered the necklace where she wore his wedding ring. "I know it's been over a year, which some people say is enough time, but it's not. He was everything to me."

A shadow crossed Vito's face, and for the first time she realized that he didn't talk much about Gerry. She wondered why. They'd been close comrades, right? Close enough for Gerry to come home with Vito on leave from the army. "You know what he was like," she persisted. "What a great guy he was."

Vito nodded once. "I know what he was like."

"So you can see why...well, why it's hard to get over him. He'll always be my hero."

A muscle worked in Vito's scarred face. "I understand. And believe me, the last thing I want is to displace that feeling in you. So please, stay and care for Nonna and don't worry about Charlie and me."

He stood and walked quickly out of the room.

And Lacey stared after him, wondering why it seemed that he was leaving a lot unsaid.

Eight

Vito was deep into finishing a research paper on the educator John Dewey when Charlie barged into his room. "Nonna's bored," he announced.

"Bored?" Vito came slowly back to twenty-first-century Ohio. "You're bored?"

"Well, yeah," Charlie said thoughtfully, "a little. But I came to tell you that *Nonna* is bored."

That brought Vito to full attention. "Did she ask you to get her sweets again?"

"No." Charlie shook his head vigorously. "She wouldn't. But she wants me to play a card game called Briscola, and it's too hard. And she wants me to watch TV with her, only I don't like her shows."

"I'll go spend some time with her." Vito ruffled Charlie's hair. "You probably want to go outside and ride that bike, don't you?" He'd fixed up an old one for Charlie over the weekend.

"Yeah," Charlie said, looking relieved that Vito understood. "Can I?"

"Let's see who's outside. If you stay on this block and be careful of cars, it's okay."

After he'd walked out with Charlie and made sure there were several parents in yards up and down the street, keeping an eye on the kids, Vito went back inside and headed toward Nonna's room. He'd stayed up late working on his research paper and spent most of the day on it, as well, and he felt like the letters on the computer monitor were still bouncing in front of his eyes. But it was all good. He was finding all the teaching theories extraordinarily interesting and it made him certain he'd done the right thing, enrolling in school.

Distracted, he tapped on the edge of Nonna's open door and walked in before realizing that Lacey was there, sitting beside Nonna, both of them engrossed in a television show.

A week had passed since Nonna's health scare and their talk, and they were settling into a routine in which Lacey spent more time at home. A routine that most emphatically did *not* include strolls to Lover's Cave. In fact, it barely included being in the same room together.

Lacey glanced up, saw him and looked away.

Nonna clicked off the television. "I can't believe he picked the blonde. I'm very disappointed in that young man."

"Well, she *was* the prettiest," Lacey said, laughing. "But you're right. I don't see the relationship lasting very long."

"Hey, Nonna." Vito bent over to kiss his grandmother's cheek, conscious that it was the first time he'd seen her that day. He'd been neglectful, working on this paper. He'd do better tomorrow.

The silver lining was that Lacey was spending more time with Nonna, staying home more. He'd heard her up at all hours, working on the renovations. Now, he realized guiltily that one reason she might be staying up late was that Nonna was needing her companionship during the day. Which was partly her job, but also partly his responsibility.

Lacey stood up. "I should go get some stuff done." It was clearly an excuse to get away from Vito.

Perversely, that made him want her to stay.

Apparently, Nonna felt the same. "Could you wait just a minute, dear? There's something I want to talk to you two about."

"O-kaaay." She sat down again with obvious reluctance.

Vito focused on his grandmother. "Charlie says you're bored, Nonna."

"Oh, my, bored doesn't begin to describe it." She patted Lacey's hand. "Although it's not for this one's lack of trying."

"I can't hang out as much as I'd like," Lacey said apologetically. "I've got to finish the renovations before the end of the summer, and there's so much to do. But I was thinking, maybe you're well enough to do more of the activities over at the Senior Towers."

"That's a great idea," Vito said, relieved. "Don't they have a bridge group?"

"Yes, and a drop-in lunch program, as well." Lacey smiled at Nonna. "You'd definitely get more exciting lunch choices over there than you get when I fix lunch. And it would get you walking more, which would be great for your health."

"How does that sound, Nonna?"

She shrugged. "Good, I guess," she said. "But..." She trailed off, plucking at the edge of her blanket.

"But what?"

She looked up. "I need a project."

"Like what, a craft project?"

"No, I want to start something new. With people."

That made sense; Nonna wasn't a sit-home-and-knit type of person, or at least, she hadn't been. "Like when you started your baking club that burned everything? Or that barbershop quartet, back when we were kids?" Vito smiled, remembering the off-key singing that had emanated from the big old house's front room when the ladies came to practice. Both groups had been disasters, but entertaining for all involved. Everyone wanted to join in Nonna's projects because she was so much fun as a person.

It made all the sense in the world that she would want to do something like that again.

"Do you have any ideas of what you might want to do?" Lacey asked her.

"Well…" She smiled winningly.

Vito shook his head. "Nonna, when you get that look on your face, I get very afraid."

"What's the idea?" Lacey sounded amused.

Nonna pushed herself up, looking livelier than she'd been the past week. "All right, I'll tell you. You know the show we were just watching?"

"*Bachelor Matches*, sure," Lacey said. "But what's that got to do with you having a project?"

Nonna clasped her hands together and swung her legs to the side of her bed. "I want to start a new matchmaker service in Rescue River."

"What?" Vito's jaw about dropped. "Why?"

"I don't think—" Lacey began.

"You remember the stories from the old country," Nonna interrupted, gripping Vito's hand. "My Tia Bianca, she was a *paraninfo*. Known for matchmaking throughout our village and beyond. She continued until she died at ninety-seven, and the whole region came to her funeral."

Vito nodded, frowning. He did remember the stories, but he wondered what was behind this.

"I need to start with some test clients," she continued, "and because of all you two have done for me, you can have the honor. For free!"

"Oh, Nonna, no," Lacey said. "I don't think this is a good idea. I don't want you to overexert yourself."

"She's right." Vito moved to sit beside his grandmother. The last thing he needed was Nonna trying to match him up with some unsuspecting woman who would be horrified by his scars.

"If I don't do this, then what do I have to live for?" Nonna's chin trembled. "Why do I even get up in the morning? Of what use am I to the world?" She buried her face in thin, blue-veined hands, her shoulders shaking.

Vito looked over at Lacey and saw his own concern mirrored on her face.

"Nonna, you have so much to live for!" she said.

"So many people who love you," Vito added, putting an arm around her shoulders.

"But none of it *means* anything!" she said, her face still buried in her hands.

Tears. Vito couldn't handle a woman's tears. "Oh, well, Nonna, if it's that important to you…"

"I could maybe see it if you get someone else involved to help you," Lacey said. "Someone sensible like Lou Ann Miller or Miss Minnie Falcon."

Nonna lifted her head, her teary face transformed by a huge smile. "Yes, they can help, both of them!"

"Good," Lacey said. "And not too much at once. Don't get carried away."

"It'll be just the two of you to start. Now, Vito. What do you want in a woman?"

Vito blinked. How had she recovered from her tears so quickly? Had he missed something?

Or had Nonna been hoodwinking them?

"Could you get me a tablet of paper, dear?" Nonna said to Lacey. "I don't want to miss a word."

"Here you go," Lacey said, handing Nonna a legal pad and a pencil. "And now I've got to get to sanding woodwork."

"Oh, stay, dear. I want to talk to you, too."

Lacey laughed. "Don't you think these interviews should be private?" She spun and walked toward the door.

Vito watched her go, thinking of Nonna's question. The truth was, he wanted someone like Lacey. But because of the secret he had promised to keep, he could never, ever have her.

The next Saturday, Lacey climbed out of her car at A Dog's Last Chance, Troy Hinton's animal rescue farm. As she stretched her arms high, she felt like a weight was gone from her shoulders.

Grasses blew in the soft breeze and looking off to the fenced area by the barn, she could see one dog's shiny black fur, another's mottled brown and white coat. Beside her, the creek rushed, a soothing sound, and red-winged blackbirds perched on the fence.

It was good to get away from the guesthouse. Good to do something for others.

Good to get away from Vito and the constant tension of trying to avoid him.

He'd been in her thoughts so much lately, and in a confusing way. He was so hardworking—up late most nights at his computer, making steady progress toward finishing his degree. He spent time with Charlie every evening, getting involved in the life of the town, even lending a hand with the youth soccer team when one of the coaches had a family emergency.

And he was so patient with Nonna, whose matchmaking service was going full speed ahead, obviously giving the woman something fun to do, but in the process, making Lacey uncomfortable.

A shiny new SUV pulled up beside her car, and Lacey was surprised to see her friend Susan getting out. "Nice car!" she said, remembering the rusty subcompact that Susan had driven when she'd lived for a year at the unrenovated guesthouse.

Susan made a face. "Sam. Just because we're expecting, he thinks we need to have a huge vehicle. I had to talk him down from a full-size van."

"How are you feeling?" Lacey could now ask the question without even a twinge of pain, and that told her she was moving forward, getting over her miscarriage and ready to celebrate other people's happiness.

"I'm feeling great, but Sam treats me like I'm made of glass." Susan rolled her eyes. "He didn't want me to come today. He's afraid one of the big dogs will knock me down. Like I haven't done this eighty thousand times before. And like a stumble would hurt the baby!"

"He loves you."

"He does." Susan's eyes softened. "And he's a control freak. But speaking of men…how's Vito?"

Lacey shrugged. "He's fine. Seems busy."

"You don't see much of him?"

"Well, since he's staying at the guesthouse, of course I see him. But we keep to ourselves."

"By choice, or would you like to see more of him?"

Lacey met her friend's perceptive eyes and looked away. "It's by choice. He makes me nervous."

"Nervous? Why?"

Lacey shrugged. "I don't know. He's so…"

"Big? Manly?"

Lacey laughed and shook her head a little. "Something like that. Come on, you've got to show me the ropes before all the kids arrive."

Susan was a longtime volunteer at the Kennel Kids, and she'd talked Lacey into getting involved. Lacey's therapist thought it was a good idea, too—a way to be involved with others and kids, not necessarily babies but with people. Making a difference.

"Speaking of Vito…" Susan said as they approached the barn where the sound of dogs barking was more audible.

Or at least, that was what Lacey thought her friend had said. "What?" she called over a new wave of barking.

"He's here. Vito." Susan gestured toward the barn, where Vito and Charlie stood talking to Troy Hinton, who ran the place and the Kennel Kids.

Lacey swallowed. What was he doing here?

Just then, he turned around and saw her. "What are you doing here?" he asked, sounding surprised.

"My question, too." They both looked at each other,

and Lacey saw in Vito's eyes the same ambivalence she felt herself.

Susan nudged her. "I'm gonna go get set up. Come over when you're ready. No rush."

"Charlie's doing Kennel Kids," Vito explained.

Relief washed over Lacey, along with something like disappointment. "Oh. So you're just dropping him off?"

"I'm...actually staying to help. Unless that's a problem?"

She lifted her hands, palms out. "No! No, it's fine."

Across the barn, Troy Hinton was hoisting a dog crate to his shoulder. "If anyone has a free hand, we could use your help here," he called.

Lacey moved forward at the same time Vito did, and they jostled each other. And then bounced apart like two rubber balls. "Sorry!" they both said simultaneously, and Vito stepped back to let her go ahead.

Lacey blushed as she hurried toward Troy. She started to lift a crate.

"Vito, could you help her with that?" Troy nodded her direction. "It's a heavy one."

So she and Vito took ends of the crate and followed Troy.

"Put it down there. We like to have a few crates out here for the dogs to get away from the kids. It's a tough gig for them. Could you two bring one more so I can get started with these kids?"

"Sure." Vito headed back, and then turned to see if she was coming.

She followed reluctantly. Why had she and Vito ended up together? Why wasn't it Susan over here with her?

"Hey, look, why don't you go ahead and help Susan?" Vito said, apparently reading her mind. "I can get that last crate."

"No, it's okay. I'll help you. It's too heavy."

Vito gave her a look. "I'm every bit as strong as I used to be, even if I do have a few injuries."

"I know that!" Then, ashamed of her exasperated tone, she followed him into the barn and took the bull by the horns. "I'm sorry if this is awkward, Vito. I wish it wasn't."

"You don't want to be around me?"

"It's not that. I just…" More seriously, she was worried he didn't want to be around her.

"Hey, D'Angelo, c'mon! We don't have all day here!" Troy sounded impatient.

Lacey flinched and stole a glance at Vito. That kind of thing had always made Gerry livid; he'd hated to be corrected. It was a guy thing.

Except, to her surprise, Vito laughed. "That's rich, coming from you, Hinton." And then he hustled over to the crate. "Guess we'd better get a move on."

She hurried to help him, wondering as she did what it meant that Vito hadn't gotten angry.

Had Gerry been unusually touchy?

She went to the crate and lifted the other side, breathing in the good smells—hay and animals. And maybe it was the thought of hay, but her necklace felt itchy on her neck.

"Dad!" Charlie ran over, his whole face lit up in a smile. "Can I get a dog? Mr. Hinton said they need homes." He jogged alongside them as they carried out the large crate.

Vito went still, looking at Charlie, then at Lacey. "It's the first time he called me 'Dad,'" he whispered.

Lacey wanted to hug both of them, but her hands were full, so she settled for a *"Wow"* mouthed across the crate as they continued carrying it out.

"Hey, Lacey," Charlie added, coming up beside her, obviously unaware of the emotions he'd evoked. "Want me to help with that? That's no job for a girl."

Lacey chuckled. "Girls can do a lot of jobs, including moving things. But yes, if you'd like to, you can take that corner." She winked meaningfully at Vito, warning him to slow down.

He gave a subtle nod, and something arced between them. It was nice to be able to communicate without words sometimes.

After they'd put the crate down, Charlie grinned at her. "*You* wouldn't mind having a dog around, would you, Miss Lacey?"

He was way too cute with that grin. She couldn't resist ruffling his hair. "I won't answer that on the grounds that it might incriminate me with your dad," she said, "but confidentially...I do like dogs."

"See, Dad?"

"Way to throw me under the bus," Vito complained, but there was a smile in his voice.

"Can we get one?"

Vito held up a hand. "That's not a decision we're going to make today."

Charlie looked like he wanted to whine, but shouts from a couple of newly arrived boys distracted him and he ran off. Vito watched him go, shaking his head. "It's hard for me to deny him anything."

A man Lacey knew vaguely emerged from the barn with two pit bulls on leads. As he approached the boys, Charlie took several steps back in obvious fear.

The man clearly noticed. "Hey, Troy," he called, "we have some new Kennel Kids here today. You want to give the bully breeds talk?"

She and Vito drifted over and listened while Troy explained that it was all in how the pit bull was raised, how some were taught to fight while others were raised in a gentle environment, how one always had to be careful in approaching a dog like this.

Troy's words triggered a thought. Charlie had apparently been raised in a rough environment, and he, too, acted out sometimes; he needed to be approached with care. But with love—the kind of love that Vito was so unselfishly offering him—he was starting, even now, to grow into his potential and to become the person God had made him to be.

She watched as one of the smaller pit bulls, a white female named Gracie, was brought out and went from boy to boy. The group started dissolving, some of the boys playing with puppies, others learning to clean kennels, others helping to leash and train dogs. Charlie knelt, and the white pit bull approached him slowly, cautiously.

"Hold out your hand so she can sniff it," Vito encouraged, and after a moment's hesitation, Charlie did.

Watching Vito, she saw someone so much more than the handsome older boy who'd protected her from school bullies when she was younger. He was fatherly now, a man, a hero. He accepted what had happened to him and ran with it, growing into a person of value.

But then again, the seed of the man he'd become had been present in the kind, handsome boy next door.

"Lacey!" Susan gave her a light punch on the shoulder, and she started and turned to her friend. "I've been trying to get your attention forever." She looked where Lacey was looking, and then a slow smile broke out across her face. "Are you *sure* you don't have feelings?"

"No! It's just Vito."

"Somehow, I'm not convinced."

"No way! The truth is, I keep thinking about Gerry."

One of the other volunteers turned. "Gerry McPherson? Boy, that guy was a piece of work."

Lacey cocked her head to one side, feeling her smile slip a little.

"What does *that* mean?" Susan asked, her voice protective.

Lacey looked at the other volunteer, and suddenly, she didn't want to hear what he was going to say.

And then Vito stepped up beside her. "Gerry McPherson was my friend and Lacey's husband." He put an arm around her, a tense arm. "And he died serving our country." His chin lifted a little and he gave the man a level stare.

The other guy raised his hands. "Hey, didn't mean anything." He turned and walked rapidly away.

Susan gave Lacey a curious look and went over to help one of the younger Kennel Kids, who was having trouble unhooking a black Lab's leash.

"Thanks." Lacey sidestepped away from Vito so she could see him better, and immediately he let his arm drop from her shoulders.

A chill ran over her where his arm had been.

What had the man meant, that Gerry was a piece of work?

She didn't want to face the tiny sliver of doubt that had pierced her.

A couple of hours later, Vito stood up from repairing a broken crate and was startled to find himself surrounded: Susan on one side and Troy's wife, Angelica, on the other.

"So, Vito," Angelica said, "what's going on between you and Lacey?"

"Not one thing. Why?"

"Oh, just wondering." The two women sat down beside him, each working on one of the broken crates.

He wasn't lying about nothing going on, at least not in a guy sense; there wasn't anything of the dating variety going on, that was for sure. On the other hand, there was a lot going on emotionally, every time he saw Lacey.

Man, that had been a close one with that stupid guy almost revealing something bad about Gerry. Lacey had looked so shocked and stricken that he hadn't been able to handle it.

She for sure still believed the best about Gerry. And that was good. He'd always remain a hero in her eyes.

And Gerry *had* definitely had a heroic side. In battle, there wasn't another man in the world Vito would've trusted more. They'd saved each other's skins more than once.

But the home front—specifically, women—had been Gerry's downfall. Something rotten in the way he was raised, or maybe the fact that he'd been so handsome and suave. Too many women had flocked to him, and Gerry hadn't ever been taught how to treat women with respect. To him, a woman who threw herself at him was fair game.

Any woman was fair game. Lacey definitely hadn't thrown herself at him; she wouldn't have known how. But she'd gotten swept away and before Vito could turn around and warn her, she'd gone and fallen for Gerry.

Vito had tried to talk her out of it, but that had been a miserable failure. Once someone was that far gone, you couldn't bring her back.

At that point, the only thing he could do was to insist that if Gerry wanted Lacey, he needed to marry her, not just use her and throw her away.

It had just about killed him to do it, because by that time, he'd thought Lacey was something pretty special himself. Talking his friend into marrying her was like cutting off his own arm. He'd had to admit, just to himself, that he'd been waiting for Lacey to get old enough that he could honorably ask her out.

Gerry had beaten him to it, had gotten in there and stolen her heart.

And he'd treated her despicably.

And now Vito was in a position of hiding Gerry's wrongdoing from the woman he still, if the truth be told, carried a torch for.

"Earth to Vito," Angelica teased, and he snapped back into the here and now. "You *sure* there's nothing going on?"

"I'm sure," he said heavily. "And there never will be anything going on."

Nine

The next Friday, Vito heard a high-pitched shout from Nonna's room. "Vito! Lacey!"

He scrambled up from the computer and down the stairs on Lacey's heels. "What's wrong, Nonna?" she was asking as they both entered Nonna's room.

"Are you okay?" he asked his grandmother, who was sitting at the small writing desk looking perfectly fine. In fact, her color was better than he'd ever seen it.

Lacey put a hand on Nonna's shoulder. "You scared us. What's going on?"

"It's my first success," the older woman said. "I found you both dates for tonight!"

Vito had to restrain himself from rolling his eyes. Just what he needed, a blind date.

"Tonight?" Lacey sounded just as distressed as Vito felt. "I…I have plans."

Nonna's eyes sparkled behind her glasses. "The same plans you've had for the past three Friday nights, young lady? A date with a paint can?"

Lacey smiled ruefully. "Actually…yes."

Nonna rubbed her hands together. "I hope you both

have some dressy clothes. You'll need to be ready at six o'clock."

Vito groaned inwardly. The last thing he wanted was to put on a suit. "Why dressy? This is Rescue River."

"You both have reservations with your dates at Chez la Ferme."

"No way!" Vito said.

"That's not how you do a blind date, Nonna." Lacey's forehead creased. "For one thing, it's really expensive."

"You get coffee first," Vito added. And then he processed what Lacey had said and looked over at her. How would she know? Was she doing online dating?

He found her looking back at him with a similar question in her eyes, and he felt himself flushing. The truth was, he *had* put his profile up on a Christian dating site a couple of times. And he'd gotten no results worth pursuing, which he attributed to women being turned off by his ugly mug. Or his lack of wealth.

"What if we don't like them, Nonna? Then we're stuck spending hours together." Lacey sank down onto the edge of Nonna's bed, facing them both.

"Whereas with coffee," Vito added, "you can escape after half an hour."

"You're taking a negative attitude," Nonna said. "Why do you think you'll want to escape?"

Vito looked at Lacey, and she looked back at him, and they both laughed. And then he narrowed his eyes at her. So she *had* online dated. But when?

Nonna steepled her hands and stared down at the floor. "I'm sorry," she said. "Do you want me to cancel the whole thing?" Her tone was desolate.

Vito looked at her bowed head and slumped shoulders and his heart melted. "No, Nonna, it's okay. I'm game. But just this once."

"Me, too," Lacey said with a sigh. "Who's my date?"

Nonna smiled gleefully up at them. "It's a surprise! You won't know until you get to the restaurant."

"Wait," Vito said. "We're *both* at Chez la Ferme tonight? Why there?"

"It's the only nice place in town. I'm so excited for you. You're going to have a wonderful time."

There was no trace of her former sadness, and Vito studied her narrowly. He had the feeling he'd just been manipulated.

"Be ready at six. You're meeting your dates at six thirty."

As they walked out, Vito couldn't help shaking his head. That Nonna. She really was a matchmaker, and she was also someone to whom he, at least, couldn't say no.

At five minutes before six, Vito came out of his room at the guesthouse. He'd driven Charlie over to a new friend's house, and as a result, he'd had to get ready quickly. Not that it mattered. Less time to spend in this necktie that felt like it was strangling him.

He needed to work on his attitude, he knew that. Maybe Nonna's matchmaking was God's way of finding him a partner, someone who'd help him fulfill his dream of building a loving family. Lacey wasn't the only woman in the world, despite what his heart said.

Halfway down the stairs, he caught his breath.

There was Lacey in a sleeveless blue dress that highlighted her figure and her coloring. She stood in front of an ornamental mirror, attempting to fasten a necklace.

Breathe. She's not for you.

He walked slowly the rest of the way down the stairs, watching her struggle with the small clasp. "Need some help?"

"Oh! Um, sure." She held out the ends of the necklace, her back to him, bowing her head.

Her neck looked slender and vulnerable. Her short hair brushed his fingers, soft and light as bird feathers.

He could smell her sweet, spicy perfume.

Breathe.

He fumbled a little with the tiny clasp, dropped one end, had to start over. "Sorry. Big fingers." But that wasn't really the problem. He knew how to fasten a necklace; he'd been doing it for his women friends forever.

Why did it feel so different with Lacey?

Why was he going slowly on purpose, trying to extend the moment, to stay close to her?

He finished and stepped back quickly, forbidding his hands to linger on her shoulders. "Whoever you're meeting tonight is going to be very happy."

She turned toward him, a smile curving her lips as she gave him an undisguised once-over. "Your date will be, too."

He laughed a little, shook his head. "My date is going to be in for a surprise, but not such a pleasant one."

"You look good, Vito." She reached up and, with one finger, touched his face. The bad side of it. "Except that there's a little shaving cream…right…here."

Their eyes met and her touch lingered on his face.

That soft, small finger, touching a place no one had ever touched, except in a medical capacity, made him suck in a breath. "It's hard to shave with…this." He gestured toward the ridged, scarred side of his face.

She let her hand open to cup his cheek. "I'm sure."

The moment lingered. He felt like he couldn't look away from Lacey's steady, light brown eyes.

Until Nonna opened her door and clapped her hands. From her room came strains of opera music. "Don't you both look gorgeous!"

Vito took a step backward and Lacey let her hand fall to her side.

"We clean up okay," he said, clearing his throat, trying to keep his cool. "How are we going to know our dates?"

"It's all set up at the restaurant."

Vito bit back a sigh and slid his hands into his pockets. "You're not going to tell us who, are you?"

"And spoil the anticipation? Of course not. That's just one of the things that will be unique about my matchmaking service. Now, you two had better get going."

That brought up another angle he hadn't considered. "Would it be awkward if we walked together to dates with other people?" he asked Lacey. "Or would you rather drive, with those heels?" *Which look spectacular*, he thought but didn't say.

"They're wedges—they're fine." Her cheeks were a little pinker than usual. "Um, sure, we can walk."

So they strolled together through the downtown of Rescue River, all dressed up. The evening air was warm, and shouts from the park indicated that families were enjoying the evening. Vito leaned just a little closer to Lacey to catch another whiff of her perfume, wishing with all his heart that he could spend this evening with her, as her date.

His thoughts toward his old friend Gerry, who'd made him promise to keep Charlie's parentage a secret, were becoming more uncharitable by the minute. The man had been a hero and a friend, and Vito mourned the loss of him, but he couldn't deny resenting the promise that stood like a wall between him and the woman he was coming to care for more each day.

"Who do you think our dates are?" she asked, looking up at him with laughter in her eyes. "Will it be people we know or complete strangers?"

"Bound to be people we know. It's Rescue River. And Nonna knows the same people we do." He actually hoped it was someone who knew what he looked like, just to spare himself the awkward moment that often happened when people met him for the first time.

They approached Chez la Ferme to discover a small crowd of people waiting outside. "Looks like they're backed up. Hope Nonna really did make a reservation."

"Or not." Lacey made a wry face. "I do have that paint can waiting for me at home."

He chuckled. She wasn't any more into this whole game than he was. "Look, there's Daisy."

"And Dion." Vito lifted an eyebrow. Were the police chief and the social worker officially admitting they were a couple? Because being together at Chez la Ferme pretty much guaranteed that they'd be perceived that way.

"Hey!" Lacey hugged both of them, first Daisy, then Dion. "Long wait?"

"Not if you let them know you're here." Dion

punched Vito's arm lightly. "Get with the program, my brother."

So Vito walked in to the hostess stand and gave his name.

"Oh, yes, Mr. D'Angelo. We've been expecting you." The hostess gave him a broad smile. "Your table will be ready in just a few minutes."

Obviously, she was in on Nonna's secret.

Almost as soon as he'd exited the restaurant, while he was still walking toward his friends, the hostess came behind him. "Dion Coleman?" she called. "And Lacey McPherson?"

A slow smile crossed Dion's face. "Oh, your grandma," he said to Vito, shaking his head. And then he crooked his arm for Lacey. "Shall we?"

Lacey's eyebrows lifted as she looked up at the police chief. "Well, okay, then." She took his arm and the two of them turned toward the restaurant.

Vito's stomach seemed to drop to his toes as he watched the pair. He couldn't help noticing the details: the large squared-off college ring that glinted against Dion's dark skin, the expensive cut of his suit, the suave way he put a hand on the small of Lacey's back to guide her inside.

They were good-looking enough that several people in the crowd turned to watch. Or maybe the raised eyebrows were because Dion was linked with Daisy in the town's collective, gossipy mind.

Vito had known he couldn't be with Lacey himself, on account of Charlie. He'd almost—not quite, but almost—accepted that.

What he hadn't anticipated was how seeing Lacey

with someone else would feel like a punch in the stomach.

And he should have known, because it had happened before, with Gerry. This exact same feeling: *You're not going to get her. She's going to choose someone else. And you're going to have to stand there and be a man about it. Do the right thing.*

Speaking of doing the right thing, he was being rude to Daisy, standing there watching Lacey and Dion disappear inside the restaurant like a hungry dog, tongue hanging out.

He schooled his expression before he turned to Daisy. Was that a similar look on her face?

That brought him out of himself. He couldn't have Lacey, and it was wrong to think she should save herself for him, that she shouldn't find happiness with someone else. Dion was a good man, respected by everyone in town.

And now, he needed to go through with the evening's plans as if he didn't feel gutshot. He didn't know Daisy well, but he assumed that if Dion was set up with Lacey, Daisy was probably set up with him. He turned to her. "Any chance you're here for a blind date, too? Set up by my grandma?"

"Yeah." She nodded. She didn't look enthusiastic.

He soldiered on, as he'd been trained to do. "Well, you didn't get the prize," he said, "but you'll get a good dinner. I think I'm your date."

"Oh. Okay." She didn't sound thrilled, but not horrified, either. "What do you mean, not the prize?"

He gestured vaguely toward the scarred side of his face. "Only a doting grandma could love this mug."

She didn't deny the ugliness of his scars, but she

shrugged them away. "Most women care more about what's inside. Whereas men…" She trailed off, and then glanced down at her own curvy body. "I'm not the prize, either, compared to her." She gestured toward the door through which Dion and Lacey had disappeared.

It was true. Vito didn't find Daisy as attractive as he found Lacey. But then, he didn't find *any* woman that attractive. For better or worse, his heart had attached itself to Lacey, and he was realizing more every minute that his wasn't the kind of heart that could easily change directions. Still, Daisy—blonde, vivacious and with a killer smile—was something of a showstopper herself. And he wasn't going to be rude to her. "You *are* a prize. Anyone with any sense would wonder how someone like me got to go out with a knockout like you. I'm honored to be your date."

The crowd by the door was thinning out, and a bench opened up. "Want to sit down?"

So they sat, and talked about her work in social services, and his desire to become a teacher. She was a good conversationalist, easy to talk to. He found himself confessing his worries about scaring kids, his desire to work with them in person, and his pretty-sure decision to go with online teaching. When the hostess called them to go inside, she had to do it several times, apparently, from her expression when she came out to get them.

As they followed her into the restaurant, replete with stained glass and low lighting and good smells of bread and prime rib, they kept talking.

"Don't do online teaching if your heart is in the real classroom," she urged him as they crossed the restaurant behind the maître d'. "Kids respond to the whole person, not just how you look. I used to worry about them teasing me about my weight, but they're completely fine with it."

"As are most men," he assured her. "Women think we all like stick-skinny women, but that's not the case. You're beautiful."

"Your table, sir." The maître d' gestured, and Vito held Daisy's chair for her.

Only then did he realize that Dion and Lacey were just around a small corner from them, probably within earshot of most things they would say.

Not only that, but the two of them were leaning toward each other, sharing an appetizer and appearing to have a marvelous time.

Ten

Lacey looked at the handsome man across the table from her and tried to ignore Vito and Daisy being seated practically right behind them.

Unfortunately, she couldn't ignore what she'd heard. "You're a beautiful woman," Vito had said to Daisy.

Which was true, and she didn't begrudge Daisy the praise, but the way it stung alerted her to something she hadn't quite realized before: she wanted Vito for herself.

"Hey," Dion said. "What's going on?"

She shrugged and toyed with her water glass.

"All of a sudden you're not comfortable," he said. "Is it something I said?"

"No! No, you're fine. What were we talking about?" She laughed nervously. "I'm sorry, I'm a little intimidated."

His forehead creased. "Intimidated? Why?"

"You're kind of known for your wisdom," she said, "not to mention that you're the police chief."

"Which is all a nice way of saying I'm an old man,"

he said, "who's fortunate to be out with a fine-looking young woman."

The words were gallant, but Lacey could tell Dion wasn't interested in her in *that* way. Rather than feeling insulted, she felt relieved and suddenly more comfortable. This was a little awkward, especially with Vito and Daisy so close, but at least she knew she wasn't misleading Dion.

"I'm the fortunate one," she said. "I might pick your brain about some Bible stuff. You're said to know everything there is to know."

"Who says that?"

"Angelica's husband, Troy. He thinks you're the font of all wisdom. And my brother's a fan, too."

"Don't you be thinking I'm perfect," he warned. "Nobody's perfect. Nobody's even close, right? That's what the good book says."

"See, you're making my point for me, quoting scripture at the drop of a hat." She frowned. "Anyway, of course, you're right. But I've spent my whole life trying to be good. Trying to be perfect."

"We all try," he said, "and that's not bad."

She did her best to ignore the rumble of Vito's voice behind her, but it played along her nerve endings like an instrument. She forced it away, forced herself to talk with Dion about her brother, with whom he'd had a good deal of official contact until Buck had dried out and they'd become friends. She forced herself to rave over the delicious, beautifully presented food: Dion's prime rib, her own organic grilled salmon.

"That was great," she said when they'd pushed away their plates.

"Yes, it was," he said, "but let me ask you something. Are you in this matchmaking thing for real?"

She looked at him and slowly shook her head. "Not really. I'm just doing it for Nonna. You?" She only asked the question to be polite, because she was pretty sure of the answer. "I always heard you were with Daisy."

"Everyone thinks that," he said, smoothly changing the subject. "You're a newish widow. It makes sense you're not ready to do a lot of dating."

"Yeah. I…I really loved my husband."

Dion didn't say, "He was a good guy." That would normally be the remark you made, wouldn't it? But instead, he said, "That's obvious. Gerry was blessed to have you. But—" he raised a finger and pinned her with a steady gaze "—at some point, you're going to have to move on. You're too young of a woman to give up on life."

She wasn't going to tell him about her infertility. Instead, she turned the tables. "Do you take your own advice?"

Dion cocked his head to one side, smiling at her. "Touché. I've been on my own a lot longer than you have, and I should probably be letting go of some baggage by now."

She wanted to ask him about his past, but the way his face closed when he mentioned it told her she shouldn't. "Moving on isn't as easy as it sounds, is it?"

"No," he said. "But let your feelings lead and you'll be fine. Your feelings and your heart. And most of all, the Lord."

Well, if she were to let her feelings lead… Involuntarily, she glanced over at Vito and then back at Dion.

"I'm ashamed to say that I haven't spent much time consulting the Lord about this," she admitted.

The server took their plates away and promised to be right back with the dessert tray. "There's no time like the present," Dion said, "to take it to the Lord. Want to?"

So she let him take her hand in his, closed her eyes, listened to Dion's quiet words and said a few herself. Asked for forgiveness that she'd neglected to seek God's guidance in her feelings. Asked Him to lead her in the right direction.

When they were finished, she felt cleansed.

"And now," Dion said, "if we can get their attention, do you think we should move our table together with our friends for dessert?"

"I, um, I don't know if Nonna would approve."

"Nonna's not here, is she? Hey, Vito." Dion caught his attention and made the suggestion, and the servers rushed to help, assuring them it was no problem.

Once they were all sitting together, there was a slightly awkward silence, broken by the approach of the dessert tray. The waiter began to describe the offerings.

Lacey looked over at Daisy. "I need chocolate. Now. You?"

"I agree."

After a restless night, Vito woke Charlie up early, figuring they'd grab breakfast and go burn off some energy on the basketball court. But even before they reached the main floor of the guesthouse, delicious smells of cinnamon and bread wafted toward them.

Could Lacey be up baking cinnamon rolls?

But when they walked into the kitchen, there was Nonna in her Kiss the Cook apron, bending over to check on something in the oven and looking like her old self.

At the table was Miss Minnie Falcon, matriarch of the Senior Towers and former Sunday school teacher to almost every child in Rescue River. Next to her was Lou Ann Miller, stirring sugar into a cup of coffee.

"You're looking good, Nonna," he said, walking over to the stove and giving his grandmother a kiss.

"And that smells good!" Charlie came over as Nonna removed the pan from the oven. "Can I have some?"

"Five minutes, *cùcciolo*." She patted Charlie's shoulder, smiling.

Vito felt a great weight lifting off him, a weight he hadn't known he was carrying. Nonna was going to be okay. Suddenly he could see it and feel it and believe it. Not only that, but she'd called Charlie by the same affectionate name she used to use on Vito and his brother. That, more than anything, meant Charlie was becoming part of their family. He swallowed against a sudden tightness in his throat and walked over to greet the ladies at the table.

As good as her word, Nonna brought a steaming loaf of cinnamon bread, along with small cups of butter and jam, and placed them in the middle of the table.

"Italian breakfast like the old days." Vito put an arm around Nonna, still feeling a little misty-eyed.

Charlie's hand froze in the act of grabbing a piece of the bread. "Why is it brown?" he asked.

"Because I used the healthy flour. It tastes just as good, so eat up."

Charlie grabbed a piece, slathered it with butter and

jam and took a huge bite before anyone else had even secured a piece. "It's good, Nonna," he said, his mouth full of food.

Vito leaned close to Charlie's ear. "Good table manners will get you more food," he whispered.

Charlie raised his eyebrows. "What'd I do?"

"Don't talk with your mouth full." They'd cover the grabby behavior later. First things first.

Miss Minnie put a clawlike hand on Vito's arm. "I understand you were our first matchmaking client," she said.

"Yes, tell us all about it." Lou Ann Miller raised a slice of bread to her nose and inhaled, closing her eyes. "Fabulous, dear. You've outdone yourself."

As Nonna beamed, the door from the backyard opened and Lacey breezed in. She wore a red-and-white-checkered shirt and cutoff shorts and she looked as carefree as she had at twelve.

And he was a goner.

"That smells amazing, Nonna D'Angelo," she said, approaching the table. "And look, whole grains! I'm impressed."

"Hey, Miss Lacey, you're not wearing your necklace."

Lacey's hand flew to her throat. "Oh, wow, I'll run up and get it before I eat."

"Want me to get it for you?" The words were out of Vito's mouth before he realized that he didn't, in fact, want to get her the necklace. Didn't want her to wear Gerry's wedding ring around her neck anymore.

"Oh, it's okay. I'll get it." She half walked, half skipped out of the kitchen.

"My Vito." Nonna pinched his cheek—the second

time someone had touched his scars in the past two days. "Always too nice for your own good."

"That's right," Miss Minnie said unexpectedly. "Being kind isn't all there is to life. Take a stand!"

"What are you ladies talking about?"

Lou Ann Miller glanced over at Charlie, who'd grabbed his handheld game and was immersed in it, still chewing on a huge mouthful of bread. She turned back to Vito. "Your love life is what we're talking about."

Vito looked from Lou Ann to his grandmother to Miss Minnie. "Seriously? Is that what I'm doing wrong? Being kind and nice?" But of course, they didn't know about his Charlie deception, which wasn't nice at all.

"Tell us about last night," Nonna said instead of answering his question. She removed her apron and sat down at the table and looked up at him expectantly.

"It was…fine. Daisy is great."

"And you don't want to date her."

"Well, of course he doesn't. For one thing, she's attached to Dion Coleman at the hip."

"And then there's the fact that Vito's affections are elsewhere."

"That's obvious. The question is what can we do about it?"

The three women's conversation was spinning out of control. "Nobody needs to do anything about it," he protested. "I can handle my own life."

The only good thing was that Charlie wasn't listening; he was just eating bread and playing with his game.

Lacey came back into the room and Vito didn't

know whether to be glad or sorry. He got busy cleaning up the breakfast dishes and washing mixing bowls and bread pans.

"How was your date with Dion?" Lou Ann asked her.

Vito couldn't help tuning his ears to hear what she would say. They'd all ended the evening together, on a friendly note and laughing about various people's efforts to play matchmaker over the years, but Vito still had a sinking feeling he couldn't compete with Dion, suave and good-looking and successful.

And he *couldn't* compete, he reminded himself. He couldn't have Lacey, because telling her the truth would destroy her world. Destroy her image of the husband whose ring she wore around her neck.

"It was great," she said easily. "He's a lot less intimidating on a date than when he's being the police chief. Mmmm, this bread is good."

Vito glanced over to see three gray heads turn toward Lacey. "So," Nonna said, "do you like Dion?"

"She means *like* like," Charlie supplied, his mouth full. "Like a boyfriend."

It seemed like everyone in the room—except Charlie—was holding their breath.

"No, I don't think so." Lacey seemed unconscious of how much interest her words were generating. "And I don't think he likes me that way, either, but I'm glad to get to know him better as a friend. He's a good guy and a wonderful Christian."

Vito let out a breath and his tight shoulders relaxed. He grabbed a dish towel and started drying cutlery with great energy.

"I'm not really ready to date," she continued, fingering her necklace. "I'm afraid you're going to have to find some other clients."

There was a little commotion outside the door, and then it opened, framing Buck, Gina and little Bobby, who toddled across the room toward Lacey. "Laasss," he crowed reverently, crashing into her leg and hanging on.

"Hi, honey!" She lifted him onto her lap and tickled his stomach, making him laugh.

She looked beautiful with a baby.

She would look beautiful with *his* baby.

Man, he had it bad and he had to stop.

"Mind if the dogs come in, Lace?" Buck asked.

She glanced down at Mr. Whiskers. "Run while you can, buddy," she said, and then beckoned for Gina to let the dogs in.

Immediately, Crater, a large black mutt with a deep scar on his back, galloped in. At his heels was a small white mop of a dog, barking joyously.

Charlie threw himself out of the chair and started rolling and roughhousing with them.

Vito looked at the ladies to see if they found the ruckus disturbing, but they were watching and laughing. Bobby struggled out of Lacey's lap and toddled fearlessly into the fray.

Buck and Gina came over to the table and talked above the kids and dogs, and all the noise created a dull roar Vito couldn't really follow, given his hearing loss. His aids worked well with individual conversations, but big noisy groups were still a challenge.

He was wiping down counters when Charlie came over and tugged at his arm. He bent down to hear what the boy had to say.

"Can we get a dog now, Dad?"

That had been predictable. "Of these two, which kind do you like?"

"Can we get two?"

"No!"

"Then, I like the big one. Can we get one like that? With cool scars?"

The phrasing made Vito lift an eyebrow. Cool scars, huh? That scars could be cool was a new concept to him. "We'll start thinking about it more seriously," he promised.

Given how strong his feelings for Lacey had become, he had some serious thinking of his own to do, as well.

When there was a knock on the front door, Lacey hurried to answer it, relieved to escape the busy kitchen and the probing questions of Nonna D'Angelo, Miss Minnie and Lou Ann. Not to mention Vito's thoughtful eyes.

It was Daisy. "Hey, I was walking by, and I thought I'd take the chance that you were here. Do you have a minute?"

"Um, sure." She and Daisy knew each other, but they weren't drop-in friends. She came out on the porch and gestured toward a rocking chair, tucking her feet under herself in the porch swing. "What's up?"

"I just wanted to make sure we're okay about last night."

Lacey forced a laugh. "We were clearly all victims of the grandma matchmaking brigade. What happened isn't your fault or mine, or any of ours."

"And it was fun in the end, right?"

"Sure." As she thought back, she realized that it *had* been fun, sitting and laughing with Vito and Daisy and Dion. Except for that nagging anxiety at the pit of her stomach.

Daisy was watching her, eyes narrowed. "But..." she prompted.

Lacey shrugged. "Nothing."

"It's not nothing. I *knew* something was bugging you last night. What's going on?"

"Nothing's going on." She paused. "If you're worried about whether I like Dion, I do, but not as a boyfriend."

Daisy waved a hand. "I know. I could tell. And it's not my business, anyway. I *wish* Dion would meet someone."

Lacey lifted an eyebrow, but didn't comment. She couldn't tell if Daisy meant it or not.

"And I'm not interested in Vito that way, either."

Lacey tried to school her facial expression, but she couldn't help feeling happy. "I...wasn't sure."

"I mean, he's great," Daisy said, "but I'm pretty sure he only has eyes for you."

Lacey had thought she couldn't get any more joyous, but an extra wave of it washed over her at Daisy's words. "You really think so?"

Daisy nodded. "I sat and had dinner with him, and he was great, he really was. So nice and flattering and kind. But he couldn't stop himself from looking over at you guys every time you and Dion laughed."

A breathless feeling took Lacey over then. Maybe this—her and Vito—could really happen. Maybe it would. "Do you think it's wrong for me to think about another man, so soon after losing Gerry? As a social worker, I mean?"

Daisy studied her thoughtfully. "It's been over a year, right?"

She nodded.

"And what have you done to get over the loss?"

"Well…" Lacey thought about it. "I've had counseling, with a psychologist and with Pastor Ricky. And with some of my friends, too, unofficially. I'm doing desensitizing things about kids, because…did you know I lost a baby, too?" She was amazed that she could say the words openly now, with only an ache instead of a sharp, horrific pain.

Daisy nodded. "I heard, and I'm sorry for your loss. That must have been terribly hard to deal with."

"Well…yeah. The worst. And I never thought I'd heal, but Buck, and little Bobby, and the church… Lots of people have helped me, and life goes on."

The door flew open and Charlie emerged. He threw his arms around Lacey and said into her ear: "I think Dad's getting me a dog!" Then he ran down the stairs and across the street to the basketball hoop where a couple of neighborhood kids were playing.

Lacey looked after him and blinked. "That came out of nowhere. I thought he didn't like me."

"If you seem to pose a threat to his relationship with Vito, he may act out. On the other hand, he might very well need a mother figure." Daisy leaned back in the chair, rocking gently.

"A mother figure?" Lacey laughed. "Why would he think of me that way? I'm not even dating his dad."

"Yet. Charlie may see something that the two of you won't yet acknowledge."

Heat suffused Lacey's cheeks and she didn't know how to respond. Because the truth was, she was interested in dating Vito. After last night, watching him with Daisy, she was sure of it.

There was a fumbling sound at the door and Miss Minnie Falcon made her way out, struggling a little with her rolling walker. Both Lacey and Daisy jumped up to help her.

"Would you like to sit a spell on your old porch?" Lacey asked. She'd bought the house from Miss Minnie two years ago when it had become too much for her to handle, and she tried to encourage the older woman to maintain her connection. It made Miss Minnie happy, and as her brother's wife, Gina, had discovered, Miss Minnie and the house itself were full of stories. Besides, Lacey enjoyed the sharp-tongued woman's company.

"Thank you, dear. I wouldn't mind."

Lacey made sure Miss Minnie was settled comfortably while Daisy folded her walker and put it against the porch railing.

"It got a little too noisy in that kitchen. I like children, but in controlled circumstances."

"I hear you," Daisy said. "It's probably just as well I don't have children." Then Daisy's eyes went round and she looked at Lacey apologetically. "I'm sorry. I guess this is a sensitive topic for you."

"Kind of," Lacey said. Then, to her own surprise, she added, "Especially since I can't have kids."

"Never?" Daisy's eyes widened, and she reached out to give Lacey's hand a quick squeeze.

"That's what they say." She lowered her head, and then looked from one woman to the other. "Please don't tell anyone, okay? I...I'm still getting used to it. And it's not common knowledge."

"It shouldn't be," Miss Minnie said, her voice a little sharp. "Young people share far too much about themselves these days. Some things are simply private."

Daisy laughed. "I take it you're not baring your soul on social media, Miss Minnie?"

"My, no." The older woman turned back toward Lacey. "There are other ways to nurture children, besides bearing them."

Lacey opened her mouth to disagree, and then realized she was wrong. Miss Minnie knew what she was talking about from personal experience. "You taught Sunday school for almost all the kids in Rescue River, so I guess you're right. That's one way."

"And you're sure getting close with Charlie, from the looks of things," Daisy said. "Kids need all kinds of people in their lives to grow up right. Not just their parents." She turned to Miss Minnie. "Did you ever regret not having kids?"

Lacey flinched a little. That was definitely a personal question. Daisy was the type to ask them, but Miss Minnie was the type to offer a sharp reply.

"Not that it's commonly known, but of course I did," the older woman said. "That's the reason I taught Sunday school all those years. If you don't have a family, you have to do a little more figuring to build a good life for yourself."

"You may not have much family, but I hear you do have a boyfriend," Daisy said slyly.

Lacey smiled, remembering what she'd seen at the Chatterbox. "Mr. Love, right?"

"You young people and your gossip tire me out. I

need to get back home." But a faint blush colored Miss Minnie's cheeks.

"We're sorry." Lacey stood to help the woman to her feet. "We don't mean to tease. It's just nice to see…" She paused to clarify her own thoughts. "It's nice to see a single person having a fun, active social life."

"That's right," Daisy contributed, picking up Miss Minnie's walker. "We single ladies have to stick together. And what's more, it's crazy that any time you're friends with a man, people start linking you up romantically."

Lacey and Miss Minnie glanced at each other as they made their way down the steps. Was Daisy talking about Dion? Was she or wasn't she involved with him?

After they'd walked Miss Minnie back to the Senior Towers, they stopped on the sidewalk to talk before parting ways.

"You going to the fireworks tonight?" Lacey asked.

"Yeah, I love the Fourth of July. You?"

Lacey shrugged. "I'll probably watch them from the front porch, with Nonna."

"And Vito?"

"Stop trying to match-make," Lacey scolded. "You heard what Miss Minnie said. We all share too much about our personal lives." But even saying that felt hypocritical, because the thought of Vito, of watching fireworks under the stars together, made a delicious excitement fill her chest. "I'm sure he and Charlie will watch the fireworks, one way or another."

"Then I'm sure you'll enjoy plenty of fireworks," Daisy teased.

"Hey, now!" She watched the woman—who was

maybe going to become a closer friend—wave and stroll down the street.

A fluttery excitement filled her. Maybe it *would* be a night to remember.

Or maybe not. She herself was starting to feel like a relationship with Vito might be possible. But she wasn't sure how he felt. With Vito, it always seemed to be one step forward, one step back.

406   *** *** *** ***

to the guests to become comfortable at way and stroll down the street.

A flutter, excitement filled him, butterflies

Eleven

On Monday afternoon, Vito was tempted to turn down his hearing aids as he drove home from the dog rescue with Charlie and his new dog going crazy in the back. Had he just made a big mistake? What was Lacey going to think of this new, and very loud, guest?

At a stop sign, he looked back to check on them. Wolfie, the new white husky mix, stood eager in the giant crate Troy had lent them, bungee-corded in place in the bed of the pickup. Charlie was turned around as far as his seat belt would allow, poking at the dog through the open back window, talking nonsense to it, turning back toward Vito to shout "look at him, *look* at him." The disbelieving thrill in his voice and his eyes melted Vito's heart.

Whatever the challenges, he thanked God that he could do this for Charlie.

When they pulled into the guesthouse driveway, Lacey was outside on her knees, weeding the narrow flower garden that fronted the house. Dressed in old jeans and gardening gloves, she looked up and smiled, brushing blond bangs out of her eyes with the back of her hand.

Vito felt an unbelievable warmth just looking at her.

They'd finally relaxed around each other, watching the fireworks together, eating Nonna's new, healthy concoctions, hanging around the house. Homey, domestic stuff. It was dangerous territory, but he couldn't resist reveling in it for a little while, at least.

He stopped the truck, and Charlie jumped out. "Miss Lacey, Miss Lacey, come see my new dog!"

She stood easily and pressed her hands to the small of her back, smiling, then headed toward the vehicle where Vito was opening the back hatch. "I can't wait to meet him!"

Vito opened the hatch and the crate, and Wolfie bounded out. He leaped up on Lacey, his paws almost to her shoulders, nearly knocking her down. Then he ran through the yard in circles, barking, his big feet tearing at Lacey's flowers. Finally, he approached Charlie in a play bow, his blue eyes dancing, his mouth open in a laughing pant.

"Sorry, sorry!" Vito ran to hook the new leash on to Wolfie's collar, but the dog darted away.

Charlie tackled the dog, and the two of them rolled on the ground together like a couple of puppies, while Vito struggled to find the ring on the dog's collar to hook on the leash.

Finally, he attached the leash and put the looped end in Charlie's hand. "Hold on to him!" he told Charlie, and then stepped back beside Lacey to watch the pair. "I'm sorry about your garden. I'll fix it. He's a little excited."

"So what happened to the concept of a small dog?" she asked drily.

Vito inhaled the scent of wild roses that seemed to come from Lacey's hair. "I know. I'm sorry. I should have called to make sure a bigger dog was okay. It's just… We were playing with a bunch of the dogs, and it was as if they chose each other."

"He was the one, Lacey! Isn't he cool?" Charlie rose to his knees as the dog bounded around him in circles, barking.

A smile tugged at the corner of Lacey's mouth, and in that moment, Vito saw her tenderness for Charlie and fell a little bit more in love with her.

"Well…we did have Crater here, and he was as big as…what's this guy's name?"

"Wolfie!" Charlie shouted, pouncing on the dog again.

"Hold tight to that leash while I get his stuff out," Vito warned, and then turned back to the truck and started unloading dog food and dishes. Rather than an expensive dog bed, they'd stopped by the Goodwill store; a big blanket would do for the dog to sleep on.

He was carrying it all up to the porch when Nonna came out.

"What have we here?" she asked, smiling.

"It's Charlie's new dog." Vito looked over in time to see the dog pull out of Charlie's grip and head for the porch.

Before Vito could do anything, Lacey dived for the leash and held on. The dog actually pulled her for a couple of feet before she was able to stop it. "Sit, Wolfie!" she commanded, but the dog just cocked his head at her, his mouth open in what looked like a laugh.

Lacey sat up cross-legged and held the leash firmly. "Nonna, this dog's a little crazy. Make sure you're sitting down when he's around, and wear long pants until he settles down." To Vito she added, "He's strong and he's got big claws. He could knock Nonna down in a second, and those claws could scratch her up pretty bad."

"He knocked me down," Charlie said, almost proudly. "And he scratched me, too." He held up an arm. Even from this distance, Vito could see the thin line of blood.

They'd definitely start training Wolfie today.

"Why was Wolfie at the shelter?" he heard Lacey ask Charlie. "He looks like a purebred, and he acts like a puppy."

"He's two years old, and the people who had him said he was un, un…" He looked up at Vito.

"Unmanageable?" Lacey asked drily.

"That's it!"

Lacey rolled her eyes at Vito, looking exactly like she had as a teenager.

He put down the supplies and spread his hands. "I know. I know, and I'm sorry. It was just something in his eyes."

"Wolfie's, or Charlie's?"

"Both. Charlie fell in love with Wolfie as soon as he saw him, for whatever reason." He noticed the "I found a home" placard they'd gotten at the shelter. "Supposedly, we have two weeks to test everything out. If he doesn't work for us, we can choose another dog."

"And two other families tried him and he didn't work out, so he was really sad," Charlie said. "I hope we can keep him. We can keep him, can't we, Dad?"

Vito blew out a breath. "We're going to do our best to give him a good home. With love and attention and discipline, he should settle down."

"Like me," Charlie said offhandedly, and went to hug Wolfie. "Don't worry, guy. Dad let *me* stay."

Lacey's hand flew to her mouth and Vito felt his throat tighten. They glanced at each other, and it was as if they agreed without words: this *had* to work.

His phone buzzed in his pocket, and seeing that the dog was safely under Lacey's control, he pulled it out for a quick look.

He didn't recognize the number, but it was local. "Hey, I'd better take this just in case it's about a job," he said to Lacey. "Can you…" He waved a hand at Charlie, the new dog and Nonna.

"Got it," she said instantly. "Come on, Charlie. Let's see if we can teach him how to walk nicely on a leash."

The fact that she had his back so readily and without complaint made Vito's heart swell with gratitude. He clicked on the call.

"Vito D'Angelo? This is Sandra Sutherland, head of the school district's summer programs. You interviewed with one of my people last week."

"That's right." He sank down onto the porch step to focus. "What's up?"

"I'd like to talk to you about a job opening for this summer, with a possibility of extending into fall. How are you with special needs boys? Older, say from eight to sixteen?"

Without even thinking about it, he laughed. "That's getting to be my specialty." He looked down the street at Charlie.

She went on to detail the job of Vito's dreams: part-time for now, sports centered, mentoring and counseling a small group four mornings per week. "We thought you'd be perfect for it."

"Can I ask why?"

She spoke slowly, thoughtfully. "Your background as a veteran, your leadership experience and the fact that you're familiar with the foster care system all play into it. And…" She hesitated.

Why would she sound so uncomfortable? Even as he thought of the question, Vito's hand went to his face and he knew the answer. "Do some of the kids have physical disabilities? Visible ones?"

"That's it," she said, sounding relieved. "We actually have two boys, siblings, who were in a terrible house fire. They lost their mother, and they have some disfiguring burns. They've been acting out, even within the small group, so when Marnie came to me and said she had a good interview with you, and she mentioned your scars…"

Vito blew out a breath and looked skyward. Was this what God was doing? He'd never thought his scarred face would be an asset.

"Look, if you're interested and available, we could set up a time to talk. Sooner rather than later, though. Their current group leader just quit."

He couldn't help chuckling again. Between Charlie, and Wolfie the dog, and these boys, it looked like he was headed toward a career in rehab. "I'm free later today," he said, and they set up a time.

He clicked his phone off and just sat a minute, thinking.

He wanted a career in education, with children. But with his looks, he'd figured he couldn't do anything but online teaching. Now, come to find out, there was a perfect job within reach—partly *because* of how he looked.

Special ed. Physical limitations. He hadn't thought about it before, but he was definitely strong enough to lift kids in and out of wheelchairs. At the VA, he'd gotten to know guys with all kinds of disabilities. And with his own very visible scars, the students would know instantly that he understood.

Father God, You work in mysterious ways.

His heart beating faster, he looked down the street and saw Lacey and Charlie coming back toward the house, laughing, trying to manage the unruly Wolfie. He stood up and headed toward them. He wanted nothing more than to tell Lacey the good news.

A job, Charlie, and maybe Lacey. Everything he wanted was within reach. Under one condition: he had to figure out a way to tell Lacey the truth about Charlie.

Lacey looked up from trying to contain Wolfie's enthusiasm and saw Vito walking toward them, face alight with some kind of excitement. The call he'd gotten must have been good news.

"Dad! Dad!" Charlie bounced toward Vito, leaving Lacey to try to hold Wolfie back with both hands as he lunged after the boy he seemed to know already was his.

Vito ruffled Charlie's hair. "How's it going? We better help Lacey, huh?"

They came toward her and Vito took hold of the out-of-control dog's leash. "We need to figure out how to work off some of his energy," he said.

"That's what me and Lacey were trying to do! Only,

he's so crazy and he doesn't know how to walk on a leash and he ran after a squirrel and we almost couldn't hold on!"

"He's excited, buddy. We'd better let him run in the yard at the guesthouse, if that's okay with Lacey."

"Good idea," she said. "He was about to yank my arm off!"

Once they'd gotten him inside the fence, they all ran and played with him. It didn't take long to discover that the fence had a broken section; Charlie and Lacey ran after the dog and brought him back while Vito did a makeshift fix. After Wolfie's energy finally started to calm, Vito and Lacey sat down on a bench together while Charlie lay beside the dog, holding tightly to his leash.

"So, finally I can ask. What had you looking so excited after that phone call?"

Vito's face lit up. "I might have a job."

As he told her about the offer, Lacey nodded. It sounded perfect for someone as nurturing—and strong—as Vito.

"I'm going to have to set up some doggie day care for Wolfie, I think, and Charlie has his park program, so we'll be out of your hair a little more if this all works out."

She tilted her head to one side, studying him. "You're the least self-centered guy I know."

He looked blank. "What do you mean?"

"Most men would be crowing and bragging about getting a job, but you're all about how to take care of your responsibilities and how it'll affect other people. That's…refreshing."

His eyes narrowed. "You sound like you've had some experience with another type of guy."

She looked at the ground, nodding, feeling guilty. Lately she'd been having some realizations that were altering her view of her marriage, and it wasn't at all comfortable.

"Gerry?"

She hesitated a moment. But she could tell Vito, couldn't she? "Yes. I hate to say it, but he tended to think of himself first. When the time came to reenlist, he didn't even ask me—he just did it and bragged about it. And I was pregnant!"

"You're kidding. That wasn't right. You deserved better." He touched her chin, forcing her to look at him. "You deserve the very best."

She met his warm brown eyes and her heart beat faster. She didn't know about deserving the very best, but she had the feeling that being with Vito would *be* the very best. Maybe even, in some ways, better than being with Gerry. It was a disloyal thought that made her look away from Vito, but that lingered in her mind long into the night.

Two days later, Vito set out lawn chairs at the lake and pulled a picnic lunch—courtesy of the Chatterbox Café—out of the back of the pickup.

It was his way of making it up to Lacey for all the hassles of having a giant new dog in her guesthouse. He'd talked her into taking the day off with them— his last day off for a while, as his new job started tomorrow.

"I wish we could've brought Wolfie," Charlie said, his face pouty as he reluctantly helped unload the picnic basket. Since Monday, he and the dog had been inseparable.

"This is a good way to test out the doggie day care where he's going to spend mornings. And Lacey needs a break."

Charlie made a face, and Vito sighed. The boy and Lacey had been getting along great, but when he was in a bad mood, he tended to take it out on everyone. He hadn't wanted to come to the lake because it meant being separated from Wolfie. And probably because Vito's new job started tomorrow. Even though it wouldn't mean much of an adjustment for Charlie, even though he liked his summer parks program, anything new was tough on a kid who'd had too many changes and losses in his young life.

"I'll take over if you want to check out the water," Lacey said to Charlie, coming over to the table. "Man, it's hot! I'm coming in as soon as we get our stuff set up."

She was wearing a perfectly modest black one-piece and cutoff denim shorts. With her blond hair and sun-kissed, rosy face, the combination was striking.

Very striking.

"Hey, Charlie!" came a boy's shout from the beach area.

"Xavier's here!" Charlie's bad mood dissipated instantly. "Cool!" Without asking permission, he ran down toward the water.

"Stay in the shallow part," Vito called after him. He waved to Xavier's mom, Angelica, who was sitting with several other women right at the dividing line between grass and sand. He pointed at Charlie and she nodded, indicating she'd keep an eye on him.

"Can he swim?" Lacey asked.

"Not real well. His old life wasn't conducive to swimming lessons."

She spread a red-and-white plastic tablecloth on the splintery picnic table and anchored it with mustard, ketchup and pickle bottles. "Speaking of his other life, how are his visits with his mom going?"

"Okay, when she shows up sober." She and Charlie had had two supervised visits since the first Sunday one. One of the other planned visits she'd canceled, and once, she'd shown up high, causing the social worker to nix her seeing Charlie. "Whether the visit works out or not, he gets upset. Tuesdays are rough."

"Well, let's make his Wednesday better." She flashed a brilliant smile at him as she set out a big container of lemonade. "Man, I'm hot. I'm going to go say hi to Angelica and dip in the water."

"I'll probably be down." Vito wiped his forehead on his T-shirt sleeve.

Before Iraq, he'd have whipped off his shirt and jumped in the water in a heartbeat. Now, though, he hesitated.

For one thing, he'd have to take out his hearing aids. And while he could still hear some, especially if a person spoke clearly and was close by, he couldn't keep up with conversations, especially when there was a lot of background noise.

Add to that the dark, raised scars that slashed across his chest and back, ugly reminders of the plate glass window that had exploded beside him that last violent day in Kabul. He'd taken the brunt of the glass in his chest, with a few choice gashes in his face and back.

Outside of a hospital, the only person who'd ever

seen the scars on his torso was Charlie, and he'd recoiled the first time Vito had taken off his shirt in his presence.

To have a whole beach full of people do the same might be more than Vito could handle.

It wasn't that he was vain, but he hadn't yet gotten used to turning people off, scaring kids. And mostly, he couldn't stand for perfect, gorgeous Lacey to see how he looked without his shirt.

Hearing young, angry voices shouting down at the water, Vito abandoned his load of beach towels and headed toward where Charlie and Xavier seemed to be in a standoff.

"It's not *fair*." Charlie clenched a fist and got into fighting position.

"Charlie!" Vito shouted, speeding up to a run.

"Take that!" Xavier let out a banshee scream and brought his foot up in an ineffectual martial arts kick, at the same moment that Charlie tried to punch him.

Somehow, both boys ended up on the ground, which seemed to end the disagreement.

Vito reached the boys. "Hey, Charlie, you know hitting doesn't solve any problems."

Angelica came over, not looking too concerned. "Xavier. You know you're not to practice karate on your friends. You need to apologize."

"You, too, Charlie."

Identical sulky lower lips came out.

Identical mumbles of "Sorry."

Then Xavier's face brightened. "C'mon, let's get in the lake!" he yelled, and both boys scrambled to their feet and ran to the water as if nothing had happened between them.

Getting in the lake sounded really refreshing. "Sorry about that," Vito said to Angelica. "I didn't see how it started, but I'll speak to Charlie."

"Don't worry about it. These things happen with boys, and they don't last but a minute." She smiled at him. "How's Wolfie working out?"

"He's a handful," Vito said, chuckling. "Bet Troy's glad to have him off his hands."

"There's a sucker born every minute," she teased. "Actually, he's a great dog. He just needed to find the right home." She nodded toward the other women. "Come on over and say hi."

The sight of Lacey, hair slicked back, perched on the end of someone's beach chair, was all the magnet he needed. He went over and greeted Gina and a woman named Sidney. They had their chairs circled around three babies, and as he watched, little Bobby held out his arms to Lacey and she lifted him up. "Such a big boy!" she said, nuzzling his bare stomach and blowing a raspberry on it, making the toddler laugh wildly.

Vito's heart seemed to pause, then pound. Lacey looked incredible with little Bobby, like she was born to be a mother. And suddenly, Vito wished with all his heart that she could be the mother of all the children he wanted to have.

If only he could tell her the truth about Charlie, cutting away the huge secret between them, he could let her know how he felt and see if there was any chance she'd be interested in him. But telling the truth would destroy her happy illusions about her husband and her marriage. Not to mention the impact the truth would have on Charlie, if he could even understand it.

And Vito didn't take promises lightly, especially deathbed promises.

The trouble was, he was having a hard time imagining a future without Lacey in it. Somehow, in these weeks of living at the guesthouse, she'd become integral to his life and his happiness.

"Dad! Come in the water!" Charlie and Xavier were throwing a beach ball back and forth.

"You should get in." Lacey smiled up at him. "The water feels great."

The sun beat down and he was sweating hard now, partly from the heat of the day and partly from the warmth he felt inside, being here with Lacey.

"Let's take the babies down to dip their feet in the water," Angelica suggested. The other women agreed, and soon they were all at the water's edge, wading.

"You're not worried about getting burned, are you?" Lacey asked him. "You're dark skinned. But I have some sunscreen back at the car if you need it."

"Why d'you have your shirt on, Dad?" Charlie asked, crashing into Vito as he leaped to catch the ball.

Vito's face heated, and to avoid answering, he splashed Charlie. That led to a huge splash fight and Vito was able to cool off some, even though he didn't dunk to get his shirt entirely wet. It was white, and his scars would show through.

When they got hungry, they headed back up to the picnic tables and Vito grilled hot dogs. The women and babies had declined to join them, but Xavier had come over to get a hot dog. It was fun and relaxing, just the kind of day he'd hoped they could have, a gift to Charlie and to Lacey, too.

"You nervous about starting your job tomorrow?" Lacey asked as they ate.

"A little," he admitted. "It's definitely going to be a challenge. I expect some testing."

"You'll handle it well," she reassured him. "You're great with kids."

Charlie grabbed the ketchup and squirted it on his hot dog. The bottle made a raspberry sound which Charlie immediately imitated, laughing.

"Let me do it!" Xavier cried, grabbing for the ketchup. As he tried to tug it from Charlie's hand, he accidentally squeezed the bottle. Ketchup sprayed around the table, painting a line across Charlie, Lacey and Vito's chests.

"That's enough!" Vito plucked the squirt bottle from Xavier's hand and set it at the other end of the table, away from the boys.

"I'm sorry," Xavier said, looking serious and a little frightened as he surveyed the damage.

"It looks like blood!" Charlie said. He and Xavier looked at each other. Charlie made another raspberry sound, and both boys burst out laughing.

Vito rolled his eyes. "Sorry," he said as he handed napkins to Lacey, and dabbed at the mess on his own shirt.

She shrugged and met his eyes, her own twinkling, and he was struck again with how great she was. She didn't get bent out of shape about boys and their antics. What a partner she'd be.

"This isn't coming off, and it stinks," she announced, gesturing to the ketchup on her shirt. "I'm getting in the water. And I bet I can beat you two boys." She jumped up from the picnic table and took off.

Immediately, the boys followed her, laughing and yelling.

Vito watched from the picnic table, alone and sweating in a now-even-smellier T-shirt. More than one male head turned to watch Lacey's progress. With her short hair and petite figure, laughing with the boys, she looked like a kid. But if you took a second look—as several guys were doing—she was all woman.

He dearly wanted to take his shirt off and follow her into the water. To be an easy, relaxed part of things. A partner she could be proud of.

He let his head drop into his hands, closed his eyes and prayed for insight and help. Insight to understand what to do, and help to do the right thing. Not just now, in regards to his ultimately silly shirt dilemma, but overall, in regards to his promise.

The smell of warm ketchup got to him, though, and he lifted his head again without any answers.

Except a memory from his time rehabbing at the VA: had *he* ever lost esteem for someone because they had scars?

And the answer was glaringly obvious: of course not. He respected the way they'd gotten them, and he looked beyond.

Charlie and the other kids might not be mature enough to do that, but Lacey? Of all people, she was one of the least superficial he knew.

On the other hand, he wasn't just interested in gaining her respect. He wanted more. He wanted her to be drawn to him physically, as he was to her.

And why was he so obsessed with what Lacey thought of him, when their relationship couldn't go anywhere?

Like a slap in the face, it hit him: he was in love with her.

Not just a crush, a remnant of high school attraction.

Full-fledged, grown-up *love*.

Wow.

He just sat and tried to wrap his mind around that concept for a while, until the boys got out of the water and started throwing a football and Lacey came back toward the table.

"Hey, lazy," she said, grabbing his hand and tugging it. "The water feels great. Come get in!"

He let her pull him up and she laughed and let go of his hand, walking toward the water with a flirtatious smile over her shoulder.

All of a sudden, he didn't want to be the good friend anymore. For once, he wanted to follow his instincts and desires, to be the main man. To try and see whether his scars were really the turnoff he feared they'd be.

He pulled off his T-shirt, removed his hearing aids and located their case, all the while psyching himself up for an encounter in some ways more terrifying than heading into battle.

Twelve

Lacey's cheeks heated as she headed down toward the lake. Had she been too forward? What was she thinking, insisting that Vito come swimming?

She glanced over her shoulder to see if he was following her. When she saw him fiddling with his ear, her hand flew to her mouth.

She usually didn't even remember that he wore hearing aids. But of course, he couldn't wear them into the water.

Was that why he'd been reluctant to come in?

She glanced again. Or was it the scar that slashed across his back, dark and very visible?

Pushing him had been a mistake. He was such a good sport he'd come if begged, but she hoped she hadn't caused him to do something he didn't want to do.

Kids shouted as they ran and splashed in the shallow part of the lake. As she walked by a group of teen girls, she inhaled the fragrance of coconut oil, something every dermatologist in the world would blanch at. Some things never changed.

She just hoped the kids and teens would be tactful about Vito's scars.

She waded into the lake, waist deep, then looked back to see whether he was following. And sucked in her breath.

The front of his chest, which she hadn't seen before, was crisscrossed with scars. Long ones and short ones, visible even with his dark Italian skin.

Their eyes met, and Vito's steps faltered a little.

Should she say something? Walk back toward him? Tell him his battle scars didn't affect her feelings toward him, except maybe to warm her heart that he'd sacrificed for his country?

But instinct told her to treat him just as she always had. Meaning, how they'd all acted at the lake as kids, since they hadn't been here together since.

He'd reached the water's edge now, and she grinned in invitation and flicked water at him with her hand. "Scared?" she taunted.

"A little." There seemed to be a double meaning in his words. "But I can play scared." He took a few steps toward her. Suddenly, he dived underwater. A few seconds later, she felt a hand wrap around her ankle, and then she was under, giggling into the green water.

She surfaced, shaking her wet hair out of her eyes. Hooked a toe around Vito's ankle and pushed hard.

He toppled backward and came up, grinning and holding up his hands. "Truce! Peace!"

Their playfulness attracted Xavier and Charlie, who came splashing toward them. "Dad, gross—put a shirt on!" Charlie yelled loud enough for the whole beach to hear.

And apparently, despite his hearing impairment, Vito could make out the words, too.

Around them, a few kids and teens stared openly at Vito. One boy, a little older than Charlie and Xavier, said something that made the nearby kids laugh.

A flush crawled up Vito's face. "I never claimed to be a beauty queen," he said to Charlie with a half smile.

He was handling it well, but she ached for him. He'd earned those scars defending his country, and she honored him for it.

Xavier studied him thoughtfully. "Kids used to tease me for being bald, when I had cancer. Mom said to ignore them."

Vito didn't respond.

Charlie went up and tugged his arm. "Hey! Are your hearing aids out?"

Vito looked down at Charlie. "What?"

"Can't he hear?" Xavier asked.

This was getting to be a little much, and Lacey decided to intervene. "Have you boys ever heard of chicken fights?"

Neither had, so she knelt in the water and told Xavier to climb up on her shoulders. "Get on your dad's shoulders, Charlie," she said, deliberately speaking loudly. "The game is, try to knock each other off."

"Get down, Dad!" Charlie yelled into Vito's ear.

Vito grinned at her, kneeled and took Charlie onto his powerful shoulders. When he stood, he and Charlie towered over Xavier and Lacey.

"Come on, Xavier. We may be short, but we're fast," she said, and went in low.

They splashed and played for a while, with both boys getting thoroughly and repeatedly dunked. Lacey's shoulders ached from carrying a heavy, wiggling boy, but she didn't mind. The water was cool and she hadn't laughed so hard in a long time.

Most of the rest of the swimmers drifted away, except for a few kids who talked their parents into participating.

Best of all, nobody was talking about hearing problems or scars.

Finally, Angelica called the boys to come and rest, and when she offered up watermelon as an enticement, they splashed their way to shore.

"Do you want to go get some?" Vito asked.

She shook her head. "I'm not hungry."

"Swim out to the dock?"

"Sure, and I'll beat you!" Lacey plunged her face into the water and started swimming fast.

It felt good. She seemed to have some extra energy saved up, a shaky excitement that made her want to move.

She was starting to feel such a mix of things for Vito. Admiration. Desire to protect. Caring.

Maybe even love.

She shoved that thought away and swam faster. She couldn't be falling in love with Vito, could she? Vito, her old friend and high school crush. Vito, the guy who'd always been around, always ready to lend an ear or a smile or a hand with whatever you were working on, be it figuring out algebra problems or speaking up against bullies or healing a broken heart.

Was he spending time with her now just to help her get over Gerry? It seemed like, in his eyes, she'd been seeing something more.

She reached the dock at the same moment he did, but touched it first. "I won!" she crowed into his ear.

"You did." He grinned at her as he hoisted himself out onto the wooden platform.

She found the ladder and climbed up, narrowing her eyes at him. "Wait a minute. Did you try your hardest?"

"Let's just say the D'Angelos are swimmers. And gentlemen."

"You *did* let me win!"

He didn't admit to it, but he flashed a grin that took her breath away. Standing above her dripping wet, his teeth flashing against dark skin, his eyes laughing, he looked like a hero from some ancient, epic tale.

She couldn't seem to move. She just knelt there transfixed, halfway up the ladder, staring up at him.

He extended his hand toward her. "Come aboard, milady," he said, and helped her to the dock.

She needed the help. She couldn't seem to catch her breath.

They lay side by side, faces toward the blue sky, the sun warming their wet bodies. Beside them, a little railing shielded them from those on the beach, though their shouts were still audible. Lacey was exquisitely conscious of Vito, the warmth of his arm close to hers, the even sound of his breathing.

She couldn't understand what was going on inside her. This was Vito, her old neighbor, comfortable and safe. Vito, who'd always seemed out of reach because he was older.

Yet he was someone else, too, someone new. The things he'd been through had forged him into a man of strength and valor, a man she couldn't help but admire. It was starting to seem like she both wanted and needed him in her life.

"Do you remember coming out here as kids?" he asked unexpectedly.

"Sure." She watched a cloud laze across the sky, and then turned so she could speak into his ear. "Buck and I came with Dad pretty often when we were little."

"How come your mom never came? Was she…sick, even back then?"

"I don't know. She never wanted to do family things. Always busy with her dreams and plans, I guess."

Vito didn't answer, but he reached over and patted her hand, warm on the dock beside her.

"I don't know when she started with the pills." Lacey followed the swooping path of a dark bird, thinking about it. "I think she was okay when I was real small, but then she just started going in her bedroom and shutting the door." As she said it, she got a visceral memory of standing outside the closed door, hand raised to knock. She'd tried not to do it, knowing that Mom didn't like to be disturbed, but she hadn't been able to stop herself from knocking, then pounding on the door.

Where had Buck and her father been? Why had she been there alone for so long, with just her mother?

"If I had a kid," she said, still speaking into his ear to help him hear her, "I just hope I'd have more sense than to leave her to fend for herself like Mom did to me."

"You would. You're great with Charlie."

His automatic, assured response touched her. "Thanks, Vito."

"It's not about having the sense, it's about heart," he said with a shrug. "And heart, you've got."

His words surprised tears into her eyes. "I appreciate that."

He propped himself on one elbow to look at her, shading the sun. He was all she could see. "I can't say enough about you, Lacey. You were always sweet, and likable, and cute…"

She snorted. "Cute like a little brat, you mean."

He cocked his head to one side. "No, not exactly. I found you…appealing, as you grew up."

"You *did*?"

"Uh-huh." He reached out and brushed back a strand of her hair.

"Why didn't you ever, you know, ask me out?"

His eyebrows drew together. "You were three years younger! That wouldn't have been right."

She laughed up at him. "You're such a Boy Scout."

His eyes narrowed. "If you could read my mind, you'd know that's far from true."

"Then, or now?"

"What do you mean?"

"Are you talking about what was in your mind then, or now?" Something, some magnetic force field, drew her to reach toward his chest, the thick, luxuriant mat of hair sliced through by scars.

He caught her hand, held it still. "Don't."

"Why not?"

Shaking his head, he continued to hold her gaze.

"Because of this?" She tugged her hand away from him and traced the air above one of the multiple fault lines on his chest. Almost, but not quite, touching it.

He sucked in a breath, his eyes still pinning her. "Do you have any idea of what you're doing?"

"What am I doing?"

He caught her chin in his hand and let his thumb brush across her lower lip.

She drew in a sharp breath, staring at him. Every nerve felt alive, every sense awake.

"You have no idea how long I've wanted to do this." He leaned closer, studying her face as if trying to read her thoughts, her mood, her feelings.

"Do what?" she asked, hearing the breathy sound of her voice.

"This." He slid his hand to the back of her head and pressed his lips to hers.

The next Saturday, Vito's head was still spinning.

Kissing Lacey had been the sweetest and most promising moment of his life. Now he just had to figure out what was next.

He'd been busy with his new job for the past couple of days, and Lacey had been taking up the slack, spending extra time with Nonna and Charlie. She hadn't said anything about their kiss, but she'd given him some secret smiles that burned right into his soul.

He had to talk to her, and soon. But this morning, to give her privacy and time to get some detailed renovation work done, he'd taken Nonna and Charlie out for breakfast at the Chatterbox.

Now, seeing Charlie wave to a friend, hearing Nonna's happy conversation with a woman at a neighboring table, he felt full to the brim. His new life in Rescue River was working out, and he had a lot to be thankful for.

"Hey, Dad," Charlie said. "Am I still seeing Mom on Tuesday, now that you're working?"

"Yes. I'll drive you, and then we're going to see if the social worker can bring you home. If she can't, I can take off early." He'd explained his commitment to Charlie's schedule during his job interview, and his new employer was willing to be flexible.

"Mom said maybe she could drive me, only there's a lady she doesn't like in Rescue River."

"That's nice of her to offer, but your mom isn't allowed to transport..." All of a sudden Vito processed what Charlie had said and his heart skipped a beat. "Did she say anything about the lady?" he asked, carefully keeping his voice even.

"I think it was because of my dad. My other dad," Charlie clarified around a mouthful of pancakes. "Hey, Rafael asked if I could go to the park and play basketball, and they're leaving now. Can I?"

"Um, let me talk to his mom." His thoughts spinning, Vito slid out of the booth and made arrangements with Rafael's mother, forcing himself to focus. Charlie's social skills were improving rapidly enough that he felt okay about letting the boy go play some ball without him—after a stern warning about sportsmanship and manners.

Once that was settled, he paid the check and escorted Nonna out of the restaurant.

As they walked slowly toward the guesthouse, Vito wondered what Krystal had said to Charlie. If she was talking that openly about the past—what did it mean?

He took Nonna's arm when the sidewalk got bumpy. Quite possibly, it meant the whole truth could come out soon.

The woman in Rescue River whom Krystal had told Charlie she didn't like—and who was connected to Charlie's other dad—could be no one else but Lacey.

But Krystal didn't know Lacey, did she? Was there a chance she'd say enough that Charlie would put it all together?

He looked over at Nonna. "What if there were something you needed to tell the truth about, only you'd made a promise not to?"

"Ah, difficult," she said, looking at him with sharp, curious brown eyes.

Clearly she was waiting for him to say more, but he didn't. If he was going to tell the truth, it had to start with Lacey. So he focused on watching a couple strapping twin babies into a double stroller.

A pang of envy swept through him. He wanted what they seemed to have. A happy, uncomplicated relationship of raising children together.

"Have you prayed about this problem?" Nonna asked.

Had he prayed? He nodded slowly. He'd sent up some urgent, brief pleas to God, for sure.

"And listened to the response?"

He blew out a breath. "Not really. I guess I need to."

They reached the guesthouse in time to see Lacey hauling a big load of trash to the curb, struggling a little. Vito jogged over and took the boxes out of her hands, earning a smile.

Lacey went to Nonna. "Are you going around the block another time? I can walk with you if Vito's got things to do." Lacey didn't look at him, but her cheeks were pink and he didn't think it was just the exertion.

There had been a tentative, sweet promise in their interactions since their kiss earlier this week.

Nonna put a hand on Lacey's arm and another on Vito's. "I've had enough for now. Why don't you two walk?" She gave Vito a meaningful look, and when Lacey turned away, she mouthed *"Tell her!"*

How had Nonna guessed that his secret had to do with Lacey?

Was he supposed to tell her *now*?

As soon as they'd gotten Nonna settled on the porch with her latest large-print library book, Vito and Lacey headed out, strolling toward the park. Behind them, Wolfie barked a request to go along.

"Should we go back and get him?" Lacey asked, clearly unaware of Vito's inner turmoil. "He's about to break through the fence again."

"Not this time. I put another nail in it yesterday."

"Thanks. I'll have to get somebody to do a real repair soon." Lacey lifted her face to the sun. "I've been inside all morning, painting woodwork. The fresh air smells good."

"I'm glad you could come." He wanted to put his arm around her. He wanted to build a family with her! But the wretched secret stood between them.

Should loyalty outweigh love? He pondered the question, watching a jogger and his golden Lab loping across the park.

"We haven't had a chance to talk since you started your new job," Lacey said. "How'd it go, really? Did the kids give you a hard time?"

The cowardly side of him was grateful for the distraction. This was territory he could handle. "It went well. The kids are a challenge, for sure, but I liked working with them."

"And your scars didn't make one bit of difference, did they?" She was smiling smugly, obviously sure she was right.

And she *was* right. "The kids made a couple of comments, but it was no big deal. I didn't overreact and the whole discussion just went away." He hesitated, then added, "You've helped me feel okay with how I look, especially because of…of how you responded to me the other day, at the lake."

She stared down at the sidewalk, but the corner of her mouth curved up in a smile.

He needed to tell her the truth about Charlie. He was going to tell her.

"I admire your being able to handle a big group of kids like that," she murmured, so quietly he had to lean down to hear her.

Thinking about how he could break the truth gently, he gave a distracted answer to her comment. "I like big groups of kids. In fact, that's my dream—to have enough kids of my own to form a baseball team."

He was about to add "with you" when she stopped still. The smile was gone from her face.

"You know what," she said, "I just realized I left something cooking on the stove. I need to run back and get it. You keep walking, okay? I don't want to interrupt your morning exercise."

She turned and hurried back toward the guesthouse.

Vito looked after her, puzzled by her abrupt departure. His *morning exercise*? And he was surprised to learn she had something cooking when she'd been painting woodwork.

He'd been about to tell her the truth. Was that God, letting him know it wasn't the right time yet?

And if so, why had Lacey suddenly started acting so weird?

Thirteen

Numb from Vito's comment about wanting a large family, Lacey stirred canned soup on the stove and tried not to think.

If she didn't think, maybe it wouldn't hurt so much that she could never, ever give Vito what he wanted.

"Miss Lacey! Miss Lacey!" Charlie barged through the screen door, letting it bang behind him. He threw his arms around her. "Guess how many baskets I made today in one-on-one?"

She clung to him for a minute, relishing the feel of sweaty boy, and then resolutely untangled herself from his arms and stepped back. Charlie was getting way too close to her, given that she'd just learned she and Vito should never, *could* never, be a couple.

"Maybe you and Dad can come watch me play," he continued, unaware of her turmoil. "And Dad said sometime we could go see a real live Cavaliers game, all three of us!"

There is no "us."

She needed to be truthful. That was kinder in the long run.

Wolfie whined at the back door and Lacey let him in, figuring the dog could comfort Charlie in the face of what she was about to say. "I don't think that's going to happen," she said, crossing her arms, deliberately keeping her distance. "You and your dad are going to move out soon, and then we won't all see so much of each other."

Charlie visibly deflated, sinking down to put his arms around Wolfie's neck. "But I don't want to move."

How quickly he accepted the truth of what she said, and her heart broke for this child who'd seen too much change and loss. She didn't know much about Charlie's background, but she knew his mom wasn't reliable enough to raise him. That had to hurt him right at the core.

And it meant he shouldn't get overly close to Lacey, because she was just going to be another loss. "You and your dad are going to be a forever family," she said, resisting the urge to hug him. "But that's not going to happen here." She forced herself to add, "It's not going to happen with me."

He looked at her with wide, sad eyes and she felt like she'd kicked a puppy. And even if her words had been for Charlie's own good, she hated that she was hurting him.

"Later," he said, then turned and straightened his shoulders. "Come on, Wolfie." And then both dog and boy ran up the stairs.

Tears rose in Lacey's eyes, and one spilled over and ran down her cheek. She wanted to call him back, to hug him and tell him that yes, they'd still be close, and yes, they could do things together in the future.

But that would just prolong the pain. Vito needed

someone who could give him and Charlie a family, and he *would* find someone.

And that someone wouldn't be her.

Automatically, for comfort, she felt for her necklace. But she wasn't wearing it. After kissing Vito, she'd decided that it was time to remove it. Time to stop focusing on Gerry, and start focusing on life ahead.

She'd been wrong.

She turned off the soup, for which she had no appetite, and trudged up the stairs. Went into her room, opened her old jewelry box and pulled the chain back out.

She'd thought she was going to make new memories with Vito and Charlie, but she was going to have to stick with the old memories. Of Gerry and the child she'd lost. Memories that didn't seem like nearly enough to build a life on now that she'd tasted what love and family could mean at Vito's side.

But Vito wanted a big family. He'd be wonderful with a big family, and she wasn't going to deny him that.

The chain and ring settling around her neck felt heavy in a way they never had before.

Suddenly bereft of energy, she closed her bedroom door, pulled the shades and lay down in the semidarkness, too tired and miserable even to pray.

Saturday afternoon, Vito arrived at the church food distribution late and out of sorts.

Lacey had been scheduled to volunteer, too, he was sure of it; she'd come out onto the porch, car keys in hand.

But when she'd realized that he and Charlie were

planning to go, she'd turned abruptly and gone back inside, shutting her door with a decisive click.

Not only that, but Charlie was on his worst behavior. After Lacey's defection he'd refused to go and, when Vito had insisted, he'd let loose with a tantrum that had surely roused the neighborhood. Now he wore a sneer better befitting a teenage delinquent than an eight-year-old boy.

"Hey, Charlie's here!" Angelica waved from where she and Troy were sorting out boxes of doughnuts and pastries. "C'mon, the Kennel Kids scored the best place on the line. We get to give out the desserts, and eat whatever's left over!"

Charlie scowled, but he walked down to the end of the line where several other boys from the group stood joking and roughhousing. Troy and Angelica seemed to have them under control, though, and Xavier greeted Charlie enthusiastically.

Relieved, Vito scouted around for a role that didn't involve a lot of chitchat. He wasn't in the mood today. As the line of food bank patrons entered the church's fellowship hall and picked up boxes to fill, Vito started carrying crates of produce from the loading dock at the back of the building to resupply those on the front lines.

He tried to distract himself from his gloomy thoughts by focusing on the scent of sun-ripened tomatoes and bundles of green onions, but it didn't work. He kept going back to Lacey's pale, strained face, to the definitive click of her door closing.

Had their new connectedness been an illusion? Had she had second thoughts about pursuing a relationship with someone who had disabilities and a challenging child to raise?

Was there some way she could have found out the truth about Charlie?

But they'd walked together this morning, and she'd been perfectly fine, seeming interested in him, his job, their conversation.

"Hey, Vito!" The father of the migrant family who was renting Nonna's house—was his name Vasquez?—took the empty crate Vito handed him and started filling it with bundles of kale. "Thanks for working today."

"Thank *you*." Vito tried for a good humor he didn't feel. "I'm impressed that you're helping, as busy as you must be with the new baby."

"The bambino has not arrived yet, and my wife, she is very uncomfortable." The man worked deftly as he spoke, lining up the bundles for maximum space in the box. "She cannot work now, so I will have to join the food line this month. But at least I can help others, too."

"Good plan." Vito took the crate from Mr. Vasquez and reminded himself that his weren't the worst problems in the world. Some families struggled to scrape together enough food to eat.

He walked back toward the line, focusing on the friendly chatter between helpers and recipients. Interesting that the line between the two sometimes blurred, as with Mr. Vasquez.

He'd just put the crate down when a highly irate voice sounded behind him. "Vito! I need to talk to you!"

It was Susan Hinton, and she tugged him over toward a quiet corner of the fellowship hall. "What did you say to Lacey?"

"What do you mean?"

Susan's hands were on her hips. "She's been doing

so well, but when I stopped by the guesthouse to pick her up for volunteering, she looked awful. Said she couldn't come, and when I asked her if she was sick, if she needed anything, she said no and went back in her room. She *never* misses."

Vito lifted his hands, palms up. "I could ask you the same question. She's backed off from me, just today, and I don't know why."

Susan's eyes narrowed. "Since when? What went on?"

"I have no idea."

She actually smacked him on the arm. "Come on. Don't be a typical guy. What did you say to her?"

"I don't know." He leaned against a stack of boxes, trying to recreate the scene of their walk this morning in his mind. "I was talking about my new job. And not just because I was going on and on about myself. She wanted to know. She was fine one minute, and then boom, she lit out of there like I'd insulted her best friend."

"What, exactly, did you say?" Susan leaned back, crossing her arms over her chest. "And I'm not just being nosy. Lacey's had a lot happen to her, and she went through a pretty bad depression. I'd hate to see her sink back into that."

"Me, too." He frowned, thinking. "I was talking about working with the kids, and she said she didn't know how I could handle working with that many. I told her I love kids, want to have a passel of them myself someday, and it was about then that she seemed to back off. Was that...do you think I somehow offended her?"

Susan threw her hands up and snorted with disgust.

"Vito!" Several people turned to look at them, and she tugged him closer and lowered her voice. "Look, I don't know that it's my place to tell you this, but Lacey *can't* have kids."

That hit him like a blow to deflect, news that had to be wrong. "But...she got pregnant with Gerry, right?"

She looked from one side to the other, making sure they weren't overheard. "When she miscarried, there was some damage. She's infertile now, and that's been really, really hard for her to deal with."

Pain sliced through him just as if it were he, himself, who couldn't have kids. Lacey would be such a great mom. Sometimes, life just wasn't fair.

"And so when you said..." Susan trailed off.

Understanding broke through. "Did she back off because I said I wanted a lot of kids?"

"I don't know. She's the type who'd sacrifice her own desires so other people would get what they wanted."

"Wait a minute, I'm confused. What *are* her own desires?"

"She really likes you, Vito, if you haven't wrecked it. Talk to her. That is, unless her infertility means you aren't interested in her, like some ancient king who only likes women so he can get a son."

Vito lifted his hands, palms up. "Whoa. That's not me. Not at all." His mind was reeling, but this was something he could maybe fix. "Look, I have to go. Can you tell them... Do you think they can handle the rest without..."

"Go." Susan actually shoved him toward the door. "The line's short today and it's almost done."

"Thanks. Thanks, Susan. Let me get Charlie, and I'm outta here."

Despite the sad news he'd learned about Lacey, hope was rising in him. If she cared for him so much that she'd sacrifice her own desires so he could have kids... But didn't she see that what he wanted was her? Kids came into families in all kinds of ways. Just look at Charlie.

The boy wasn't with the rest of the Kennel Kids. "He said he needed to talk to you," Angelica said. "Didn't he come over?"

"No..." Vito turned and scanned the room. "I'll find him. Thanks."

Alongside his excitement about possibly working things out with Lacey, self-blame pushed at him. He'd been paying so much attention to Susan's story that he'd forgotten to keep an eye on Charlie.

Finally, he thought to talk to the other Kennel Kids. "He said he was outta here, going home," one of the younger ones finally volunteered.

"Thanks." Vito blew out a breath, quickly left the church and walked the three blocks to the guesthouse at record speed. He'd told Charlie he had to stay and help the whole time. What did this new wave of defiance mean?

Nonna was at the front gate, headed out for lunch with Lou Ann Miller. "Did you see Charlie come in?" Vito asked.

"No, but I've been getting ready. I wouldn't have heard him if he went right upstairs. Is anything wrong?"

"Everything's fine. He's just in trouble."

"Don't be too hard on him, dear." Nonna patted

Vito's arm, and then the two women headed down the sidewalk.

He trotted up the stairs. Noticed the door to Lacey's room was still closed. Was she in there?

He *really* wanted to talk to her, but he had to deal with Charlie's disobedience first. He pounded on the door to Charlie's room, and when there was no answer, flung it open.

The lecture he'd been about to give died on his lips.

The room was empty. Not just empty of people, but empty of stuff. Charlie's stuff.

He opened the closet door. There was a hamper of dirty clothes, but the clean ones were gone. As was Charlie's suitcase.

His heart pounding, he ran out onto the landing. "Charlie! Charlie!"

No answer, but Lacey's door opened. "What's wrong?"

He looked from window to window, searching the yard on both sides of the guesthouse, but they were quiet, empty.

"Vito? What's going on?"

"Have you seen Charlie?"

"Not since you guys left for the church. Where is he?"

"That," Vito said grimly, "is the million-dollar question. I think he's run away."

Fourteen

Vito continued searching even as he explained the situation to Lacey, trying to stay calm.

"I just can't believe he'd run away. He's so happy here, and with you." Lacey walked into Charlie's room. She opened the closet door, and then squatted to look under the bed—all places Vito had already checked.

Vito strode into his adjoining room. He flung open the closet door and checked it top to bottom. "I never thought of him running, either, but he's not here. And his suitcase is gone." Quickly and methodically, he searched the rest of his room. News stories of all the bad things that could happen to kids played through his head, one after another.

A thought struck him and he went back to the window, lifted the screen and leaned out. He gave a whistle, and Wolfie trotted over to that side of the yard, panting, looking up expectantly.

"It's okay, boy," he said, and shut the window. Surely Charlie wouldn't have left without his beloved dog.

When he looked back into the room, Lacey was at

Charlie's little desk, rifling through papers and magazines and empty potato chip bags.

"I'd better call Dion." He had his phone out to punch in the police chief's number when Lacey cried out softly.

"Look at this. Is this his handwriting?"

Vito took the torn piece of notebook paper from her and scanned it quickly, his heart sinking with every word he read.

I thot I cud have a mom and dad. I need a mom.
Take care of Wofie.

And he'd signed it, "Love, Charlie."

Vito's heart seemed to stop in his chest.

"What does it mean?" Lacey clutched her arms around herself. "'I need a mom.' And who did he think would be his mom? Was it…was it me?"

"Maybe." He caught Lacey's eye, held it. "Believe me when I say I didn't try to plant that idea. But right now I'm more worried about where he's headed."

"Could he have gone to his mom?"

"That's what I'm afraid of." He turned toward the door. "I can't even imagine how upset he was, to leave without Wolfie."

"But you said she's an addict…"

"She is, and she isn't very selective about her boyfriends. I've got to find him." He headed down the stairs.

She followed behind. "Where does she live? Where has he been meeting her?"

"He's been meeting her at a center in Raystown. But

she actually lives in Barnsdale. Way too far to walk, and he knows that."

Lacey grabbed his arm, stopping him. "There's a bus that goes to Barnsdale. We were talking one day, Charlie and Nonna and me, and we looked over the bus route together. He was sounding out the words, and when he came to Barnsdale, he said that's where he used to live."

Vito groaned. "I have a feeling that's exactly what he did. Is the bus stop still at the front of Cramer's Drugstore?"

She nodded. "Let's go. Maybe we can catch him before he gets the bus. I don't even know the schedule anymore, but the bus can't run very often."

They each grabbed phones, wallets and keys and rushed out to Vito's car. As they climbed in, Wolfie howled his distress at being left behind.

"Let's drive slow and watch. He could be headed back home. I doubt a bus driver would even take a kid as young as Charlie."

"I don't know. He can be pretty smart about figuring out ways to do things and making up stories."

They were at the drugstore in minutes, and Lacey got out of the car and rushed in before Vito even had a chance to park. By the time he got inside, seconds later, she was in heated conversation with a teenage clerk.

"Why didn't anyone stop him?" she was lamenting. "A little boy, alone?"

"Kids eight and over can ride unaccompanied." The young woman shrugged. "He had the right paperwork, looked like. The driver always checks."

Vito's heart sank. Charlie was perfectly capable of

talking an adult into filling out a form for him. "How long ago did the bus leave?"

The teenager looked at the wall behind her, taking what seemed like an extremely long time to skim over a schedule. "Must've been about…an hour ago?"

He and Lacey looked at each other. "Let's go," she said.

As they reached the truck, the ramifications of what might be in front of them rushed into Vito's mind. Krystal, Lacey, Charlie. All together. "Lace…you might not want to go along. Someone should stay back at the guesthouse, in case he comes back."

"I'll call Lou Ann on the way and ask her and Nonna to go back."

"It's not safe—"

"*Charlie's* not safe. And you need backup."

He pulled out of the parking lot and headed toward Barnsdale. "I need backup I don't have to worry about. You can only come if you stay in the truck and be ready to call the police if needed. That's it, Lacey. I don't want you tangling with Krystal and her boyfriends, or whoever else is crashing at her place."

"Fine."

As they drove in silence, Vito's mind hopscotched from topic to topic. How would Charlie get from the bus stop to his house on the poorer side of town? Should he explain the whole situation about Charlie and Krystal and Gerry so that Lacey could be prepared? Why had Charlie run away, really?

He heard a small sound from the seat beside him. When he glanced over, he saw Lacey brushing her forefinger under her eye. "What's wrong?"

"I think I know why Charlie ran away," she said with a hitch in her voice. "I think it's my fault."

"How could it be your fault?" He kept his eyes on the rural road before him, pushing the speed limit.

"Because I told him we couldn't keep doing things together." She fumbled in her purse, found a tissue and blew her nose. "I told him we couldn't be a family."

Whoa. "How did you get into that conversation? When?"

"Just this morning." She paused, took a breath. "He came in from basketball, talking about all the things we three were going to do together, and I thought...I thought he'd better not expect that. So I just...told him it wasn't happening."

"Why?"

"Because it can't." He could barely hear her voice, low and hoarse.

He risked taking a hand off the steering wheel and gave her arm a quick squeeze. "We have to talk. Susan told me some stuff."

"What stuff?" She shifted to face him, sounding uneasy.

A passing road sign told Vito they were halfway to Barnsdale. "Look, I'm sorry if this is none of my business, but apparently Susan thought I should know about your infertility."

She drew in a little gasp, her hand rising to her mouth.

There was probably a tactful way to have this conversation, but he didn't know it, not now. "I'm sorry, hon. That's got to be tough, maybe the toughest thing for a woman."

She didn't say anything, and when he glanced over,

her lips were pressed tightly together and her body rigid.

"But there are all kinds of ways to be a parent. It's not just biological. I mean, look at me and Charlie."

She didn't answer, and they rode without talking into Barnsdale, passing the automobile factory on one side of the road and a couple of small machine shops on the other.

He tried again. "When all this is over, when we find Charlie and get him home safe, I want to have more of a conversation about this. Okay?"

She nodded, reached over and squeezed his arm. "We'll find him."

Vito pulled onto the street where Krystal had been renting a place, the last address he had for her. Dingy cottages and overgrown yards lined both sides of the street. "This isn't going to be pleasant. Remember, I want you to stay in the car."

"I know. I'm ready to call the cops." She looked around uneasily.

He stopped the truck in front of Krystal's place. "And Lace…"

"What?"

He hooked an arm around her neck, pulled her to him and gave her a fast, hard kiss. Then he pulled back to look into her eyes. "Remember, whatever happens, I want this with you." He got out of the truck before he could say too much.

There was a bang as the screen door flew open and back on broken hinges, slamming into the front of the house.

"Hey, what's going on, my man Vito!" Krystal came

out on the front stoop, started down the concrete steps, and then grabbed the railing and sat down abruptly.

A man appeared in the doorway behind her, the same one Vito had seen driving the SUV. The balding, bearded one who'd made Charlie cringe.

Vito strode up the narrow walkway. "Is Charlie here?"

"Yeah, he's here." Krystal held up a can of beer like she was making a toast. "Decided he'd rather live with his good old mom after all."

Relief that he'd found Charlie warred with worry about the situation the boy had gotten himself into. "I'd like to talk to him."

The bearded man came out onto the stoop, his face unfriendly. "What's your business here?"

"Just looking for my son." Vito visually searched the place, glancing around the weedy yard, up at the little house's windows.

A curtain moved in one. Was it Charlie?

"You been stepping out on me?" The man nudged Krystal with his knee, none too gently.

"Aw, cut it out, Manny."

"You've got it wrong." Vito kept his voice calm, because he could tell that the man was volatile. "I'm just an acquaintance of Krystal's. Taking care of her son."

"You the daddy?" Manny asked.

Behind him, Vito heard the window of his truck being lowered. Lacey.

"I'm not his dad yet, but I'm going to adopt him. Let's just get him down here and I'll be on my way."

"Maybe I don't like the way you look." Manny shoved past Krystal and came down the steps. "Maybe I want you to leave right now."

Vito automatically straightened up, his fists clenching. He wanted to punch the jerk, but for Charlie's sake he couldn't. He needed to stay calm and keep things peaceful. "I'd be glad to leave you people to your own business as soon as I have Charlie."

Then everything happened at once.

Manny drew back a fist, but Krystal rushed up and grabbed it. Manny shook her off and shoved her back, roughly, causing her to fall back onto the steps. At the same moment Charlie came running out of the house. He crashed into his mother, who reached out reflexively to grab him.

Manny, unaware what was going on behind him, threw a punch that Vito dodged, but landed a second one on Vito's shoulder, knocking him back.

Behind him, the truck door opened. "Charlie!" Lacey cried. "Over here!"

Manny advanced on Vito, and with no time to regret the violence, Vito threw a one-two punch, connecting with Manny's ribs and then the side of his throat. Manny fell to the ground, gasping for air.

Vito spun to help Charlie just in time to see the boy extract himself from his mother's grip and run to Lacey. She was turning to usher him into the truck when Krystal spoke up.

"Hey!" she called, her voice slurred but plenty loud. "Wait a minute. I know who you are!"

Vito's heart skipped a beat and he ran toward Lacey and Charlie, intent on getting them into the truck so they didn't find out the truth this way.

Her heart pumping, her adrenaline high, Lacey ushered Charlie into the backseat. Then she turned to see where Vito was. She'd drive Charlie away herself if she needed to, even if it meant temporarily leaving Vito behind. He could fend for himself better than Charlie could.

Vito was approaching the truck at a run, so Lacey went around to get in the passenger's seat.

The dark-haired woman, Charlie's mother, reached the truck just as Lacey opened the passenger door. "I know who you are," she said, her tone angry.

Vito came back around from the driver's side. "Come on, Krystal, we'll talk another time. When you're sober."

"I'm sober enough to recognize *her*."

Lacey studied the woman. "How do you know me? I don't think I've met you."

"Krystal—" Vito started.

She held up a hand and interrupted him, still glaring at Lacey. "*You're* the woman who stole my man away."

That was so far from anything Lacey expected that she could only stare at Krystal.

"Hey, now," Vito said, "this can wait. Charlie doesn't need to hear this."

Lacey stepped away from the truck door. Before she could close it in an effort to block Charlie's hearing them, Krystal slammed it shut.

Someone clicked the locks. Vito.

She looked past Vito to Krystal, filled with a sinking feeling she didn't understand. "How do you know me?"

"Guy named Gerry McPherson sound familiar?"

"Ye-e-e-s," Lacey said slowly. "He was my husband."

"Well, he was *my* fiancé. And the father of my child."

"The father of your…"

"Him." Krystal pointed toward the backseat. "Charlie."

Lacey looked at Vito, who should be denying what this madwoman said, but Vito's face was a stone.

The edges of her world started to crumble. "Gerry was Charlie's father?"

"That's right. I gave him more than you ever did."

The words stabbed her, but she ignored the pain. She had to explain to the woman how wrong she was. "But Charlie's eight. I was married to Gerry when…" She stared at Krystal.

Krystal threw up her hands. "You didn't even know, did you?"

Slowly Lacey shook her head. What she was hearing couldn't possibly be right.

"Yeah, he was seeing me on the side. At first, I didn't know about you, either." The anger was draining out of the woman's voice. "When I figured out that he was married, I tried to break it off, but he said your marriage was on the rocks and he was leaving. It was only when I saw that photo in the paper that I realized he'd been lying. You two were hugging each other like lovebirds, all happy." She shook her head, her expression bitter. "He wasn't worth the time I put into him."

"At least you got…Charlie." She heard the choked sound of her own voice as if from a distance.

Gerry had been cheating on her?

Could it be true?

She cleared her throat. "How long were you seeing him?"

"Couple of years. He didn't come around as much

after Charlie was born. To be fair, he was overseas a lot after that."

"Don't be fair to him!" Lacey snapped. "Did he see you when he came home, too?"

"Yeah. Some. Not much." Something like compassion had crept into Krystal's voice. "Charlie doesn't remember him."

Lacey sagged back against the truck, unable to process what she was hearing.

Gerry had been unfaithful during the whole course of their marriage.

He'd conceived a son with this woman in front of her.

He'd met the son and seen the woman when he came home on leave.

And she'd known none of it.

She put her hands over her face, trying to block it out, trying to preserve the memory of the husband she'd adored, of the happy marriage she'd thought she had.

Vito cleared his throat.

The sound brought a whole new betrayal into focus, and she dropped her hands away from her eyes and turned to stare at him. "You knew."

Slowly, he nodded.

"You knew, and you stayed in my house, brought Gerry's son into my house, and you didn't tell me."

"Cold, Vito," Krystal said.

"Lacey, I wanted to tell you. Started to, so many times. But I promised Gerry I wouldn't."

Krystal snorted. "Yeah, well, we all made promises, didn't we? And look how much good that did."

Lacey stared from Krystal to Vito, trying to process it all.

Vito was still talking. "I promised that I'd take care of Charlie and look out for you, too. He knew how much it would hurt you…"

"Oh, that's rich," Krystal said.

Lacey just stared and shook her head. He'd kept the truth from her so as not to *hurt* her? At Gerry's behest?

There was a sound from inside the truck, and she turned to see Charlie knocking on the window and mouthing words, his face anxious.

Lacey just stared at him, the boy she'd come to care for so much. The boy whose eyebrows arched high and dark, just like Gerry's had.

He was Gerry's son.

Gerry *had* a son. She herself had had so much trouble conceiving, and when she'd finally gotten pregnant, it had been too late: Gerry had been killed, and she had lost the baby.

Charlie was rattling the truck door now, and Vito and Krystal were arguing about something, but the words blurred into a mishmash she couldn't understand.

It was all too much. She had to get out of here.

She spun away and started walking down the road, faster and faster until she was nearly at a run.

Fifteen

For a few seconds, Vito was paralyzed, watching Lacey disappear down the street.

Charlie's rattling of the door and the sounds of Krystal's voice speaking to Manny, who was waking up, snapped him out of it.

He needed to go after Lacey. He needed to reassure and help Charlie. And he probably needed to make sure Krystal was okay, too.

The confusion of prioritizing made his military training kick in. *Secure those closest and most vulnerable.*

He opened the truck door and leaned in toward Charlie. "Listen, we're going to talk this through and figure it all out."

Charlie slumped. "Am I in trouble?"

"Yes, you're in trouble, but everyone gets in trouble. It's okay." He knew what Charlie would ask next, and he held up a hand to forestall it. "You're not getting sent away. You're still going to be my son and you can still see your mom every week."

"What about Miss Lacey?"

Vito blew out a breath. No dishonesty. That was what had gotten him in trouble in the first place. "I just don't know, Charlie. She's pretty mad at me right now."

"How come?"

"Grown-up business. We'll talk about it later." He stood, patted Charlie's shoulder, and then reached in and gave the boy a hug. "Sit tight. I've got to check on your mom and then we'll go make sure Lacey is safe."

He shut Charlie's door gently, and then walked a few steps toward Krystal. "You going to be okay?" he asked, nodding toward Manny. "I can call the cops for you."

"I got this," she said. "Go after her."

He took her word for it and drove out in the direction Lacey had gone, scanning the road. It was late afternoon and clouds were rolling in, thick and ominous. He had to get her before this storm started—or, given the neighborhood, something worse happened. "Help me watch for Lacey," he told Charlie.

A moment later, Charlie leaned forward in the seat and pointed. "Is that her?"

He could see her yellow shirt. She was desperately waving down a truck. No. She wouldn't get in a stranger's vehicle. Would she?

Did she want to avoid him that badly?

The truck stopped. The passenger door opened, and Lacey climbed in.

Vito hit the gas. "Do you know anyone who drives a blue pickup?" It seemed to have writing on the side, but Vito couldn't read it.

His stomach was lurching. If something happened to Lacey...

He got behind the truck, which was traveling at a normal rate of speed, and was relieved to see it was headed toward Rescue River, rather than away. Maybe she'd known the person and was getting a safe ride. But he still followed, just to be sure.

His head was still spinning from the way it had all gone down. Lacey had found out the truth about Gerry in the worst possible way.

Why hadn't he told her before? The betrayal in her eyes had just about killed him.

How awful for her to find out about her adored, war hero husband from his lover, screaming jealously at her.

And normally, she'd have turned to him for comfort. But instead, she'd looked at him as the betrayer, and rightly so.

Except he'd promised Gerry he wouldn't tell.

He tried to think of how it could've worked out differently. What all he'd done wrong. He shouldn't have made the promise. He shouldn't have moved in with Lacey. But that had been for Nonna...

There was a sniffle from the seat behind him, and Vito pulled his attention away from his thoughts and to Charlie. "Hey, buddy. What's the matter?"

"I thought Mom would want me," Charlie said in a subdued voice. "But when I got to her house, she told me to go away because Manny would get mad. And then Manny saw me."

"Did he hurt you?" Vito would kill the man if he had.

"No, but he made Mom shut me in the bedroom. And they said I couldn't come out. And they were gonna call you, but then they started fighting and kind of forgot about me."

"You can't do that, buddy. You can't run away. And you can't live with your mom." As he spoke, he was watching the truck in front of him, relieved to see it taking the exit that led to the guesthouse.

"I know." Charlie's voice was subdued.

"We're gonna figure this out, talk about it." Vito reached over and ruffled Charlie's hair. "Right now, though, we've got to check on Lacey."

He followed the truck, and when it pulled up in front of Lacey's place, he pulled up behind it.

"Do I have to stay in the truck again?" Charlie's voice was quiet.

"No, buddy, but you have to let me talk a little bit to Lacey. Grown-up business. Go see Wolfie. Okay? Take him out and walk him down the street, but stay where you can see me. We'll go inside in just a minute."

"Good, because I'm hungry."

They both got out of the truck, and Vito watched to make sure Charlie was safely out of earshot. He turned in time to see a dark-haired man walking beside Lacey toward the front door.

Jealousy burned inside him. He didn't want anyone else walking with Lacey. Especially not some tall, buff, thirty-ish guy with no scars and, probably, no baggage.

He followed them up the steps. "Lacey, I need to talk to you."

She ignored him and turned to the dark-haired man. "Thank you for the ride."

"Would you like me to stay?" the man asked in a courteous voice with just a trace of a Spanish accent.

She glanced toward Vito without meeting his eyes. "Maybe for a few minutes, if you don't mind. I just need to talk to…my other boarder, without him bothering me, and make a couple of arrangements."

"It's no problem." He sat down in the porch chair Vito had begun to consider his own.

Lacey turned to go inside.

Vito started to follow. "Lacey—"

"The lady prefers that you don't come in," the other man said, standing up to block Vito as Lacey continued on inside.

Vito stopped, lifted an eyebrow, wondered if he was going to have to fight again that day.

"She's an old friend, and she told me on the way home that she doesn't want you around. Not my business why." The man shrugged. "Sorry, man."

Vito sat down heavily on the front steps. He could smell someone barbecuing for Saturday dinner. He and Lacey had done the same just last week.

Before everything had fallen apart.

Charlie came back into the yard, tugging Wolfie. He started up the steps. "Let's go in. I'm starving."

"Can't. Not yet."

"Why not?"

"Lacey is… She doesn't want us to come in just yet, but we can in a little while."

Charlie's lower lip began to stick out. "I want to go to my own room."

Except it wasn't his own room. "Just a little while, buddy."

The dark-haired man stood and went down to his truck. He came back with a sandwich encased in plastic wrap and an apple. "Here," he said to Charlie. "It's good. Turkey and cheese."

"Thanks!" Charlie grabbed the sandwich and started unwrapping it.

"That's your lunch, man," Vito protested.

"I have kids. I understand." He sat back down in the same porch chair.

"Hey, you don't have to wait around. I won't bother her."

"I said I'd wait," the man said quietly. "No offense."

So they sat in silence while Charlie scarfed down the sandwich, and then played in the yard with Wolfie. It was another forty-five minutes before Lacey came out the door.

"Thanks, Eduardo," she said, still not looking at Vito. "I'm sorry to keep you from your work. I'm fine now."

"You're sure?"

"I'm sure."

They both watched as Eduardo trotted down the steps and swung into his truck. Charlie came over, holding Wolfie tight on his leash, in control for once. "Hi, Miss Lacey," he said uncertainly.

She knelt in front of him, giving Wolfie a quick head rub, and then turning her full attention to Charlie. "I need to talk to you about something serious," she said. "Can you listen?"

He nodded, eyes wide.

"I like you a lot," she said. "I'm really sorry it didn't work out for me and your dad, but that's not your fault."

Charlie swallowed hard, and Vito did the same.

"You always have a safe home with your dad. That isn't changing. You don't run away from him anymore, okay?"

"Okay." Charlie's voice was low.

"And because I really like you, this is hard, but...you and your dad are going to need to move out."

Charlie looked down at the floor, nodded and turned

away, nuzzling his face in Wolfie's fur. Wolfie, seeming to understand the boy's sadness, whined a little and licked Charlie's face.

Vito felt like he'd been punched in the stomach, hard.

Lacey stood and faced him. "Vito, I've made arrangements for Nonna to stay at the Senior Towers. They have a room open for her for however long she needs, and they can help her move in tomorrow. I have a call in to a friend of mine, a nurse, who'll check on her every day."

"You didn't have to—"

"Let me finish." She held up a hand. "You're going to have to find another place for you and Charlie to stay. I'm going away for a few days, and I want you out when I get back." Her voice was cold and distant.

She didn't wait for an answer, but turned and walked into the house, letting the door bang behind her.

Vito's shoulders slumped and he felt like collapsing down onto the porch and burying his head in his hands.

She was really, truly rejecting him. He loved her, and he'd lost her. Despair clutched his stomach with strong, cold fingers.

But he had a son to care for.

He swallowed the lump in his throat and straightened his shoulders. Looked out across the lawn.

There was Charlie's basketball. They couldn't forget that.

He walked down the steps, heavily, to pick it up.

"We gonna play, Dad?" Charlie asked eagerly.

"No, son." Vito carried the basketball up the stairs, not even bouncing it. "We're going to have to start packing, and I have to start looking for a new place for us to live."

He went to the front door, held it open for Charlie, and then followed the boy inside.

He felt utterly broken. And the only reason he was standing upright, trying to be strong, was because Nonna and Charlie depended on him.

It was Lacey's fifth day at the Ohio Rural Retreat Center, and she was finding some small measure of peace.

She'd cried so much that her eyes felt permanently swollen. She'd prayed almost continually. She'd sought counsel with the center's spiritual advisors.

She knew now that she needed to put her faith in God, not men.

She knew she wasn't healed yet, not even close.

The thought of Fiona Farmingham coming to visit with her today was terrifying. It wasn't that she didn't like Fiona; she barely knew her. And she had Fiona to thank for the idea of coming here. When she'd blurted out a piece of an explanation to Eduardo in that horrible truck ride home—"my husband wasn't who I thought he was"—Eduardo had urged her to get in touch with Fiona, who'd had something similar happen to her. And then he'd gone further and called Fiona, who'd texted her the address of the retreat center where she'd stayed when her world had fallen apart.

There was a knock on the door of her small, monk-like cell. "Your visitor is here," came the quiet, soothing voice of the retreat receptionist.

Trying not to show her reluctance, Lacey went out to the reception area and greeted Fiona with a handshake, then an awkward hug.

"Would you like to walk?" Fiona asked. "When I was here, I always liked the trail around the pond."

"Um, sure." She hoped Fiona didn't plan to stay long, that she wouldn't say anything to burst the fragile, peaceful bubble Lacey had built around herself.

But it couldn't last forever, of course. She was going to have to get back to renovating the guesthouse. To rebuilding her life in Rescue River as a strong single woman.

That had been her goal all along. When and why had she let that fade? But she knew the answer: it was when Vito and Charlie had come. Ever so gradually, they'd slipped into her heart so that now, having lost them, she didn't feel strong. She felt weak and vulnerable and raw.

"Thanks for agreeing to a visit," Fiona said as they walked toward the center's small pond, separated from the main building by a stand of trees. "I just felt really led to talk to you. And if your nights have been anything like mine were, you're not sleeping well, so I figured an early morning visit would be okay."

"I appreciate it," Lacey lied politely. "Where are your kids?"

"With the nanny," Fiona said, sounding apologetic. It was no secret that she was quite wealthy after her scandalous divorce settlement, but she didn't flaunt her money; in fact, people said she didn't like mentioning it.

A red-winged blackbird, perched on a cattail at the pond's edge, let out its trademark "okalee, okalee" before taking flight, bright red and yellow wing patches flashing in the early morning sun. "This is an amazing place," Lacey said, meaning it. "Thank you for telling me about it."

"Of course. How are you doing?" The question wasn't a surface platitude, but a real inquiry.

"I'm...managing, but barely," Lacey admitted.

"That's normal," Fiona said matter-of-factly. "When I found out my husband had a whole other family, it took a year to even start to feel normal again."

Her blunt words reached Lacey in a way the retreat counselors' soothing tones hadn't. Fiona had been there, had experienced the loss and humiliation Lacey was going through. "Did you ever feel like it might have been a dream, like you were going to wake up any minute and none of it would be true?"

Fiona nodded. "All the time. And then you keep on realizing, no, it's true, my life wasn't at all like what it seemed to be."

"Exactly. It's like my memories were stolen. The happiness I had with Gerry was all a huge lie."

"Well." Fiona reached out to run her fingers alongside the reeds that rimmed the pond. "I don't know if it was all a lie. My therapist said that men who lead double lives can really believe they love both women. Or in my case, both families."

Lacey inhaled the rich, damp-earth fragrance of the wetlands. "I don't know how you stood it, with four kids to watch out for. I'm barely managing with just myself."

"You do what you have to do. For me, the betrayal was the worst part. It messed with my whole image of myself as a woman, like I wasn't enough."

Lacey looked over at Fiona, tall, with long, wavy red hair and an hourglass figure. *She* had felt like she wasn't enough? "Did you get over that?"

Fiona shook her head. "You will, I'm sure, but I didn't. I've got my hands full with my kids and starting a business. Even if I felt like I could trust a man again—which I don't—I wouldn't have time for it."

"I hear you. My guesthouse is yelling for me to get back to renovations."

They walked in companionable silence for a few minutes. Green-headed mallards flew down and landed on the pond, skidding along. Overhead, the sky turned a brighter blue.

"I just wonder if everyone in town knew but me," Lacey burst out finally.

"I wondered the same thing, and I found out as soon as the truth started getting publicized. People *did* know, and they rushed to tell me how they'd suspected, or what they'd heard." She sighed. "That was bad enough, but when my kids started getting teased and bullied, I'd had it. I had to leave. It's why I moved to Rescue River."

"Oh, how awful for you *and* your kids!" Lacey felt almost ashamed for being upset about her own situation. Fiona, with her four kids suffering, had it so much worse.

"It was awful, but things are better now. Much better. What happened with your husband? How did you find out?"

So Lacey explained the whole situation. "And then Vito, he brought Gerry's child into my home! He was living there all along, knowing that secret."

"Ouch."

The sun was rising higher, and Lacey slipped off her sweatshirt and tied it around her waist. "He was an old friend, but he lied to me."

"Did he actively lie? He seems like a really nice guy, but you never know."

Lacey thought back. "No, he never actively lied. I

think the subject of Charlie's dad might have come up once, but he told me Charlie's father had died. And that he was Vito's war buddy. All of which was technically true. But—" she lifted her hands, palms up "—why did he come to live in the guesthouse—with my husband's son—when he had to know how much the truth would hurt me? And then we…" Tears rose to her eyes and she blinked them back. "We started getting close. I thought he cared for me." She almost choked on her words.

Fiona put an arm around her, giving her a quick shoulder-hug. "That sounds so hurtful. But do you think he did it on purpose, to be mean?"

Unbidden, an image of Vito's kind face swam before Lacey's teary eyes. She thought back over the time when he'd decided to stay at the guesthouse. "Nooooo," she said slowly. "He was actually reluctant to stay, and only agreed because his grandma was so keen on it."

"So he didn't exactly come knocking on your door, looking for a place to live."

"No. But he should have told me the truth!"

"He should have." Fiona hesitated. "That's a pretty hard thing to tell."

"I guess." Lacey didn't want to look at Vito's side, not yet. She was still too angry at him.

"And the thing is, were you perfect? That's what my counselor made me look at, in my situation. Were there any mistakes you made, in your marriage?"

"I was stupid," Lacey said bitterly.

"Well…yeah. You kind of were."

Lacey blinked, surprised. Not many people would speak that bluntly to someone who wasn't an old friend.

"We weren't wise as serpents, were we?" Fiona

stared off into the distance. "Neither of us. And people suffered because of it."

Lacey had never thought of it that way. She'd focused on how she was an innocent victim, not on how she'd had a responsibility to be wise as well as gentle and kind.

And yes, people had suffered. She thought of Charlie's hurt face when she'd told him she wouldn't be doing things with Vito anymore. It was a big part of why he'd run away.

Kicking him and Vito out on the street… Making Nonna move to the Towers… Yeah. "I've made a lot of people miserable, dragged them down with me."

They were coming to the end of the loop around the pond. "Don't beat yourself up. That's not what I mean at all. I'm really sorry for what happened to you. It's just…we're all a mix, right? Nobody's perfect. Not your husband, not you. And not Vito, either."

"True."

They walked quietly for a few more minutes, and when they reached the parking lot, Fiona stopped. "I've got to get back to the kids. But I just want you to know, there's life after this. You can come back, live well. Keep on praying, and I'll pray for you, too."

They hugged, for real this time. "Thanks for coming to see me," Lacey said. "It helped. A lot."

And as she waved, and then headed back inside, she felt better. Not healed, but better. And it was a good thing, because tomorrow she had to go back to town, hold her head high and probably encounter Vito and Charlie.

Sixteen

A week later, Vito parked in front of the Senior Towers and headed inside. He'd been so busy with Charlie and his job that he hadn't visited his grandmother for the past couple of days, and he felt guilty.

That wasn't the reason for the heaviness in his soul, though. *That* came from his unresolved issues with Lacey. Even now, if he looked down the street, he could see her on the porch of her guesthouse, talking and laughing with a couple of visitors.

He hoped to catch her eye, but she didn't even glance his way.

He trudged inside the Senior Towers, trying to look at the bright side. Charlie was doing well; Vito had explained the whole situation to his social worker, and a couple of sessions with her, Vito, and Charlie had helped the boy to understand as much of the truth as an eight-year-old needed to know. They'd talked over running away, and Charlie had promised to make a phone call to his social worker if he ever felt like doing it again.

They'd found half of a double to rent on the edge

of town, with a huge fenced yard and a dog-friendly neighbor in the other half of the house. So that was another good thing.

His course work was going well, and his new job even better. He loved working with the at-risk boys, and already his supervisor had talked with him about a possible full-time opening once he had his degree.

The scars weren't really an issue, in the job or otherwise. In fact, he felt almost foolish about how much he'd let them get in his way when he'd first returned to Rescue River. Now if a newcomer stared or a kid made a comment, he could let it roll off him, knowing that to most people, it was what was inside that mattered.

Lacey had helped him see that first. He owed her a debt of gratitude, but it was one he couldn't pay. To approach her again, after what he'd done, would be an insult to her.

He straightened his shoulders and ordered himself to focus on what he could do, not on what he couldn't. He'd go spend time with Nonna, help her feel better and recover from the move.

He walked into the Senior Towers and crossed the lobby. He was about to push the button on the elevator when he distinguished Nonna's voice, and he turned to see her emerging from the exercise room in the midst of a crowd of women. She wore hot pink sweats and a T-shirt that said... He squinted and read the words, Vintage Workout Queen.

She walked to him and gave him a strong hug. "My Vito! Come on. Sit down here in the lobby. I can spare a few minutes before I meet with my business partners."

Vito blinked. "Business partners?"

"Yes, Lou Ann and Minnie. The matchmaking business is taking off. Now, tell me what's new with you, and you know what I mean."

He tried to deflect the conversation to his work, and to Charlie, but Nonna saw right through it.

"I'm glad those things are going well, but what about Lacey? Have you mended that fence yet?"

He shook his head. "No, and I don't think it's going to get mended. Some things just can't be fixed." Nonna didn't know the details of what had happened between them, didn't know about Charlie's parentage, but she knew something serious had split them apart.

"Bella? Are you ready?" It was Lou Ann Miller, and it took Vito a minute to realize she was talking to Nonna. He'd almost forgotten his grandmother had a first name. "Oh, hello, Vito."

"Go rouse Minnie," Nonna instructed the other woman. "We have to do a quick consultation with our first client, Vito, here, before we start working on our business plan."

That was the *last* thing he needed. "Nonna... I was really just coming to check on you, not to talk about my own troubles. How are you feeling?"

She waved a hand. "I'm fine. Better every day, and these ladies—" she waved toward Lou Ann and Minnie, now both coming down the hall, talking busily "—they keep me in the loop. Lou Ann knows about all the news outside the Towers, and Minnie knows what's going on inside. I love it here!"

Vito felt a pang. He wasn't really needed by his grandma, not anymore. Nonna was making a new life for herself.

The other two women reached the cozy corner where Nonna and Vito sat, and Lou Ann pulled up chairs for both of them, leaving Vito surrounded and without an escape route.

Immediately, Nonna launched an explanation. "Vito, here, is estranged from the woman he most loves, because of some kind of fight. He thinks the relationship is doomed."

"Do you still have feelings for her?" Lou Ann demanded.

He was torn between telling the three interfering woman to go jump in the lake and embracing them for taking his troubles seriously. He chose the latter. "I still have feelings. But I did something that hurt her terribly."

"Did you apologize?" Miss Minnie asked.

"Yes, of course. But she kicked me out of the guesthouse, and she isn't speaking to me."

"Why did you do it?" Lou Ann asked.

He shrugged helplessly. "Loyalty, I guess. Loyalty to an old friend."

"Loyalty is an important value," Miss Minnie said. "But love...remember your Bible, Vito. The greatest of these is Love."

It was true. He saw that now, too late.

"So he's just backing away. Out of politeness!" Nonna leaned forward and pinched his cheek. "My Vito. Always the best friend. Always so nice."

"Too nice," Miss Minnie declared.

Lou Ann Miller looked thoughtful. "If you give up on her, maybe you just don't care enough. Why, I know a couple right here in Rescue River who had to keep huge secrets from each other. But they pushed through their problems. Now they're happily married."

Happily married. If there was any possibility at all of that for him and Lacey...

"The choice is yours," Nonna said. *"Coraggio, ragazzo mio."*

Lacey was what he wanted most in the world. Could he risk another try, a heartfelt apology, a grand gesture that might sway her back in his direction?

What did he have to lose?

Nonna seemed to see the decision on his face. "If you need any help," she said, "we're here for you."

He stood and kissed her cheek. "I will most definitely take you up on that."

From a high-backed chair that faced away from their corner, Gramps Camden stood and pointed a finger at Vito. "For once, the ladies are right. Being polite doesn't get a man much of anything."

As the ladies scolded Gramps for eavesdropping, Vito waved and headed for the door, feeling more energy with each step he took.

He had some serious planning to do.

A week later, Lacey hugged Nonna at the door to the Senior Towers, glad to feel that the older woman was gaining weight and strength. "Don't worry," she said. "I'll take you to the party next week. Are you sure you don't want me to walk you upstairs?"

"I'm fine. And I'm sorry I got the date wrong. Maybe I'm losing my marbles." Nonna shrugged.

"It's all right. I enjoyed spending some time with you." Truthfully, the excursion had filled a gap in Lacey's week. Even though she'd tried to rebuild her life, to spend time with girlfriends and focus on her work, she still found herself lonely.

Still found herself missing Vito and Charlie.

Nonna reached up and straightened Lacey's collar, plucked a stray hair off her shoulders. "Do you know what we always said in Italy? *Si apra all'amore.* Be open to love."

"Um, sure." Maybe Nonna *was* getting a little confused, because that remark had been apropos of nothing.

She drove the half block to the guesthouse and parked in the driveway, taking her time. She didn't want to go inside an empty house. Without Charlie roughhousing and Wolfie barking, without Vito's deep voice, the place felt empty.

But delaying wouldn't solve her problem. She clasped the cross she'd hung around her neck, in place of the wedding ring she'd worn before. It was a reminder: she could do all things through Christ.

Including survive loneliness.

She climbed out of the car and walked slowly toward the front entrance, checking her flower beds, which were doing great. Looked reflexively at the broken fence. She really needed to...

She stopped. Looked again.

The makeshift fix they'd done weeks ago, when Wolfie had escaped, wasn't there. Instead, the fence was repaired.

She knelt down, awkward in her dress and heels, and examined it. The two broken pickets had been replaced with new ones, painted white. Only when you were very close could you see that the paint was a little brighter on the new pickets.

She frowned. Who would have repaired her fence?

Wondering, she walked toward the front of the house. As she rounded the corner, she heard music.

Opera music. *Italian* opera music.

What had Nonna called it? *The most romantic music on earth.*

What in the world?

The wonderful smell of Italian food—lasagna?—wafted through the air.

As she climbed the front steps, she saw something pink.

Her heart pounding, she reached the top of the steps. A trail of rose petals led her across the porch to a table set for two, topped with a white tablecloth.

She stared at the centerpiece, and tears rose to her eyes.

A ceramic rooster, exactly like the one Charlie had broken the day she'd met him.

No longer could she doubt who was responsible for what she was seeing.

She turned toward the front door. At the same moment, Vito emerged through it, a bowl of salad in one hand and a tray of pasta in the other. He wore dress trousers, a white dress shirt and an apron. Focused on balancing both dishes, he didn't notice her at first, but when he did, a strange expression crossed his face.

"Lacey," he said his voice intent. "Wait." He turned and carefully put down the two items on a side table.

Then he undid his apron and took it off, his eyes never leaving hers.

"How did you…" She broke off.

Walking slowly across the porch, he stood before her, not touching her. "I trespassed. Nonna gave me her key."

"Nonna…" She cocked her head to one side and reviewed the afternoon. Nonna's sudden invitation to a party, her insisting that Lacey dress up, the realization that it was the wrong date… "She was in on this. And you fixed my fence."

"For a good cause."

"What do you mean?"

He walked around her and pulled out a chair. "Explaining will take a minute. Would you like to sit down?"

She hesitated, feeling a little railroaded, but curious, too. "Oka-a-a-ay."

He poured iced tea, the raspberry flavor she always ordered at the Chatterbox, looking for all the world like a handsome Italian waiter. But then he pulled a chair to face her and sat down, close enough that their knees almost touched. Almost, but not quite. "The good cause is…an apology. Lacey, I am so sorry for what I did to you. There's no excuse for dishonesty."

She wanted to forgive him instantly. The music, the tea, the rose petals, the mended fence, the ceramic rooster—all of it created a romantic little world. But she couldn't just succumb to it. She needed to be as wise as a serpent, not just gentle as a dove. Not just go with her heart. "I would like to hear why you did what you did. I wasn't in a condition to listen before."

He drew in a breath and nodded. "Of course. You deserve that." Still, he seemed reluctant to speak.

"I can take it, Vito! Whatever happened, it's probably better than what I've been imagining."

"Right." He reached for her, then pulled his hand back. "It was only in the last couple of months of Gerry's life that I found out he'd been unfaithful to you."

The word stung, even though she knew it was true. "How did you find out?"

"He was burning letters," he explained. "Building a fire was dangerous over there, so I went to stop him. He said he had just a few more to burn, and he was turning over a new leaf. I still had to stop him—I was his commanding officer by then—and I happened to see a…suggestive card. It didn't look like something you'd send, so I asked him about it."

The thought of another woman sending racy cards to her husband made Lacey's face hot with anger and humiliation. Was that what Gerry had wanted in a woman? Hadn't her tame, loving letters been enough?

Vito was watching her face, and he reached out and wrapped his hand around her clenched fist. "He was *burning* it, Lace. He'd had a couple of risky encounters that had made him think about his life, and he wanted to get a fresh start."

"Either that, or he was afraid of getting caught."

"No, I think he was sincere. He really did love you. He just wasn't used to…" Vito seemed to cast about for the right word. "To monogamy, I guess. That's why I regret introducing you two."

"That's why you tried to warn me about him. You knew what he was like."

Vito nodded. "But you were in love, and I hoped marriage would change him. And it did. It just took a while. When you let him know you were expecting a baby, it made him want to change his ways, be a better husband and father."

"He already had a child!"

"Yeah." Vito sighed. "I found out about that at the very end. You sure you want to hear?"

"Tell me."

"Okay." He looked out toward the street, his shoulders unconsciously straightening into military posture. "Three of us were cut off from the others, and both Gerry and Luiz were hit and bleeding pretty bad. When Luiz died and Gerry realized the medics might not get there in time for him, either, he told me about Charlie. He asked me to take care of Charlie if Krystal couldn't. And he asked me to look out for you, and to keep you in the dark about who Charlie was, because he thought it would kill you to know. Before I could make him see it wasn't possible to do all those things together, he was gone."

Lacey just sat, trying to process what Vito was saying.

"I tried to save him, Lace. And I tried to do what he asked, though I didn't succeed very well." He sighed. "I thought things were okay for Charlie and Krystal. I thought it might be best for you if I stayed away. But then I got injured, and there was the rehab, and then everything hit the fan with Krystal and I found out Charlie was about to be put into the system... Well, first things first, I thought. Charlie is a kid."

"Of course." Lacey stared down at the porch floor. "It was my own fault I was so foolish, marrying Gerry. I was vulnerable to anyone."

"I was foolish, too, but I've learned. I've learned that honesty and...and *love*...trump loyalty to a bad cause."

She froze, not daring to look at him. "Love?"

He squeezed her hand, then reached up to brush a finger across her cheek. When he spoke, his voice was serious. "I love you, Lacey. I... Maybe I always have, kind of, but now it's grown-up and serious and forever."

Cautiously she looked at him through her eyelashes, not wanting to let her joy and terror show. She drew in a breath. "I have an apology to make, too. I was wrong to kick you and Charlie out. I was angry at Gerry, really, and at myself, and I took it out on you."

"Understandable."

"Is Charlie okay?"

He nodded. "We've had a few sessions with his social worker to talk it all through. She helped me understand how much to tell Charlie. Right now, he knows that his dad was a hero, but made some mistakes. That he felt ashamed he wasn't married to Charlie's mom. And that none of it is Charlie's fault. That seems like about as much as he can take in, right now."

"That's good." She bit her lip. "I shouldn't have taken out my hurt on you, and especially on an innocent child."

"For whatever you did wrong, I forgive you."

"And I forgive you."

They looked at each other. "Are we good?" he asked.

"We're good." She felt a strange breathlessness as he stood and pulled her gently to her feet.

And into his arms.

Being held by him, seeing and believing how much he cared, soothed some deep place inside her that wanted to be cared for and loved.

His hand rubbed slow circles on her back. "I hated being at odds," he said, and she felt the rumble of his voice against her cheek. "I want to be your friend. At *least* your friend. I want to be more."

She pulled away enough that she could look up at his face. "What kind of more?" she murmured in a husky tone that didn't even sound like her.

"This kind." He leaned down and pressed his lips to hers.

After a long while he lifted his head, sniffing the air, and then pulled away.

Lacey smelled it at the same time he did. "Something's burning!"

They ran inside and Vito pulled a scorched cake from the oven. "Oh, man, it was chocolate, too!"

She burst out laughing.

And then they were both laughing, and crying, and hugging each other, and kissing a little more. "It was so awful being apart from you. I never want that to happen again," he said.

"I don't, either." She pulled back. "But Vito. That nice meal is getting cold."

He laughed. "It'll warm up just fine. Come here."

He was right, of course. She stepped forward into his arms. "I love you," she said.

Epilogue

One Year Later

"I predicted this as soon as I saw you catch that bouquet," Susan Hinton said, looking around the guesthouse lawn with satisfaction.

"You couldn't have!" Lacey laughed. "Vito wasn't even back yet."

"I saw him come up behind you and I knew."

Gina, Lacey's sister-in-law, came over to where Lacey and Susan sat, under the party tent they'd put up against a summer shower. "Vito and Buck are exchanging fatherhood tips with Sam."

Lacey craned her neck and saw Sam Hinton, holding three-month-old Sam Jr. as if he were made of glass. Buck squatted to wipe the cake from little Bobby's face. And Vito was bending down to speak to Charlie, who looked adorably grown-up in his junior tux.

Lacey felt fully recovered from the devastating news about Gerry being Charlie's father. There even seemed to be a strange rightness in her helping Vito to raise Gerry's child.

Nonna approached Vito and took his arm, pulling him toward Lacey. She seemed years younger than she had after her heart attack; indeed, she was helping to teach heart attack recovery classes at the Senior Towers and was so happily enmeshed in the social circles there that she'd decided to live at the towers full-time.

"I need to talk to the bride and groom," Nonna said as she reached Lacey and her friends. "Alone."

Vito lifted an eyebrow and reached to pull Lacey from her reclining position. The very touch of his hand gave her goose bumps. They'd spent glorious time together during the past year, getting to know each other as the adults they were now. Vito had finished his online studies and student teaching, and had the offer of a job for the fall. Meanwhile, he'd been working with Lacey at the guesthouse, which had become so successful that she'd had to hire help—help that would now manage the place while she and Vito honeymooned.

The thought of their honeymoon on a South Carolina beach made Lacey's skin warm. She couldn't even regret that they could only manage a long weekend, with the guesthouse to run and Charlie to parent. She was so, so ready to begin married life with Vito.

"I'm afraid I've been interfering again," Nonna said, a twinkle in her eye.

"Nonna! What now?" Vito's tone was indulgent.

"You have that look on your face," Lacey added. "What have you been up to?"

Nonna looked from Vito to Lacey and bit her lip. "First, I have a confession to make." She hesitated, then added, "My interfering has been going on for a while."

"What do you mean? The matchmaking date?" Lacey had suspected for some time that Nonna had arranged for her and Vito to go out with Daisy and Dion, knowing it would push them into acknowledging their feelings for each other.

Nonna patted Lacey's arm as if she were a bright student. "Yes, the whole matchmaking service was a scheme to get the two of you together. Of course, it's grown beyond that." Lou Ann and Miss Minnie had become Nonna's first lieutenants, matching up the singles of Rescue River.

"I'm just wondering when you three ladies will do some matchmaking on each other," Vito said. He didn't sound particularly surprised about Nonna's interference, either.

"Oh, no!" Nonna looked shocked. "We're having far too much fun to weigh ourselves down with cranky old men."

That made Lacey burst out laughing. "You're incorrigible."

"Well, and it didn't begin with the matchmaking service, either."

"What else?" Vito put on a mock-serious tone. "Tell us everything."

"I...well, I may have arranged for Lacey to take care of me, and my home to be unavailable, when I found out you were coming home, dear." She looked up through her glasses at Vito, her face tender. "You're going to be a wonderful husband, but I was afraid you'd be my age before you figured it out. When I ended up on Lacey's floor at the hospital, and heard about her history, and saw how lovely she'd grown up to be... well, I may have done a little scheming."

"Nonna D'Angelo!" Indignation warred with laughter in Lacey's heart. Laughter won on this glorious day.

"I have a way to make it up to you," Nonna said hastily. "You both know I came into a small inheritance when my cousin Paolo died last year."

Vito nodded, and Lacey just looked at Nonna, wondering where this was going. What would Nonna think of next?

"I've been trying to decide what use to make of it. What can I do, at my age? I have a few plans, but the first one is I want to give you this." She reached into her handbag and pulled out a small, gift wrapped box. She handed it to Lacey. "Open it."

The box was featherlight, and inside, there was nothing but paper. "I think you forgot to put the gift in—"

"Nonna!" Vito had pulled out the papers and was scanning them. "You can't do this!"

"I can, and I've already done it. You're booked for a week at a villa in Tuscany, and then a week in Rome and Venice. You leave tomorrow." She crossed her arms and smiled with satisfaction.

"But…our reservations in South Carolina…"

"Canceled. That was the interfering part." Nonna looked only slightly abashed. "You'll still get a wonderful honeymoon. It's just the destination that'll be different."

Lacey stared at Nonna and then at Vito. "Italy?" she asked faintly. "I've never been out of the country."

"And that's why your brother had to check into whether you had a passport. You do. Some trip to Canada that didn't materialize?" Nonna waved her hand as if the details didn't matter.

Lacey looked at Vito. "Italy."

"Together." A smile spread across his face. "I've never been, either."

"And that's why you need two weeks," Nonna said firmly. "Everything's all arranged. The guesthouse, Charlie, reservations in *Italia*."

Lacey looked up to see Buck, Charlie, Susan and Sam all crowded together, looking at them, coming over to congratulate them on their changed honeymoon schedule and destination. It looked like everyone had been in on the surprise. Even Charlie knew that he and Wolfie would get to spend a little longer at the dog rescue farm with Xavier.

A regular clinking and ringing sound came, the traditional instruction to kiss. Vito pulled Lacey into his arms and kissed her tenderly, then held her against his chest.

"Is this what it's going to be like to be married to you?" he rumbled into her ear. "Surprises and adventures?"

"Enough to keep you on your toes." She laughed up at him as he pulled her closer, and then looked beyond, to the clear blue sky. Vito was amazing, and life with him and Charlie was going to be an adventure.

But she knew deep inside that none of this was a surprise to her heavenly father, who'd orchestrated all of it and would guide them through the rest of their days.

* * * * *